THEY'D KILL HIM FOR WHAT he'd done. And what he hadn't done. And who he was.

The boy retreated into the shadows. He would need a plan, carefully constructed. Earning trust in a situation like this wouldn't be easy.

The boy breathed deeply, envisioning every stairwell and hallway and turn he'd need to navigate before moving. Then he pushed off the railing and ran.

CONTAGON

ERIN BOWMAN

HARPER TEEN
An Imprint of HarperCollinsPublishers

For those both awed and terrified by the
incredible vastness of space

Library of Congress Control Number: 2017951096

ISBN 978-0-06-257416-9

Typography by Erin Fitzsimmons

20 21 22 23 PC/LSCH 10 9 8 7 6 5 4 3 2

❖

First paperback edition, 2019

UNITED PLANETARY COALITION

KNOWN ALSO AS THE UPC, OR SIMPLY, THE UNION

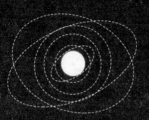

THE CRADLE
(NEW SOL)
MER
PIERRA *
NEW EARTH *#
LARISSA *
DEE
NIMBUS BELT
JUSAURNE

THE TRIOS
(SOL II)
ELPIS
EUTHERIA *#
SOTER *
LETHE BELT

THE FRINGE

FRINGE-1
(F1)
ACHLYS
KERES

FRINGE-2
(F2)
BEV
CASEY *#
SAL

In the ransacked Black Quarry base, the boy climbed into an over-head vent and secured the cover behind him. Peering through the crosshatched metal, he watched the engineer consider the pistol in his lap. Blood dripped from the man's brow.

"Go," he'd said to the boy just moments earlier. "If you want to take your chances, go now. Otherwise . . ."

Otherwise I'm shooting you.

Because he blamed the boy, maybe, or because of the undeniable truth: they were both doomed. The shot would be a mercy killing, before he saw to himself. Help wouldn't arrive for ages, and they were out of time. Even now, the boy could hear their final reinforcements being breached, the screech of metal hot in his ears.

He watched the engineer hook his foot beneath a utility cart, pulling it nearer so he could retrieve a damaged Tab. The screen was cracked. The signal, weak. It had barely worked when they tried to contact the drilling crew that morning, but the man booted it up and began to record an SOS.

Another screech of metal ripped through the base, so close it rattled the vents and set the boy's pulse on fire.

The engineer swore, tossing the tablet aside. He looked at the gun, the door, the gun again. He knew what was coming, how he'd be unable to hold his ground.

With a trembling hand, the engineer brought the gun to his temple.

And the boy fled, scrambling down the air vent on all fours.

I

THE EVACUATION

Northwood Point Research Facility

Soter, Trios System

ALTHEA SADIK HAD BARELY FINISHED positioning a new slide on the microscope stage when the evacuation alarm blared, reverberating through Northwood Point.

"Red alert!" someone shouted behind her, as if the distinctly red-colored lights flashing across the research lab's metallic counters didn't communicate just that. A more helpful response would have been what "red alert" meant. Thea raked her memory. What had the Company officials said in orientation? Red signified . . . a breach in the ice sheet? A fire? No. Inclement weather. That was it. The radio had been crackling about a brewing arctic storm all morning, and Northwood Point was finally being evacuated. Two storms had blown through the base in the four weeks since Thea arrived, but neither had required evac. This weather system must be unusually dangerous.

Thea's mentor, Doctor Lisbeth Tarlow, leapt to her feet and scrambled to gather their samples. Her trembling fingers fumbled the small vials of salt water, sending them scattering over the countertop.

"I'll get them," Thea said, catching one before it could fall. "You submit the logs."

The doctor nodded and turned to the computer. She suffered from a benign tremor—an annoying side effect of age, but one that made tasks requiring fine motor skills incredibly trying. It was the reason Hevetz Industries had hired an intern to assist her, and not a day went by that Thea didn't thank her lucky stars that she—an orphan from Hearth City—had won that position.

It wasn't unearned, of course. Thea had slaved for her exceptional grades. Labored over essays, sacrificed social gatherings like her junior gala. She'd even broken up with Mel. *Me or the internship*, he'd said at the end of the school year, and Thea had chosen her dreams. Now a single storm was threatening to cut the internship of a lifetime short.

She focused her attention on the remaining vials, threading them into the metal carrying case as Dr. Tarlow pecked frantically at the keyboard. Behind them, the rest of the lab workers hurried to stow away samples and back up research.

The small crew had spent the past month monitoring water temperatures and ice sheet thickness, ensuring that Soter's caps would be an ideal site for Hevetz Industries's next drilling venture. As the Union's largest supplier of corrarium, the energy company was ruthless about staying on top. Every potential location was studied and scrutinized, risks and benefits weighed, and that research had to be protected.

Thea slid the water samples into the fridge. "Now what?" she called as she entered her four-digit PIN to lock the door.

"Now you board *Odyssey*," came an authoritative voice.

Thea spun to see Dylan Lowe standing beside the doctor. The forewoman rarely made appearances in the lab, but she looked no different than she had the few times Thea had crossed paths with her over meals or in the halls: pissed off and irritated. Her pale nose was scrunched up as though she'd just smelled something foul, and her short, dark hair fell to her jawline, the cut as severe as the glare she was currently shooting them.

"She's determined," a brown-skinned Hevetz temp named Nova had told Thea during her first week on-site. "Takes her job seriously."

Thea could appreciate determination. Illogical orders were another issue.

"*Odyssey* won't hold everyone," Dr. Tarlow argued, which was precisely Thea's concern, but she wasn't about to openly question a superior.

"I've got most of the crew boarding the *Muriela*," Dylan said, "but Hevetz is requesting you and, by extension, your intern, at the Black Quarry base."

"Black Quarry?" the doctor echoed. "Never heard of it."

Neither had Thea.

"It's a newer project. I'll update you in transit. Right now, we've got twenty minutes to evacuate. Hevetz is saying this blizzard's gonna pummel Northwood for nearly a month straight. If you don't want to freeze when the generators fail, I advise you get your things in a hurry."

Thea didn't care *where* she completed her internship, just that she did. The Black Quarry base would be fine. Maybe it would even be located somewhere warm. She missed the humidity of home, the thick heat Hearth City always provided.

Perhaps the storm hadn't ruined everything after all.

Nova Singh tossed items into her duffel, attempting to block out the headache-inducing evacuation alarm. They were five hundred kilometers from the nearest town, and with a Cat-5 blizzard closing in on them fast, the window for an easy evacuation was shrinking. Flying in this would be a bitch.

At least she'd finally get to prove her worth at the yoke. If everything went smoothly, Hevetz Industries might consider hiring her as a full-time employee months ahead of schedule. There was no glamor in being a temp, and the pay sucked, too.

The door to her bunk burst open. "Ever hear of knocking?" she grumbled.

"I'm not in the mood, smart-ass."

Nova snapped to attention at the sound of her boss's voice. Dylan Lowe was never in the mood—not for sarcasm or relaxing or basically anything but work. That one night of cards the day they arrived at Northwood was clearly an outlier. Dylan had the most serious demeanor of anyone Nova had ever met, and Nova had spent eighteen months training with the best fighter pilots in the Union. She knew plenty of uptight asses.

But *this* uptight ass was her boss, and Nova spun to face the door, the duffel forgotten.

Dylan said, "Hevetz lost contact with one of their drilling crews and just issued a distress call on their behalf. We're the nearest team, and they gave us orders to investigate."

Nova muttered a swear. "What happened?"

"That's what we're going to find out. Come with me."

Nova yanked the zipper closed, slung the duffel over her shoulder, and grabbed her parka. Then she darted after Dylan, jogging up the hall. The doors to most quarters were open, crew members scrambling to pack their things and make it to the hangar.

"I need you to get *Odyssey* prepped while I round up a team," the forewoman said as they shoved between two research techs. "Tarlow and her intern might already be onboard."

"Intern meaning . . . Thea?" Nova had eaten lunch with the girl a few times in the break room. They'd bonded over being the only two at the base who couldn't legally drink.

"You're bringing an intern to investigate a distress call? That sounds kinda risky."

"So is having a temp do my flying, but Anderson's the only other pilot on site, and he doesn't have interstellar training. So he'll do the evac, and you'll do this."

"Touché," Nova said, trying to hide her excitement at the word *interstellar*. A chance to finally do some *serious* flying.

"I'm gonna pull together a small crew," Dylan continued. "Cleaver and Toby, probably."

"Toby's had a mustard stain on his polo for the last three days," Nova pointed out.

"He's our only on-site tech admin. He doesn't have to be coordinated at eating, just good with computers." She pulled up just outside the communications room. Nova stopped, too, the weight of her duffel sagging into her back. "Any other suggestions?"

"Sullivan," Nova said.

"No way."

"Come on, Dylan. Please?"

Sullivan Hooper was the only reason Nova even had this trial of a job. He'd been a mechanic with Hevetz for about five years, and being the universe's best cousin, he'd pushed her application onto the right desks when she'd needed it most, praising her skills.

But while Sullivan thought highly of Nova, his opinion of Dylan could not be more opposite. In fact, Sullivan seemed to make it his mission to gripe to Nova constantly, arguing that Dylan didn't deserve her promotions and that her father was the only reason she'd climbed Hevetz's corporate ladder so quickly. Even Nova could admit that running research ops—and now captaining a possible rescue mission—was a lot for a twenty-three-year-old, but Nova suspected Sullivan didn't see Dylan fairly. The woman was a blunt, uptight ass, sure, but she was also effective. She got things done. Nova had worked a site evaluation job in the tropics of Eutheria with Dylan a few months back, now this one on Soter's polar caps. Dylan's harsh shell had become a challenge to Nova, a game. *Two smiles*, she'd tell herself. *I bet I can make the uptight ass smile twice today.*

After working with Dylan for half a year, Nova's record was still just a whopping three. With the exception of that night of cards, which Dylan had made clear didn't count.

"We *will* need a mechanic," Dylan said, fiddling with a thin silver bracelet on her wrist. "I'll make Sullivan an offer. But if he agrees to come, you've gotta keep him in line."

"Well, that was a quick fold. Also, I will not assume responsibility for a grown man's actions."

Dylan smirked. *That counts as a half*, Nova thought. *Today's tally: 1.5.*

"All right. I'm gonna round up the others. See you on *Odyssey*?"

"Yes, ma'am."

Dylan shoved into the comm room, and Nova carried on for the hangar, her heart beating wildly against her ribs. She shouldn't be this excited. Not when the blizzard was a threat to everyone at Northwood Point and Hevetz had spent good money to ensure the location was a viable site for future drilling. Plus, this unresponsive Black Quarry crew could mean nothing good.

But Nova hadn't dropped out of high school at sixteen to taxi workers to research bases, twiddling her thumbs until everyone needed to be shuttled home again. She'd dropped out to enlist in the military, to serve and protect. She was supposed to be a decorated fighter pilot like her late father, only she'd developed a rare, degenerative eye condition that had robbed her of everything.

Not even a semester into her second year of training, her top scores suddenly meant nothing. Her skills at the yoke became worthless. When your peripheral vision gets compromised, the military won't touch you, not even when laser treatment stops the progression of vision loss and reverts it to nearly where it was before. *Surgically altered eyesight disqualifies anyone,* they'd told her. *It's not personal.*

It seemed a sham. Every damn bit of military tech was state of the art, advanced and enhanced, and yet this was where officials decided to become traditionalists—only allowing unaltered, pure eyes to sit in a pilot's chair?

It was bullshit to the fullest degree.

But it didn't change the fact that she'd become ineligible to ever fly in combat.

Her mother, who had been furious with Nova for dropping out of school, refused to take her back in. "This is your mess," she'd said. "You wanted to be an adult so badly, thought yourself too good for school? Well, now you can deal with finding work and paying rent."

Nova had turned to private companies, hoping a job as an interstellar pilot might satisfy her need to be in the air. It didn't matter that only the smallest fraction of her peripheral vision was damaged. No one wanted to take a risk on her. No one but Hevetz Industries. The multibillion-unne drilling conglomerate had said she could shuttle their workers around for a year, and if she didn't screw up, they'd consider bringing her on full-time. Maybe even get her a job in shipping, where she could expect to be in transit most of the time, always among the stars. So here she was, just a few months from nineteen, fighting tooth and nail for a job that would pay the bills while everyone else her age was training and studying for a promising career.

Nova burst into the hangar. The main doors were already open, the deathly cold of Soter's caps whipping through the space. She shouldered her way through the throng of workers trying to board the *Muriela* and raced up *Odyssey*'s gangplank.

On the bridge, she stared at the pilot's seat.

This was her chance.

Battling her way through snow and hail to get off-planet. Flying through the dark expanse of space. Touching down as smoothly as a dragonfly on water.

She was prepared for it.

She could do it with her eyes closed.

She'd impress the hell out of Dylan, who'd mention it all to her father, and Hevetz would hire her immediately. The chains would be off. Her wings reinstated.

Nova felt lighter already.

"You've never heard of Black Quarry?" Thea asked Dr. Tarlow as they raced for the hangar, packed bags flung over their shoulders.

"Never." A harsh line had appeared on the doctor's brow. It aged her slightly, but the truth was that Dr. Tarlow always looked decades younger than her nearly seventy years. Part of it was her wardrobe—fitted trousers and designer flats that always peaked from beneath her lab coat. The rest, Thea assumed, was just good genetics. Even now, with her pale hair pulled into a tight bun, Thea thought Dr. Tarlow's cheeks looked flushed with youth, her green eyes lively. It was as if decades of fieldwork and late nights staring at a screen had barely affected the woman. As if her body had decided to stay shy of forty forever.

"But Hevetz's drilling ops are always on the news," Thea said.

"The ones funded by the Union are. But the Company has plenty of private contracts, too, and the details of those operations are never disclosed. Same with surveys for future drill sites. Wouldn't want competitors sweeping in to steal a fertile corrarium vein, would we?"

Come to think of it, Thea hadn't seen a drop of coverage on the Northwood Point project, and even the job listing for her internship hadn't disclosed a location. She'd only learned she'd be spending her summer on Soter's ice caps *after* she'd accepted the position. Black Quarry could be anywhere. She could be headed from one pole to another. Or back to her home planet of Eutheria, even.

A sharp burst of wind whined around Northwood Point, and the base plunged into darkness. Thea froze, putting a hand on the wall to steady herself. A second later the backup generators kicked on. Floor lighting illuminated with white markers, and doorways gleamed teal. She couldn't get Dylan's warning about failed generators out of her head. How long would these run before powering down?

The doctor pushed her way into the hangar and Thea followed, a gust of frigid air cutting right through her. The *Muriela* was gone, and the world beyond the external hangar doors was a whirlwind of thick, heavy snow. A shiver racked Thea's body. Forty below was not something you got used to— not even in an industrial parka.

Odyssey's landing lights were on, and a massive security detail who went by Cleaver was driving a rover up the low- ered gangplank. Dylan stood in the mouth of the cargo hold, barking directions to him.

"There you are!" she shouted when she spotted Thea and Dr. Tarlow approaching. "Winds have turned for the worst. Nova says we've got about five minutes to get out of here, so get your asses buckled in."

Dr. Lisbeth Tarlow fumbled with the straps of her harness.

Just a year ago, her tremor had been barely visible, a whis- per of a twitch that would appear at random. She'd chalked it up to stress and exhaustion. Now it was a constant. She couldn't eat dinner without pieces of her meal flying off a quivering fork. Her signature had grown sloppy. Preparing slides and entering data into the computers took twice as long as it used to.

Hevetz had put their foot down and demanded she get an assistant. The pool of job applicants had been dismal— Lisbeth hadn't approved of a single one—and so the Com- pany had hired an intern while they continued the search. "We'll look for one more quarter," Aldric Vasteneur had said through the vidscreen. "One more quarter and then if no one's up to your standards, you're getting whoever I deem best. It will be nice to have a dedicated, full-time assistant," he'd gone on. The words were forced, laced with insincerity, but that was always true of CEOs. "Someone to talk to. Less time spent alone."

But Lisbeth Tarlow liked quiet. She liked solitude. This was what Hevetz never seemed to understand. She worked best alone—*had* to be alone. Assistants only slowed her. The Hevetz family had understood this. But they'd sold the Company a few years back, and the new management had been trying to convince Lisbeth to hire help ever since.

Probably she shouldn't complain. Another employee in her shoes might have been replaced by now; a more cost-efficient solution than adding an assistant to the payroll. But she was Lisbeth Tarlow, renowned microbiologist, an expert on a type of microbe that thrived in the Trios oceans and played an intricate role in the balance of the ecosystem. She'd been running environmental assessments at drilling sites before, during, and after Hevetz drilling ops for over forty years. She was the reason they continued to receive government grants and impressive Union contracts. Science and technology could work together. They could do good, but also do it responsibly. *Protect the future,* the Company slogan said, but that was only possible if they continued to monitor the ecosystem, if they were deliberate and careful in selecting drilling sites.

Hevetz *needed* her.

In fact, it was concerning that they had another assessment in the works that she'd never even heard of—this Black Quarry project. Research gigs commonly overlapped in schedule, but Lisbeth was always consulted before they began. She always knew what was happening and where.

Lisbeth made a fist and again shook it out, then returned her attention to the harness. Using every bit of focus, she guided the anchor plate into the latch. When it gave a satisfactory *click*, she leaned back in her seat, smiling. Halfway there.

Someone nudged her with an elbow. Lisbeth glanced up to find Thea nodding at the harness, her brows raised in offering.

This was what Lisbeth loved about the intern. The girl was polite and professional and didn't ask questions unless they pertained to the job at hand. In the month they'd worked together, they'd developed their own language, Lisbeth able to communicate *next slide, please* with a nod at the microscope, or *bring that closer, if you don't mind* with a beckoning finger. Most days, they rarely used words. It was a pity Thea was still a student. Lisbeth would have liked to hire *her* permanently.

"I can manage," she said to Thea, "but thank you."

Lisbeth readjusted her grip on the remaining strap, hand wavering. As she slid the buckle home, she considered that her condition, while benign, could also be hereditary. Her father had suffered a tremor like this. It appeared shortly before his death.

Liftoff wasn't as loud as Thea had anticipated. There was a roar, yes, but the sensation was worse than the noise. Even the pilot's warning—*this is gonna be rough*—didn't prepare her for the full force of the storm.

Positioned on the bridge and strapped into one of several chairs behind the pilot's seat, Thea braced against the turbulence. The ship rattled and shook, the rest of the crew bouncing in their seats beside her. Thea's teeth chattered, her ears hummed, her vision bounced. For one brief moment she feared she might be sick. She clamped her eyes shut, feeling as though her stomach had fallen into her feet, that her eyes were loose inside her skull, that the harness holding her in place was going to snap her in two.

As suddenly as the pain began, it dispersed, the pressure dissipating as the inertia dampeners activated. Thea's chair ceased to jostle. She felt suddenly weightless, almost in free fall, and then the artificial gravity must have kicked in because she was merely sitting in her chair.

Thea opened her eyes.

The world beyond the bridge window was so drastically opposite the scenery she'd experienced in the last month that she felt temporarily blinded.

Space.

Stars.

Nothing but inky black and pinpricks of light as far as she could see.

The charcoal leather of the pilot's seat was cool and familiar against Nova's spine, the glow of the cockpit controls comforting as she gripped the yoke.

It had been too long since she'd flown like this. Too long since she'd felt free.

Odyssey was only a UT-800, a standard small-class transit ship. It didn't have a fraction of the kick or power of the fighter jets she'd flown at the Academy. But she was sailing with the stars again, and it was better than nothing.

Behind her, she heard Dylan request a debriefing, ordering the crew from the bridge. Harnesses unlatched and boots stomped off.

"I need you to chart a course to the Fringe," Dylan said, sitting beside Nova. "Achlys, to be exact."

Nova gaped. There had to be some type of mistake. Achlys was an uninhabitable, storm-ravaged rock in F-1, and roughly two months from Soter, even with an FTL drive. Plus, every drop of corrarium Hevetz had ever extracted had been pulled from a planet in the Trios. You needed thriving oceans for corrarium. You needed complex *life*. Of all places to find the sustainable energy source, Achlys seemed as unlikely as a gas giant.

"You're kidding," Nova said. "Did they find corrarium on Achlys?"

Dylan merely frowned. Nova should have seen it coming. At Northwood, Dylan had mentioned *interstellar* flying. Of course they were leaving the Trios. But to head to the Fringe . . .

As respectfully as she could manage, Nova said, "What the heck is Black Quarry?"

"Just chart a course and come to the debriefing. I'd prefer to only explain this once."

He could hear it. Everything. The screeching metal and the crash of colliding bodies and the blast of the engineer's gun.

The clamor echoed in his mind. He heard it with his hands clasped over his ears. He heard it even when he made it to engineering, where the whirr of Celestial Envoy's power units thrummed around him.

It had been a nightmare getting there. Once he'd exited the vents, he'd been a rat in a maze. He crept carefully, listening at every corner and adjusting his route accordingly. More than once he'd been forced to backtrack—moving away from his destination before heading for it again. It took twice as long as it should have to reach the engine room, but he'd arrived in one piece.

Now, standing before the row of breakers, the boy considered his options. Cutting the power wouldn't change the fact that one of their pilots had flown for help, or that the engineer's SOS might have gotten out. But if someone tried to hail Celestial Envoy and couldn't make contact, maybe that would be enough to keep them from returning. Maybe Hevetz would consider the entire Black Quarry op a lost cause, an unfortunate sacrifice on a planet too dangerous to risk revisiting.

The breakers were yellow, wide, and heavy. They'd require two hands.

It would be worth it, the boy reasoned. He knew he wouldn't last until help arrived—he'd be lucky if he made it through the night—and it wasn't worth subjecting more people to this place, to that darkness . . .

He reached out and grabbed the first breaker.

II

THE TRANSIT

Odyssey

Interstellar Airspace

TOBY CALLAHAN HADN'T EXPECTED *Odyssey* to be so similar to Northwood Point, but here it was, overwhelming him with its uninspired blandness—industrial angles, narrow corridors, and rugged stairwells, all illuminated by sharp fluorescents. The ship even smelled similar—metallic and a little bit stale, despite the air he could feel filtering through the vents. But there was no ignoring that exit signs here would lead to escape pods, not ice sheets. Only a carefully engineered hull and fully functioning air locks separated the crew from the endless and deadly expanse of space.

A shiver slid over his limbs. Toby had read about ship manufacturers on New Earth who were using weakened materials to build the rigs they exported to the Trios, saving the best-made vessels for the Cradle. It was just a theory, of course, yet to be proven, but it sounded about right. The Cradle was the heart of the Union, and so they got the best, while the Trios was just a series of veins, being bled dry for their corrarium.

"Everyone grab a seat," Dylan said as they approached a lounge area just opposite the galley. Toby crashed on an armchair, kicking his feet up on the table. Sullivan did the same, and the intern sat beside Tarlow on the couch like a loyal lapdog. Hevetz had been on the doctor about getting an assistant for ages, and now they'd let a high schooler play the part, forcing Toby to set up accounts and passwords for an underqualified teenager who'd be gone by the end of the summer. A complete and utter waste of time and resources, if you asked him, but no one had.

"Long story short," Dylan began, "Hevetz lost contact with Black Quarry."

"That another drilling op?" Cleaver asked.

Dylan nodded. "My father's overseeing it, actually." Which meant it was important. Toby leaned forward in his seat, suddenly interested. "The crew failed to report yesterday, and Hevetz issued a general distress call on their behalf today. We were the nearest crew, so based on Company policy, we've been tasked with responding to it."

"But we can't be nearest," the intern said. *Well, look at that, she speaks!* Toby thought. And clearly she had a spine after all—or was just plain dumb—because everyone knew better than to argue with Dylan Lowe.

Dylan jerked her jaw toward the intern, her glare pointed.

"Well, we're off-planet," the girl said quietly, her dark eyes downturned as her pale fingers laced together. "There must be a closer team already stationed on Eutheria, right?"

"We're not headed to Eutheria," Dylan said. "Black Quarry's stationed on Achlys."

A confused murmur passed through the group and Toby watched the intern's face scrunch up, her too-thick brows dipping as her lips puckered into a pout. He knew what she was thinking. It was what they were all thinking: There was nothing *on* Achlys. It was tidally locked to the red dwarf star, F_1, meaning one side of the rock always faced the sun, burnt out, and the other side was plagued by nightfall. There were theories that if you stuck to the terminator—the area between the night and day sides—you might be able to avoid the worst of the planet's storms, but the Union had long ago deemed it not worth the risk (or efforts) of colonization. It was basic knowledge, taught in every universe history class.

"I thought we ran environmental assessments *before* drilling?" Cleaver asked. The bulky security detail was still hovering behind Dylan, his semiautomatic ray-rifle held so the barrel pointed at the floor.

"We do," Dylan said. "Did you forget Witch Hazel?"

Cleaver's face went as contorted as the intern's had a moment earlier, and Toby didn't miss how Lisbeth Tarlow bristled at the mention of the past project.

"Witch Hazel," Toby repeated to Cleaver. "The first and

only environmental survey that Hevetz ran on Achlys. It made our Dr. Tarlow here a legend." He nodded at the woman, but Cleaver remained perplexed. "Come on, man. Everyone knows about Witch Hazel. Even the intern knows, don't you, Thea? Wanna give us all a rundown?"

She shook her head adamantly, causing her dark hair to ripple like an inky river.

Toby had been pestering her about the doctor's history every chance he could get. *Did Tarlow tell you how she survived yet?* he'd say over meals in the break room. *I heard she killed the whole crew in their sleep.* It wasn't the nicest way to initiate someone, but the girl was just so criminally easy to toy with. Toby could pick any crazed conspiracy theory—from Tarlow being a murderer to Achlys's air turning toxic—and throw it at Thea, and she never told him off. She had to be smart to have snagged her internship, and yet she rarely showed it.

"Oh, you mean *that* Witch Hazel," Cleaver said, drawing all the vowels out about twice as long as necessary. "Wasn't that, like, fifty years ago, though?" His mouth pinched with suspicion as he eyed Lisbeth Tarlow. Even Toby could admit that the doctor didn't look old enough to have been a part of the op. Maybe she'd undergone some pricey skin rejuvenation procedures.

"I was only a kid at the time," the doctor said, "allowed to stay with my parents in their bunker because of the duration of the three-year survey."

"And the only one to survive," Toby said.

A massive storm had struck while the crew was taking samples, and when the rescue team finally arrived, they found Lisbeth Tarlow locked in the bunker, shaking like a leaf.

She'd been all over the news, a headline to fascinate a generation—the girl who survived a survey no adult had. The bodies were never found, and while no foul play was discovered, the entire operation had left a bad taste in everyone's mouths. Speculations flooded the Interhub and continued to pop up on forums to this day. While Toby didn't put much stock in the "Tarlow was a kid serial killer who murdered the whole crew" conspiracy, he maintained that the public hadn't gotten the whole story. Bad tastes were like foul odors—they meant something was being covered up.

Even now, he felt like Tarlow was hiding something, her hands clasped in her lap, her posture ridiculously sharp. She was too calm. She'd lost her parents on Achlys—lost her entire crew—and she had nothing to say about revisiting the place?

Boots clanked back near the bridge, and Nova joined the group.

"What did I miss?"

"Hevetz must have found corrarium on Achlys," Toby said.

It was the only explanation for why a crew might be there.

The doctor bristled again, but when she spoke, her voice was calm. "Witch Hazel found conflicting evidence regarding the possibility of corrarium veins, and Hevetz declared Achlys unsuitable for drilling just months after I came home. Unpredictable weather, an insurance nightmare, profit margins too small to outweigh the risks; all the same reasons the Union never seriously considered colonizing the planet. It makes no sense for a crew to be drilling there now. If they'd bothered to ask me my opinion on the matter, I'd have said to avoid the place. Indefinitely. It's too dangerous."

"Yeah, but corporations are no better than governments," Toby said. "Greedy bastards trying to line their pockets at the expense of everyone else."

"This again?" Nova moaned. "Not everything is a conspiracy, Toby."

"Right. If we just sit around ignorant, we won't notice the corruption, and it will almost be as if it's truly not happening."

"Can it, both of you," Dylan spat. "I've had to listen to your bickering over every damn meal at Northwood Point, and I'm not about to do it again on this ship. Look, Hevetz is five billion unnes stronger than they were at the time of Witch Hazel. There's enough red tape and confidentiality records around *any* mission, and maybe circumstances we don't fully understand are at play here. Maybe Hevetz has a very good reason to deem Achlys 'worth the risk.' It doesn't matter *why* they sent a crew, just that they did and that now they're not responding. We have an obligation to look into that." Her eyes moved over them one at a time as she spoke, boring in, daring someone to challenge her. "Black Quarry has been on Achlys for several months, but they only broke ground a few weeks ago. Setting up the drilling site took longer than expected because of poor weather. There's a good chance the weather is also to blame for their failure to report, causing an equipment malfunction or blocked signal."

"Shouldn't they be able to fix that themselves?" Sullivan asked.

"After the Witch Hazel disaster, Hevetz didn't want to waste any time getting a crew out. We were nearest, and luckily, we were able to hit the skies before that storm kept us grounded."

"Yeah, so lucky," Toby deadpanned. "A crew of novices is speeding off to the Fringe."

"Watch it, Callahan," Dylan barked.

He didn't know what had gotten into him—talking back like this. It was Sullivan who ran his mouth, complaining about Dylan behind her back and rolling his eyes when he didn't think she was looking, and one of these days, it was going to get him fired. Or maybe, if Sullivan was really lucky, just suspended for a few months. Toby had always taken the safest route: fuming in silence. Until today.

"It's not as if you have decades of experience under your belt either," Dylan added.

"But that's exactly my point," Toby said, working to keep his voice calm. "Look, with all due respect, you've got one half-assed crew here. I'm only a year out of university. Cleaver's so trigger-happy Hevetz only stations him at isolated bases where there's no civilians to mistakenly shoot. Plus, we've got a high school intern and a temp pilot rejected by the military?"

"That doesn't mean my skills aren't top-notch," Nova gritted out, brown arms folded across her dark green jumpsuit.

And you, Dylan, Toby felt like saying. *A Company darling, on account of your father, who runs surveys and is highly underqualified to captain a rescue mission.*

Instead, he only said, "This still doesn't feel like a rescue crew."

Sullivan grunted in agreement.

"I don't care what you think it feels like," Dylan said sharply. "Hevetz initiated this distress call on Black Quarry's behalf, and while we don't have details right now, Hevetz assured me they will keep us informed while in transit. As for our crew, I rounded up the best-looking team that Northwood Point had to offer, and that included our only interstellar pilot, and yes, a high school intern, because Hevetz strongly suggested I bring Tarlow."

"Because of her previous experience?" Toby muttered. "From when she was *ten*." He had the wits to say it quietly enough that Dylan couldn't hear, but Tarlow's eyes flicked his way.

"I don't like it." Sullivan ran a hand over his shaved head. "We should turn around, have them send a more qualified crew. I'm a mechanic. I do EVA repairs and calibrate FTL drives. I don't search barren wastelands for storm survivors."

"We don't even know if there *was* a storm," Dylan snapped. "If a specialized crew is needed, Hevetz will send them. They'll make that call in the next seventy-two hours. But in the meantime, I'm not turning my back on Black Quarry."

On him, Toby thought. This wasn't about the crew—it was about Dylan's father. He was the only reason she had her job, and she had to protect that. Maybe she even cared for him a little, too, but Toby doubted it.

"I am following Company orders," Dylan continued. "If anyone here has a problem doing the same, please let me know so I can draft a letter to Hevetz advising for your termination. As for all those bullshit horror stories you've heard about Achlys? Get them out of your head. Right now. They're not real. The air doesn't burn people up. People don't disintegrate during storms. Black Quarry has software to predict volatile weather, and the crew knows when to hunker down. We're not going to have to 'search barren wastelands for storm survivors.'"

If that was true, Toby didn't see why Hevetz would need to send a crew to Achlys in such a hurry to begin with.

Sensing that her argument wasn't winning over the crew, Dylan turned to the doctor. "Tell them, Tarlow. Please."

The doctor ran her dainty hands along the front of her white lab coat, smoothing the material in her lap. "It's a dangerous, desolate place," she said finally. "But we'll be fine, so long as we're careful and keep an eye on the weather." Her fingers shook, and though Toby knew it was the product of her tremor, it was far from reassuring.

After adding water to the three compartments of her dehydrated dinner pack, Thea was rewarded with soggy peas, runny mashed potatoes, and bland pork, all of it the same watery consistency. While most of the crew sat crammed around the mess table, she remained in the lounge, eating beside Dr. Tarlow while attempting to stifle her anger.

Dylan Lowe had just stolen *months* of Thea's life—four, to be exact. Maybe Hevetz employees were used to sacrificing time like this. It was merely a long commute, a lengthy meeting, time on the clock. But to Thea, it was her world, and Dylan Lowe had just hijacked her future. A future in which every step mattered.

Thea had planned it out oh-so carefully. Having grown up in a foster home, Thea knew she had to fight for herself. She'd been hoping the Hevetz gig would help her stand out when she applied to Linneaus Institute in the fall, especially if Dr. Tarlow wrote her a favorable reference letter. Maybe it would even earn her a healthy scholarship. As it was, Thea couldn't even afford airfare to the Cradle where Linneaus operated on New Earth, let alone a single credit.

But none of that seemed to matter. All her carefully laid plans were collapsing, imploding like a dying star, and by the time she returned from Achlys, the application deadline for Linneaus would have passed.

The foster warden back home would be so smugly pleased. He'd needed to approve Thea's travel visas for the Hevetz internship, and he'd laughed when reading the details. "Hevetz?" he'd said with a snort. "A research gig off-planet? You're not qualified, Althea."

"It's Thea, sir." He glanced up, brow pitched. "My name. I prefer Thea." She'd told him this a hundred times.

"The sooner you learn that kids from Hearth City don't amount to nothing, the better off you'll be. You following? You're not going nowhere. You're not qualified for this gig. Just move on already. Accept that this is the best it's gonna be."

Those words had stung like salt water in a wound, nudging

at a very real insecurity that forever lingered in the back of her mind.

She felt it again now.

She *was* unprepared. She *was* in over her head.

"What do you think happened to Black Quarry?" she asked Dr. Tarlow, shoving that negative voice aside.

The doctor scooped up some runny potatoes, her fork wavering in her grasp. "It's probably something small—an equipment failure, a jammed signal. I wouldn't be surprised if Black Quarry makes contact with Hevetz in the next few hours and Nova has to turn this boat around."

Did she truly believe this, Thea wondered, or did she hope it? With her history on that planet, Thea suspected it might be the latter.

"And if they don't call us off? I signed up for a summer-long internship on Soter's ice caps, not investigating distress calls. I'm supposed to be back in school by September. I have university applications due in early fall."

"Thea," the doctor breathed. "I'm so sorry you got dragged into this. That's on Dylan."

No, it's on you, she felt like saying. *Where you go, your intern goes. I never had a choice.* But she knew that wasn't fair. The doctor couldn't control her tremor. Thea was taking out her frustrations on the wrong party.

"On the bright side," Dr. Tarlow went on, "think of how

amazing this will look to the Linneaus admissions board. I doubt most university-bound students can add 'experience in deep space and on uninhabited planets' to their resume."

Thea forced herself to mirror the doctor's weak grin. It was true that this *would* be an incredible learning experience. Working an internship alongside Dr. Lisbeth Tarlow was one thing, but assisting the doctor all the way into the folds of space? Those were the type of credentials that would make a renowned university seriously consider an application—even one submitted post-deadline.

Kids from Hearth City don't amount to nothing.

Oh, she'd amount to something. Thea would amount to so much that no one in the whole universe would be able to ignore her. Not Hevetz. Not Linneaus. Not a single damn soul.

Lisbeth Tarlow retired to bed as soon as she finished eating. She couldn't stand being around the crew anymore, didn't trust herself to keep her nerves hidden.

They couldn't go back to Achlys. It wasn't safe. And yet they were already headed there, at Company orders. Her word couldn't override Aldric Vasteneur's.

What was he playing at? Hevetz instructed Dylan to bring Lisbeth along today, and yet they'd refused to ask Lisbeth her opinion when starting the Black Quarry op? She should have known about the project when it was first proposed. She should have known the *instant* it was even being entertained. Lisbeth would have done her damnedest to see that it was never green-lit.

She stepped into her quarters, shutting the door. The room was narrow and drab. Two beds and one desk and a strip of track lighting that threw everything into a sickly yellow glow. The intern would likely share this room with her, and if Lisbeth was going to cry, now was the time to do it.

She sat on the bed and stared at her hands.

They trembled as she unbuttoned her lab coat.

There was no changing the past, but if she had to go back to that place, she would make sure the past wasn't repeated. In the process, she might even find answers. She'd been digging and hypothesizing and researching for decades in the Trios to no avail. Perhaps returning to Achlys, while terrifying, was also a blessing.

Her parents' faces flashed before her, and Lisbeth clamped her eyes shut. Even in the darkness, she saw them. And Achlys. And an inky blackness that swam and twisted and curled like ribbons.

She pressed her fingers to her eyelids until the image was gone.

Thea gathered up her dishes and took them into the kitchen. As she scraped them clean, the crew rambled behind her.

Sullivan: "Hevetz better be paying us overtime for this."

Nova: "Just be happy you've *got* decent pay, Sull. My temp wages are criminal."

Toby: "We'll all get better wages if the Trios goes independent."

Nova: "Says who? If we pull out of the Union, the import taxes on pharm and tech products from the Cradle alone would bankrupt us."

Cleaver: "Pass that pork."

Toby: "So we up export taxes on corrarium in return."

Nova: "And slowly bleed each other dry? How does that—"

Dylan: "I think we have bigger things to worry about right now."

Sullivan: "Oh, like your father's unresponsive crew and how you didn't bother to tell us we were answering a distress call until it was too late for us to bail?"

Cleaver: "The potatoes, too."

Dylan: "I was out of options with that storm slamming us. You would've done the same thing in my shoes."

Sullivan: "I'll never be in your shoes, 'cause I don't have a father working for Hevetz who can promote me before I deserve it."

Dylan: "That same father could get your ass fired, Sullivan. *I* could get you fired."

Cleaver: "Toby, you gonna finish that meat?"

Dylan: "Actually, I think I'll go write that letter documenting your insubordination, Sullivan. How's that sound?"

Sullivan: "No, don't. I'm sorry. This whole thing's just gotten me riled. I didn't mean it."

Cleaver: "Toby! Your meat. Are you gonna eat it?"

On and on it went, as Thea dried and stowed away the dishes. She'd listened to similar bickering in the break room at Northwood Point. Sullivan was constantly criticizing Dylan, though never to her face like this. Nova and Toby were always arguing about politics. Thea was of the same mindset as Nova: the planets that made up the Trios were strongest when they were part of the United Planetary Coalition. Leaving the Union would only create new problems, and she didn't understand how the Radicals—a long-standing and ever-growing group of Trios citizens angling for independence—couldn't see that. But even if Thea *didn't* share the pilot's opinions, she would have sided with Nova during these debates—anything to get back at Toby for teasing about Dr. Tarlow's past and spewing nightmarish fiction.

Thea had just hung up the dishtowel when a signal blared from the bridge, halting the bickering behind her.

"Proximity alert," Nova said, standing. "See you clods on the other side." She tossed her napkin down and took off running, Dylan calling after her, "Thread the needle, Nova-Girl!"

Thea watched the pilot disappear from the mess, her dark braid flapping behind her like a rope.

"When will she sleep?" Thea asked no one in particular.

"When we're through the asteroid belt," Dylan answered, "which should be in a few hours. Impressive accelerator drives might have us cruising at a twentieth of the speed of light right now, but that's not gonna get us to the Fringe any time soon. Once we're sufficiently beyond the Trios, we'll engage FTL."

"Which is when we'll all sleep, right?" Sullivan asked. "I'm tired as hell."

"You're not sleeping for the long haul until you've run checks on every last component. I'd say tomorrow around oh nine hundred we'll lock in for good."

"For good?" Thea echoed.

Sullivan pointed a fork her way. "Sedation, kid. Cryostasis. Even traveling faster than light, it'll take us roughly two months to make the trip to Achlys. You think there's enough food on this rig to sustain us that whole time and once we're there? Nah, we'll go under and sleep our way to the destination. It's the best way to travel, really. Feels as quick as a yawn."

It was difficult to wrap her head around. The flight from Thea's home planet of Eutheria to Soter had been thrilling, but had taken place at the interplanetary speeds Dylan had mentioned. Thanks to the relatively close position of the planets at that time, they'd covered 116 million kilometers in roughly two and a half hours.

But to engage FTL, to speed between star systems, covering sixty light-years in roughly two months . . .

"You better wipe that starry, dazed look off your face before people realize you're just a confused intern and not a legitimate member of this crew. Oh, shoot!" Toby put a hand to his chest in mock regret. "Did I give away your secret?"

This was precisely why Thea preferred science to people. Numbers and data made sense, but people were impossible.

She left without acknowledging Toby's dig.

"I heard you're bunking with the doctor tonight," he called after her. "Stay safe in there. Wouldn't want Witch Hazel 2.0."

Nova reclined in the pilot's chair as *Odyssey* hurtled toward the Lethe Belt. She'd already adjusted their course and wasn't really needed anymore. The shields were up to deflect smaller matter, and the larger asteroids in the belt were roughly fifty thousand kilometers apart—nowhere near a threat. In fact, the ship was already back on autopilot. But

Nova remained in the chair, staring into the abyss. Once they passed the belt, they'd be completely out of the Trios, tearing for the Fringe, getting farther from civilization with each passing second.

Just chart a course and come to the debriefing. I'd prefer to only explain this once.

Had it been wrong of Nova to expect Dylan to be upfront about Black Quarry's location? The captain could have told her back on Soter, during Northwood's evac. Yes, time was of the essence due to the incoming blizzard, but Nova was the only person capable of piloting *Odyssey* and she was now flying them toward a planet known for weather so volatile it had claimed the lives of the entire Witch Hazel crew, minus Tarlow. Hell, it might have already claimed the lives of some of the Black Quarry drillers. What if Nova couldn't handle the winds while landing? What if she got them on the ground but couldn't get them out again? It was a lot of responsibility to shoulder, and the very least Dylan could have done was explain *exactly* what was at stake to begin with.

So turn around. Hevetz will send a different crew.

Nova's subconscious presented this option as though she had a choice. As if disobeying orders wouldn't cost Nova her job. Besides, what kind of asshole didn't answer a distress call? A coward. Not the type of person Nova wanted to be.

She heard someone on the stairs outside the bridge, and a

moment later, hands cupped her shoulders, squeezed reassuringly. "How you feeling, Nova?"

She beamed up at her cousin. "Like a star made for streaming."

The corners of Sullivan's lips lifted, brightening his entire demeanor. His skin was tawny—lighter than hers—and with his shaved head, broad shoulders, and sharp nose, Sullivan's exterior presented something sterner than the cousin Nova knew him to be. He'd recently turned twenty-eight, but working for Hevetz had aged him. Or maybe it was just working for Dylan. There were creases around his eyes that Nova didn't remember him having a few years ago, and back then, he'd worked exclusively for Hevetz's shipping department, running maintenance for rigs that hauled corrarium from the Trios to the Cradle. It was a thankless job, with strict schedules and lots of time spent in transit. He'd transferred to this current research position so he'd have more time at home with his family, and now he was on *Odyssey*, flying away from them yet again.

"Crew quarters are going to be tight tonight," he said, the smile fading. "Our lovable captain says you and me are bunkmates."

"That sounds cramped," Nova said.

"'Cozy' was the word she used. Also: 'Family reunion.'"

"She would twist it like that." *Odyssey* was equipped with

five bedrooms—two with double capacity and the rest, singles. The obvious solution was to pair off the women: Dylan and Nova, the doctor and the intern. But if Nova had learned anything about her boss these past few months, it was that Dylan Lowe could talk her way out of every corner, turn a catastrophe on its head, somehow make you believe the worst thing to ever happen to you was actually the best. She was queen of silver linings.

"She should have bunked you with Toby or Cleaver," Nova said to her cousin, "and doubled up with me."

"She had her own room as a forewoman at Northwood Point. She wasn't about to demote herself now that she's captaining *Odyssey*."

Nova rolled her eyes.

"Ah, come on, Nova. I'm not that much of a drag to hang out with. You could at least try to mask your disappointment."

"It's not you, Sull. I promise."

"Oh, I know," he said. "It's Dylan. You like her."

"That's not true." But even as she said it, her heart beat wildly in her chest.

That night of cards flashed in her mind. Dylan betting bold, throwing back drinks, shooting coy smiles across the table. She'd kissed Nova before staggering to bed, then claimed the next morning that it was a mistake. "It can't happen again," she'd said. "I can't be involved with my subordinates." Nova had agreed. She hadn't gone looking for the kiss, but after it happened, she kept thinking about it constantly. Watching Dylan's mouth whenever she spoke, imaginging it pressed against her own.

She looked away from Sullivan, her cheeks feeling warm.

"A word of advice: never get involved with your boss," her cousin went on. "Murky waters. Tragic endings."

"Don't waste your breath, Sull. There's nothing there."

"Whatever you say." His boots clanked off.

"That's how you're gonna leave things?" Nova called after him, swiveling in the chair. "Where the hell are you going?"

Sullivan paused in the doorway. "I gotta record a message for Mikko, let her know I'll be gone for a while. I'm gonna miss the twins' birthday again. Working research was supposed to fix this problem."

"Mikko will understand," Nova said. "It's not like you can control distress calls."

"It's not her I'm worried about. It's the boys. They're just four, and all they're gonna see is Daddy missing another party." He prodded the doorframe with the butt of his fist, mouth in a hard line. "Anyway, I'm serious about that advice, Nova. Dylan's not worth it. She's selfish, and even if she wasn't, she'd manage to get you fired if things ever went south."

"I appreciate you helping me get this job, but I can take care of myself from here." She turned back to the window.

"I'd just hate to see you—"

"Good night, Sull."

Long after the din of his boots faded on the catwalks, Nova was still staring at the stars.

At 0900 the next morning, Dylan called for cryostasis.

Thea reported to a small room positioned below the bridge and at the very nose of the ship, where cylindrical glass compartments lined the perimeter. As she'd been settling in the night before, the ship had engaged FTL. Thea had felt a subtle pressure as they accelerated, then nothing. When she'd found a window to peer from come morning, the stars outside were thin white streaks. Now, in the windowless cryostasis room, there was no way of sensing that *Odyssey* was barreling toward Achlys at nearly one hundred times the speed of light.

"System check?" Dylan barked at Sullivan.

"FTL drive running steady at eighty percent. That's the fastest I feel comfortable pushing *Odyssey* for a trip this long. Anything more could weaken the inertia suppressor, and then we're bugs on a windshield."

"Course?"

"Plotted," Nova confirmed. "We'll be pulled out of

FTL—and stasis—as we close in on Achlys."

"Perfect," Dylan said. "Until then, sweet dreams." She entered some commands into a processing unit in the middle of the room. The doors to each chamber slid open.

Thea chose one beside Dr. Tarlow. After she stepped inside, the doors slid shut, and Thea leaned back, resting her head in the designated area, her arms in the wrist cuffs. A fan kicked on. A few minutes later, she sensed reality shifting. It was like that moment between dreaming and waking, a realm of limbo. Thea grew vaguely cold. Her eyelids became heavy.

Through the chamber's glass door, she saw Dylan close her eyes across the room.

And then Thea, too, was drifting.

It was not as quick as yawning, like Sullivan had promised.

Thea moved in and out of sleep. If she dreamed, she didn't remember the details, and when she was awake, her thoughts weren't much better than nightmares.

The distress call.

What they might find on Achlys.

Where she'd find herself in a few months.

Thea could think, but she couldn't see or hear or feel. She only knew that she existed, that her body filled space, that she was trapped as the ship drew steadily nearer to its destination.

Thea was floating.

Suspended.

A sample in a jar of formaldehyde.

Nova dreamed of stars and flying.

She was alone on a small transport ship, chasing a beacon that led her to a space station with a massive breach. Inside, objects floated in zero gravity—droplets of water, droplets of blood, a thin silver bracelet.

Something hovered near the far air lock. A person, wearing a leather jacket and fitted pants. Short, dark hair splayed out around their head like a halo, and a stun gun was holstered at their thigh.

Dylan.

Nova pushed through the space station, propelling herself off ladders and walls until she reached the woman. She grabbed her, spun her around.

Dylan's eyes were missing, replaced with gaping holes.

A scream tore from Nova's throat, and then she was back on her ship, drifting among the safety of stars. Time passed at a rate she couldn't calculate, her memories fogged. And then there was a beacon again, and a space station on the radar.

The dream repeated.

● ● ●

Lisbeth Tarlow swam through darkness. It was thick, viscous. It choked and smothered.

Just before snatching her last breath of air, the liquid thinned, transforming into clear water. Dark seaweed danced below, tendrils glinting. Lisbeth's toes grazed the uppermost blades.

There was a voice in her head—*Don't tell them, don't tell, don't*—and then an echo, from somewhere deep in the water. *Tell, tell them, tell them now.*

Waking was what felt like yawning. Satisfying, eager, an overdue stretch.

When Thea opened her eyes the world was blinding. Her limbs felt detached from her body and heavy. So heavy.

The door to her chamber was open, and she could hear a distant sound, ebbing, flowing. As it grew clearer, she recognized it as the proximity alarm from when they'd approached the Lethe Belt.

Two months ago.

Had it really been that long?

Nova shot by her line of vision, a blur of brown skin and moss-green jumpsuit as she tore for the stairs. The others descended from their chambers, stretching and groaning.

Thea stepped onto the metal floor of the cyrostasis room, surprised that she didn't find the weight of her own frame a labor. She'd expected her knees to buckle beneath her, to have lost all her muscle. Didn't hospital patients have to relearn how to walk after months in a bed? But Thea only felt a vague tightness in her joints; a stiffness that suggested she'd dozed off in an awkward position for a few hours.

"Bridge," Dylan snapped, and Thea told her legs to move, following the others from the room and up a flight of stairs.

On the captain's orders, everyone strapped into their seats on the bridge, but Dylan lingered near the window a moment, fiddling with a silver bracelet on her wrist.

Achlys loomed in the distance. The day side was a scorched expanse of barren, endless brown; the night side was bathed in shadow, seemingly black from their position. Thea didn't think the terminator looked very habitable. If there was water along that meridian, it wasn't in any large quantity. From *Odyssey*, the land between the day and night sides simply looked brownish gray.

"I reviewed the updates that came in from Hevetz while we were under," Dylan said. "They've confirmed that Black Quarry is still unresponsive, and shortly after we entered stasis, an additional backup crew was shipped out. They will be arriving in roughly twenty-six hours. In the meantime, we're to set down and get in touch with Black Quarry, figure out what happened."

Dread laced through Thea's body. Backup should have been reassuring, but all it did was make her wonder why backup was even needed to begin with. Wasn't the *Odyssey* crew enough? Did Hevetz know something they weren't sharing?

This all felt suddenly much larger than her internship and the experience point she was hoping to add to her applications when returning home. Toby had been right all along, just like the foster warden.

I'm really not qualified for this.

The planet reminded Nova of a massive eyeball, the terminator roping around the rock like a murky, brown iris. It stared, and she stared back.

She double-checked *Odyssey*'s radiation shields. Active and running strong. F1 was only a red dwarf star—cooler, smaller, and far less luminous than the Trios's and Cradle's suns—but it was just as capable of burning them up if they flew too close for too long. She kept them on course, and soon the pilot's chair was shuddering against Nova's back, *Odyssey* entering a dance with gravity.

Here comes the fun part.

She engaged the rear thrusters and the ship roared. Inertia suppressor readings spiked on the dashboard during entry, then dropped off as the g-force exerted on the ship also lessened. The pressure came from all angles, though, her blood beating like a fury in response. Grip firm on the yoke, Nova pulled them out of their dive, and her heart hammered in her chest. God, she'd missed this.

Cruising some three thousand meters above the scorched side of the planet, Nova turned her attention to the radar.

"Tracking software," Dylan prompted, as if she'd thought of it first.

"Already on it." A beacon blipped on the screen—somewhere in the terminator. Nova grabbed the radio.

"*Celestial Envoy*, this is *Odyssey*. Do you read me?"

Silence.

"*Celestial Envoy*, this is the Hevetz-manned *Odyssey* responding to a Company-issued distress call. Do you copy?"

Nothing.

"Let's go to them," Dylan said.

Nova adjusted their course and flew on. As they left the scorched side of the planet behind them, visibility grew worse, slipping into something akin to twilight. What Nova could make out of the planet below appeared rugged—mountains and ravines, crevices and craters—and the sonar mapping depicted something similar on her dash. The infamous Achlys storms were absent. For now.

Well into the terminator and nearly on the dark side of the rock, they finally came upon the research and exploration ship that had transported the Black Quarry crew to Achlys months earlier. *Celestial Envoy* stood out against the rugged landscape, the polished exterior winking under *Odyssey*'s lights. But nothing winked from within. No lights, no signs of activity.

"Set us down at a distance," Dylan ordered.

Nova took *Odyssey* in wide circles, searching out a place to land. Achlys was a mess of crevices and cracks and spears of rock that shot upward from the ground like angry blades, but with careful work at the yoke, she eventually set them down several kilometers west of *Celestial Envoy*.

"Nicely done," the captain said, giving Nova a rare smile. It was the first of the day and should have brightened Nova's sprits, but her stomach was uneasy.

She powered *Odyssey* down. The sound of harnesses releasing filled the bridge.

Nova knew what would come next. Gear and stun guns and flashlights. Search and rescue.

This was what she'd wanted—to prove herself a worthy and skilled pilot who Hevetz couldn't wait to get on their payroll. She'd just expected to do it by more traditional means.

It was too late for wishful thinking. The only way out was through.

Nova released her harness.

● ● ●

Thea waited in the cargo bay alongside the others as Sullivan suited up and stepped into the air lock. After opening the exterior door to the elements, he checked Achlys's atmosphere with a handheld device, then returned to the cargo bay.

"Everything looks stable. Roughly seventy-six percent nitrogen, twenty-three percent oxygen, and sixty-nine thousandths of a percent carbon dioxide. Plus, trace amounts of argon, methane, and helium."

"CO_2's a touch high," Nova pointed out.

Dylan batted a hand. "People have worked in worse."

"For an hour or two," Sullivan said, tucking the device into his pocket. "Not indefinitely."

"Well, we're following Black Quarry's protocols while on Achlys, so it's environmental suits for everyone so long as we're exposed to the elements." Dylan pointed to one of the lockers lining the perimeter of the cargo hold.

Thea located the smallest suit and pulled it on. The material was thin but durable; not quite skintight, and not an impairment to her mobility, either. Compared to the numerous layers she'd been used to wearing the past month while gathering water samples at Northwood Point, it felt almost freeing. A utility belt built into the suit hugged her waist, and reinforced panels lay across her chest and biceps to monitor her vitals. The bulkiest and heaviest part of the suit fell across her shoulder blades, where the oxygen reserves were stored.

"Everyone start your clocks," Dylan continued. "We've each got about ten hours of oxygen and should be back long before those run low, but keep an eye on the time."

On Dylan's cue, Thea reset the watch that was built into the wrist of the suit. Milliseconds began ticking off. The crew pulled on their helmets, and Thea hurried to do the same. When it clicked into place, creating a seal with her suit, her vitals flickered on the helmet's glass visor, just in the corner of her vision.

It was fancy tech, but also intimidating. Having her pulse and blood pressure constantly displayed only made Thea think of all the types of employees to have worn these suits before her—the situations they saw themselves in, the need to even have vitals monitored to begin with.

I'm not qualified for this, she thought, and her pulse readings spiked in response.

Thea exhaled through her nose, forcing away the thought as she tried to steady her breathing. The last thing she needed was to burn through her oxygen too quickly. The numbers fell, stabilized.

One thing at a time.

That was how Thea had gotten here, after all—one assignment at a time, one aced test, one perfect essay, one application, one internship, and now one foot after the other yet again. Toward *Celestial Envoy*, then through it, then back to *Odyssey*. Back home. Back to her life, her future.

She could do this.

Dylan punched a button to open the air lock. They all stepped in. Another punch to seal it, a third to open the exterior door.

The gangplank lowered.

And Achlys beckoned.

He'd seen them coming. In the endless state of near darkness, it had been impossible to miss. First, the emergency tracking software had been engaged remotely. He'd been scavenging the ship again, restocking his supplies, and the steady beep-beep-beep drew him to a halt. When he'd raced for the observation deck, he could make out the ship in the distance, a tiny star shooting toward Celestial Envoy.

It held a search and rescue crew; he was sure of it.

They'd kill him for what he'd done. And what he hadn't done. And who he was.

The boy retreated into the shadows. His eyes adjusted, almost instantly now. The last two months had forced him to adapt, this much was certain.

He would need a plan, carefully constructed, foolproof. Earning trust in a situation like this wouldn't be easy.

The boy breathed deeply, envisioning every stairwell and hallway and turn he'd need to navigate before moving. Then he pushed off the railing and ran.

III

THE SEARCH

Celestial Envoy

Achlys, Fringe-1 System

"THIS ISN'T RIGHT," SULLIVAN SAID as they drove, his voice crackling in Thea's ear. The helmets were linked for wireless communication, and it was strange hearing him when he wasn't even in Thea's rover. "It's too dark. They're not answering. I got a bad feeling."

No one said anything. Not even Dylan, who Sullivan's words were surely meant for.

"Look, I got a family to think about," he went on. "Maybe we just wait for the backup crew. They're only twenty-something hours behind us."

"Twenty-six hours," Dylan snapped from out of view. "And I've got family who's *part* of Black Quarry. Now, for the love of god, shut up. Driving around all these craters is harder than it looks."

Thea was relieved when he fell quiet. Sullivan's fears mirrored her own and were making her pulse readings jump again.

Dr. Tarlow gave Thea a nudge with her elbow, followed by a reassuring nod that seemed to say, "Don't worry." Thea had always respected the doctor, admired her greatly, but this lie was so obvious that a tiny ember of resentment began to burn inside her. How could anyone not be worried right now?

Never meet your idols, Thea remembered Mel saying. *They rarely live up to your image of them.*

As Cleaver drove, following Dylan's rover toward *Celestial Envoy*, Thea tilted her head back, looking out the moonroof that spanned the entire length of Rover2. A star-pocked blanket stared back. The rover was heavy-duty, a true all-terrain vehicle, unlike the drafty, glorified golf cart she'd driven around Soter's caps back at Northwood. Behind the bench seat she and Dr. Tarlow occupied was a spacious rear for hauling equipment, accessible by a hatchback door. Its window was narrow, and through it, Thea could see *Odyssey* shrinking in the distance, the cloak of twilight and wafting dust swallowing it whole.

When *Celestial Envoy* finally entered the glow of the rover's's headlights a few minutes later, it looked nothing short of ominous. Where *Odyssey* was small and slender, with rooms stretched out over the course of two levels and a cargo bay, this ship was monstrous. The gangplank was already lowered and the ship's innards bared to the night.

Rover1 lurched to a halt, and Cleaver stepped on the brake, halting Rover2 just a few meters back.

"It's open," Sullivan said from the first vehicle, his voice again as clear as though he was sitting beside Thea in Rover2. "It shouldn't be open like this."

Ignoring Sullivan's concerns, Dylan climbed from Rover1 and motioned for everyone to follow her on foot. *Maybe Sullivan has a point*, Thea felt like saying. But she wouldn't. Didn't. One thing at a time. Follow this order, then the next. She would get through this.

She scrambled from the vehicle and, with the wind nudging at her back, followed the rest of the team up the gangplank. Cleaver had his ray-rifle out, and everyone else from Rover1 held stun guns at the ready. Thea flexed her fingers around the flashlight she'd taken from *Odyssey*, unsure what to do with her hands. At Northwood Point, she'd carried a stun gun on the ice caps, to protect against lynx and wolves, yet here she was, in a situation where she truly might need a weapon for once, and she was unequipped.

As the crew moved up the gangplank, lights from their helmets bobbed like cautious fireflies, the flashlights mounted to their pistols and rifles cutting into the depth of the cargo bay.

"Can someone get the power back up?" Dylan asked.

"On it," Toby responded. His footsteps clanked off, a lone flashlight beam moving deeper into the cavernous ship.

Thea scanned the hold. As far as she could tell, it was

65

empty. And overrun. Storage crates and drilling gear were strewn about. Shuttles and rovers would have made sense, but there were no vehicles, at least not that Thea could see.

The floor was awash with raked markings, like a giant garden till had torn open the metal. Wires from the overhead utility lights hung like sweeping jungle vines. She'd seen enough horror movies to know Toby shouldn't have gone off on his own. Actually, now that she'd had a decent look at this part of the ship, it seemed safest that they all turn around and return to *Odyssey* immediately.

"What the hell?" Sullivan had paused in the middle of the hangar, his flashlight falling on something decidedly human shaped.

Thea edged closer, freezing when she saw what lay there.

A corpse.

Thea staggered, alerts flashing in her visor.

The middle-aged man lay on his back, pale skin shriveled and sunken eyes staring vacantly. An angry slash had torn open his neck, and the front of his drilling uniform was stained reddish black.

Sullivan stood quickly, his flashlight trailing over the blood beneath the body, following more smudges and spatters across the floor. Another two bodies lay crumpled near the base of a set of stairs that led deeper into the ship. Their throats were also slit, their eyes wide and lifeless. All three corpses were frozen solid, the Achlys elements having pre-served them before much decomposition could occur.

Thea gagged. She'd never seen a dead body before—let alone three—and the corpses might have made her truly sick if it weren't for the alerts flashing in her visor. They slammed her back to reality, ordering her to regain control of her breath.

"We should fall back," Sullivan said.

"We were instructed to sweep the ship," Dylan responded.

"It looks like we just walked into a war zone!"

"Then maybe instead of yelling at me, you should get your gun out and start searching the place. There could be sur-vivors."

One moment Sullivan was standing in the middle of the cargo bay, and the next he was towering over Dylan, the glass of his helmet grazing hers. "I am *not* dying for you, Dylan. This is bad. Something bad happened, and you need to get your head out of your—"

Dylan kneed him in the gut, and in the time it took Sul-livan to mutter a curse, she threw her hands into his chest, sending him stumbling backward.

"Here's how it's going to be," she said, addressing the entire team as Sullivan gasped for air. "We're splitting into two groups and scouring this ship from top to bottom. If you don't like that idea, I will escort you back to *Odyssey* and put you under cryo until this is over. I don't need cowards right now; I need people who can follow orders. And right now, those orders are to search for survivors."

Sullivan glared. Thea thought it was good they were all suited up, or else Sullivan's fist might be finding a new home in Dylan's cheek. She thought also that being in cryo right now might be a blessing.

"So," Dylan continued, "does anyone agree with Sullivan?"

Cleaver hoisted his ray-rifle. "Only in the fact that I'm not dying."

"Right you are. You take half the crew and search top, down. I'll handle bottom, up. Sullivan, I don't even want you in my sight. You and Tarlow go with Cleaver. Nova and the kid are with me."

Nova hesitated, looking between the two teams. "And Toby?"

"Toby, sweep the engine room while you're there, then join whichever group is closest."

"Roger," he said in their ears.

"You don't think maybe we should all stick together?" Nova said, her eyes still on the first corpse.

"It'll be faster this way. Two decent shots per group."

"I can shoot if you give me a gun," Thea told Dylan. She'd never fired a stun gun at a live target, but she'd been required to take a basic firearm safety course and log twenty hours of target practice before starting her internship. She liked to think that she was proficient enough to at least defend herself without posing a risk to others.

"Look, kid, until I actually see you shoot, I'm not blindly trusting that you're a good shot." Dylan jerked her chin toward the pilot. "Let's move."

Thea almost left it at that. She almost nodded and accepted Dylan's words as law. That's what she would have done in the classroom. But as her eyes swept the hold again, she was reminded that they were very far from a classroom. They were on a distant planet, searching a ship that looked like it had witnessed war. There were bodies at her feet. Bodies with slit throats. They'd died at the hands of someone else, and everyone but Thea and Dr. Tarlow was armed. Even Toby, a scrawny communications tech who couldn't manage to keep mustard off his shirt, had a stun gun.

Thea had just as much right as anyone to protect herself.

She was soft-spoken, but not meek.

She followed instructions, but not if they were flawed.

She was not going to die on this rock because someone as petty and shortsighted as Dylan Lowe refused to arm her own team.

"Quit calling me *kid*," Thea said, barely recognizing her own voice, "and give me a stun gun."

Dylan blinked at her.

"You know, I've been thinking," Thea continued, knowing her words were transmitting to everyone. "Maybe you're too close to all of this. Maybe your father being a part of Black Quarry is affecting your ability to—"

"Enough!" Dylan spat. "Here." She pulled a spare gun from her belt and passed it to Thea, grip first. "This is the safety," she said, pointing, "and this—"

"I know how to use it."

Dylan pushed a spare battery mag into Thea's chest. "Just don't kill anyone."

Thea didn't point out that she would have to squeeze the trigger a dozen or more times to cause any serious damage to a grown adult. She'd made herself heard, and in the moment, that was enough.

Well, shit, Toby thought as he stared at the ship's corrarium reactor.

He'd had little trouble getting to the engine room, and despite its massive scale and series of catwalks, even less trouble finding the reactor. It was on the first level, directly off the hangar. What was puzzling was that it was intact.

He'd seen the blood on the hangar floor same as everyone else, noted the botched state of the supplies held there. One look at that mess and Toby had suspected pirates. When

Sullivan started yelling about dead bodies, he was damn sure of it. Corrarium was the life force of the entire Union, powering reactors that made FTL travel possible and fueling cities for durations that put the capabilities of Earth Era energies to shame. It wasn't uncommon to hear that a freighter hauling corrarium had been robbed. Pirates would even take the ship, if they could manage. A corrarium reactor could fetch a fat sum on the black markets, after all.

Celestial Envoy was a research ship, not a freighter, but it didn't seem unreasonable for a pirating crew to try to steal the reactor, assuming they'd picked up some of Black Quarry's activity. Criminals tended to lurk in the uninhabited quadrants of space, and Achlys was pretty far off the grid. Hell, the whole of the F-1 system was considered off-grid. But here sat the corrarium reactor, covered with a thin layer of dust, the sides of the three-meter cube plastered with radiation signs, and every last piece of piping and tubing still connected.

No one had even breathed on the reactor, let alone tried to steal it.

Toby turned quickly, the light on his stun gun feebly scanning the room. The door he'd entered still stood ajar in the distance. Dylan had been shouting orders about splitting up to search the ship when he first reached the engine room.

Now the crew was silent, except for the occasional "clear" or "that way" resounding in his ear.

He backed away from the reactor, pulse readings ticking up slightly. *It was just pirates*, he was supposed to be saying right now, the crew laughing along with him. *Nothing but a band of space thieves.*

The lights. Dylan had asked for the lights.

Toby tilted his head back, following the piping that snaked to the upper levels of the engine room. He found the nearest stairwell and climbed.

Several flights and a catwalk later, he located a row of breakers. All three of the main power grids were off, along with the backup generators. Someone had deliberately killed the power, and then turned the backup supply off, too. That didn't make much sense. Reactors had fail-safes installed so that they automatically powered down if they malfunctioned. No one should have needed to completely cut the power. And to kill the generators, too . . .

Toby's eyes darted between the breakers, his pulse reading climbing another two points.

"Clear," Cleaver barked through the intercom, and Toby dropped his weapon in surprise. It clattered onto the grated metal floor, echoing through the engine room.

Sullivan should be here, he thought as he retrieved the weapon and holstered it at his thigh. *I know computers, not power grids. There's gotta be a reason they manually powered down every last system.*

This was Toby's punishment for wanting to be the hero, for thinking the engine room would provide an easy explanation to Black Quarry's silence, a magic bullet he could relay to his crew. And now he had to get the lights on before Dylan ate him alive.

Toby straightened to face the breakers. He'd bring the generators back up, he decided. It would be enough to get some lights on, and maybe after a search of the ship, they'd know why the Black Quarry crew cut their own power—and if it was safe enough to reinstate.

Toby reached for the lever labeled *Emergency Generators*. Using both hands, he began to prime the breaker.

They found more dead bodies as they continued. Not in large numbers, Thea noted, which was concerning in itself.

The crew quarters had been empty save for a few deceased. One strangled in his bunk, bedsheets disheveled. Another with his head bashed in near the showers. It wasn't that Thea wanted to see hundreds of corpses, but if only a handful of the crew were dead, they should have come across survivors by now.

Entering the mess hall, Thea panned the cavernous room with her weapon. Holding her flashlight alongside the barrel, she found overturned chairs and trays. Maybe a half-dozen bodies scattered throughout. Nova checked them all, prodding at them with her ray-rifle. "More of the same," the pilot said, her voice crisp in Thea's helmet. "Stabbed. Slit throat. This one was strangled and—hey, look at that."

Thea followed the pilot's flashlight, which moved from the strangled corpse to the plates of food on the tables. Shriveled fruit and scraps of bread were covered in a fine blanket of white fuzzy mold. Frozen solid, it almost looked like crystalized snow.

"How'd this grow in the cold?" Nova said.

"Maybe it grew earlier," Thea offered. "Before the ship was exposed to the elements?"

She didn't mean for it to come out a question. Even now, the exterior temperature reading on Thea's visor read -11°C, just a single degree warmer than when she'd walked up the ship's gangplank. Definitely not prime mold-growing temperature.

Dylan's brow furrowed behind the glass of her helmet as she swept the room a final time. "Clear," she announced, and exited the mess.

Nova followed, and as Thea brought up the rear, new questions rattled in her mind: Why had someone exposed the entire facility to the elements, and where were they now?

The deeper they moved into the ship, the more uneasy she

grew, and Thea's fears were not diminished by the fact that she was now armed. In fact, she was starting to worry that a stun gun wouldn't help her at all. There didn't seem to be anything to shoot: no enemies, no survivors, *nothing*.

The suspense of sweeping each room and hallway grew unbearable, and by the time they reached the aeroponics facility, Thea could no longer keep her pulse readings steady. Vertical racks of arugula, Bibb lettuce, and other leafy greens sat shriveled and crystalized, their overhead lights dead and their roots as frozen as the microfleece membrane from which they grew. The nutrient-rich mist that once fed the plants had left the ground slick with a thin layer of ice, and as the women moved carefully through the vertical farm, their flashlights glinted and bounced off the frozen surface, causing shadows to stretch eerily across the room.

Thea used to find similar moments in horror movies comical, but now she wished it was that simple; that this graveyard of a ship was nothing more than a scene in a film. That any second something would scare her senseless, but it would only be a member of the Black Quarry crew. A farm tech, appearing from behind a rack of spinach, happy to see them.

Exiting the aeroponics farm, they found another dark hallway. "Bridge should be that way," Nova said, pointing with the light mounted on her weapon. "Nearly everything on this ship is automated, right down to flight control and—"

A screech filled Thea's helmet. She flinched and tried to cover her ears, but by the time her hands hit her helmet, the noise had stopped. Thea's ears rung in the newfound silence.

She looked to the others. Nova was shaking her head, and Dylan still had one hand pressed to her helmet. Her lips moved, forming a swear Thea could read, but not hear. The intercoms were dead. Barely a half hour after leaving *Odyssey* and their gear was already failing. But no . . . Thea's vitals were still flashing in the corner of her visor, so it wasn't an issue of power. It was an issue specific to communication, which wasn't much of a silver lining.

"What the hell just happened?" Dylan appeared to be shouting, but her words were muffled and barely audible.

"No idea," Nova yelled back. "Maybe something failed on *Odyssey*. Toby would know."

"This is exactly why I keep telling Hevetz they need to update *all* their gear, not just give the latest and greatest tech to select rigs. Piece of . . ." Dylan trailed off in favor of smacking at the side of her helmet. As if that would suddenly make the intercoms work again.

"Switch to external mics," Nova shouted, toggling a switch on the side of her helmet. "Testing, testing. Can you guys hear that?" The pilot's words now projected into the hallway. They were nowhere near as crisp as when the comms had transmitted directly into Thea's ear, but it was preferable to having to shout through their helmets. Thea gave the pilot a thumbs-up, then made the switch to her external mic as well.

"What I was trying to say," Nova continued, "is that *Celestial Envoy*'s bridge is massive and has a double-cased, reinforced doorway. If the crew was looking to take shelter, they might have gone there."

Dylan nodded her on.

Thea brought up the rear, the darkness right on her heels, her pulse still hammering. How had she ever enjoyed horror movies with Mel? They used to curl up together on the couch, limbs entwined beneath a blanket as they took bets on who would die first. Usually, it was the poor schmuck bringing up the rear.

The floor suddenly vibrated, and Thea froze. Dylan did, too. They glanced at each other just briefly—the pounding underfoot getting faster, closer—then spun, weapons ready. A figure rushed them, blinding light where his face should be, like his head was a mirror reflecting their flashlights back down the hall. But it wasn't a mirror, it was his helmet. Because it was . . .

Thea barely had time to shove Dylan's arm up, sending

the fired wave of electricity at the ceiling instead of into the man.

"Shit!" Toby said, pulling up short. "You nearly dropped me."

"What the hell were you thinking?" Dylan shouted. "Creeping up on us like that?"

"I was looking for you guys. My intercom stopped working"—he tapped the side of his helmet—"so I had to run to catch up."

"You're *supposed* to be getting the lights back on!"

"I threw the generators a little while ago."

"What? Toggle your external mic. I can barely hear you."

Toby complied. "I said I already threw the generators," he repeated, his words now much clearer. "Emergency lights should boot any minute."

As if on cue, they flickered to life. *Celestial Envoy* illuminated in the same manner Northwood Point had before they left Soter. White lighting lined the floors and hugged the doorways, casting everything in a cool glow. Thea wasn't sure if she preferred pure darkness or this new level of slim visibility. She'd still need her flashlight, only now she could see far enough behind Toby to mistake hanging ceiling panels or dropped gear as signs of life.

Toby raised a hand. "See?"

"Throw something next time. Call out. Use your damn

flashlight to signal us. But if you go sneaking around like an idiot, you're gonna get a shock blow to the chest. And I'm not gonna be apologizing when you're lying on your back gasping for air. You read me?"

"Loud and clear, Captain."

Dylan spun on her heel and marched toward the bridge.

"Bitch," Toby muttered, but only Thea was near enough to hear it.

The hallway led to a half flight of stairs, which the group took two at a time, Thea still bringing up the rear. On the landing, the reinforced doors Nova had mentioned were already open, the locking mechanism mangled and blackened.

"Electrical fire," Toby offered as Dylan bent to inspect the damage. "Or maybe pure force. Sullivan would know better than me."

"You said this would be the safest place," Dylan said, glancing at Nova, "that it was secure."

The pilot shrugged and Toby offered, "You can override anything if you're desperate enough."

How reassuring, Thea thought.

She reluctantly followed the others onto the bridge. It was easily five times larger than *Odyssey*'s, with command stations spread out in a stadium fashion, the rows of stations descending as they approached the front of the room.

Where Thea expected to see a windshield there was only a wall of vidscreens. She assumed they typically projected star charts, flight data, system reports, and whatever else the *Celestial Envoy* crew needed to keep their ship navigating smoothly, but now they were merely black.

"Systems are still booting, I think," Dylan said from one of the command stations. "Toby?"

He moved to help the captain, and Thea, desperate to no longer be at the tail end of their search party, descended the levels toward the front of the bridge. Nova did the same, her weapon held with precision, her movements quick and methodic as she cleared behind each station. Thea was so used to seeing the pilot lounging in the break room at Northwood—long legs kicked up on the table, contagious laugh resounding as she threw her head back at something Sullivan had said—that it was easy to forget she had military training.

Improving her own grip on her weapon, Thea rounded another station. Her boot caught on something and she toppled forward, the gun skittering out of her hands as she crashed to the floor. She rolled over to see what had tripped her and yelled out.

Red alerts flashed in her visor.

"We got another body!" Nova shouted.

Thea scrambled away from the corpse, heart pounding.

The cold had stopped the worst of the decaying process, and like all the bodies they'd crossed so far, it was impossible to guess at how long the man had been dead. His skin had shrunken and shriveled, his eyes recessing into his skull. He was wearing a set of Hevetz coveralls and an unzipped jacket, but no environmental suit or helmet. A dusty Tab lay across his shins. There was no knife wound on this corpse, no sign of strangulation. Instead, there were two holes in his skull—small near one temple, larger at the exit point on the other side.

That was when Thea noticed the pistol resting near his knee.

She couldn't stop staring at it or wondering how the man had gotten his hands on something that shot bullets. Hevetz Industries certainly didn't supply any. The company's founder, Julian Hevetz, had been a pacifist, a lover of nature and animals, and was strongly against firearms. He'd passed nearly a century ago, but his surviving family had upheld his values, and even when the company's ownership transitioned to the first non–family member a few years ago, all of Julian's policies were still followed. This was why Thea had been trained with a stun gun, not a handgun. Why people like Dr. Tarlow were employed to monitor the environmental impact of their drilling. Why even in the most dangerous drilling locations or top-secret research facilities, workers were protected by security details boasting long-distance ray-rifles. Employees shot to stun, not kill. They did due diligence both before *and* after. They valued life. *Protect the future.* Hevetz truly wanted to leave the universe better than they found it.

"Evans," Nova said, reading from the name patch sewn onto the man's uniform.

"He left us a note," Toby said. Standing a few paces from the body, Toby's flashlight shone on a section of the floor where Evans had smeared a finger-painted message. Only the paint appeared to be blood.

> *It got in us and most are dead.*
> *Decklan flew for help.*
> *Don't trust the kid.*

Thea read it once, twice, again.

Dylan dropped to a squat beside the body and reached out.

"Don't touch him!" Thea shouted, her brain stuck on the first four words of the message, the analytical side of her jumping through the worst possibilities: disease, infection.

"I'm in an airtight enviro suit and I'm picking up the damn Tab, not frisking the corpse," Dylan said. "Do I need your express permission?"

Thea shook her head adamantly, even though the question

was rhetorical. The captain retrieved the Tab, ran her gloved hand over the front to clear away the dust, and toggled it on. The screen remained dark.

"Dead," she said. "Let's try to find a charging pad. Could be some useful info on this."

"Hang on," Toby argued. "What about the rest of this message? *Decklan flew for help*? Who's Decklan? And *It got in us*! Do you think the air's toxic after all?"

Everyone's gaze drifted to Thea, intent and expecting. It took her a moment to realize they were waiting for a response and then a moment longer to realize Dr. Tarlow wasn't going to burst onto the bridge to offer her professional opinion.

"There could be something in be the air, I guess," she said finally.

"You *guess*?"

"Well, I don't have much to go on. The readings Sullivan took when we landed were fine. If it *is* something in the air—something that manifests after prolonged exposure—we're not going to know unless someone volunteers to ditch their helmet, which would obviously be incredibly stupid."

The group stared, mouths thin.

What more was she supposed to say?

"It could mean anything," she concluded, folding her hands together. "I honestly don't know."

"Interns," Toby muttered.

You're not qualified for this.

"Decklan's probably a pilot," she offered, wanting to help *somehow*.

"Clearly, if he flew for help," said Nova. "But I don't understand where he flew. He couldn't have gone anywhere in a short-range shuttle, and if *Celestial Envoy* was equipped with any long-distance transport models—a UT-800 like *Odyssey*, or similar—I didn't see any in the hangar. If he took the only one, we could have passed him during cryo. Maybe we flew right by each other without even knowing it."

Dylan rubbed the back of her neck.

"We should contact Hevetz," Thea said. "If Decklan was headed for the Trios, he's likely there by now."

Toby tapped a foot near the message. "*Most* are dead. Does that mean some of the team is still alive?"

"It has to," Dylan said. "He'd only have written *Don't trust the kid* if 'the kid' was alive." There was hope in her eyes. While Thea wanted to feel it, too, her optimism was fading, and unlike Dylan, Thea didn't have a family member in Black Quarry to fan those feeble flames.

"Except I doubt there were *kids* involved in Black Quarry," Nova pointed out. "Trained Hevetz employees, sure. But not kids."

"I still think we should contact Hevetz," Thea said, this time loudly enough that no one could ignore her.

Dylan raised the Tab. "After we get this thing charged. Communications will be slow this far into the Fringe, so there's no point contacting Hevetz until I can give them a conclusive report. Let's regroup with Cleaver." She stooped to retrieve Evans's pistol, then straightened and led the way off the bridge.

Lisbeth Tarlow was worried. Not for herself, but for the others.

"The standard diagnostics program is accessible," she told the men, "but we're locked out otherwise." She straightened from the medical bay computer. Cleaver was sifting through cabinets, though most of the equipment seemed to be scattered across the floor and counters, bloody fingerprints covering everything from gauze to scalpels. A shock rod lay forgotten by one of the isolation chambers. Sullivan stood watch at the medbay's sliding glass doors, though his eyes kept drifting to the mud-red smears on the regenerative beds and the footprints tracked between them.

The tension in the air had been palpable when their intercoms had failed after leaving the observation deck. They'd switched to the external microphones and worked their way down through the administrative quarters, finding the hall empty and each suite locked. They'd come across maybe a dozen dead bodies in their sweep, but not a single survivor.

Lisbeth could practically feel the apprehensiveness dripping off the men now. They hated the quiet, despised being cut off from Dylan's group, but the silence was a blessing to Lisbeth. Comforting, like an old friend.

"And that means?" Cleaver asked, nodding at the computer.

"Black Quarry medical files are secured, but third parties can still run blood work or body scans if someone gets injured."

"Third parties?"

"Us," she said. "We're the third party. Anyone not in Black Quarry can still use the lab for medical purposes. It's just that Black Quarry's research and medical files—the stuff that would be incredibly useful to us right now—are protected."

"Ahhh," Cleaver said, but given the way his brow wrinkled, Lisbeth still wasn't certain he was following.

"There's nothing here," Sullivan growled. "Let's keep moving."

She saw no reason to argue. Confidential or not, Lisbeth could guess what the medical files would say. Telling the others would only create panic.

It was better this way—the silence, the unspoken words.

It was safer.

They left and moved down the hall, finding a research

laboratory. It was in as poor a state as the medbay. Its far wall was lined with standing freezer units, one of which had a shattered front door, shards of glass littering the honeycombed floor tiles. The adjacent walls were home to display mounts currently flickering start-up prompts on account of Toby rebooting the generators. Computer stations and the occasional storage unit underneath them basked in the electronic glow.

"Dead," Sullivan said, snatching a Tab off a large metallic table in the center of the room. He grabbed another, knocking a plate of frozen, half-finished food aside. "Dead also." And another. "This one, too."

"There's a charging caddy behind you," Lisbeth said, pointing.

Cleaver grabbed it and wheeled it over, and as the men started loading Tabs onto it, she moved past them, drawn to the standing freezers. Inside were at least a dozen cylindrical canisters, filled with what appeared to be dirt or mud extracted during drilling. Even without power, the contents had been more or less preserved by Achlys's frigid environment. One canister had been knocked on its side, but its mud-colored substance was still solid, dangling between the wire racks like dark icicles. It must have melted when *Celestial Envoy* first lost power, then refroze as the ship cooled.

Lisbeth leaned in for a closer look, the visor of her helmet scraping the glass door. The contents of several canisters in the back looked remarkably like corrarium—viscous and dark.

Something clicked beside her, then hummed.

Lisbeth turned slowly, locating the sound. It was coming from a steel-gray, waist-high freezer in the corner. A temperature gauge on the side was set to 2°C. Not a freezer, then. Just a very cold fridge. A passcode keypad was positioned just beside the handle, but the word UNLOCKED flashed up at Lisbeth. Perhaps it had been reset during the power reboot. She grabbed the lid and heaved it up, expecting to find more drilling samples. There was only an aquarium inside, roughly a meter wide and perhaps a half meter tall and deep. Suspended in the water was a long, leathery piece of black seaweed.

She jumped back, visor flashing red.

"Something wrong?" Sullivan called.

"No, sorry. I just lost my footing on some of this glass." She toed the shards on the floor for emphasis.

"What's in the freezers?"

"Drilled samples. And this fridge is empty." She lowered the lid.

NEW PASSCODE? the keypad display prompted.

Lisbeth glanced over her shoulder. The men were again

focused on the Tabs, their backs to her. She entered her Hevetz ID into the keypad.

CONFIRM PASSCODE.

She entered it again.

ACCEPTED AND SECURED.

Nova was growing uneasy, but she kept her grip steady on the ray-rifle, her eyes keen as they moved through the halls. Once you put your nerves on display, you were only more likely to fail—a lesson that had been hammered into her by her flight instructors at the Academy.

Dylan led the way up to the next level, where shadows flickered over the threshold of an open doorway. A jerk of the chin from the captain, and Nova stepped forward, the rifle aimed into the room.

Three heads snapped toward the doorway. Sullivan, Cleaver, and Tarlow, gathered at a table in the middle of the disheveled research lab, sifting through Tab data.

Nova lowered her rifle.

"Find anything?" Dylan asked as she pushed past Nova and strode in. She set the Tab and pistol from the bridge on the table.

"Maybe," Cleaver said.

"*Maybe?* Are you looking at the same reports I am?" Sullivan tossed one of the devices to Dylan. "They've been drilling in a canyon due north of here. That Tab has records for a dozen different drill points, and the log from the most recent drill was two months back."

"And?" Cleaver said.

"And that's roughly when Hevetz issued the distress call on Black Quarry's behalf," Dylan answered. She looked back to Sullivan. "There's nothing else? They drill that day and never bother to record another thing?"

"Not that I can see," Sullivan said. "Comm logs show their last report to Hevetz was sent on June thirtieth at around oh eight hundred. It was just one line: *Complications—stand by.* There are updates on previous drilling progress. And on construction. They finished the drilling base but recently broke ground near it to start work on a more permanent living structure. Based on corrarium finds, it sounds like they're gonna get a colony of Hevetz workers stationed here in the future, but nothing else."

"Wait, so they found corrarium?" Toby interrupted. "Tarlow said it didn't exist."

"I said Witch Hazel found conflicting evidence," the doctor clarified.

Dylan's brow wrinkled. "Anything else?"

Sullivan shook his head. "Most of the Tabs are outta juice. We've got a bunch of them charging, and if everything was synced properly, that could give us answers. But right now everything looks pretty basic. Standard reports, standard comm records, then radio silence. But for any privately logged data, the computers are our best bet."

"I could try to poke around," Toby offered, "see if there's any info that's been logged privately. I don't have clearance for this project, though, and it'll take some time."

"Fine. Meanwhile, let's take a rover down to the canyon," Dylan said. "Maybe we'll be able to glean a bit more if we survey the drilling setup."

"I think we should update Hevetz first," Nova said, glancing at Thea, who'd argued the case earlier. The intern's gaze was downturned now, perhaps too shy to make a stand against Dylan twice. Luckily, Sullivan joined in, offering a gruff "Yeah."

"If I wanted your opinions, I'd ask for them," Dylan said.

Nova actually laughed. It was as if her body had forgotten formalities and betrayed her. She was used to Dylan being uptight and blunt, but not foolish.

"Is something funny?" Dylan asked with a glare.

"We've found a few corpses but no survivors, and Sullivan has drill logs that disturbingly end when Hevetz called us in. Thea already pushed for contacting them on the bridge, and I'm siding with her. We need to update Hevetz. Right now."

Toby muttered something that Nova couldn't quite make

out, but it sounded an awful lot like, *You* would *side with the intern.*

"She spared you from a shock blast to the chest, Toby."

"She wouldn't have had to if our captain wasn't so trigger-happy!"

"Hey, guys?" Thea said.

"And that's Thea's fault?" Nova continued. "What is your problem, Toby? Because I'm a temp and she's an intern we can't possibly be smart or capable? Is it our job titles that offend you or our age? Are you threatened by people who might outshine your mediocrity?"

"Enough!" Dylan roared.

"Guys!" Thea tried again.

"I'm not the one with the mediocre vision barring me from the aero force," Toby said.

"You fucking asshole!"

"WILL EVERYONE SHUT UP!" Thea yelled.

Nova fell silent. So did Toby. In fact, the whole crew went still. Nova had never heard the intern raise her voice, and now she'd just yelled at them. Screamed, really. Behind her visor, Thea's cheeks were flushed with heat.

"I think we should watch this," she said firmly, nodding at the Tab they'd found on the bridge. It had been set on a charging pad, and the cracked screen was now illuminated with data.

Everyone huddled nearer. Peering over Thea's shoulder, Nova could make out the following:

Sent: July 1 at 14:05:45
From: Pitch Evans, Engineer (#LD49203)
Subject: SOS
Operation: Black Quarry
Location: Achlys, Fringe-1 (view coordinates)

"That's barely five hours after we entered cryo," Toby said.

Thea let out an exasperated sigh. "I know. That's why I was trying to get everyone's attention."

"Play it," Dylan said, nodding at the arrow icon.

Thea reached out and tapped the prompt.

Static overtook the screen, flickering before it revealed a choppy shot of a young man sitting against a wall of brushed aluminum, the Hevetz logo stamped into it at even intervals. This was Pitch Evans, Nova realized. He was still slumped against that command station, only he was now unrecognizable as the man in the video. On-screen, sweat coated Evans's brow and dripped from his bangs. The collar of his Hevetz coveralls was torn, revealing a tattoo of the Union flag on his neck. His head hung forward. Each breath seemed a labor. When he finally looked up at the screen, Nova shuddered. His eyes already seemed empty, sunken.

"It's bad," he said, voice husky and pained. The video flickered. "—Li's dead, the rest of the crew's—" Another flicker, followed by a long break of black. Then Evans again, panting, grimacing. "—and if you come, don't come without the best scientists. Bring a microbiologist, or a geneticist. Also, some guns. Actually, no. . . . If I'm honest—" The whole of his body twitched with the static, pulled left, then right. The audio faltered, then returned. "—call Black Quarry off. Forget about *Celestial Envoy* and don't ever set foot here again. We're as good as—" From somewhere offscreen there was the sound of screeching metal, like a cargo bay opening against its will. Evans's gaze darted from the screen. "Shit! Shit-shit-shit." He leaned back. What felt like ages later he looked directly at the screen, his eyes boring into Nova. "Pretend I never sent this. Trust me. It's for the best."

Another shriek of noise, angry and murderous, and the video cut out.

"This is why they sent backup," Toby murmured, his face ghost white. "This came through a few hours after we went under cryo, and they're throwing us to the wolves. The Company knows just how bad things are here, and they sent us in anyway."

"We need to abort," Sullivan said, his eyes flicking toward Nova. She could see the fear there, how his thoughts were already drifting to his family. "Dammit, Lowe, what have you gotten us into?"

"I don't know!" Dylan snapped. "This is news to me, too. Hevetz never mentioned an SOS transmission when they told me backup was being sent."

"Really?" Sullivan countered. "They sent a specialized backup crew, likely with doctors just as this SOS calls for, but didn't tell you why those doctors were needed? I bet you saw this exact message in their updates and didn't bother to tell us because you were too worried about your father!"

"Are you insinuating that I've kept information from you?" Dylan roared. "That I knowingly risked all our lives?" Her eyes flashed with authority, and Sullivan fell silent.

For a long moment no one said anything, but Dylan kept glaring at Sullivan in a way that made Nova uncomfortable. The rage that had first sparked through her blue eyes had faded, replaced with something uneasy, something fearful. Dylan's brows remained furrowed. It was almost as if she was terrified Sullivan might repeat his accusations, as though Dylan didn't want the crew thinking too hard about what he'd said.

But that couldn't be it. Dylan wouldn't lie about something like this. She was stubborn and proud, but there was no way she could have seen this SOS message in Hevetz's updates and still ordered the crew to case Black Quarry's ship.

"Didn't that drill report mention someone named Li?" Cleaver asked, breaking the silence.

"Jon Li," Sullivan supplied. "That final drilling log listed him as one of the techs. There was an equipment malfunction. Li was injured. And then . . ."

"Complications—stand by."

The men exchanged a worried glance.

"Well, let's get the rover and head down to the drill site," Dylan said.

"Have you lost your mind?" Sullivan said. "You heard what he said. *Call Black Quarry off. . . . Pretend I never sent this.* He requested scientists and guns!"

"Which we have," Dylan interjected, tapping the weapon holstered on her thigh and then throwing a hand toward Tarlow.

"We need to get our asses back to *Odyssey* and keep them there."

"And turn our backs on any potential survivors?" Dylan roared. "They could be out there, Sullivan. My *father* could be out there. And if the most recent manifest is correct, there were two workers who stayed behind at the drill site when the crew brought Li to the medbay for his"—she referred to the Tab Sullivan had handed her—"head injury and abrasions."

This was getting out of control. Nova stepped forward.

"Look, Dylan. It's been two months since that incident, and with all due respect, there's no way those crew members are still out there."

"There's only one way to know for sure."

"Even after the SOS that Hevetz kept from you? Even after Evans's body and the note he left on the floor? It's just plain stupid, and I know you're not stupid." The captain's chin jutted out, her glare almost daring Nova to continue. Nova had seen this expression before. It came from flight instructors at the Academy when a pilot was getting out of line. But this was a line that needed to be crossed, right now, before Dylan led them straight off a cliff.

"I have never questioned your orders," Nova went on. "I have always listened to every command you've given me. I'm asking you now to consider that maybe your concern for your father is clouding your judgment. We should fall back to *Odyssey*. Everyone on your crew—*everyone*—is pushing for us to fall back."

"What was the message?" Tarlow asked. Nova had almost forgotten the doctor's presence. The woman was leaning against one of the glass-doored freezers, kneading her hands together anxiously. "From the dead man—Evans. You mentioned a note."

"*It got in us and most are dead. Decklan flew for help. Don't trust the kid*," Nova recited. "My guess is he was worried the

SOS wouldn't get out, so he put a warning on the floor, too."

"And then put a bullet through his own brain," said Toby.

A myriad of emotions flicked over the doctor's face, there and gone so fast that Nova couldn't get a good read on any of them.

"I don't know why that engineer took his own life," Dylan snapped. "Anything we theorize is speculation. But here's what I do know: we were sent here with a job to do and I am not running back to *Odyssey* like some spineless coward. We will continue our search for the Black Quarry crew, and we will exercise extreme caution until the backup team relieves us."

"Exercise *caution*?" Dr. Tarlow said, pushing off the freezer. "Captain, what would make a highly trained Hevetz engineer ask for a microbiologist and geneticist? Infection? Disease?"

The team bristled.

"As for the guns he requested . . . maybe he didn't mean stun weapons. Perhaps he meant weapons like the one he used to end his own life." A pause. "Now, the SOS requested a microbiologist, and you have one," Tarlow said, touching her own chest. "And since Hevetz likely suggested me for your crew because of my previous knowledge of this site, allow me to share some of that knowledge:

"Achlys is brutal and unforgiving. Its sun, F_1, is a red dwarf with a luminosity less than a hundredth of what we're used to in the Trios, and our tidally locked position creates a host of problems. Achlys's orbital period is exactly as long as a single rotation. Like a moon to its planet, the same side always faces the sun, which means there are no sunrises or sunsets. The day side is baked out. The night side is essentially in an isolated ice age, and winds constantly blow from the west. There'll be horrific, unpredictable weather. Here in the terminator, we're somewhat protected, but given our temperature readings, I'd say Black Quarry is positioned along the edge of the night side. That means we're dealing with excessively poor lighting—not just twilight, but something more akin to the final moments of dusk. Plus, aggressive winds and subfreezing temperatures. And that's not to mention unpredictable solar flares and sunspots off F_1, which can throw Achlys into a state of blinding light or sudden blackness for weeks on end. Witch Hazel spent a lot of time at this longitude, researching along the night side's edge, and trust me when I say the last thing you want to test is the power of nature."

Bracing her palms against the table, Tarlow leaned forward, exuding a type of authority Nova had never seen from the willowy doctor. "Now, if that's not enough reason to exercise caution, how about the fact that nearly an entire Hevetz team has seemingly up and vanished? The few employees we've found are all dead—murdered, it seems. Their rig is trashed, their labs overrun. These samples"—Tarlow waved a thumb over her shoulder—"look basic enough. Achlys's version of limestone, shale, and sandstone. The dark samples in the back might even be corrarium. But we don't know that for certain. Frankly, we know nothing. I strongly suggest you give me time to run tests on these samples and allow Toby a chance to access the systems. We should thoroughly evaluate all the logs before we go running into some canyon where contaminated matter might have been drilled."

Dylan eyed the samples, one of which had spilled and frozen all over the freezer's wire shelves. "If that shit is contaminated," she said, "I think we're all in a bad place."

"We're fine, because we're fully suited," Tarlow replied. "But the Black Quarry crew might not have been—not while on *Celestial Envoy*."

"Which is all the more reason to stay put," Nova said in agreement. "Wait for the backup crew to land or a debrief to come in from Decklan and Hevetz."

"It's all the more reason to look for survivors," Dylan said.

"With our intercoms down?" Tarlow argued. "With everything I just told you and our helmets no longer linked, you want to go digging around in Achlys canyons in the dark? You're going to get us all killed."

Thea fidgeted beside Nova. Toby let out a nervous laugh.

"No one is going to die," Dylan said. "Not if we're smart

about this. And smart people follow orders. Do I make myself clear?"

Silence.

"I'll pretend you all said *yes*. Sullivan, show me everything you found on the drill sites."

As the team dissolved into planning, Thea stood in the doorway of the lab. Dylan had put her on watch, despite it being obvious that there was nothing on *Celestial Envoy* outside sparking wires, flickering lights, and a few dozen frozen corpses.

Thea was vaguely aware of the discussion unfolding behind her. Dr. Tarlow would glean what she could of the still-frozen freezer samples while everyone else went to the drill site. Only Sullivan would stay behind. "For protection," Dylan had said, despite the fact that Cleaver was the security detail and Thea was the most fit to aid the doctor in any lab work. But she'd heard Sullivan's begging. He hadn't been quiet about it.

"I'm not going looking for trouble, Dylan. I won't do it. I've got my boys back home, my wife. Let me stay here and sift through the Tabs, see if I can learn anything new."

Did he think his own life was more valuable than everyone else's because he had a family? They were *all* trying to get home. And while for Thea that meant a foster home, it didn't mean she had nothing to live for. She kneaded her fingers together. Her mother had never seemed farther away.

Orphans don't have mothers, she could hear Toby chiding. *By the very definition of the word, your parents are dead.*

But there'd been no body, no official close to the missing persons case, and Thea's mother was only *presumed* dead. That's what her file said, and the social worker Thea was required to meet with every month had been urging Thea to accept her mother's death for years.

She couldn't, wouldn't. Not until she hired the galaxy's best private investigator and they told her otherwise.

Thea had been four, sitting on a bench at a bus stop when she'd last seen her mother. The woman had gone to the bank. Or maybe it had been the pharmacy. Or the pawn-shop. Thea couldn't remember. All Thea knew then was that when Mommy went off to run an errand, you sat and waited for her to return.

Thea sat through the #4 bus and the #17, and then the #32, #25, and #4 again. It started to rain. Dusk set in. And then the cop car had arrived, every millimeter of the water-slicked streets suddenly pulsing red from the vehicle's strobes.

"Althea," she told the officer when he asked for her name.

"Where do you live?"

"I don't know." She did, it was just that the car was stolen and she didn't want to get her mother in trouble.

"Who do you live with? Parents? Grandparents?"

"My mommy."

"What's her name?"

"Mommy." It was actually Naree, but Thea knew her mother sometimes had to do not-quite-legal things to scrape together meals, and she was worried the cop might lock her up for that instead of reuniting her with her daughter.

"Get in the car," the officer said.

Thea blinked rainwater from her lashes. "Mommy says I'm not supposed to go with strangers."

"Yeah, well, it doesn't look like your mommy's coming back. And I'm not a stranger, I'm a cop." He pointed at his badge for emphasis. "Now get in the car."

It was one of Thea's very first memories. She'd searched long and hard for earlier ones, trying to recall her mother's face or a happier moment. She could see the car they'd called home, the food credits on the dash, a blanket on the back seat. But not her mother.

After being placed at the foster apartment in Hearth City, Thea spent the following years searching news articles and scouring the Interhub for traces of Naree Sadik. The woman didn't seem to exist. Thea began to wonder if that was even her mother's real name. All Thea knew for certain came from her child services files: Thea was of mainly Turkish and Korean descent. She had O negative blood and a gluten allergy. Her mother was presumed dead.

Still, some small part of Thea believed that if she was good enough, impressive enough, *special* enough, her mother might find reason to love her again, to reappear. She might come back.

It was why Thea had thrown herself into her schoolwork and studying. It was even why she'd first approached Mel. He was two years older, also placed at her foster apartment, and she'd asked to borrow his textbooks so she could read up a few levels. Mel was the only good thing about that place. They'd been best friends for years, and then more than friends, and then nothing.

Thea was alone again. She had her schooling, and her longing for family, and if she ever got back to the Trios, she would find that shadow of a mother and never let her leave again; because Thea was certain, somehow, deep in her soul, that her mother was out there. If she was dead, Thea would know. She'd feel it.

"Shouldn't we be getting the comms back up before we do this?" Nova argued behind Thea.

"I can't do three things at once," Toby snapped. "You gotta pick: I go to *Odyssey* and try to get the comms up *or* I stay here and attempt to access the Black Quarry system *or* I come with you to the drilling site in case something needs to be hacked or overridden there."

"The last one," Dylan said. "I don't want it to be a wasted trip."

Thea steeled herself, squared her shoulders. There was no arguing with Dylan Lowe. If the acting captain wanted to visit the drilling site, the crew would. What concerned Thea was what they might find.

Warnings from Pitch Evans's SOS replayed in her mind as well. Requests for a microbiologist or geneticist and for weapons. Then for the Company to simply abandon the entire project.

It got in us.

Thea's pulse kicked up, and she reminded herself that she was wearing an environmental suit. She was protected. She just had to let Dylan case the drilling site, and then they'd return. The true rescue crew would arrive. She'd go home.

One thing at a time.

"Looks like roughly a half-hour ride to the drilling base," Nova said. She was bent over the Tabs, studying what could only be a map, her bronze skin tinged cool by the screen's glow.

"Not far from the old Witch Hazel bunker," Dylan agreed. "This blueprint shows a couple drill platforms. We can divide and conquer." She clapped Nova on the shoulder, then straightened from the table. "Let's move. I want to sweep the drilling stations and be back before the sun rises."

"It doesn't rise," Dr. Tarlow said impatiently. "The same side of Achlys constantly faces the sun. It's dusk until we leave this place. Weren't you listening?"

"It was a euphemism. Come on, people!"

As the crew filed into the hallway and Thea moved to follow, someone squeezed her arm. She spun, startled to see Dr. Tarlow there.

"Be careful, Thea. Hang back, okay? Don't touch anything, not even survivors, if you find them. We have no idea what happened here, and you've got nothing to prove. Let Dylan be the hero."

All Thea could hear was the woman's reassurances the night before they entered stasis: *It's probably something small—an equipment failure, a jammed signal.*

The doctor's new tone terrified Thea. It was understandable after what they'd learned from the SOS message, but still terrifying.

"I'll be careful," she promised, and she meant it. One step at a time, Thea would be painstakingly careful.

Lisbeth would have to work quickly.

She'd been hypothesizing for years—decades even—and now she could finally act. It wasn't without risk, of course. The crew was running off to the drilling base against her advice, and Sullivan was staying behind with her. If he grew nosy about her work, started asking questions, she'd have to lie.

Lisbeth's gaze drifted to the frozen samples in the freezer, to the fridge with the dark seaweed.

She didn't want to make things worse. Then again, her decades spent at cold-water research sites had yielded nothing. Not yet. And she was here now. She was on Achlys after all these years, and she'd be a fool to waste this opportunity.

As Sullivan started his work on the Tabs, Lisbeth opened the freezer and removed the first drill sample, the cylinder shaking in her unsteady grasp.

Their ship was called Odyssey. A standard UT-800, a boat for small crews.

He'd cased it, walking through the rooms with a wave of dread surging in his stomach. Nothing about the vessel screamed rescue specialists. There were no weapon stores on board, no heavy artillery. The crew had severely underestimated what they would find on *Achlys*.

He'd checked their comm transcripts, too. They'd told Hevetz they'd landed, nothing else. Hevetz hadn't responded, but a delay was standard this far into the Fringe. In fact, it was unlikely the crew's first message had even reached its destination yet.

They'd visit the drilling stations, he reasoned. It was only a matter of time.

He should have moved the engineer's body.

He should have washed away the warning.

He should have done so many things he hadn't, but it had been a long time since he believed help might be coming, and he'd grown sloppy.

The boy considered if it was worth turning things on again,

sending a drill bit down-down-down into Achlys's depths. It might serve as a solid distraction from the truth. But it could also awaken that darkness again, bring devils to the surface.

A new possibility dawned on him. He considered leaving this rock, starting over. His food stores were almost gone. And there was the reason he'd joined Black Quarry to begin with, an objective he might still be able to complete.

He reviewed plans mentally, until he found the one with the best chance of success. Perfect execution would be key, and with any luck, the crew could be his ticket off-planet. He'd just have to convince them to take him. He'd have to lie.

And he was okay with that.

He'd done a lot, lot worse.

IV

THE GRAVE

Black Quarry Drilling Base

Achlys, Fringe-1 System

SHOWING WHAT TOBY THOUGHT MIGHT be her first bit of foresight since landing, Dylan refused to leave Sullivan and the doctor without transportation. The result was a very crowded ride to the drilling site.

Toby sat crammed in the back of Rover1 with Nova and the intern, bouncing and jolting as the vehicle navigated the harsh terrain. Dylan drove about as aggressively as she had when she transported them from *Odyssey* to *Celestial Envoy*—lots of sudden braking and harsh acceleration. Even Cleaver, who sat in the spacious front passenger seat and was almost impossible to shake, had a hand braced against the window frame.

There were no tracks to follow. Probably they'd been swept away in the storms Tarlow had mentioned. Their destination flashed on the dashboard navigational system, but when Toby searched the horizon, Achlys was nothing but murky shadow beyond the glow of the rover's headlights.

They bucked over a particularly rough patch of ground, and Nova was not quick enough to brace her hands against the seat in front of her. Her helmet bounced off the seat and she cursed enthusiastically. "If we die on this planet . . ."

"We'll be just like the Black Quarry crew," Toby said. "And Hevetz will still get what they want."

"What does that mean?" the intern asked.

He side-eyed her through his helmet. For someone so smart, she sure was ignorant.

"The corrarium. They found it, so what do they care if the entire crew died? They've got an untapped vein—no, *planet*—of corrarium to stake their claim in."

"But they can't possibly *want* their crew dead," the intern went on.

"True, but I doubt they really care, either. Remember the underwater Hab that breached on Eutheria last year? Four dozen drillers and technicians crushed by the pressure of the Paxica Ocean, and Hevetz didn't bat an eye. They settled lawsuits and paid off families and kept right on drilling. The corrarium harvested far outweighed their legal fees, especially when the Union keeps throwing grants and funding their way. It's always about the bottom dollar."

"So why do you work for them?" she countered. "Why work for a company you clearly despise and think is unethical?"

"They pay well," Toby answered with a shrug.

"Ah," the intern said, cocking up those too-thick eyebrows. "So it's all about the bottom dollar."

Nova smirked.

Okay, so maybe the intern was sharp after all.

"You wanna know what I really think about all this?" Toby said.

"Please, no." Nova groaned.

"I think Hevetz is in a powerful position and they better act before it's too late. Before there's no Trios to call home."

The intern's face pinched up.

"Toby's convinced we're gonna get ourselves blown up," Nova explained. "That if the Radicals don't commit to their cause and instead keep running these weakly backed export strikes, the Cradle won't even bother intervening. They'll just give the order to blow the Trios to stardust."

"That'd be counterproductive," Toby said. "We've got the corrarium. They're not going to blow us up when they need us to mine and export it."

"I don't see how the Radicals expect to accomplish anything when their last strike failed after twenty-four hours," Thea said.

"Because the military intervened," he countered. Clearly an unfair advantage, but the intern didn't look convinced.

"Look, this entire universe is due for a shake-up," he went on, "and it's coming whether we like it or not. Hell, it already happened over in F-2, on Casey. Those Fringe colonists fought for independence a few years back, and they

115

don't even *have* corarrium. Granted, that's probably why the Union let them cut loose. There's nothing to be gained from that rock. Still, those colonists understood how important independence is. They knew they were better off relying on the Earth Era energies they had than dealing with the UPC. If we don't follow suit, and fast, the Union is gonna step in and fire every government official serving in the Trios and replace them with their own loyal lapdogs, till our little paradise of a system is completely at their mercy and we have no chance at independence." He paused for dramatic effect, then added, "That is, unless the Radicals get their act together first and stage a coup from within."

"How?" The intern actually laughed, the noise jolting as the rover pitched over a series of ruts. "The last distribution strike was ended by our own military vessels—vessels that serve the Trios but also the Union. That's how powerful the Union is, Toby. It stretches across systems and planets, has ties within every level of any organization, and has been growing since the colonization of New Earth."

"Sort of like the Radicals," he countered. "They've been growing since we founded the Trios, infiltrating key positions and public offices, and even serving in the Trios military. We've got our own fleet, just like the Cradle. They all serve the Union, but if enough Trios ships defect, they could stage one hell of a revolution."

"And start one hell of a war," the intern argued.

"Not if they managed to get Hevetz onboard first. Now that the Company's found an uncolonized rock that's possibly rich with corrarium, they can hold Achlys, cease drilling in the Trios, maybe even destroy the wells there. Exports to the Cradle will run out, and then we've got the Union officials right where we want them. The Trios can renegotiate taxes and regulations, and if all else fails, we just cut 'em off. Regain our independence."

"God, your dedication to conspiracy theories is riveting, Toby. Truly," Nova said.

He smirked behind his helmet. Debating with Nova was so much easier than the intern. All he had to do was strike a nerve and the pilot lashed back with personal attacks and emotion. He always knew he was winning when her pretty face went dark with anger.

"Do you even realize how far-fetched that is?" Nova went on. "How much brainpower did you dedicate to dreaming that up?"

"Just think about it, Nova," he said. "For one tiny moment, try to imagine that Hevetz might not be our friend. I want independence as much as the next Radical, but we might end up being sacrificed in order to secure it."

"Not everyone even *wants* independence!" Nova spat. "I tend to like the protection we get being in the UPC. People die when there's war. My *father* died trying to calm the uprisings on Casey a few years back and . . ." She exhaled hard. "That's not why we're here, Toby. It's just not."

Toby shrugged, unswayed. "No one's set foot on Achlys since Witch Hazel, but now Hevetz is suddenly interested again? They've lost contact with the Black Quarry crew and—let's be honest—seen a fucking terrifying SOS, but they still told us to case their ship, *and* sent another crew to follow up. That sounds like they're protecting an investment to me. You don't put that much energy into something unless it's gonna pay off tenfold later."

"It's all about the bottom dollar," the intern quipped. Nova smirked beside her.

"Go ahead and laugh," Toby said. "Just remember that I don't want to be right on this. Not this time. 'Cause if I am, we're all in a bad place."

"Almost there!" Dylan called from the front.

Thea squinted, trying to make out anything in the poor lighting. Through the windshield she could see what looked like a steep crater or perhaps just a gully. Whatever the obstacle, the Black Quarry crew had erected a bridge to cross it, and the ride was momentarily blessedly smooth. Then the rover bumped back onto the terrain, and it was more bucking and pitching. A few meters ahead and barely visible in the vehicle's headlights, was a squat, one-story structure. The drilling base, Thea assumed. For all the talk of it being positioned along a canyon, there was no sign of one. Maybe it was on the opposite side of the building, hidden from view.

"We go on foot from here," Dylan said, tugging on the emergency brake. She cracked her door only to have the wind wrench it fully open.

Thea put a hand on Rover1 for balance when she exited the vehicle. Dirt and pebbles pinged against her suit.

"Incoming storm?" Nova screamed over the din.

"Could be," Dylan yelled back. "We better be quick."

Dr. Tarlow had mentioned that strong winds were a constant, so Thea tried to remind herself that this gale blowing from the west might be perfectly normal. Harmless, even. But she'd never had to work so hard to simply *walk*.

As they approached the drilling base, Toby's words echoed in her mind.

I don't want to be right on this.

Thea didn't want him to be, either, because as much as she hated to admit it, this was one of Toby's theories that seemed based in reality—at least somewhat.

For as long as Thea could remember, the Trios had been angling for independence from the United Planetary Coalition. *Unity ≠ Freedom* was spray-painted on a dumpster behind the foster home in Hearth City, and the even shorter ≠

constantly appeared on subway cars and billboards. The Trios had needed the Union's assistance once, back when the system was first founded, but that was eons ago. Rich with corrarium, they were now self-sufficient—and also required to provide corrarium to all colonized planets in the Cradle under the UPC's Responsible Energy Statute. In theory, the law was sound. If sustainable energy sources exist, they should be used whenever and wherever possible to extend the life of Union planets and avoid overharvesting as seen during Earth Era. But the pro-independence mindset thought of the Cradle as freeloaders, leeching off the Trios's corrarium and not paying nearly enough for the precious resource.

With the failed export strike behind them, maybe the Radicals *had* approached Aldric Vasteneur. No one really knew what direction the new owner intended to take Hevetz Industries, and it was possible he was protecting an investment, like Toby had implied.

The thought terrified Thea. What did the Radicals think would happen if they staged a coup and managed to hold corrarium reserves hostage—that the Union would let the Trios secede peacefully? It was laughable.

The Trios and Cradle militaries were evenly matched, but the Trios would never be allowed to cut loose. And even if the Trios *did* somehow manage to win independence through a war, what would they lose in exchange for it? Most ship manufacturers were based in the Cradle, as were a decent number of pharm corporations, which produced invaluable vaccines and had patents on med-gear. Would these things still be affordable to Trios citizens once they were no longer in the UPC? Travel visas could be banned, too, making an attendance at Linneaus Institute impossible for Trios citizens like Thea. And that wasn't even considering the complications that could arise from Union loyalists within the Trios, many of whom were bound to be in military positions.

It was a giant, nightmarish mess, and Thea prayed Toby was wrong. He had to be, because the alternative wasn't pretty.

A particularly strong gust of wind sent Thea jogging sideways, and she righted her course, focusing her attention on the building ahead. Up close, the drilling base looked a lot like Northwood Point's hangar: plain, dark, and unadorned save for the Hevetz logo painted across the sliding door.

Dylan and Cleaver hauled it open, and the group crossed the threshold, finally protected from the wind. In the span of a few steps, Thea's body felt half as heavy, the world twice as quiet.

She brought up her stun gun, flashlight held alongside it as she scanned the dark.

What she found was an equipment graveyard, rovers and forklifts and utility cases spread throughout the hangar. The floor was divided like a giant yellow-and-white checkerboard, and each piece of equipment sat in a numbered space, aisles and rows cutting between them. A central aisle—wider than all the others and covered in muddy bootprints—cut straight for the rear of the garage.

Nova used her rifle to point at it repeatedly, jerking her head for emphasis.

Thea looked again. It wasn't mud. It was blood. Or maybe a mix of both.

Dylan snapped her weapon up, the mounted light following the prints. Something groaned in the rear of the garage.

The crew froze, all their lights snapping toward the sound.

There it was again. A low groan, a high-pitched squeak, then a bang. It repeated, the iteration uneven, like someone was dragging a pickax across the floor, lifting it, and slamming it against the walls.

Dylan sidestepped into a row of machinery, leaving the bloody footprints in favor of a narrow row of forklifts. She skirted between them, weapon at the ready, moving silently toward the sound. The others trailed after her, fanning out into other aisles.

Thea forced herself to follow.

The flashlights made the forklifts cast long, sharp

shadows, which shrank and expanded as the crew continued forward. Thea kept looking behind her, mistaking the flickering shadows for life.

The rows of equipment finally ended, the far wall of the hangar glinting under the crew's lights.

And then movement to the left. A long, horrible creak.

Thea swiveled toward the noise.

A door slammed shut. Wind somehow caught it, throwing it open again, so that it swung on its hinges, groaning for a second before banging shut another time.

Dylan ran forward, propping the door open with her foot as she scanned beyond with her weapon.

Thea crept nearer, and when she got a glimpse of what waited past the doorway, the wind suddenly made sense.

The drilling base had indeed been constructed along the rim of the canyon, and here the door opened onto a ravine so narrow, Thea could easily make out the far side. Beyond the door was a small landing and a set of grated stairs that snaked downward. She knew the structure would have to be strong to withstand Achlys's storms, but it looked like little more than scaffolding.

"Found the reactor!" Cleaver shouted from inside. "It's not running."

Thea backed away from the door and followed Dylan in the direction of Cleaver's voice, until the Portable Corrarium

Reactor came into view. Every ship in the Trios was powered by one, and most remote research posts and drilling excursions used them, too. It was the energy Hevetz was drilling for, contained in a box and powering the whole of the Black Quarry operation.

The large alloy cube was positioned in the rear corner of the garage, maybe three meters tall and just as wide and deep. Bolts and couplings secured the container in place, and warning labels were plastered on every surface. Pipes and tubing ran from the reactor through the rear wall of the garage, connecting to what Thea could only assume would be the drilling equipment below.

Northwood Point had a Portable Corrarium Reactor, too, but it was secured in a dedicated room somewhere on the administrative side of the research facility. Thea had never seen it, but she knew the PCR provided them their every convenience, only to be shut off in favor of antiquated backup power in the cases of extreme storms. There was nothing more dangerous than a damaged reactor. They were in a critical state even while running normally. But with damage, a breach, the smallest hiccup . . .

Thea took a step backward.

"Should I reboot it?" Cleaver nodded at a series of breakers along the wall.

"Not with the chance of a storm," Nova argued.

"It's go through that door and climb down two dozen flights to the drill deck," Dylan said, "or take the elevator." She pointed to a panel of metal fencing. Beyond it, Thea could see an empty car waiting in the shaft. "The reactor's got a built-in fail-safe. It'll power down if the storm gets too intense, but right now, time is of the essence." Dylan walked to the elevator and slid open the gate. "Power it up, Cleaver."

Toby leaned against the wall as the car ratcheted down, the thrum of the reactor fading. A flash of yellow light outside the fenced gating announced each new level.

This was all decidedly bad: another intact reactor, bloody footprints, no survivors.

He stretched his neck, feeling antsy. Toby wanted the uprising, the fight back, the reclaiming of their system. He'd be happy if this Black Quarry gig wasn't only about the bottom dollar, but independence, too. But that, in itself, was part of the problem. Because if Hevetz's presence on this bleak, deserted rock was as complicated as Toby expected . . . Well, so long as the Company assumed control of the place in the end, they wouldn't care much if *Odyssey*'s crew disappeared just like Black Quarry's.

The elevator came to an abrupt halt. Dylan threw the door open to reveal the drilling tier. Steam hissed and sputtered.

Toby stepped from the elevator and onto a narrow catwalk.

Waist-high railings ran along the length that bordered the chasm, and just ten meters or so across the yawning gap, he could make out the opposite ravine wall. One look through the grated catwalk surface and Toby felt slightly dizzy. Black. Nothing but darkness as far as he could see; but it had to end somewhere. This was the drill deck after all.

Bumped and prodded as the others filed out of the elevator, Toby brushed against a series of pipes that ran along the chasm wall. Steam rippled from them. He couldn't feel anything through his suit, but the pipes were clearly heating up. Another catwalk was suspended overhead, but like the chasm wall behind him, it seemed to serve no purpose other than to support pipes and tubing.

"Drill sites one through five are to the left," Dylan said, pointing down the catwalk. "Six through ten to the right, and I'll check those with Nova. You three case the others." She tossed a handheld radio to Cleaver. "Swiped those from the rover. Radio if you find anything."

With the intercoms down, it would be their only method of communication once the groups separated. Dylan and Cleaver picked a channel and tested the radios. The audio crackled lightly.

"I don't really think we should split up," the intern argued, but Dylan had already grabbed Nova at the triceps, leading her off toward drill sites six through ten.

"Let's just get this over with," Toby said, giving Cleaver a prod in the back. "The sooner we're out of this dank hellhole, the better."

Thea was sick of bringing up the rear.

She followed Cleaver and Toby down the catwalk and away from the elevator, knowing arguing would make no difference. Cleaver was the skilled security detail. He should go first. And Toby . . . Well, she knew how highly he thought of interns.

The external temperature readings in her visor flicked from -12°C to -11. Now that the reactor was up and running, the piping beside her was giving off some heat. Not that she could feel any of it. Her suit was a pleasant 20° and had been since stepping off *Odyssey*.

"Drill point up ahead!" Cleaver called.

She jogged after the men, leaving the catwalk for a half-moon landing that extended out over the chasm. In its center, the drilling apparatus stood like a stoic obelisk, extending below the landing and out of sight. The wellheads surrounding it all bore a stenciled 5.

Toby leaned over a waist-high railing that made up the perimeter of the landing, and Thea joined him there, scanning over the edge. Something twinkled at the bottom of the narrow ravine. Water, she realized, just a story or two below them. The icy river cut through the channel, flowing from east to west. It appeared almost black, taking on the color of the dark earth surrounding it.

Odd, Thea thought to herself. In only very few instances was corrarium found in lake beds or river deltas, but the Black Quarry engineers must have determined this to be the best location to drill. That, or perhaps weather on the night side was too intense to risk drilling through the ice sheets to access Achlys's ocean. Without seeing their data, it was impossible to know. Dr. Tarlow's warning echoed in Thea's mind.

We should thoroughly evaluate all the logs before we go running into some canyon where contaminated matter might have been drilled.

She backed away from the railing.

Cleaver made a circular motion with his finger, wrapping up their work on the landing, and they moved on.

About halfway between drill sites five and four, the stairwell from the garage joined the catwalk. It was covered in the same bloody footprints from above, only the prints were now subtle and smeared.

"Rain coulda washed 'em away," Cleaver suggested. He tilted his rifle back, shining the light through the gaps in the overhead catwalk.

"Let's radio Dylan," Thea said. "Tell her the prints lead to this level."

"It's nothing she doesn't already know about," Toby responded. "She saw those prints leading down the stairs, and she's just gonna tell us to keep sweeping and call if we find survivors."

Cleaver shrugged in agreement but drawled sarcastically as they pressed on. "Follow the bloody footprints, they said. What could go wrong, they said."

Thea fanned at the steam coming off the pipes as they continued. Between the light on her helmet and her flashlight, navigating the catwalk had become as treacherous as driving through thick fog with high beams engaged. Their lights were only making things worse. She trained her weapon and flashlight down, letting the light fall near her feet, and used Toby's small frame as guidance.

At each drilling point, she eagerly stepped onto the landing, momentarily escaping the onslaught of steam. Cleaver scanned the deck and overhead catwalks while Toby and Thea leaned over the railing to check the service ladders that ran down around the drill.

By the time they reached the final drilling point, the footprints had long since been scrubbed clean from the catwalk. Cleaver grumbled something unintelligible as he stepped onto the landing, rolling his eyes. Thea wished she could feel as frustrated, as disappointed. Instead, she felt only a clawing, uneasy dread in her stomach. It wasn't as if there were tons of places where the Black Quarry crew could have retreated for safety. If the crew's survivors weren't on *Celestial Envoy* or here at the drill site . . .

"Over here!" Toby yelled. "Holy shit! Get over here!"

Thea bolted across the landing to join him, adding her light to the beam he'd already projected downward. And there, at the bottom of the chasm, piled high in the Achlys river, lay the remains of the Black Quarry crew. And not just one or two of them, but presumably *all* of them. There were too many to easily count. Not a single person wore a space-suit or helmet. Instead, they were in standard work clothes, mechanic coveralls or medic uniforms, their exposed skin blistered with cold.

"Oh my god," Cleaver breathed.

Thea scanned the mass of frozen flesh as best she could, her pulse spiking in her visor. Only a few of the bodies were faceup, and their eyes were closed as though they were merely sleeping.

"Why would the crew move their deceased here?" Toby asked, still staring at the atrocity.

"Isn't there an incinerator on *Celestial Envoy*?" Cleaver added.

"Yeah. That'd be a hell of a lot easier than dragging them all this way."

"No one moved them," Thea said. "They walked here themselves. We saw their footprints."

"Impossible." Toby shook his head. "No suits or provisions—it's a death wish. They'd be condemning themselves."

"Maybe they were sick. Maybe whatever they caught messed with their heads."

"And then they just fell asleep in their watery trench-grave? I mean, their eyes are closed," Toby said, throwing a hand at the bodies. "That suggests they either died in their sleep or someone closed their lids for them and then moved them here. Which again, makes precisely zero sense."

"Only one way to know for sure," Cleaver said. "We take a body back for autopsy."

"No way!" Thea spat. "That pile is at least a hundred bodies deep—some drenched in water that could be contaminated—and you want to go get one of them? After you saw the state of *Celestial Envoy*? After Evans's message? *It got in us.* No. We shouldn't touch anything."

Clearly not fond of being ordered around by someone half his age, Cleaver snatched the radio from his waistband. "Found deceased crew members," he said. "Advise?"

"Confirm their status," came Dylan's choppy reply. "If dead, haul one up so we can transport it to—"

She cut out, overwhelmed by static.

Thea looked up to the sky. Clouds were gathering, angry and heavy. "Storm must be interfering."

"Well, you heard Dylan," Cleaver said, tucking the radio

131

away. "Let's go fishing." He located a first aid case bolted to one of the landing's rail posts and wrestled it open, pulling free a body bag. Thea shuddered. The life of a driller was never a safe one. They lost their lives on occasion, but this, here on Achlys . . . Presumably every member of the drilling crew had died. Every scientist and maintenance worker and company official—from pilot to mess cook—had lost their life. There wouldn't be enough body bags for them all.

"I still don't think we should do this," Thea said.

"We're in full gear," Toby argued. "And besides, what do you propose—we wait for Dylan to show up and tear us a new one?"

"We're not waiting," Cleaver said, reaching over the railing to grab the harness and belay system used to service the drilling shaft. "She probably started running this way as soon as we radioed, and I sure as hell am gonna have a body hauled up by the time she gets here. Aw, shit." He glanced up from the harness, which didn't have enough belt for his wide frame. "Damn grease heads. Just 'cause they have to be small and fit in tight places doesn't mean *every* harness should be sized to fit girls."

Toby, who wasn't much larger than Thea, rolled his eyes.

"Well, which of you is gonna go?"

"No one should go, is what I'm saying," Thea argued.

"You then, Tobs?"

"Of course, me," he snarled. "Dylan will have both our heads if we let an intern handle something this important." He took the harness from Cleaver, staring at it a moment before adding, "Throw down some flares so it's not just me and my one light, 'kay?"

Nova stood on the platform of drill site nine, her ray-rifle aimed at the catwalk. "You sure you don't want to regroup with the others?"

"In a minute," Dylan said. She was leaning over the guard-rail, scanning the base of the ravine. They'd already cased sites six through eight, each providing a slightly better view of the river running through the chasm below. But that's all there was to see—the chasm, the river.

"They found *bodies*," Nova argued.

"And we're casing these drill points before we leave, in case there're bodies out this way, too." Dylan shoved off the guardrail. "Let's move. One site left."

Nova clenched the rifle to calm her fingers. There was no denying she was on edge. Granted, Nova was always on edge unless she was flying, and she wasn't trained for this type of search and rescue. The only person who was, was Cleaver, and he wasn't what Nova would consider the smartest or most cautious of their group. And now Dylan had ordered him to reel in a deceased Black Quarry member as if they were on a harmless fishing trip.

Nova followed Dylan back onto the catwalk.

"With all due respect," she said as they walked, "I think we should turn around."

"We will. After we see to the final drill site."

"We shouldn't have come to the drilling base, period. I know you're worried about your father, Dylan, but we should have updated Hevetz already. We should be acting on their orders."

"I'm in charge here, and we're acting on *mine*."

"You think that's what your father would want? For you to charge forward without—"

Dylan spun so suddenly that Nova nearly collided with her. "You know nothing about what he'd want," Dylan hissed through her teeth. Her eyes were icy behind her visor, her jaw clenched.

"True," Nova admitted. "Come to think of it, we worked that job on Eutheria, then Northwood Point, now this, and I still don't think I know a damn thing about you, Dylan. I've spent the last six months shuttling you to operations, living in the same claustrophobic base, and all I know is your name, rank, and that you smile less than my flight instructor back at the Academy."

Dylan smirked.

Nova needed to start counting smirks as full points, not

half points, or she was never going to break that three-smiles-in-a-day record. Still, that put today's tally at one and a half.

The captain steeled her expression, raised her chin. "My father would want me to not be a failure."

"Overseeing Hevetz research ops at the age of twenty-three is a failure?"

"Go ask your cousin. He's on to the truth."

It didn't surprise Nova that Dylan knew what was being said behind her back. The woman was smart. The surprise was that she was bothered by it. Nova had always assumed Dylan had skin too thick to care what others thought.

"I got kicked out of the Academy, too, you know," she said, glancing sternly at Nova. "My father's done everything in his power to cover it up, to pretend it never happened, to give me the kind of position I might have had if I'd graduated. Research forewoman sure isn't on par with flight captain, though."

"You were training to be a pilot, too?"

Dylan nodded.

"What happened?"

"Rix."

"Holy shit," Nova mumbled.

Rixtokin was the drug equivalent of a massive energy drink. It gave an insane boost of energy and laser focus, and

Nova had heard stories of desperate Academy pilots taking it to boost their scores. But the stuff had nasty side effects with prolonged use, including short-term memory loss and blackouts. It was highly addictive and grounds for immediate expulsion. Most pilots knew it wasn't worth the risk.

"I'd never *not* been the best at something," Dylan went on, "but suddenly I was competing with the most skilled pilots in the whole damn Union, and I needed an edge to put me ahead. Rix kept me sharp in the beginning. My scores jumped. I was top of the class for a few months. Then I started getting sloppy. My roommate confronted me about it, and I shrugged her off, told her she was just jealous that I was finally outscoring her. I blacked out during a training drill a week later. Came to before crashing or doing any damage to others, but she still ratted me out to our superiors. They ordered a drug test and I was gone. Out. Blacklisted forever." Dylan shrugged like this wasn't a big deal. "Dear ole dad put me in rehab till I was clean, then got me a job at Hevetz. Paid some buddies to wipe my name from Academy records and told me to start going by my middle name."

"Dylan's not your real name?"

"It's Alexa," she said. "Alexa Dylan Lowe."

It didn't suit her.

"It's all still there if you dig enough, of course. Hevetz knew I was a risk. They're just doing my dad a favor, and so I've gotta impress. We're alike in that way," Dylan said. "Damaged goods. Liabilities. One fuckup, and we're out."

"I'm not a liability," Nova said. "I was top of my class, and I'm *still* a damn good pilot. It's the Academy that has shit rules and lets administration lackeys who've never logged a single flight hour decide that surgery somehow makes you unfit to pilot for the military."

Dylan rolled her eyes, as if Nova was being overly sensitive at having her eye condition lumped in with expulsion for drug use. Nova didn't choose to get that degenerative condition and lose some of her peripheral vision. But Dylan chose Rix. She *chose* to put that needle in her arm.

"Look, I don't talk about this shit much, but I need someone to have my back," Dylan said. "And I know I can trust you. So just help me find my dad or the crew or whatever the hell happened here. And once we've got answers, I can update Hevetz, and we'll both be in their good graces. Maybe they'll even offer you permanent work."

It *was* what Nova was after. But as she continued to follow Dylan down the catwalk, her stomach twisted. For months now, Nova had been feeding info about her own life to Dylan in hopes that Dylan might offer something in return. And now here was this dark secret, a blemish on Dylan's otherwise perfect resume, and she'd shared it with Nova along with a declaration of trust.

It should have made Nova's insides beam. It should have been worth twenty smiles, but instead, Nova felt as if she'd been dealt a negative blow.

Dylan was still trying to prove herself. It was like Rix all over again, an unpredictable risk taken with the hopes that it would put her ahead. The difference was, this time, she wasn't merely playing with her own life, she was playing with *everyone's*.

"Did you see the SOS on *Odyssey*, in the updates Hevetz sent?" Nova asked. "Did they order us to sit tight and wait for the backup crew?"

"Is that what you really think of me?" Dylan snarled, whirling on Nova, her blue eyes flashing behind her visor. "That I'd knowingly put my crew in danger?"

Yes, maybe, I don't know.

"You tell me."

"I'm the captain, Nova. I don't have to answer a question like that." She turned and marched on, and the truth coiled and tightened in Nova's stomach, making her nauseated.

Whether Dylan trusted Nova was irrelevant.

Nova couldn't trust *her*.

Toby pushed off the maintenance ladder and swung out over the chasm, one hand curled around the belay line as the body bag dangled from the other. The harness was riding up between his legs with more force than was comfortable, and the pile of bodies looked a lot farther off now that he wasn't standing on the landing.

I better get one hell of a raise for this.

Cleaver worked the belay system, adjusting the speed. Toby tried not to look down. He'd never much liked heights, but when the intern tossed three flares after him, he couldn't help but follow their glow to the pile of deceased below. The flares landed without a sound, forming a small triangle that flickered and glinted. The red glow danced over the nearest corpses in a way *just* creepy enough to make their icy skin suddenly appear tinged with life.

He could see blood now—on their uniforms, their hands and necks and faces. Most didn't appear to have obvious wounds. It was almost as if the blood was merely paint, smeared across their skin for reasons he couldn't fathom. Toby's stomach twisted. He hated blood. There was a reason he stuck to computers and databases, why he hid behind a desk. Code couldn't cut a person.

Far sooner than he was ready, his feet touched down. The bodies were frozen solid, and Toby's boots went sliding off a torso. The belay line tightened and the harness caught him, jerking uncomfortably around his crotch. He found his footing, and the line let up a little, the harness relaxing.

The man between Toby's feet was facedown in the pile.

He wore a pair of coveralls—a driller or mechanic, most likely—but the material making up one of the sleeves had been ripped open, and where blood didn't stain the man's exposed skin, Toby could make out a sleeve of tattoos.

Don't think about what happened, or how they ended up here. Don't psych yourself out. Just get the guy in the bag and be done with it.

Toby shook out the body bag and laid it alongside the corpse. Then he grabbed the man beneath the arms and hauled him toward the bag. Or tried to. The pressure of the oxygen reserves on Toby's shoulders seemed to have tripled, and the frozen body might as well have weighed a metric ton. He'd died—and subsequently frozen—in an odd position. One leg was straight. The other had rolled outward at the hip so that no matter how Toby tried to shove him into the body bag, that damn leg was always going to be cocked to the side, impossible to zip in. He wrestled with the limbs, the zipper, the limbs again. Sweat beaded on Toby's brow, dripped into his eyes.

With the corpse halfway in the bag and the zipper mostly secure except for that damn leg, Toby reached for his harness. The plan was to unfasten, clip the body bag in, and have Cleaver haul it up. Then they'd drop the line again to retrieve Toby.

But with the clip in his grasp, Toby paused. The thought of staying down here—truly alone as the line towed up the body bag—was terrifying. His footing no longer seemed steady. Granted, it had been hell to find a way to balance on this heap of death to begin with, but now he felt as if the ground was shifting beneath him, like the pile was sand in an hourglass and he was about to fall through. No, it wasn't just in his head. Toby could really feel something.

He froze.

Looked down.

The bodies jolted beneath his feet. Toby's ankle sank into the corpses. And then something pulled him.

He plunged down, the belay not locking until he was waist deep in the bodies.

"Pull me up!" he screamed. "Something's got me. Pull me up! PULL ME UP!"

Pain seared across his leg and he felt burning cold. His visor went wild with alerts. Spiked pulse. Erratic breathing. Oxygen levels plummeting.

He flailed, grabbing at the belay line, trying to pull himself up. Above, the landing was a small dark smudge, barely visible through the feedback in his helmet. The harness heaved around him, and for a brief second Toby worried he might be torn in two, but then he lurched free of the corpse pile. He swung and spun on the line, the world still red, the pain everywhere. A warning about oxygen levels flashed. The words and numbers blurred.

Don't pass out, don't pass out.

Hands grabbed beneath his shoulders. He felt the railing strike his thighs, heard Cleaver request backup into the crackling radio, and then he was being lowered onto the landing's metal grating.

"Something grabbed me," he muttered. "Something grabbed me. It grabbed me. Something grabbed me. . . ."

Over and over he repeated it, as Cleaver and the intern appeared behind the red alerts, their faces blurry and the sky above them an indigo-black slash just barely lighter than the dark chasm walls.

"Nothing grabbed you," Cleaver said. "You just slipped and got spooked."

"My foot. I was grabbed. It had me. Something had me. Something—"

"Toby!"

Black danced in his peripherals.

Then the intern's voice: "Cleaver, his leg. Look at his leg."

Toby's vision tunneled. The air was thin. He couldn't get enough of it. His lungs were screaming. His heart about to burst from his chest.

"We have to get him to medical," she said.

It was the last thing he heard before everything went dark.

Drill site ten provided the best view of the ravine so far. Here, the gorge was widest, and standing on the platform,

Nova could easily see down to the bottom.

"Must be flowing fast to not be frozen," she reasoned aloud.

She swept the light of her ray-rifle across the water. Her helmet put the external temperature at roughly -12°C, but the water was moving quickly west, toward the day side, just as Dr. Tarlow had told them ice melt would. Nova scanned along the edge of the river, expecting to see ice where the water met the ravine walls. There was none. Even fast-moving rivers in the Trios usually had ice along their edges in the winter. Unless . . .

Over the holiday break during her first year at the Academy, Nova had left New Earth for a vacation at the Bleyti Resort on Larissa with her then-girlfriend, Aileen. It had been completely outside Nova's budget, from the planet-hop flight to the cost of every last meal. Aileen paid for it all, making a show of her wealth, but Nova's favorite part had cost them nothing: a hike to Bleyti's hot springs, where they swam in a comfortable 35°C pool, surrounded by snow and ice.

Perhaps this Achlys river was the same, heated by a geo-thermal spring. This water lacked the murky, pale-blue color of the Bleyti hot springs though, and there was no steam rising off the surface, either. Maybe this water was somewhere in the middle, heated just slightly so as to keep from freezing, but still quite cold.

Nova brought her light over the water again. The light on

Dylan's weapon momentarily crossed hers. "Wait! Bring it back. Do you see that?" Nova said as the beams joined again. Something was moving just beneath the surface, dancing in the water's current. A series of flat, wide ribbons. "What is that?"

The radio crackled at Dylan's hip, Cleaver shouting something unintelligible.

"Say again?" Dylan responded.

The unit hummed static.

And then, one word cut through, impeccably clear: *backup*.

Dylan sprinted from the landing, and Nova tore after her.

Thea saw her own horror and confusion mirrored in Cleaver's expression. The suits were incredibly durable, made for planetary exploration. They shouldn't simply tear. But there was no denying that Toby's suit *had*, that the material was shredded at the ankle. That Toby was now exposed to atmo. And bleeding everywhere. If the blood loss didn't kill him, the cold could.

Toby's eyes fluttered shut. His body slumped onto the landing.

"Cleaver, we have to get to medical," Thea said again.

"Hold this." The security detail passed her the radio he'd used to contact Dylan, then unhooked Toby's harness clip and heaved the man onto his shoulder. Thea bolted upright, glancing into the chasm. Everything was as they'd left it, the bodies frozen solid, the tattooed man half zipped into the body bag. As the flares died, flickering and sputtering, it almost made the corpses appear to move.

Thea turned and ran.

She sprinted after Cleaver.

Through clouds of steam.

Toward the elevator.

A whooping alarm suddenly kicked on. *Adverse weather conditions*, a robotic voice announced as lighting mounted along the catwalks flashed red. *Reactor powering down in five minutes. All personnel must evacuate and seek shelter immediately.*

Thea kept running. Past drill landings. Over bloody footprints. Through more steam. All the while, her visor flashed updates. She was sweating profusely. Her blood pressure had reached a questionable high.

"Dylan!" she yelled into the radio. "Toby's injured and we're heading for medical. Get back to the rover ASAP."

Silence.

"Dylan, do you read me?"

Nothing. Nothing but the alarm and the lights and that looping warning.

Adverse weather conditions. Reactor powering down in four minutes. All personnel must evacuate and seek shelter immediately.

Thea's skin prickled. She glanced over her shoulder and saw only steam and flashing lights.

Cleaver stopped unexpectedly, and Thea barreled into his back.

"It's just us!" someone shouted.

Dylan and Nova emerged through the steam, hands held in surrender. They must have received Cleaver's original request for backup after all.

Adverse weather conditions. Reactor powering down in three minutes. All personnel must evacuate and seek shelter immediately.

Everyone ran to the elevator, and Nova slammed the grated door shut. Cleaver set Toby on the floor as the car rattled to life. It seemed slower than before.

"What the hell happened?" Dylan dropped to her knees beside Toby. His eyes rolled, head rocking side to side. He was going into shock—from pain, maybe blood loss. The visible portion of his leg was red with cold, and the blood was oozing everywhere. "Why didn't you report an injury?"

"We tried," Thea gasped out. "Storm must have interfered."

"He said something grabbed him," Cleaver explained.

"Grabbed him?" Dylan glanced up.

Thea explained what they'd witnessed—how Toby had sunk into the bodies as though they were quicksand, then begun screaming.

146

The robotic voice announced that they had only two minutes of power remaining. If they got stranded in the elevator . . .

"What could have possibly grabbed him?" Nova said. "Nobody can tear an environmental suit with their hands."

"Maybe it was cut open on some gear we couldn't see. . . ?" Cleaver said.

"Maybe." But Dylan looked unconvinced. "Did you get a body for the autopsy?"

"Does it look like it?" Cleaver growled.

Adverse weather conditions. Reactor powering down in one minute. All personnel must evacuate and seek shelter immediately.

"All right, all right," Dylan said. "Let's get Toby to medical. Soon as this storm passes, we're coming back for a body."

It was a ludicrous suggestion. They needed to get Toby stabilized and comfortable in an isolation chamber, and above all they needed to contact Hevetz. But there wasn't time for an argument now. Thea could make her case in the rover.

Lights outside the gate flashed as the panel inside the elevator refreshed: LEVEL 5 . . . LEVEL 4 . . .

Reactor powering down in five, four . . .

LEVEL 3

Three, two . . .

LEVEL 2

One . . .

The digitized display went blank and the car lurched to a standstill. Dylan threw the door open, revealing a waist-high wall. It took Thea a second to realize this was the floor of the garage, that they'd crawled to a stop barely a meter shy of their destination.

Dylan hoisted herself up and out of the car, then reached back in for Toby, who Nova and Cleaver lifted to her. The floor was smooth and slick, Thea's hands unable to find purchase, but with a boost from Nova, she swung a leg up and managed to scramble into the garage. Nova came next, followed by Cleaver. He picked up Toby, and again, the group was running—through the garage and into the storm beyond.

The sky had filled with dark clouds that crackled with electricity, and as soon as Thea stepped from the shelter of the hangar, the wind pushed her violently. Each step became three or four, the magnitude of the storm shoving her east, toward the night side.

She struggled to stay on course.

Thea could see the rover just ahead, its form glinting as lightning clapped. But as the others reached the vehicle, Thea was propelled right past it, her hands flailing wildly for a door latch but coming up short.

They should have parked the rover *inside* the garage.

They should have turned around the moment Nova sensed a storm.

They should have contacted Hevetz immediately after finding Pitch Evans.

There were a lot of things that should have been done differently, but none of that would get Thea to safety. She crouched down, regaining her balance, then turned and leaned into the wind. Head hunched, she half crawled, half walked toward Rover1. A voice carried through the raging wind, urging her on.

Dirt and rubble flew, slamming into Thea like a downpour of rain. Her helmet sheltered her from the onslaught, but it was almost impossible to fight the instinct to keep her head down, to protect her face and eyes. Thea forced herself to glance up, squinting, searching. A faint blue-white light glowed through the dust. *Headlights.*

Lightning flashed, and she saw them just briefly, only a few meters ahead. Cleaver was holding the door to the rover open with his back, both arms reaching for her.

Her visor flashed warnings.

She lunged with her last bit of strength.

A piece of debris flew at her head. She turned to dodge it, and it clipped her in shoulder, throwing her backward. The momentum of her fall combined with the force of the wind sent her tumbling end over end. Thea was weightless longer than felt natural, and when she slammed to a halt, her back flared with pain.

The world had gone dark. Any lighting that had existed in the state of dusk was now completely blotted out by the storm. Around Thea, the air danced with particles of dirt.

Had she been thrown into the crater that Black Quarry's bridge spanned? It wouldn't have been a long fall—a meter or two—but the rover wouldn't be able to follow. She had to get back to them. If she could just locate their headlights again . . .

Thea pushed to her feet, straightened.

Something dark hurtled at her head.

This time she was too slow.

The rock hit her helmet with a nasty crack, and she fell to her knees, stunned.

"He's losing too much blood!" Cleaver shouted beside Nova.

"I *know*," she shouted back, and used a long piece of gauze from the rover's medkit to tie a tourniquet high on Toby's leg. "Shut up and let me focus."

Nova peeled the liner off a Seckin bandage. The adhesive side shone, and she positioned it over Toby's wound, trying to steady her hands against the constant rocking of the rover. Short for Second Skin, the nanomesh dressings were designed to quicken clotting and draw out bacteria, preventing infection and slowing bleeding until further medical attention could be received.

"It's not gonna help him if you don't fucking apply it!" Cleaver roared.

"Shut up!"

Everything had gone to hell, and Nova couldn't help but blame Dylan. If she'd only waited to search the drilling sites or turned to Hevetz for their instruction, they wouldn't have lost the intern and Toby sure as hell wouldn't be bleeding all over the rover.

His leg was a mess, but the suit was shredded enough to reveal most of the wound. All she had to do was slow the bleeding. Nova lowered the bandage, hands shaking. The rover bucked over a rut and she was flung forward, the dressing clinging to Toby's suit rather than the wound. Nova swore as she tried to peel it off Toby's suit, but it was ruined, useless.

"He still got a pulse?" she asked Cleaver as she reached for the medkit.

"Yeah, but at the rate he's bleeding . . ."

"I know, I know."

She found a new Seckin bandage and stripped off the liner. The wind let up momentarily, and before Nova missed her opportunity she slapped the bandage down. Success. Running her gloved hand along Toby's leg, she secured it in place. The dressing seemed to dissolve beneath her fingers, adhering to Toby's skin.

"How much farther?" she shouted to Dylan.

"I can't see shit!" came the reply.

Nova glanced up. Sleet and hail the size of golf balls bounced off the rover. Two cobwebbed cracks that weren't there earlier now marred the windshield. How the hell was Thea going to survive this? Nova had begged for Dylan to wait, insisted that they needed to search for her. But they couldn't find Thea's helmet light in the madness, and Dylan had made the executive decision to bring Toby to medical and return for the intern later. Nova feared there'd be nothing to find. It wasn't right. Nova would have picked saving Thea over saving the enormous prick bleeding before her, and yet here she was, bandaging his leg.

"Pulse?" she again asked Cleaver.

"There, but faint."

Nova looked down at Toby. His eyes were closed but twitching behind the lids.

Thea Sadik heard the alerts before she saw them. The beeping noise brought her out of a fog, and she forced her eyes open, one after the other.

Consciousness lost for 0:00:13.

Her vitals flashed, all relatively stable considering her

predicament, but then her eyes caught a new alert, and everything began to spike.

Suit breach. O_2 reserves at 70%.

She searched the tempered glass, eyes burning in their sockets as she stretched the limits of her vision. And there, above her left eye, up near her hairline, was a small crack. The rock that had struck and stunned her.

She looked beyond the glass, desperate to find the rover's headlights. There were none. The only bit of light that now existed in the raging storm was the small glow provided by her helmet's headlamp and the crackling of electricity in the overhead clouds. She'd lost her flashlight during the fall, but had possessed the sense to holster her stun gun when they first left the drilling base's garage. Not that the weapon would do her any good now. It was the flashlight she needed most.

The alert in her visor updated. *O_2 reserves at 66%.*

She needed to find shelter. If the atmosphere didn't kill her when her oxygen reserves ran out, prolonged exposure to the cold might. Would a hairline fracture in her helmet be enough for her to freeze to death? She didn't want to find out.

Thea pushed upright only to have the wind beat her back to all fours. She tried again, staying hunched over as she attempted to run. The wind tossed her like a rag doll. She cartwheeled end over end, thrown farther east until she slammed to a halt against sloped earth. The air went from her lungs, and she gasped wildly. When it returned, she felt along the curve, finding a lip. A shallow crater.

Thea heaved herself up and over.

She couldn't fight the wind—that much was obvious—so she decided to move with it. If she could only find some shelter—a cave, a shallow ravine—she might be able to wait out the storm and find her way back when the weather cleared.

Each step sent her running forward, the wind shoving her on. At least now the ground was blessedly even—rolling slightly, but free of craters or fissures. It started to sleet, sheets of icy water assaulting her, making the earth beneath her feet slick and treacherous. Unable to see anything, she stumbled on, hail piercing her shoulders and back like knives.

Lightning flashed, revealing something large and smooth just ahead. Clearly man-made. What was it Dylan had said when reviewing maps just earlier?

Not far from the old Witch Hazel bunker.

The wind pushed at her back, moving her like a leaf toward the structure. It was a storm wall, she realized. She closed in on it with frightening speed, and then she was upon it, throwing her hands out to minimize impact.

Thea's wrists flared with pain but she ignored the ache,

feeling along the wall. It was smartly angled, allowing the wind to ride up and over it. She walked beside it until she discovered it was actually a multitude of walls, each section recessed slightly from the next, leaving enough room for a rover to gain passage. Likely in preparation for the very predicament she now found herself in. A researcher caught in poor weather could still gain access to the bunker while the bunker remained protected from the storm.

Thea slipped between two walls and found the space on the other side spared from the worst of the wind. A low and sprawling construction sat ahead, shaped like an off-kilter pinwheel. The entire thing was as dark and unadorned as the Achlys landscape.

O_2 reserves at 62%.

Thea ran, now propelled by only her legs. They ached with exhaustion. Sleet pummeled her shoulders, threatening to beat her to the ground.

She felt cold, suddenly. Deathly cold. At the end of the bunker's nearest spoke, Thea found an air lock. A faded Hevetz logo adorned the door.

Please still have power, please.

She slammed her fist into the access panel. Miraculously, the door slid open. She stumbled into the bay. Pressed the button to close the door behind her.

It sealed shut.

The sound of depressurizing air was the most glorious song she'd ever heard.

Every muscle shaking with relief, ready to give out, Thea pressed a third button, and the interior door opened to the safety of the bunker.

She stepped through, gasping with relief.

It was dark, quiet.

Feeling blindly, she searched for a panel to activate the lights, the heat. Her hands twitched with cold as they grazed a set of breakers.

Odd that the air locks were powered and the bunker was not. Then again, the entrance could be supplied by emergency power. There was no sense heating a bunker if no one was in it. Well, she was here now. And she needed heat. Desperately.

She threw the breaker and white-hot agony roared, scorching every limb, the cold she'd felt replaced with monumental pain. A dozen alerts flashed in her visor. Her heart rate skyrocketed, then dropped to zero.

Thea Sadik hit the floor, dead.

He'd retreated to safety at the first sign of the storm. Even now, after two months alone on Achlys, the boy knew better than to test the fury of nature.

When the storm reached a dangerous intensity, he'd cut all but the emergency power. Weather like this didn't last forever, and he could go without lights or heat.

But then she'd come.

From his section of the bunker, his skin had prickled, and when he peered through the reinforced grated windows, there she was; a member of the rescue crew, running for the northwest air lock amid the raging elements.

He'd padded soundlessly to the bunker's core, then taken the corridor to meet her. When he arrived, it was too late. Then again, he hadn't truly hurried.

The boy looked down on the girl. Her mouth was caught in a shape of surprise behind her visor, her brown eyes dazed and lifeless. Dark hair clung to her sweaty neck. She should have known better than to try to reinstate power during an electrically charged storm, but she was young. Far younger than he'd guessed any of the Odyssey crew might be. Perhaps she had no clue what she was up against. Perhaps she was ignorant.

He cocked his head in thought.

The others would assume she'd perished in the storm. Probably they wouldn't even look for her.

It would be easy to let her die.

But if he tried to revive her . . . if he succeeded and earned her trust . . .

He needed an ally, someone who believed him decent and good and worth saving.

The boy unfastened her helmet.

V

THE SURVIVOR

Witch Hazel Bunker / *Celestial Envoy*

Achlys, Fringe-1 System

THEA CAME ALIVE GASPING, LOOKING into a set of foreign eyes.

She felt the ghost of pressure the young man's mouth had made against hers, and her palms flew to his chest. Before she could shove, his hands closed over her wrists and he moved away from her, sitting back on his heels.

"You're welcome," he said, and let her go.

She scrambled away, feeling at her face, the neckline of her suit. "You took off my helmet."

"Again, you're welcome."

Inside, she reminded herself as her back hit the bunker wall. *Not exposed to atmo. Inside. Safe.*

Even still, it was cold enough that she could see her breath in the air. The corridor was illuminated only by faint orange lights that ran like piping along the edges of the floors and ceiling. Things were still running on minimum power, and whatever she'd done with the breaker had accomplished nothing but nearly killing her.

She glanced at the air lock to her right, the darkness of the bunker waiting to her left. And then the stranger crouched before her.

He wore a set of work coveralls, only the upper half was unzipped and the sleeves were tied around his waist in a makeshift belt. A security vest hung open over a stained T-shirt. Along his collarbone, the dark tendril of a tattoo crept over his tan skin.

The tattoo reminded her of Pitch Evans.

The warning.

Don't trust the kid.

But this stranger didn't look like a kid. Dark scruff shadowed his jaw. Wild hair hung to his shoulders, half of it pulled back and secured in a bun on the top of his head. Even hunched in a low crouch, forearms resting on his knees, he had an assertive confidence Thea had come to expect of adults, not her peers; the kind of confidence she was still struggling to find herself. And yet there was a youthfulness to the boy's eyes, a fullness to his cheeks.

He was her age, Thea reasoned. Maybe a little older. Certainly more adult than child. But if Pitch Evans was anything like the *Odyssey* crew—anything like Dylan or Toby—he likely defined a *kid* as anyone incapable of working a job for Hevetz in an official capacity. A student, like herself, an intern. Could this boy be an intern, too? Surely Hevetz didn't take on interns for confidential operations like Black Quarry.

"Are you Black Quarry?" she asked.

"Yes." His voice was low and scratchy, like he wasn't in the habit of using it.

"Where's the rest of the crew?"

"Dead."

Thea swallowed. She'd expected as much, but hearing it . . .

"How did—?"

"Look, if you wanna talk, I'm not doing it here. Come on." He extended a hand as he stood. He was taller than Thea expected, but leaner, too. The coveralls and vest added bulk, made him look bigger when he was crouched beside her. Dirt was wedged beneath his fingernails and pressed into the creases of his skin, but otherwise, his hand was impeccably unmarred for a drilling technician. No cuts or scars or bruises. Thea looked again at his outfit, part drilling uniform, part security detail.

Don't trust the kid.

"I'm not moving 'til you tell me what happened."

"I saved your ass, is what happened. You'd be dead if I hadn't revived you. So how about you say *thanks*, for starters?"

She said nothing.

Grunting, he reached for her, and Thea scrambled to her feet, grabbing for her weapon. His eyes followed every movement—her fingers unsnapping the holster, her hand lifting the stun gun free. As she brought the barrel up, his thick brows lifted in amusement.

"I could take that away from you before you even *started* to pull the trigger."

He was lying. No one was that fast.

But there was a calmness to his expression that unsettled her. What had he done to survive on this rock when everyone else had perished? What was he willing to do still?

"Who the hell are you?" Thea asked, leveling her aim.

"Amos Lashley," he said, showing her his palms. "Hevetz drilling crew and sole survivor of the Black Quarry op. I've had one hell of an eight weeks, but by all means, threaten to shoot me. It's not like I've had it rough or anything."

"I can see *Celestial Envoy*!" Dylan shouted from the front. "We're almost there."

Nova braced a hand against the side of the rover. There was a bump as Dylan drove them over the lip of the gangplank, and then the scream of the storm's wind was cut in half as they came to a halt inside the hangar.

"Tarlow? Sullivan?" Dylan said, trying the intercoms in desperation. "Damn, still down." She threw open the door and scrambled out. In the back seat, Nova did the same.

"Let's get him to medical." Nova grabbed Toby beneath the arms, ready to heave him from the vehicle, but he flinched beneath her touch. His eyes flew open, and Nova lurched away with surprise. "Toby!" He stared blankly at the roof of the rover. "Toby, you okay, man?"

He sat up slowly, swaying, dazed, but there was a bit of color in his cheeks again. Maybe it wasn't as bad as they'd first thought. He could have just fainted from shock, and now that the Seckin had slowed the bleeding, regained consciousness. Thea would know better.

But the intern wasn't here.

Because they'd left her.

Nova shook her guilt aside, put on a professional face. "What happened back there?" she asked as she helped Toby from the vehicle. He paused at the door, feet planted on the floor outside the rover, but body still slumped into the seat.

"I . . ." He tried to touch his forehead and simply grazed the glass of his helmet. "I fell," he said after a moment. "No, I was grabbed."

"I don't understand."

His head jerked to face Nova. "We have to get off this rock. We gotta go now." Beads of sweat lined Toby's brow, and his lip practically trembled with fear. Nova had never seen him anything but cocky and argumentative, cool and composed.

"Toby, if you're messing with us . . . If this is all some elaborate, sick joke . . ."

He grabbed her arm, the pressure viselike. "Get us off this planet." His fingers dug in hard. "Get us outta here now!"

As Nova buckled in pain, Dylan appeared at her side,

pinching just below Toby's elbow and causing him to relinquish his grip. "We're headed to medical first to get you stable," Dylan told him calmly. "The storm's too bad to leave right now regardless."

"It's not right," he went on. "It's wrong. Something's wrong."

"Callahan!" Dylan barked.

He twitched, as though he'd just received a jolt of electricity, then keeled forward. Nova grabbed him at the shoulders to keep him from falling from the rover, then pushed him back to a sitting position. He raised his head wearily, and she spotted the blood.

"Nosebleed," she said to the others. Then to Toby: "Come on, asshole. Can you walk?"

She helped him from the rover, but he walked alongside her for only a few steps before his body was raked with another tremor. His head twitched, and he shoved Nova. She went staggering aside, barely able to keep her footing.

"I want it off!" Toby screamed, pawing at the helmet. "Get it off me!"

Nova raced in grabbing at his arms. Blood now flowed freely from Toby's nose.

"What the hell is wrong with him?" Cleaver said, rushing to aid Nova.

"Toby, you have to calm down," Dylan said. "Do you

understand me? Calm down."

The technician took a few deep breaths, nodding frantically. With Cleaver's assistance, Nova was able to support Toby as they made their way through *Celestial Envoy*, Dylan in the lead. The twitching and spasms began again within minutes, and by the time they entered the medbay, Toby was struggling against them with unbelievable strength, clawing at his helmet.

"Get it off, get it off me, get it off now!"

"Tarlow! Sullivan!" Dylan shouted in the direction of the research labs.

Nova kicked Toby in the back of the leg, causing him to buckle to one knee. It gave her and Cleaver the smallest moment of relief from his thrashing, and as he attempted to stand they forced his hands behind his back. With Dylan at his feet, the three of them lugged Toby onto one of the operating tables, then forced his limbs into the wrist and ankle restraints. Even once secured, Toby continued to arch and struggle.

Tarlow burst into the medbay, Sullivan on her heels. Nova made the briefest eye contact with her cousin, his expression asking, *You okay*, and her frantic nod responding, *At the moment.*

The doctor, however, looked at no one but Toby. "We need to sedate him."

"Don't you want to know what happened first?" Dylan asked.

"It doesn't matter what happened. He clearly needs to be sedated."

"Oh my god!" Cleaver said, backing away from the table. "His eyes!"

Nova followed Cleaver's gaze. Toby's eyes were filled with blood, their whites now an unnatural, dark red.

"They're hemorrhaging," the doctor said, grabbing a syringe. "I need to get his helmet off."

Everything was blurry.

His vision, his senses, even his own thoughts. Nothing made sense.

Toby's eyes felt like they were burning. He wanted to claw them from his skull. Something warm and metallic dripped into his mouth. He wanted to claw at that, too.

He kept trying to stop himself, but his hands had their own agenda. He thrashed, his limbs fighting against his restraints. He could feel warmth around his wrists now, too, his skin surely split from his struggles. He didn't care. If he could only get this helmet off. If he could just get the blood off his face, the heat from his limbs.

He gagged, hacking on air, spitting out blood.

There was nothing else to eject.

Except there was.

He had to be sick. They needed to let him throw up.

A figure moved above him, fuzzy, gray. There was a click, and his helmet lifted free. For one blessed moment, Toby's lungs filled with fresh, clean air. He bit at it, gasped at it, tried to drink it all up.

Then the needle came down, burrowing into his neck.

Like before, he felt it moving through him, a current, a fire. He tried to sit, jump, run. He kicked and thrashed and roared. The wave was coming again, ready to overtake him.

The metallic taste in his mouth faded. The room blurred further, morphing into dense fog.

Toby leaned back on the table.

His head lolled to the side, and his eyes fell shut.

When Thea didn't shoot, Amos walked away, heading deeper into the bunker.

"We have to go!" she called out. "I need to get back to *Celestial Envoy*, regroup with my team."

"In this storm? Be my guest."

Thea peered through the air lock. "How long do they usually last?"

"Couple minutes, hours, days. They're all different."

Days? She pushed to her feet and jogged after him.

He led the way toward the bunker's hub, which housed mess quarters and a small infirmary. A hallway wrapped around the centralized facilities, providing access to the various corridors branching from it. Amos turned down one labeled *Bunk 03*. It dead-ended at a sliding door, which he gripped along the seams.

"Everything's on manual during the storm," he explained as he pried the door open.

Beyond, Thea could make out private living quarters, hexagonal in shape. Dr. Tarlow had called this room—or one like it—home all those years ago.

"I know this looks easy," he prompted, "but the door's actually kinda heavy."

She considered the room beyond, how the door would slide shut once she stepped inside, leaving them very alone.

Don't trust the kid.

But she was no less alone out here in the hall than she'd be in the living quarters. Her crew was back at *Celestial Envoy* or dead in the storm. His crew had long since perished, and besides, *she* had the gun. If he meant her harm, he wouldn't have bothered reviving her.

Thea walked through the doorway.

Immediately to her left was a bathroom, and to her right was a small storage closet holding a pair of work coveralls, a few extra envirosuits, and one ray-rifle surrounded by battery mags.

So much for being the only one with a gun.

The furniture in the sitting room was antiquated, styled with the rounded, soft angles that had been in fashion fifty years earlier. It reminded Thea of her room back home, furnished with pieces purchased at secondhand stores or donated to the foster home by others.

Amos had set up a portable emergency cooking stove on the table in the sitting area. A box of freeze-dried fruit was on one of the chairs. Was this what he'd been living off— hot water and fruit rations? Surely an operation like Black Quarry would have plenty of supplies, enough for a single survivor to eat better than this.

There were two bunk beds in the room, but only one of the four mattresses was made. Thea sat on it and stared out the window. A wind chime made of kitchen utensils bounced and flailed, sometimes connecting with the glass, but never making a sound she could hear.

Thea missed the sun, natural lighting. Her world had been blindingly, sickeningly white at Northwood Point. She'd thought she hated it, but this was worse. She couldn't wait to feel the humidity of Hearth City again, to have the air so thick and heavy that it coated her like a wet second skin.

"Here."

Amos pressed a mug of hot tea into her hands. Without her helmet, she could smell it, the sweetgrass and citrus wafting up to her nose. Fresh. Real. So opposite the sterile, filtered air of her suit, the cryo chamber, *Odyssey*. It made her think of coffee shops she used to visit with Mel. The smell was so blessedly *normal*, it nearly made her cry.

"Thanks." Thea sipped the tea. "So, Amos. I need to know what happened."

"It's Coen, actually," he said. "I'm named after my father, but Coen's my middle name, and I prefer that to the constant reminder that I'm living in his shadow."

"Oh. Okay."

"This is where you tell me what I'm supposed to call you," he prompted.

"Thea."

"Thea what?"

"I can't possibly see why that matters."

"Everything matters," Coen countered.

"Fine, Thea Sadik. Now, what the hell happened?"

"We landed, got set up, and built the drill site," he said, pouring a cup of hot water for himself. "Shit hit the fan two weeks after we broke ground."

"The water was toxic?"

"Something we touched was. It started with Li, one of our technicians, then spread."

"A virus? Bacteria?"

"Maybe. We never had the time to figure out what was happening. Not scientifically, at least. By the time we realized we needed to start quarantine procedures, the affected were out of control. Clawing at their skin, their faces, their eyes—clawing at others. They overran *Celestial Envoy* within twenty-four hours. Cut the power and sabotaged the comm gear. We tried barricading what we could—the mess, the bridge. Nothing worked."

The visuals flashed through Thea's mind. The overrun hangar deck, the halls, the fried doors to the bridge. The dead crew members spread through the ship. Coen seemed almost eerily calm given all he'd just told her.

"How'd you survive?"

"I hid."

Thea frowned. "That's it?"

"First the ship's air vents, then this bunker. I never said it was heroic, but I did what I had to." Coen set his mug on the table. "So are you really Hevetz or were you just unlucky enough to crash-land here?" Thea must have appeared confused, because he clarified with, "You don't really look like search and rescue. What are you, fifteen?"

"Seventeen."

"You look young, that's all."

"So do you."

"I'm twenty," he replied. "You wanna see my Hevetz ID?"

Don't trust the kid.

"Yeah, maybe."

"Hevetz sends me a rescue team that includes a kid bright enough to electrocute herself," he grumbled, ignoring her request. "Just my luck."

It was like the warden back home all over again, her biggest insecurity thrown in her face.

"If you don't need us, feel free to stay on this rock when we leave."

Coen pinched the bridge of his nose. "Sorry, sorry. Look, I've never really been good with people, and that's only gotten worse after being alone for two months. You're just not what I was expecting."

"And I never expected to be here. I was interning at a research base on Soter when Hevetz issued a distress call on Black Quarry's behalf. Our crew was apparently the closest, and now here I am." She went on to explain how the Company had shipped the *Odyssey* crew out in a hurry, instructing Dylan to bring along Thea's mentor because of the doctor's knowledge of the site, and how an additional backup crew was still on the way. "They'll be the true search and rescue; the crew you've been hoping for."

Coen didn't seem relieved by this. "Hold up. The doctor. What's her name?"

"Lisbeth Tarlow," Thea said.

"*The* Lisbeth Tarlow?" Coen stood so abruptly he rattled the table, sending some of his tea sloshing over the lip of the mug. "Tarlow who was stationed here with Witch Hazel as a kid? *She's* part of your crew?"

Thea nodded.

"I need to talk to her. Right now."

"But the storm—"

"Is over."

Thea twisted toward the window. It was still dark out—Achlys was always dark, she needed to get used to that—but the wind chime now hung idly, swaying in nothing worse than a breeze.

"They can clear out as quick as they strike," Coen explained. "Let me patch your helmet." He disappeared into the closet and returned with a patch kit that he applied to the fracture. His work dried almost instantly, the damage to the visor barely visible.

"No one should notice the difference," Coen said, passing her the helmet, "but if they do, pretend like the glass always had a patch. You don't need to give anyone a reason to be suspicious. Everyone with Black Quarry turned on one another. No one trusted anyone, so no one could work together."

"Right. Thanks."

"What the hell were you doing out in that storm anyway?" he asked as he began rummaging around in the closet, gathering gear.

"Dylan wanted to check out the drill point where Li was injured. We found the dead crew members, which distracted us from the storm. Our tech guy got hurt, and I was struck by debris as we brought him back to the rov—"

"Hurt how?" Coen asked, spinning to face her.

"He fell trying to gather one of the bodies for an autopsy. His leg got torn up."

"We need to go. Now! Do you have any idea what your crew brought back to *Celestial Envoy*?" He grabbed an orange backpack from the closet and became a tornado, darting from one corner of the room to the next, stuffing items in the bag. A thermos, some of the dried fruit, a framed photo from his nightstand.

"You said it was in the water," Thea said, "or the rock."

"But it was spread person to person."

"And everyone's now dead."

Coen turned to face her, bag hanging limp from his hand. "How do you think that pile of bodies got there, Thea? You think *I* moved them? That I was so bored in my solitude that I wasted precious battery charges driving the deceased to some chasm-grave?"

"Of course not. We saw the footprints. We already figured they walked themselves there."

"And now they might walk back out."

A nervous laugh shot from Thea's throat. "What are you talking about? They're *dead*. I saw them. They've been lying in a canyon for two months, exposed to freezing temperatures."

"Then how'd your technician's leg get clawed up?"

She didn't have an answer. Nothing could survive in those conditions. It didn't make sense.

"We need to get off this planet while you still have a pilot," Coen said, grabbing a pickax from the closet. He slid the tool through several loops of fabric he'd stitched onto the outside of the backpack, the carbon fiber shaft threading into place like a blade in a sheath. Then he swung the bag onto his shoulders, snatched up the ray-rifle, and hurried for the door.

"Come on!" he said when he realized she wasn't moving.

"Aren't you forgetting something?"

Coen glanced at the straps of his backpack, the ray-rifle clutched in his hand, back to her.

"A suit?" she offered.

"Oh my god!" Coen dumped the bag and stripped off his vest, threading his arms back through the coveralls and yanking the zipper high beneath his chin. Then he pulled on one of the spare suits from his closet. Helmet sealed and orange backpack again on his shoulders, Coen gave her a thumbs-up.

This was the mastermind who survived a horrific tragedy— a boy who couldn't remember to put on a suit before venturing outside?

Don't trust the kid.

Maybe it was foolish to take the advice of a dead man over that of a boy who'd survived what no one else had. But Pitch Evans had chosen his last words carefully, taken the time to paint them on the bridge's floor with his own blood. Maybe Coen had abandoned the engineer in a moment of need, left him to die. Coen had even admitted that he only survived by hiding.

Would he abandon Thea if it came to it? She was his ticket off-planet, after all. Perhaps that was the only reason he'd revived her.

"This way," Coen said, stepping into the hall.

She could venture only the slightest guess at where *Celestial Envoy* sat in relation to the Witch Hazel bunker. And what did she intend to do, walk back to it? Stagger into that unpredictable wasteland again when someone was offering to drive her back to her crew?

Whether she trusted Coen Lashley fully or not, there was no denying that he was her ticket off-planet, too. Thea pulled on her helmet. As it sealed with her suit, her vitals booted up on the visor, then faded, replaced with a quick reading on her oxygen reserves. She was just shy of sixty percent.

The suit breach was now sealed, thanks to Coen's help, and the time spent in the bunker had countered any of the reserves she'd lost earlier in the storm. She checked the watch on her wrist, which was recording how much time she'd spent on planet. It was ticking its way toward the three-hour mark, meaning her oxygen would definitely not last the ten hours Dylan had originally predicted. Hopefully they'd be back on *Odyssey* long before that became an issue. Honestly, at this rate, Thea was more worried about having to pee in her suit, not running out of air.

One thing at a time, she reminded herself.

She followed Coen to an air lock—different from the one she'd used to enter the bunker. It opened onto a sheltered loading bay, where a rover was waiting. Markings on the body read *WH-Rover1*.

"I've been using it to make runs to the ship," Coen explained as he threw his bag onto the back seat. "To restock supplies."

"Why even stay at this bunker? The ship has everything necessary to sustain a crew of hundreds."

"Because the infected figured out how to use the vents, like me. The bunker was a necessity. And then later, by the time they cleared out and went to the ravine, the aerofarm was destroyed, all the fresh food ruined. Nonperishables were fine, so I've been taking what I need when I need it. The place is too depressing to stay there. You saw it."

Thea worked over this new information but said nothing.

"You don't trust me," Coen said.

"I'm slow to trust anyone," she answered.

She'd meant for it to be a defense, a way to keep him quiet so she didn't have to talk, but as soon as she said it, she realized it was true. Thea wasn't sure if she'd ever trusted a single person fully in her whole life. She'd never believed the people who insisted her mother was dead, that Thea would be best to accept this fact. She'd been suspicious of Dr. Tarlow's claim that everything would be fine on Achlys. And she hadn't trusted Mel to not leave her when he went off to university, so she'd left him first. Trust in others was a luxury Thea couldn't afford. The only person she counted on was herself.

She climbed into the rover. It was a significantly older model than the one she'd ridden to the drilling base. The seat cushions were peeling, the dash clouded with a layer of dust. Even when she dragged a palm over it, the interface that glowed up at her was outdated; earth tones and soft angles.

As the rover jostled out of the bay, Thea watched the Witch Hazel bunker shrink in size. Coen guided them between two of the storm walls, and the facility disappeared from sight entirely, swallowed up by the darkness of the planet.

They drove in silence.

Thea noted that the compass on the dash showed them moving southwest. It matched her thinnest guess at where *Celestial Envoy* might sit in relation to the Witch Hazel bunker, and the longer the needle stayed pointing at "SW," the more at ease she felt.

Other than blowing away her crew's rover tracks, there was little evidence of the storm that had nearly killed Thea. Soter's ice caps always transformed during a storm, the caps blanketed in white, the snow softening everything. The horizon would glisten, deathly cold, yet insanely beautiful. But here on Achlys, the world outside the rover looked as ravaged as it had before the heinous weather. Craters and gullies still cut through the earth. Rock pylons and spikes still rose toward the sky.

She couldn't get off this planet fast enough.

"That's a horrible way to approach life, you know," Coen said, breaking the silence.

"What is?"

"Not trusting anybody."

"It's worked out pretty well so far."

He rolled his eyes with such force, Thea was surprised they managed to stay in his skull.

"What do you want me to say?" she snapped, patience lost.

"Nothing. I just thought maybe me saving your ass and patching your helmet and driving you back to your crew would win me a few points."

"You wanna win a few more? Tell me why the dead engineer on the bridge wrote a note saying we shouldn't trust you. Tell me why as the sole survivor, you didn't contact Hevetz once in the past two months. Explain to me how you can be desperate to see our doctor and get off this rock, but you didn't rush to meet us when we lan—"

"When you landed," he snarled, "I was in the bunker going through my rations. I didn't even know a crew was here until you stumbled through my air lock. Also, *Celestial Envoy*'s comm gear is damaged. I couldn't contact anyone."

"And the engineer's warning?" Thea nudged. It would be the first thing her crew asked about when she returned with Coen in tow. Entering *Celestial Envoy* with him might turn them against her also.

"What warning?"

"Pitch Evans. He wrote to not trust you."

"He wrote *my* name—Amos Coen Lashley?"

"Well, no."

"Then how do you know he was talking about me?"

"He said *Don't trust the kid*."

"That could be about anyone," Coen said. "How am I supposed to know why the hell he wrote what he did before— actually, no. Screw this. I don't have to defend myself. Not after what I've been through."

"Yeah, save your energy for the captain. You're gonna need it, because she sure as hell is gonna expect an explanation."

"You know," he grumbled, "I'm starting to think I shouldn't have bothered reviving you."

He squeezed the steering wheel, focusing on the terrain outside the windshield.

The girl didn't trust him.

The rest of the crew might not trust him, either.

But that was fine. He didn't need their unanimous support. Just the doctor, who might hold answers. And the pilot, who had wings.

Everyone else was expendable.

The entire Black Quarry crew had been expendable, after all, and the Company had sent a team of novices to deal with a deadly contagion. It was hard to imagine they cared for Odyssey's crew any more than they cared for his own fallen colleagues.

Initially, he'd made his peace with dying alone on Achlys. But after what Thea had told him about the approaching crew—a specialized backup team en route to Achlys—everything changed. His death would no longer be his own choice. Once a high-ranking Hevetz official saw the state of the Black Quarry op, anyone living would be shot on sight. The operation would be forgotten, reports deleted, records destroyed. The planet would be put *under galactic quarantine.*

A threat must be contained.

He'd understood that originally. It was why he'd pulled the breakers. But now it was flee and have a chance, or stay and be shot in the back, and he had no intention of being executed. If he was going to die, it was going to be on his own terms.

He could see the way now, knew what he had to do.

Every lie he'd told—every half truth he'd yet to utter—was purposeful. If the Odyssey crew didn't fight him, he could potentially save them all.

VI

THE INFECTED

Celestial Envoy

Achlys, Fringe-1 System

AS THEY APPROACHED *Celestial Envoy*, Thea spotted one of *Odyssey*'s rovers still parked near the gangplank. Storm winds had pushed it several meters, but it was still right-side up. The second rover—the one the team had taken to the drilling base—waited inside the hangar, doors open and dashboard still illuminated.

Coen parked beside it, and Thea stared at the empty interior. Her crew had made it back. They'd needed to find shelter, and driving on had likely been a matter of survival, but it still stung to know she'd been left behind so willingly.

Thea let Coen lead the way to medical, grateful for his presence. He was familiar with the ship's layout, and though she'd never admit it to him, the last thing she wanted to do was navigate the place alone. When they reached the medical floor, they found the entire level sealed off from the rest of the ship.

"They probably flushed the wing, vented the air," Thea offered. "Maybe so they could remove Toby's suit while seeing to his injuries."

"Stupid," Coen muttered, but all Thea could think about was how difficult fine motor skills were for Dr. Tarlow because of her tremor, and how Toby could be bleeding out on a table because Thea wasn't there to help.

She raced ahead, Coen now following her. The hallway was dimly lit, lights flickering, but the medbay was a glowing beacon at the end of the corridor, and soon she was upon it, bursting through the doorframe.

Barely a step into the room, Thea froze.

In part because Dylan, Nova, and Sullivan had snapped to attention at her approach and now had their weapons aimed at her and Coen. But also because the room looked like a battleground.

Cabinets hung open, surgical instruments and vials of medicine strewn across the counters and floors. Regenerative beds were open, their surfaces stained with blood and other fluids Thea didn't care to think about. Several of the overhead lights were blown out, and the one in the center of the room flickered above Dr. Tarlow, who was bent over a body on the table, Cleaver assisting right beside her.

Thea couldn't see their subject's face, but she knew it was Toby. His suit, boots, and helmet lay discarded on the floor.

"Who's the boy?" Dylan asked, jerking her weapon in Coen's direction.

"He's Black Quarry," Thea began, but Dylan was already

putting it together—Coen's approximate age and Pitch's warning. Just as Thea had anticipated.

"Isolation," Dylan snapped, motioning her stun gun at one of the chambers that lined the medbay walls.

"Wait, listen to me," Coen began. "This is important."

"Isolation!" The room flared with light as Dylan sent a shot of electricity at Coen. It caught him in the side, but rather than dropping from the charge, he simply staggered. It was Nova's shot, from a far more powerful ray-rifle, that sent Coen stumbling backward a few steps, his arms windmilling in an attempt to regain balance. In the process, he crossed the yellow-and-black chevron line on the floor that marked the divide between the medical bay and the chamber, and as he shook his head, trying to dispel the shock, Dylan slammed her fist into the chamber's door panel. The glass slid shut, cutting Coen off from the rest of the room.

"Hey!" he shouted, banging into the glass door. "Let me outta here. Listen, we have to leave. *Now!* We need to—"

Dylan punched another button, and Coen's words were cut off, no longer broadcast into the rest of the bay. He continued slapping at the door, shouting muffled protests.

"Thea!" came Dr. Tarlow's voice behind her. "Thank goodness. Get over here! I need your help."

"One second, doc," Dylan said, grabbing Thea at the meaty part of her arm. The captain's eyes flicked toward Coen, and then she said to Thea, pointedly, "Explain."

"After you *left* me in that storm," she began, "I managed to get to the Witch Hazel bunker. His name's Amos Coen Lashley, but he goes by Coen. He's Black Quarry's only survivor, drilling division, and said he's been holed up in that bunker for weeks."

"You think he's the kid Pitch warned us about?"

"He said he doesn't know anything about the warning," Thea said, "but maybe."

"Thea, now!" Dr. Tarlow yelled.

"Go on," Dylan said, releasing Thea. "I'll talk to the kid, figure out what to do with him."

"Here's what we do with him," Nova said after Thea had moved to join the doctor. "We transfer him to *Odyssey*'s isolation chamber if we don't trust him; we've done our part. Thea's fine. We're all back together. We've seen to the Company-issued distress call and rescued the one survivor. Now let's get the hell off this rock."

Since Tarlow had sedated Toby, Dylan had spent the past twenty minutes arguing that they wait to see how things progressed. But Nova didn't care what the captain thought anymore. It was obvious Toby's reaction to a simple leg injury was a sign that they needed to put as much space as possible between the crew and whatever caused it—fast.

"We've only got one isolation chamber on *Odyssey*," Dylan said. "Once we've confirmed Toby's stabilized, that's a fine plan. Or if he succumbs to his injuries, even. But I'm not abandoning one of our own in favor of Black Quarry's survivor, who turns out to be the very person Evans specifically told us not to trust."

Nova glanced over her shoulder. If the survivor named Coen was a *kid*, then Nova was a kid, too. The boy looked about her age. Maybe twenty, tops. She turned back to Dylan. "So we sit and twiddle our thumbs and wait to see what happens to Toby? What if he gets worse?"

"Nova's got a point," Sullivan added.

Nova was pretty sure he'd say whatever was necessary to get off-planet, but she appreciated the support.

"Move," Cleaver grunted, pushing between the three of them and disappearing down the hall. He looked about ready to be sick. Maybe he hadn't been kidding when the doctor asked for his help and he'd said blood made him queasy. It was almost funny. Almost.

"I'm calling the shots," Dylan said firmly, "and we're waiting."

Sullivan let out a string of expletives, followed by, "Goddamn reckless."

"No, Sullivan. It's not. It's the opposite of reckless. I am going to make an educated decision here, based on facts.

That means questioning our newest arrival while Tarlow finishes with Toby."

Dylan turned away from them and walked over to the isolation chamber, where she began to question—or based on the sound of it, interrogate—Coen.

Nova leaned in to her cousin. "She should really be letting Hevetz call the shots at this point, but it's been"—she checked her watch—"roughly three and a half hours since we landed, and she hasn't debriefed them *once*."

"Maybe that'll change depending on what the kid says." Sullivan fell in line beside Dylan to listen.

For a moment, Nova seriously considered sneaking back to *Odyssey* and contacting Hevetz alone. But she caught wind of Coen mentioning Jon Li's injury two months earlier and curiosity got the best of her. She joined Dylan at the isolation chamber door.

After Cleaver had stripped off a pair of surgical gloves that he'd been wearing over his suit and fled the medbay, claiming he was about to be sick, Thea got her first unobstructed view of the operating table.

A tourniquet had been tied high on Toby's thigh and a Seckin bandage applied to the actual wound. Thea had never seen a Seckin bandage before. They were Cradle technology and therefore had quite the price tag. The same engineering that made the bandages possible was also found in regenerative beds, which went a step further, stimulating new skin and muscle growth after a wound had successfully clotted. Unlike the beds, Seckin bandages were small and easily transportable, making them a staple in military medkits and the medicine cabinets of the wealthy.

The bandage appeared to have done its job controlling Toby's bleeding, but the wound was only part of the technician's problems. His ankles and wrists had been secured by restraints. An additional strap was buckled down tightly across his chest, the mustard-stained shirt now also stained with blood. There was more on his neck, chin, mouth—the origin point seeming to be his nose. A massive nosebleed had caused all of this? Thea looked up a bit farther. Dr. Tarlow had lifted his eyelids to check pupil dilation.

"What happened to his eyes?"

"They hemorrhaged," the doctor said plainly.

Thea stared, trying to discern where Toby's irises ended and the blood began. "Is he . . . ?"

"He's sedated. I could barely press the plunger because of the tremor. And this—well, I'm butchering this. Here, come finish it." She held a needle out to Thea, the Seckin dressing pulled halfway back so she could access the wound.

Thea felt frozen suddenly, her arms glued to her sides. "I've never worked on a person before."

"It's no different than a shark."

Thea maintained that it was actually quite different. For one, Toby didn't have gills. Plus, the lone shark she'd dissected with Dr. Tarlow at Northwood Point had already been dead when they worked on it. They'd merely been checking its eating habits, confirming the presence of expected marine life in the shark's stomach. It was a dissection, not a surgery.

"What about the regenerative beds?" Thea asked.

"They won't work unless he's conscious, and that's too risky at the moment. He's sedated and won't feel a pinch. And when he comes to, he'll probably appreciate your stitching over mine. A steady hand will result in a smaller scar."

Thea hesitated.

"I wouldn't ask this of you if I didn't think you could do it," the doctor insisted.

Thea nodded and forced herself to move. She pulled on a set of surgical gloves, then accepted the needle from Dr. Tarlow.

Slowly, gingerly, Thea pulled the Seckin bandage back completely. Beneath it, Toby's calf was a mess, torn open in three different places. Had the wounds been higher, on his thigh, they'd likely have severed his femoral artery and he'd have bled out in the rover. Dr. Tarlow had already seen to two of the wounds. Thea focused her attention on the third, which was already starting to well up with fresh blood in the absence of the Seckin bandage.

She slid the surgical needle through the skin, drawing it back together. She refused to so much as glance at Toby's face. If she saw him, he'd be a person, but if she only focused on his leg . . . The skin was red with frostbite and blistered. It made her stomach queasy, and she threw her attention to her work. Once she found a rhythm, things grew easier.

Behind her, she was vaguely aware of voices, the team discussing Toby's fate, when to contact Hevetz, and what to do with Coen. But she was too focused on the needle and thread to pick up much else. Soon the wound was closed, and Dr. Tarlow was passing over a pair of scissors with a quivering hand.

Thea tied off the stitches and cut the line. Toby's dark eyes were still staring unblinkingly at the ceiling. When he woke up—*if* he woke up—Thea wondered if he'd be grateful for "the intern's" help, or if he'd just criticize her technique.

She slumped into a wheeled stool and pushed away from the table.

"He's stable?" Dylan asked, appearing behind them.

"For now," Dr. Tarlow said.

Nova and Sullivan drew nearer as well, peering at Toby over Dr. Tarlow's shoulder.

"I've seen this before!" Coen shouted from the chamber.

"We need to go, and we need to go *now*."

Thea turned, startled. Dylan must have triggered the chamber's intercom during her interrogation.

"This is how it starts," Coen continued. "The bloody nose, the hemorrhaged eyes. It doesn't matter that you sedated him. He'll wake, and when he does, we need to be gone. We get on your ship, and we leave right now."

"Abandon Toby?" Dylan said.

"It's not him anymore," Coen argued. "That's what I'm saying. He's sick. It's turned him into something else."

"How do we know you're not sick, too?" Dylan wheeled on the isolation chamber. "Maybe that's why Evans wrote that warning not to trust you."

"Do my eyes look filled with blood? I'm telling you, screw that bastard on the table. There were Black Quarry admins that kept trying to save everyone also. Once the commander got sick, they refused to abandon him, and it just got them killed, too. You can't beat this. You fight it by running."

"The commander?" Dylan froze.

"Yeah. Ansley Lowe, Black Quarry commander." Coen's face went grim. "He's dead. They're all dead."

Dylan must not have gotten very far in her interrogation if this was news to her, Thea reasoned.

"And you ran to safety while all these people died trying to save their colleagues?" Dylan was very close to the glass doors of the isolation chamber now, her mouth curled into a snarl.

"I'm telling you, running is the only option! Now let's go to your ship and—"

Dylan's hand slammed down on the intercom button, cutting Coen off. He pounded the glass, but she turned her back to him. "I'm going to hail Hevetz for instruction. This coward," she said, throwing a hand at the chamber, "stays in isolation until we're advised otherwise."

"*Celestial Envoy*'s comm lines are completely down," Sullivan said. "I tried to get them back up when you guys were at the drilling site. I figured we'd need to debrief Hevetz eventually, but no such luck. Maybe Toby would have found a work-around, but . . ." Sullivan motioned at the sedated technician.

"Let's take a rover to *Odyssey* then," Dylan said. "I'll contact Hevetz from there. From this distance, messages will take about an hour to get to the Trios, so there's no time to waste."

Thea glanced at the chamber, her eyes locking with Coen. *Get out of here now*, he mouthed, a primal fear shining in his eyes. *Don't wait*. Regardless of the warning on the bridge, he was the only one making sense. Black Quarry was dead. He'd witnessed the outbreak of a terrible infection. And now he claimed Toby was showing symptoms of the very same contagion.

"Am I the only one who thinks we should maybe listen to Coen?" Thea said. "We should leave now, hail Hevetz from off-planet."

"If I wanted an intern's advice, I'd ask for it," Dylan said.

"I just think he probably knows a thing or two about surviving. If he says Toby's—"

"*Don't trust the kid*—that's what Evans wrote. I know Coen gave you access to the Witch Hazel bunker, but that's no reason to trust him blindly."

"Gave me access?"

Dylan glanced at Coen's chamber. "He told me he helped you get through the air lock. That there was a power issue due to the storm. Is that not true?"

There was definitely a power issue. One so intense it had stopped Thea's heart, but Coen had conveniently left that part out.

Pretend like the glass always had a patch. You don't need to give anyone a reason to be suspicious.

Thea, resuscitated by "the kid" Evans warned them not to trust.

Thea's helmet, breached, exposing her to the same atmosphere that Toby was exposed to before Coen insisted the technician was infected.

Thea's eyes darted to Coen, still standing with his hands

pressed to the glass of his chamber's door. His brows quirked upward. She could almost hear him saying, *Again, you're welcome.*

"Well?" Dylan prodded.

Thea had never been a convincing liar. When she fibbed to her classmates (*No, this shirt isn't secondhand; Yes, I have a Tab at home; Of course I've been off-planet*) they always saw through her. Sometimes they seemed to spot the lie as quickly as if she'd admitted the truth outright. It was like the rotating faces in the child services office. No matter how many times Thea told them she wasn't still searching for her mother, they never believed her. And they weren't wrong.

"I . . ." She looked between Dylan and Coen, the lie feeling sloppy on her tongue. "He . . ."

"Guys?" Cleaver appeared in the entrance to the medbay, face grave. "You all need to see this. Right now."

The research facility was cleaner now. When Thea had been at the drilling base with the others, Dr. Tarlow and Sullivan had organized the freezer samples, swept the glass that had littered the floor, and tidied up the work areas. Black Quarry Tabs were now stacked in organized piles or charging on pads or in the rolling charging caddy.

"I needed a break," Cleaver began, "and came in here to get some fresh air. Took about a minute before I was bored. I started going through the Tabs Sullivan had charging. A few of them have power now, and there's a whole report on Li's injury." He held up the device. "The crew hit gold at drill site BQ7 two days before the incident."

"Corrarium?" Dylan asked.

"Corrarium-like," Dr. Tarlow said. "I found the samples while going through the freezers. It's the dark stuff in the far back, labeled *CorrX*."

"Why didn't you mention this earlier?" Dylan growled.

"I planned to," the doctor said, "but we've all been a little preoccupied since you returned."

"Yeah, well, here's where it gets really interesting," Cleaver said, bringing everyone's attention back to him. "They continued drilling at all points and had a jam at BQ1. Li was the mechanic working that shift, and he went down to investigate. He had to wade into the river and reported feeling, and I quote, 'something like air moving through the water and up toward the surface.'"

"What does that mean?" Nova prompted. "Like a hot spring?"

"Can't be," Cleaver said, referring to the Tab. "The report puts the water at roughly negative one degrees Celsius. That's not exactly hot spring temperatures, right?"

"There are hot springs and then there are thermal springs," Thea said. She'd always been fascinated by the pressure beneath her feet, that gravity pulled her down and yet heat was always trying to escape *up*, through ocean floors and fissures, volcanoes and geysers. For a year in middle school, it was all she'd read about. "A thermal spring is defined as water just six degrees Celsius warmer than the mean air temperature. So on Achlys, a thermal spring's temperature would sound pretty cold to us."

Cleaver still looked confused.

"She's saying it's possible that heat from Achlys's core is still reaching the riverbed," Dr. Tarlow explained, "and that the heated water is rising to the surface, keeping it *just barely* warm enough to stay liquid."

"Whatever," Cleaver said. "The short of it is Li lost his footing in the river, struck his head on a rock, and blacked out momentarily. He was inspected at the drilling base, and medics found a bad gash on his head. He started exhibiting signs of some type of infection not long after."

"Did his suit get breached during his fall?" Thea prompted. "Like Toby's?"

"No," Cleaver said. "But he'd been completely submerged, and the medical team recorded some hypotheses about a contagion originating in the water, something that might have been able to get through the material. It's all kinda over my head."

"Over mine too, unless I'm missing something," Sullivan

cut in. "The suits are airtight, pressurized. If air can't permeate them, how could a liquid?"

"Maybe there was a breach they didn't catch," Dylan offered. "Cleaver, you said we should *see* something."

Cleaver tapped at the tablet, then swiveled it around so the rest of them could see the video he'd pulled up.

It showed a shot of an empty medbay. Not *Celestial Envoy*'s, but a facility Thea didn't recognize, perhaps one at the drilling site. The shot of the angle was drastic, as though taken by a security camera, and metadata in the corner dated the footage a day prior to the issued distress call. A man Thea assumed to be Jon Li entered the lab, escorted by another worker. Two medics came running into view as well.

Words were spoken. There was no sound to the video, and the camera angle didn't give her a good look at the workers' faces, but their body language didn't seem terribly worried.

Li sat on the edge of a bed and removed his helmet. His hair was slick and shiny along the crown. Blood. He reached back and prodded at the injury, cringing. A medic slapped his hand away and gave an order. Li lay down. The medic dressed the wound, took vitals, used a light to check Li's eyes. Then the medics turned away to discuss something. When they faced Li again, he didn't seem pleased about whatever they had to say.

"I figure they're telling him he has to report back to

Celestial Envoy," Cleaver said. "He says he's feeling fine. They insist."

"How do you *figure?*" Dylan asked.

He swiped ahead to another video—Li bursting into *Celestial Envoy*'s medbay.

The mechanic was now clawing at his eyes. He'd shed his suit sometime between leaving the drilling base and arriving back at the ship, and the front of his coveralls was stained with blood. When the camera managed to capture a shot of his face, Thea pressed a hand to her mouth. The whites of Li's eyes were dark, and blood dripped from his nose.

Medics rushed to his aid, but Li was convulsing now—crumbling to the ground, shaking and bucking as though suffering a seizure. His frantic gestures left swipes of blood on the shiny floor.

The medics managed to sedate Li, and when his body went limp, they wrestled him onto one of the medical beds and strapped him into place. Then they glanced at each other—the tension and worry apparent in their expressions—before racing for the intercom system on the far wall. With their backs to Li's unconscious form, they began updating . . . someone.

"That's exactly what happened with Toby," Nova said beside Thea, her voice at a whisper.

"Unbelievable," Dr. Tarlow breathed.

"We need to contact Hevetz immediately," Dylan said, gaze stuck on the Tab in Cleaver's hands. "I need them to advise."

Just like I've been saying! Thea thought. *Like we've all been saying.*

"This isn't the worst of it, though," Cleaver said. "A half hour later . . ." He scrubbed through the video, skipping a bunch of unessential footage. The medics disappearing, returning, checking Li's vitals. When Cleaver stopped, letting the video resume, three new men were entering the medbay. The one in the forefront had an air of prestige about him. A high-ranking individual, for sure. Sharp suit, short hair, confident shoulders. Before Thea could make note of the markings along the sleeve of his jacket, Dylan uttered, "Dad."

Standing just behind him were two other officers. The video showed only their backs as all three men moved closer to Li's bed. They observed him, sleeping. The medical team updated Commander Lowe.

And then Li's hand twitched.

Thea froze.

The men in the video all froze, too.

Without warning, Li's eyes flew open, and as though the ratcheted straps holding him in place were nothing but a blanket, he threw them off. His hand came up, breaking free of the wrist restraint, then snapping the longer strap across his chest.

The medic screamed something that looked like *Sedate him!* But the second wrist strap was already breaking.

Commander Lowe lunged forward, tried to hold Li's shoulders to the bed. Lowe was the larger man, by far, and yet Li batted the commander's arms away with ease. Then Li clawed at Lowe's front, dug his fingers into the man's eyes. The ankle restraints broke free as Li swung his legs off the bed. Everyone in the medbay was shouting orders now. The medics scrambled for sedatives. The two other officers tackled Li to the ground but found no success keeping him there. Thea watched the driller's shoulder lurch from its socket as he struggled to free himself. Still, Li battled on, never flinching or pausing, using nothing but his blood-covered hands to attack the others.

Scratching and clawing like a feral cat, Li somehow managing to free himself from beneath the two officers. He lunged to his feet, springing at Commander Lowe once more—and a blast sent him toppling backward.

Commander Lowe had fired his stun gun. Another blast of electricity, and Li was propelled back farther, into the very isolation chamber Coen was now secured in.

Lowe slammed a hand down on the door trigger. It closed, locking Li in place. Still, he came at the glass like a demon possessed, blood-filled eyes locked on the officers and medics panting on the other side. The commander checked his watch, then looked up at the security camera.

Cleaver paused the video.

Thea stared at the frozen frame, Commander Lowe staring back, one eye completely ruined.

The thing in the medbay stretched. First its fingers, then wrists. It rolled its ankles in circles, tilted its neck to one side, the other.

Then it opened its eyes.

It was too bright in here, too hot. The thing's eyes itched and burned. Its skin ached. If only it could relieve the pain. It needed to move. It . . .

It wasn't alone. There was a boy, standing still as could be on the opposite side of a glass panel. The thing could see him with perfect clarity. Could smell him, too. It cocked its head. No, it could smell *many*. Down the hall. If it listened very carefully, it could hear the fluttering rhythm of their hearts.

The thing lurched to a sitting position. Or tried to. Its limbs were shackled, a strap buckled across its chest. It yanked at one of the arm restraints. The boy banged on his glass door. His mouth moved and noise came out, but it held no meaning.

The thing yanked at the restraints again, rattling the metal. There was a wetness on the thing's wrist now. It was mildly pleasant, temporarily dulling the burn that seemed to cover the rest of its body.

The boy banged harder. His mouth moved faster.

He made such funny noises.

The thing watched him yell louder. And then the thing smiled.

No one spoke.

Words seemed impossible.

The only sound came from down the hall, where Coen was banging on his door again, probably yelling for Dylan to let him out.

Thea couldn't pull her eyes from the Tab, couldn't believe what she'd just seen. It had all happened so quickly.

Li. On the table.

Asleep.

Until he wasn't . . .

Suddenly, Coen stopped banging.

And Thea heard a restraint snap.

She ran. They all did.

When the medical bay came into view, Toby was sitting upright on the table, clawing at his eyes as if he thought he could scoop the burst blood vessels from them. The strap that had been tightened over his chest dangled near the floor, and the wrist cuff had been snapped open.

Thea skidded to a halt with the rest of the team, but Toby

had already sensed their movement. His head jerked toward the doorway, those dark eyes locking on them. His gaze stayed rooted there, even as he reached to loosen the straps on his legs; fresh blood dripped down his cheeks and neck from where his fingers had clawed at his own skin.

Sullivan lunged to open the medbay doors.

"No way!" Dylan roared, cutting him off.

"He'll come out here if we don't go in. We might as well get to him on our own terms, before he unstraps himself completely."

The thigh strap fell aside. Toby reached for the ankle cuff.

"Let him go after Coen," Dylan spat back at Sullivan. "We'll take him out when he's distracted."

"Coen's Black Quarry!" Thea shouted. "We were sent here to help him!"

"And Toby doesn't seem very interested in him," Sullivan added.

It was true. Toby was still looking at them in the hallway, pulling his eyes away only briefly, to hit the release on one of the ankle cuffs. It sprang open, freeing his right leg.

"I am ordering you not to go in there!" Dylan roared.

"We can't just stand here and do nothing!" Sullivan shoved the captain aside and opened the door, bursting into the room. Toby managed to release the final restraint at almost the same time. The technician sprang from the table, flying at Sullivan and tackling him around the middle.

Sullivan fired his weapon, and midfall, the men were propelled apart. Sullivan slammed onto his back, wincing. Toby hit the bed he'd just been secured to but managed to keep his feet beneath him.

"Full charges!" Sullivan ordered as he fired another shot, and Nova and Cleaver rushed to help him. "Hit him with all we got."

Thea threw the intensity level as high as it could go on her stun gun, but as she moved to join them, someone grabbed her arm. Dr. Tarlow. For being so willowy, the woman was exceptionally strong. Thea struggled against her, watching helplessly as Sullivan, Cleaver, and Nova unleashed shots on Toby. It didn't seem to matter how many times they hit him, he was tireless, springing back up, coming at them over and over again—until all three of them managed to hit him at the same time. The combined jolt of electricity sent the technician stumbling backward. He hit a regenerative bed and toppled over it, regaining his footing on the other side.

"Isolation One!" Sullivan screamed. "Someone get Isolation One open."

Thea's eyes locked on the chamber, and she immediately understood Sullivan's plan. With a bit of strategic firing, the crew might be able to secure Toby inside, just as Dylan and

Nova had secured Coen in Isolation Three earlier. That was, if they managed to get the door to the chamber open first.

But with each shot Nova, Cleaver, and Sullivan fired, Toby merely slumped to a knee before staggering upright again. It didn't make sense. No one should be able to withstand such a continued assault.

It's not him anymore, Coen had said. *It's turned him into something else.*

Toby wasn't going to tire. Eventually Sullivan or the others would slip up and he'd attack. "Do something!" Thea yelled to Dylan, but the captain stood stoic in the doorway, frozen. "We have to do something," she said again, this time to Dr. Tarlow, but the woman's grip only tightened on Thea's arm. Well, if no one was going to help . . .

Thea slammed her foot down on the inside of the doctor's foot. The woman yelled with surprise, and Thea—just as surprised that she'd lashed out at a superior—committed fully, throwing an elbow into Dr. Tarlow's stomach. The instant the doctor's hold on her slipped, Thea bolted forward. She ran, focus set on the chamber across the medbay, gaze never leaving the path she intended to take because she knew that if her eyes landed on Toby, she'd lose all her nerve. She skirted around the table he'd broken free from, vaulted over a closed regenerative bed, her feet colliding with a rolling service cart. It spun away from her, spilling tools as it went.

She found her footing and raced on. The control panel was just ahead of her, the slanted yellow rectangle that would toggle the door in her sights.

Thea could sense Toby zeroing in on her, was certain his blood-soaked eyes were turning away from the others and locking onto her back. But she wouldn't look. Couldn't. She was so close, and then she was there, her hand slamming down on the button.

The door slid open, and Thea turned, bringing up her weapon.

Toby was barely a meter away, his face a shadow of what it had once been. His nose and mouth were smeared with dried blood, his eyes dark and flooded, his teeth stained and bared.

She'd never fired at anything but a target before, let alone a person.

But it wasn't him. Not anymore. And her finger seemed to be ahead of her brain, reacting instinctively.

She pulled the trigger and held it, releasing a long shock of electricity into Toby's chest. When the fail-safe kicked in, ensuring she only stunned her target instead of sending him into cardiac arrest, Sullivan threw a charge.

Then Nova and Cleaver together.

With each charge, Toby staggered back a bit farther and farther, and then he was crossing that threshold, his boots teetering over that yellow-and-black chevron line. The instant he cleared it, Thea throttled the door's control again.

The crew stopped firing, and the chamber sealed just a heartbeat before Toby collided with the glass.

Nova Singh blinked sweat from her eyes, watching as Toby pawed at the glass doors of the isolation chamber like a madman.

The intern had just saved all their asses. While Nova's combat training had been minimal, she'd still received it, which was more than could be said for Thea, who was now shaking like a leaf. The poor girl's visor was probably flooded with alerts. Even Nova's was still refreshing, her pulse slowing in the aftermath.

Sullivan tapped at the side of his helmet, shaking his head.

"You okay, Sull?" Nova called.

"Yeah, my alerts are going wild. Have been since we ran in here."

"It'll clear," Cleaver said, breathing heavy. "Mine are coming down now."

"What about you, kid?" Sullivan asked Thea. "Doing all right?"

She gave a jerky nod, then jumped as Toby threw himself at the glass. Apparently clawing and banging at the door had run its course, and he now believed he might be able to break through with enough determination.

"I need to sedate him," Dr. Tarlow said, rushing into the room.

"'Cause that worked so well the first time," Sullivan deadpanned.

"It failed because it wore off, but I can vent a sedative into the chamber, keep the environment controlled." The doctor typed commands into a keypad beside the door. Nova heard a fan spur to life on the other side of the glass. Almost immediately, the enthusiasm with which Toby attacked the door began to fade. The blood flowing from his newest wounds—the scratches on his cheeks and neck—had slowed, but he looked like something tortured and wild. He looked like Black Quarry's Jon Li.

"This is exactly what we saw in that video," Nova said, breaking the silence. She hated that her voice came out small. "It's gotta be a contagion in the water. A bacteria or parasite or something. Li caught it when he fell."

"But his suit was never breached," Sullivan pointed out.

"Could it have survived on his suit, though?" she asked. "At least until he . . ." She touched the back of her helmet, illustrating how Li had reached back to inspect the open wound, prodding with his gloved hand.

"He infected himself," Thea said.

Nova felt sick. "And then passed it to his own crew members . . ."

"By blood," the doctor concluded. "The nosebleed, the

clawing at their skin and eyes . . . Once the infected blood is on their hands, they attack, trying to spread it."

"Toby's leg . . ." the intern said, her voice cracking. "If it's passed by blood, by scratches and gouges, that would mean that back in the chasm . . . Toby was . . . Oh my god."

A bang.

Nova jolted, expecting to see Toby still attacking the glass, but he had already fallen to the floor, unconscious. The noise had come from Isolation Three, where Coen had returned to banging on the glass. *Listen to me!* he was screaming. Nova could read his lips. Thea darted for his chamber and toggled the intercom.

"Thea's right," Coen gasped out, his words now clear.

Nova felt a sense of dread deep in her stomach. She didn't want anyone to be right. Not about this.

"Toby's leg, the chasm. He wasn't exactly swimming in liquid water," Coen continued, "so that means he came in contact with the contagion via blood."

"But they're dead," Dylan said.

That's when Thea said what seemed impossible: "Not all of them."

Nova glanced at the doctor, hoping she'd reject it, say they were mistaken, but Tarlow was observing Toby's unconscious form, impressively calm given what Thea and Coen were proposing.

214

"That's ridiculous," Dylan said. "Those bodies have been exposed to atmo and freezing temps. For *weeks*."

"Well, it's just a hypothesis, and I'm no scientist"—Coen's eyes flicked to Tarlow—"but I think they were trying to return home, in a way. They were compelled to spread whatever they'd caught, and then when they couldn't spread it anymore, they were compelled to walk right back into the chasm, to the water. This contagion . . . clearly it can live in those extreme temperatures, even if we can't."

Tarlow snapped out of her trance and turned away from the chamber. "But the bodies of the infected. *They* wouldn't be able to survive."

"Unless they were hibernating," Coen said. "Unless they don't need what you and I do to survive once infected. Maybe the heat from one another was enough to keep some of them alive, in some sort of suspended animation."

The crew bristled.

"Look, before I found the Witch Hazel bunker, I watched what I could from the vents," Coen continued. "Once the disease had spread and they had no one else to attack, they got slower, clumsier, like they were shutting down. They walked themselves out to that chasm, and I'm willing to bet you a good sum of unnes that now that they know there's fresh meat on this rock, they're going to start climbing back out."

"We need to get back to *Odyssey*," Dylan said, "hail Hevetz,

215

and evacuate immediately."

Sullivan grumbled. "Funny how I've been advocating for that all along, and yet I was the coward. I was the baby who couldn't take orders, and then you go and stand there in the doorway of the medbay, hiding while the rest of us get things done."

He had a point, and everyone knew it. But Dylan would never admit fault, because that would mean she had a weakness. She would never apologize, because it would mean she was in the wrong. She'd divert attention, change the subject, or victimize herself by making someone else the villain. Nova had seen her do it before, and she'd always made excuses for the woman. But their current situation was too black-and-white, too dire, too extreme. There was no excusing what happened here.

Nova could see it now, plain as day: in Dylan Lowe's reality, she was never wrong. She *couldn't* be wrong. Not when there was upper management to impress.

Sure enough, Dylan batted a hand at Sullivan. "We don't have time for this."

"An apology takes a whopping five seconds."

"Sullivan, I am the captain, and when I say we're leaving for *Odyssey* right this second—"

"Apologize, dammit!"

Dylan's mouth fell open, her brows dipped. Nova was

shocked. Sullivan had made Dylan Lowe pause. If he got an apology, too, it would be a day for the record books.

"Sullivan," Dylan said seriously.

"Thea deserves one also," he continued, pointing at the intern. "Hell, we *all* deserve one."

"Sullivan—your nose!"

Nova searched her cousin's face, and there it was: a small black bead of blood, dangling at the edge of his nostril. He pulled his helmet off despite a chorus of "no"s that resounded through the room, then touched the blood and stared when his fingers came away wet.

Nova took a step toward him.

"Don't!" he shouted, putting his hands up and stepping away. "Nobody touch me. Nobody come near me."

"I don't understand," Nova continued. "You're in your suit. You never . . ."

Sullivan slapped up and down his torso, feeling the material for breaches, then moving on to his arms, his legs. As he worked his way back up, he paused along the side of his torso. His head jerked up, searching the room and finally locking on something on the floor.

Nova saw it, too. A surgical, handheld laser resting on the ground beside the very table Toby had been secured to earlier. He must have grabbed it as they entered the room and lashed out when he tackled Sullivan. It was the only contact he'd had with any of them and the only type of tool capable of piercing Sullivan's suit. Nova hadn't noticed it in Toby's hand, but she'd been so focused on timing her shots perfectly, ensuring that Toby was secured.

No wonder Sullivan's visor had been acting up earlier, *going wild*. A breach to the suit, the contagion moving through him . . .

"I didn't even feel it," Sullivan said, still prodding at his side. "It must be a clean slice. And shallow."

"It won't matter," Dr. Tarlow said. "Look at Toby's palm." She nodded at the isolation chamber, and Nova saw the blood on the technician's hand. "He cut himself first, or maybe in the process of cutting you. Either way, the damage is done."

Sullivan tilted his head back and tried to slow the blood that spilled from his nose. "You have to put me in with Toby," he said, stumbling toward Isolation One.

"No," Nova pleaded. "Sull, think about this. There are other chambers. You can have your own."

"There's *one* other chamber, and I'm already showing signs. But if you're not sure someone is safe, you'll need that room. I'm already gone."

Nova hated that he was being logical, could scream at how much he made sense. He was all she had left on this rock, the only bit of family for nearly sixty light-years in any direction.

"You can have Coen's chamber then," she suggested. "We'll let him out."

"We won't," Dylan interjected. "*Don't trust the kid.*"

"He's not presenting symptoms."

"But Sullivan *is*," the captain said. "Just like Toby had."

Sullivan backed toward the chamber, and Nova reached for him anyway.

"Stop it," he said. "Dammit, Nova, if you care about me at all, you will not risk getting yourself sick. You hear me? You do everything in your power to get off this rock and never look back."

She nodded, tasting salt. She was crying.

Sullivan's head twitched against his will. Blood spattered the floor. "Tarlow," he gasped out. "Please?"

Everyone hesitated.

"You heard the man," Coen snapped from his chamber. Nova could throttle him for his lack of sympathy, for his callous tone.

"Do it!" Dylan ordered.

The doctor purged Isolation One and opened the door. Toby didn't budge as Sullivan walked inside.

Nova jogged after him.

He turned to face her, the blood flowing freely from his nose. "Tell Mikko and the boys I love them," he said.

The door slid closed. Another tremor rocked his body.

Sullivan dropped to his knees, coughing, cradling his face in his hands. His body shook. The fan kicked on, the sedative again filling the chamber, and Sullivan slumped to his side.

Tears streaming down her face, Nova Singh watched as the tremors slowed and her cousin's eyes fell lazily shut.

Pulling her gaze from the laser Toby had used to attack Sullivan, Thea inspected her own suit. Everything was intact.

Of course it was. She knew all too well the alerts she'd have experienced with a suit breach. Had Sullivan seen the same thing? *My alerts are going wild.* She wondered briefly if he'd tried to hide it from them. The answer didn't matter. Not anymore.

"We need to get off this planet," Dylan announced.

"And leave them?" Dr. Tarlow asked, nodding at the two unconscious men.

"They're screwed. The Black Quarry vids showed it, and the kid's confirmed the same thing. We need to evac immediately."

"Dylan's right," Thea said, shocked she was even having to argue this point. Of all people, Dr. Tarlow should know how dangerous this situation was, how they needed to start quarantine procedures and stick to them, how this could get away from them in seconds and infect the entire crew if they weren't careful.

"The kid said it spread before they could do anything," Dr. Tarlow responded. "For all we know it's a simple infection. We can keep Toby and Sullivan in quarantine, but at least let me take some blood samples and run a few tests, see if anything looks familiar."

Nova turned away from the isolation chamber, hope shining in her eyes. "You think you can cure them?"

"I can't promise anything. But I'd like to try. I have a hypothesis, and that's a start."

"I'll stay and help," Nova offered.

"You will not," Dylan said. "You're our only pilot, and I'll be damned if I let you within a meter of anyone experiencing symptoms."

"Screw you, Dylan."

The captain stared.

"This is your fault!" Nova went on. "You had us come barging in, go digging in the dark without updating Hevetz, and now look at Sullivan! At Toby! I wanted to trust you, tried to believe you'd pull through but—"

"If I'm recalling correctly, *you* all barged ahead!" Dylan spat. "I gave orders for us to stay out of the medbay!"

"We only ended up in this situation because you insisted on going to the drilling base to begin with. You've got your head so far up the Company's ass that you can't see warning signs that have been flashing since we left Northwood."

Dylan exhaled evenly. "What is this, Nova? Sullivan gets sick and you jump on his soapbox; is that how this works?"

"He's been right all along. We all have! We never should have left *Odyssey*."

"And right now, instead of saying 'I told you so,' we need to get back to it." The captain angled to Dr. Tarlow. "And no, you can't stay and run tests. You heard what the kid said. Those dead bodies in the chasm might not be all that dead, and I don't wanna deal with Achlys zombies."

"Zombies are fictitious," the doctor said curtly.

"What about Coen?" Thea asked.

"He stays like the other two."

"The whole reason we came here was for survivors! He's a survivor."

"A potentially infected one."

"Again," Coen called from his chamber, "do I look like I have bloody eyes and a massive nosebleed?"

"We can't confirm what he's been up to the past two months," Dylan continued, "so if we're enacting quarantine procedures, we can't in good faith bring him on *Odyssey*."

"We have an isolation chamber on *Odyssey*," Thea went on. "If you're gonna leave Toby and Sullivan behind, you could at least take the person we were sent here to help."

"I've had about enough of interns and temps arguing with my orders." Dylan made a circular motion with her stun gun, then pointed it at the hall. "Let's go."

"I'm staying," Dr. Tarlow announced. "I refuse to abandon these men, not if there's something that can be done for them."

"Then you're forcing *me* to abandon *you*," Dylan said.

"Leave me a radio. That storm was rough. If you find *Odyssey* in flying condition, I'll come join you immediately; leave these men to rot, no questions asked. But if you need repairs . . . Well, I'll see to our men while you see to our ship."

Dylan considered this a moment, then tossed a radio at Dr. Tarlow, who barely managed to catch it. It shook in her grasp, and she set it on a nearby counter, extending her trembling fingers.

"I'm not leaving you a security detail," the captain said. "Not when you're taking a risk I advised against and we might only get one shot to get out of here."

"Fair enough," the doctor said. Then she turned to Thea. "I'll need your help if I want to make good time."

Thea wanted to scream. How could the doctor ask this of her? For once, Dylan Lowe was making sense. The crew needed to get off Achlys. They never should have landed.

Thea glanced at the men. It could have been her in that chamber. Cleaver hadn't fit in the harness at the drilling site, and he'd looked to her, but Toby had volunteered. Toby, who was an ass, always heckling her, always condescending

223

toward everyone, but now unconscious on the other side of that glass. And Sullivan, too. She'd figured him to be a coward earlier, convinced herself that Sullivan thought his life and his family were more important than the rest of the crew's, and yet he'd been the first to jump to action.

If there was a way to stabilize these two men, to undo everything that had happened in the last few hours . . . Well, Thea owed it to them to at least try. And she owed Coen also. She would most certainly be dead if it hadn't been for his help at the Witch Hazel bunker.

"Thea, please," Dr. Tarlow insisted.

The woman was smart enough to know a lost cause, Thea reasoned. If there was hope of a cure, they could potentially *all* get off this planet, Coen included. There'd be no reason to leave anyone behind. She glanced at his chamber. He was leaning in to the glass door, shoulders slumped in defeat. When he saw her watching he simply raised his brows as if to say, *Your call.*

Had he known Dylan would rightly be so uptight about security, even after he confirmed that the contagion originated in water and was passed by blood? Was that why he'd covered for Thea, said he'd helped her enter the Witch Hazel bunker, not revived her?

Thea turned away, not quite caring what his answer was. She owed him, and it would be so very easy to release Coen from his chamber once Dylan was out of sight.

"I'll stay," she announced.

The reactions were varied. Dylan grumbled about interns being stupid. Coen looked surprised, Nova grateful. Cleaver, who was already sweeping the hall, shouted back, "Great, the intern wants to be a hero. Good for her. Now let's get back to *Odyssey* while we still can."

"I'll leave you one of the rovers," Dylan said, and led Nova and Cleaver out without another word.

The medbay doors sealed with a hydraulic click.

Thea thought the vacant hallway seemed more ominous now that the others were gone. Lights pulsed and flickered before plunging into darkness for a solid three seconds, then winking on again. Someone could run up the hall in that stretch of poor visibility and reach the medbay without Thea or Dr. Tarlow even seeing them coming.

The tattooed man from the chasm flashed before Thea's eyes. His purple-blue skin. His blood-soaked coveralls.

It sounded impossible—infected, hibernating victims capable of reanimating under the right conditions. Either Coen's hypothesis was wrong or the impossible was possible on Achlys.

Dr. Tarlow called for Thea, and she stepped away from the door.

"What are you doing?" Coen asked as she passed the isolation chamber. His intercom was still on, and his words resounded clearly on her side of the glass.

"Saving your ass," she said, throwing his own words back at him. "You're welcome."

"You can't save anyone if you're dead. You should have gone back to your ship."

"I don't think you're following. Dylan isn't going to let anyone on *Odyssey* if she suspects they might be sick. So if you want to get off this planet, Dr. Tarlow and I need to find a cure. Even then, Dylan will have her suspicions, and you'll end up in an isolation chamber on *Odyssey* for the whole flight home."

"I don't trust her," Coen said, dropping his voice to a whisper.

"Yeah, it's pretty hard to trust a captain who's rude, underqualified, and prone to recklessness. I told you she'd give you trouble."

"Not Dylan Lowe," Coen clarified. "Your doctor."

"What?" Thea looked over her shoulder. Dr. Tarlow was gathering equipment while one of the medical computers booted up. "Why not?"

"I've got my reasons."

"Back at the bunker, you wanted to see her."

"So I could talk to her, not sit in isolation."

"Dr. Tarlow?" Thea called. "Can I let Coen out? He wants to talk to you, and the testing will be faster with a second set of hands anyway."

Without so much as looking their way, the woman shook her head.

"He's been on this rock two months," Thea continued, "and doesn't have any of the signs the others exhibited. I don't think he's a risk to us."

Dr. Tarlow paused, head cocked in thought. Then she swiveled in her chair to face them. "You're an official Hevetz employee, are you not?" she asked Coen.

He nodded.

She considered this a moment before pivoting toward Thea. "Then we can't risk it."

"But we can risk *me*?" she erupted. "I'm expendable?"

"Of course not, Thea. But you and I . . . we have a rapport. We've worked out a system. I trust you in a situation like this. I don't trust *him*."

"Funny, I don't trust you either," said Coen, but there was no anger to his expression, no edge to his voice. It was said plainly, and Thea thought he almost looked . . . scared.

Dr. Tarlow stood, smoothing the front of her suit, as if it were even possible for the material to hold a wrinkle. "This conversation is a waste of precious time. Come on, Thea." She picked up a medical case and walked toward Isolation One.

"Ask her about her parents," Coen said as Thea moved to join her.

Thea frowned. "They died during Witch Hazel. In a storm. Everyone knows that."

"Ask her for the details."

Thea stared at him a moment. Pitch Evans said not to trust Coen. Coen said not to trust the doctor. Which was it then? Trust no one?

"Thea?" Dr. Tarlow called.

She left Coen standing there, palms pressed helplessly to the chamber's glass door.

"I fucked it all up," Dylan muttered.

Nova stared, certain she'd heard her boss wrong.

They'd made it to the hangar without incident and were now in Rover1, driving back into the Achlys night. Cleaver was in the back seat, head reclined and eyes closed. The drive to *Odyssey* wasn't longer than fifteen minutes, but he was clearly trying for a catnap. Nova wished she could join him. Anything to not think about what had just happened in that medbay, the fate that awaited Sullivan.

"You were right," Dylan said. "This is my fault, all of it— Toby and Sullivan and . . ." The captain let out a long exhale. "I was set on making sure I could impress my dad, and by extension, Hevetz. Except he's dead. We all saw that footage.

He's gone and so is Black Quarry, and now some of my crew is damned, too. I shouldn't have let Tarlow and the intern stay behind. If something happens to them, that's on me also."

Nova peered at Dylan, confused. The captain refused to admit when she was wrong. She hated looking weak. This confession was the most vulnerable thing Nova had ever heard her say.

"God, I'm so sorry about Sullivan." Dylan glanced Nova's way, a heavy line creased in the captain's brow. Was this an honest apology or simply what Dylan thought she was expected to say? Nova didn't know anymore.

"Fuck," Dylan said. She smacked the steering wheel once. Twice. Swore again.

Because Nova didn't know what else to do, she said, "It's okay, Dyl."

"How is it okay?"

It wasn't, not really. Back at Northwood Point, Nova had begged Dylan to add Sullivan to the crew. His predicament was partially her fault, but it weighed most heavily on Dylan. If the captain had been honest about where they were headed, about what might be at stake, Nova never would have dragged her cousin into this mess. And if Dylan had seen that SOS . . . Hell, even if she *hadn't*, Dylan was still responsible for pushing the team on and putting them at risk.

Nova blamed Dylan Lowe. She wanted to scream this at

her, make the woman feel the guilt, have the regret bur-
row deep into her bones. But when Nova was honest with
herself—when she looked past her anger and to the next few
hours ahead—getting off Achlys only seemed feasible if she
put that bitterness behind her. Maybe Tarlow would figure
something out back at the medbay and Nova's animosity
toward Dylan wasn't even necessary.

She had to stay levelheaded. Optimistic. Hopeful.

They had to work together.

"I don't know," Nova said to Dylan finally. "But we'll get
through it."

"There's no good outcome."

"There's no perfect outcome," Nova countered.

"It's fucked. The whole mission. It's impossible."

"Impossible is just an excuse not to try," Nova said. "You
break it down into little steps, and then it becomes a bunch
of things you can tackle. *Possible* things. So let's get to *Odyssey*
and then call Hevetz and then go from there. One possibility
at a time."

"Where the fuck did you hear that?" Dylan said. "It's so
practical I want to puke."

"My father."

"What is he—a life coach, a shrink?"

"He's dead."

"Oh," she said. "Sorry." Then a moment later: "How?"

"Trying to do the impossible."

"You mean the possible," Dylan corrected.

"Something like that." Nova glanced out her window, the rugged expanse of Achlys racing by.

The truth was that she'd never forgiven her father for picking the Union over his family, for flying wherever someone ordered him to. He'd been blown into stardust during the Casey uprising when Nova was fifteen. Her mother blamed the colonist who shot him. Nova blamed the Union for putting him in danger to begin with. He'd received the Hero's Medal after his death, the Union's highest honor for their soldiers. By moving into the line of fire, he'd saved the rest of his unit, but a medal couldn't replace her father, and every time she saw it sitting on their mantel, her anger festered and grew.

As soon as she turned sixteen and became eligible for the military, she dropped out of school to follow in his footsteps. Nova wanted unity, peace. She wanted to go back in time and tell those bastards on Casey to stop fighting what was good for them. She wanted the Trios to start seeing straight before they ended up exactly like Casey, a war erupting beyond their atmosphere, their system's future suddenly uncertain, their skies bloody. And that blood wouldn't fade. It would be a constant. The Trios was too valuable, its resources too precious, and the Union would never let them go. The skirmish wouldn't end in independence after a mere four months of fighting like it had for Casey's citizens.

Above all else, Nova just wanted to be with her father again. He was out there, in space, pieces of him sprinkled across the cosmos. When she was flying, she was home. Maybe she had a bit of a death wish, but if she ended up scattered across the void like him, would that really be such a bad thing?

Of course, the Union had gone and robbed her of even that possibility, blacklisting her from combat when her peripheral vision faltered. These days, she hated them almost as much as she hated the Radicals.

"All right," Dylan said. "One possibility at a time. Until the impossible's accomplished." She forced a smile. It wasn't large, and it was aimed at the windshield, not Nova, but it counted. And it put the day's tally at two and a half, which was really saying something given their circumstances.

"Let's start with blood work," Dr. Tarlow said, handing Thea a rack of vials and two syringes, and grabbing an electric shock rod that had been lying forgotten beneath one of the regenerative beds. "I'm not purging the chamber. When we open the door, the rest of the facility will be exposed to the sedative."

The plan was simple: enter the chamber, take several blood samples, and get out. Still, elevated pulse readings flashed in the corner of Thea's visor, especially since the doctor was bringing a shock rod into the chamber for good measure.

Dr. Tarlow opened the door.

They waited a moment.

The men remained motionless, still unconscious, still exposed to the sedative. Thea had a suit and helmet between herself and them, a filtration system that would keep her air clean and safe, and yet her knees still seemed to tremble as she walked into the chamber.

"We'll start with Toby," the doctor said. Thea readied a syringe while Dr. Tarlow straightened Toby's arm, exposing a vein. She cleaned the skin there, cotton swab quivering in her grasp.

Thea positioned herself over Toby's arm. The vein pulsed lethargically beneath his skin, reminding her that while his body was unmoving, he was still very much alive. Those blood-filled eyes could flash open and find her if the sedative failed to do its job.

Thea didn't need a pep talk from Dr. Tarlow this time, only her directions.

"Bevel side up."

Thea adjusted the needle.

"Keep it at thirty degrees as you enter."

She did as she was told.

"Hold steady. First tube."

The doctor passed it to Thea, and she pressed it into place, watching as Toby's blood filled the vial.

"Pull."

She removed the tube and was handed a new one. Thea drew more blood as Dr. Tarlow attempted to put the first tube in a rack. Her unsteady fingers found success on the third try. They continued the process in silence, Thea thinking about the doctor's failing hands. The woman was a great asset to Hevetz, this much Thea knew. The microbe Dr. Tarlow specialized in was found only in the Trios's oceans, and so far, those oceans were the only places to produce corrarium. There were theories that the two were somehow linked, that without the microbe there'd be no corrarium and without corrarium, there'd be no microbe. And with a microbe that seemed to hinge upon the entire balance of an ecosystem—well, Thea could understand why Hevetz insisted that Dr. Tarlow be involved in so many predrilling evaluations. Soon, though, the doctor's hands would fail her. An intern wouldn't be enough. Tarlow would need a full-time assistant to complete her work in a timely manner, maybe even a replacement.

When she accepted the next vial from the doctor, Thea caught sight of Coen across the lab. His eyes were strained slightly, his chin bobbing, as if to say, *Go on. Ask her.*

"What would your parents think of all this?" she said

before she could lose her nerve.

"I have no idea. They're dead."

"I know. I wasn't trying to be insensitive. I just thought that since they'd been here before, too . . . This reaction, a waterborne contagion . . ."

"I'd rather not talk about them."

"Does your family know you're back here again? I didn't get to update anyone before we left, but I'm guessing Hevetz has by now."

"I don't have any family," Dr. Tarlow said plainly. "My first love has always been my work, and it felt irresponsible to get married or start a family when I'd be away so often."

"Isn't that lonely?"

"I have my work. The lonely person would be my partner."

"So you married your work, and that's it?"

Thea had meant it as a gross exaggeration of the situation at hand, so she was surprised when the doctor nodded.

"I knew what I wanted out of life. I believed in science, in solutions and answers, and I went after them wholeheartedly. I saw no point in romance, and I regret nothing."

Thea could understand some of the sentiment—she'd sacrificed plenty, after all—but a career that forced you into isolation sounded more like a curse than a blessing. Thea loved science, but it had always been a thing to fill the void left by her mother's disappearance. It was a path that might lead her to prestige and tempt her mother out of hiding; a passion that was a means to an end.

But for the doctor, science was everything. Literally.

"That's the last tube," the woman said. "Let's move on to Sullivan."

The thing could feel them.

Their hooks in its skin, their tools eating its blood.

The world had gone dark and muddled. Each limb had become anchored and chained. A blanket of weights seemed to cover its chest. Even the thing's eyelids proved too heavy to move.

The feeding devices suddenly retreated. The women moved away.

The thing couldn't see this, but it felt it somehow, sensed it in the deepest recesses of its sleeping mind.

Free of the hooks, the thing felt lighter, looser. If it could just open its eyes, brush aside the thin, curtained veil that was intent on smothering out the world.

Light danced in the distance.

They said no more as they drew samples from Sullivan, using his jugular vein—the only easily accessible one given that he still wore his environmental suit. In the silence, Thea and Dr. Tarlow finally found a rhythm, smoothly exchanging tubes. When the final one was filled with blood, Thea handed it over with a sigh of relief.

A glance at her watch told her she'd been in the isolation chamber barely ten minutes, but it felt like hours. She couldn't wait to be back in the medbay, a glass door again separating her from the men.

She wiped down the needle, coiled up the tubing.

That was when Toby's foot moved.

Thea went still, certain she'd imagined it. But there it was again—the smallest twitch.

"Doctor," she whispered.

The woman looked up from the samples she was threading into the carrying case, her body going rigid as she saw what Thea had: Toby's boot, jerking again. His fingers flinching.

Something brushed Thea's knee. Sullivan's hand. She looked to his face just in time to see his eyes fly open. They were filling with blood—hemorrhaging before her—and his hand shot up, seizing Thea at the neck. Even with the added protection of her suit, her visor flashed with warnings. She dropped the needle and clawed at his fingers, positioned just below where her helmet sealed with the suit. She choked on her cries for help, and Sullivan stood as though Thea weighed nothing. She kicked, striking his torso, his groin. The mechanic didn't even flinch. With his free hand, Sullivan reached for her helmet, searching for the release.

Thea could hear a struggle behind her—Dr. Tarlow wrestling with Toby—and as her feet swam aimlessly, she realized with sickening dread that she was on her own. No one was coming to her aid.

Shadows danced in Thea's peripherals. Her lungs screamed in agony.

A childhood memory struck: Thea and Mel at the bottom of a pool, seeing who could hold their breath longest. She'd pushed herself, until an animalistic instinct took over and she'd bailed, shoving off the bottom. The last meter to the surface had lasted an eternity, and for a terrifying second, Thea feared she wouldn't make it. Then she was bursting into the artificial light of the pool facility, her lungs singing in relief, gasping down the air.

It was a strange thought to have now, as her pulse slowed in her visor and darkness flicked at the corners of her vision. But the feeling was the same. Thea could imagine the taste of air, the relief it would give her if she could just get to the surface, but the surface was too far away. She kicked, going nowhere.

Thea caught movement to her right. Mel, the water rippling around him. No, it was Dr. Tarlow, racing nearer, something flashing in her hand.

Sullivan released Thea without warning.

She hit the floor like a lead weight, gasping and coughing, gulping down the air. The lightheadedness subsided, and she scrambled away from Sullivan, feeling at her suit, the helmet. No breach errors appeared in her visor.

It was only then that she was able to make sense of what had happened. Toby was staggering to his feet nearby, Sullivan twitching on the floor. Dr. Tarlow held the shock rod, the end still jumping with energy as she brandished it like a sword. When Sullivan rolled over, Dr. Tarlow hit him again.

But Toby was upright now, racing in . . .

"Look out!" Thea yelled, but not quickly enough.

Toby barreled into the doctor, tackling her to the ground. The shock rod went skidding across the floor. Thea scrambled for the weapon, her fingers grazing the shaft, deflecting it farther away. She heard the click of a helmet being released behind her, then the screaming.

By the time Thea's hand closed over the shock rod, Dr. Tarlow was pressed against the wall, pinned there by the men. Her helmet rocked near their feet. Thea threw the live end of the weapon into Sullivan's back, then Toby's.

They dropped to their knees, momentarily stunned.

"Go!" Dr. Tarlow yelled. "Leave me." The woman's face was red with scratches, thin lines of blood welling up on her cheeks and neck. "Close the door behind you."

"But—"

"Go!" she shouted. "Contain it."

A hand closed over Thea's ankle. She threw the shock rod

down into the meaty flesh of an arm, not bothering to identify which man had grabbed her. She sprinted for the door, over the black-and-yellow threshold line, slammed her hand into the door switch. The glass slid shut, locking all three adults inside.

Sullivan threw the doctor into the wall with brutal force. Her head hit with a sickening crack, and she slumped to the floor, still. The men turned, their dark eyes locked on Thea.

She stepped away from the glass as they plowed into it, trying to reach her.

None of this should be possible. The chamber had been gassed, the sedative . . . had grown thin. Thea took another step away, feeling sick. With the door open, the gas had leaked into the rest of the facility. She'd only been in the chamber with the doctor for a few minutes, though, and the amount being pumped in—even with the door open—should have been enough to keep the men sedated.

But it wasn't.

Because these men weren't just men anymore. They were . . . something else.

Sullivan and Toby looked at Thea, the door, each other, the door again. Then, as though they'd shared a silent thought, they reached for the seam in unison, fingernails prying at the glass. The door groaned under their efforts.

"Hey!"

Thea turned and found Coen pounding on his chamber's glass, practically red in the face. "Open my door," he yelled, motioning at the panel for Isolation Three. "We gotta get out of here. Right now."

Whatever reasons Pitch Evans had for distrusting him didn't seem to matter anymore.

Thea triggered the door for Isolation Three, and they darted for the exit. Toby and Sullivan were still wrestling with their isolation door, and though Thea didn't think they'd be able to overpower the mechanism before passing out again, she didn't intend to wait and find out.

As Thea reached to unlock the medbay doors, the hallway lights flickered on, revealing a face. Hemorrhaged eyes. Purple skin blistered with cold.

A scream tore from Thea's throat.

The Black Quarry driller stared at them as he bumped into the glass barrier. Then his hands came up and he began to feel along the glass surface that divided them, searching for a way in.

"He can't get in here, right?" Thea asked Coen.

"No, but together they might."

"Together . . . ?" Thea followed Coen's gaze down the hall, where dark silhouettes moved in the flickering light. Silhouettes that were very much human shaped. She watched in horror as two more Black Quarry crew members joined the first. One wore the remnants of a medic's uniform, now stained with dirt and blood. The second was Commander Ansley Lowe. He stared at them with one blood-filled eye. Where Li had attacked him, an empty socket stared back. Behind the commander, more crew members shuffled up the hall. They lacked any sort of dexterity or grace, limbs stiff with cold. Commander Lowe bent to inspect where the teeth of the two doors joined to create a seam. His head jerked up, and as though he'd given a verbal order to the others, they began to pry at the doors. Just like Toby and Sullivan in Isolation One.

Thea thought of Pitch Evans's final stand, the breached entrance to the bridge. These things were going to force their way into the medbay.

"How long will it take them?" she asked Coen. His ray-rifle was missing, probably confiscated by Dylan, and all she had was the shock rod and her holstered stun gun. It wouldn't be enough.

"If they're smart enough to switch the doors to manual, a matter of minutes. Otherwise, they're fighting the hydraulics, and who knows? But it won't matter if they decide to use the vents."

"The vents!" Thea spun, searching the room. "That's what you used, right?"

"Yeah, but they started using them eventually, too. That's

why I moved to the bunker."

But Thea was barely listening. She'd located a vent in the corner of the medbay, right above a wash station. Setting down the shock rod, she grabbed a bone saw that had been discarded in the sink, then scrambled onto the counter. Using the edge of the blade like a screwdriver, Thea went to work loosening the first of several screws holding the vent's cover in place.

"Almost there," she said.

"Wait, do you hear that?" Coen had gone very still, his head tilted up at the ceiling. Thea couldn't hear anything but the scrape of nails against the medbay's door, and the grunting of Toby and Sullivan to her right, still trying to open their chamber. She turned around and continued her work on the vent cover.

"Thea, wait!" Coen shouted.

That's when she heard it, too—the scuffle of something in the ventilation system. Holding her breath, moving ever so slowly, Thea peered through the metal cover. A set of black eyes stared back. The thing lunged, and the cover snapped in half, the side Thea hadn't seen to still held in place by the screws. Thea tumbled off the counter, landing awkwardly on her left arm. Heat laced through her wrist.

A young woman's head emerged from the vent shaft, snarling and snapping like a feral dog. She hissed as her shoulder hit the still-secured section of vent cover, which blocked her from coming into the room. She lunged against it and the cover rattled. She lunged again, and again, blood dripping into the sink.

Thea scrambled away on all fours, bumping into Coen. He grabbed her beneath her arms, pulled her to her feet.

The woman kept throwing herself into the vent cover. She would sever her shoulder just to get through the small opening, and that was if the cover didn't give out beforehand.

Thea glanced desperately around the room. Sullivan and Toby were waning in enthusiasm, the sedative again thick on their side of the glass. They'd pass out soon, and Thea and Coen would be temporarily safe. But the vent cover would give eventually. Or the main doors of the medbay would. They were doomed, about to become worse than dead.

Dead!

Thea whirled, staring beyond Coen and back into his isolation chamber, to the far wall, which doubled as a door. *Of course!* The rooms were in place for quarantine procedures, but the ship's manufacturers had prepared for worst-case scenarios. Situations that might include a need to hold dead bodies, clearing a chamber's bay for new patients while in transit.

244

"The exterior door," she said, racing for it.

"What?" Coen said.

"We can climb down the hull."

She tapped at the controls. A warning flashed, reminding her that the interior door was also open. She pressed on, ignoring it. There was no vacuum to worry about, and she and Coen were both in their suits.

Behind her, she heard the vent cover break free, clattering to the floor. The woman slithered into the room, her shoulder a lump of butchered meat.

The exterior air lock hissed as it slid open. "Come on!" Thea shouted. As Coen darted into the chamber, she drew her stun gun and fired a shot at the horde of infected who were slowly crawling toward them, the woman in the lead. Then Thea backed into the chamber as well, reaching blindly around the doorway, feeling.

"What are you waiting for?" Coen shouted. "Let's go!"

There it was, that familiar rhombus button. Thea pressed it, withdrawing her arm just as the interior door slid shut. The woman collided with it barely a second later, the rest of the bodies thudding into it as well.

Thea looked beyond them, across the room. Sullivan and Toby were passed out in Isolation One, and Dr. Tarlow still lay slumped on her side, forehead bloody from when her head had struck the wall. The scratches on her neck and cheeks seemed too tiny to be damning, but Thea knew better.

"Thea," Coen urged. "Before they figure out how to open it."

She turned, finding him by the soft light of her helmet. He stood at the edge of the chamber, one hand on the frame of the open door, the other reaching for her. She edged nearer, heart plummeting when she saw what waited.

They were twenty-something floors up, the severely sloped edges of *Celestial Envoy*'s hull disappearing into the black night.

Lisbeth Tarlow felt her grasp on reality slipping.

The thump of her pulse was loud in her ears, and it was slowing. The blood on her forehead was sticky and warm. The scratches on her neck seemed to tingle and itch. Neither hurt much, but her entire body felt heavy, leaden. She'd never felt so slow, or so lost in her own skin.

Lisbeth drew an uneven breath. The pain continued to lessen.

The wound's not deep. You'll be fine.

"Thea!" she heard Coen shout. "Before they figure out how to open it."

Lisbeth couldn't keep her eyes open anymore, but she heard them leaving.

The pain was nonexistent.

Her final thought was not of home or safety or escaping this dark planet. It was the bittersweet sting of knowing her hypothesis was right and that she didn't have more time.

He leapt, landing on a narrow service walkway that roped around the ship.

It was hopelessly dark. A sunspot must have formed on F_1, blocking the bulk of their light. That, or the storm had simply kicked up a horrendous amount of dust.

Still, he could see well enough. This was not the first bout of blackness he'd been forced to navigate on Achlys, and the lights on his helmet helped tremendously. With one mounted near each temple, a hazy, murky glow radiated around his head like a halo.

He squinted. To his right, the hull of the ship. To his left, nothing. Celestial Envoy dropped off like a cliff, the jagged earth waiting below. But straight ahead . . . if they followed the walkway toward the nose, the hull would extend gradually, allowing them to reach a height they could safely jump from.

Alone, he wouldn't waste the time. He'd take his chances scaling the dangerously steep hull right here outside the medbay. The metal was stamped and sealed. There were sure to be hand- and footholds. But he couldn't risk Thea taking a deadly plunge. Arriving at Odyssey without the doctor was one thing, but arriving without both women would only make the crew more suspicious of him. And the captain already distrusted him enough.

Thea hesitated on the lip of the air lock.

There was no time for hesitation.

The darkness was coming. As they delayed, it strengthened at the isolation chamber's interior door—the bodies too excited to see the simple "open" switch, too long infected to use logic over brute force. That had been one of the first things he'd noticed about them when observing: they were smart immediately following infection. Cunning, even. That intelligence waned with time, until they became mindless, ambling corpses. Still, they'd find a way through. That was the second thing he'd learned: the things never quit.

"I'm right here," he called out to Thea. "Below you. There's a landing."

She lowered herself over the edge, dangling a moment before dropping to the walkway. He put a hand out to steady her, and she gripped his forearm, fingers like thorns.

"I can barely see," she said.

The isolation chamber door groaned. He would have to be her eyes.

"Keep your right hand on the hull"—he took her hand in his, extending them out until their fingertips grazed Celestial Envoy—"and follow me. Don't think, just run. Understand?"

She nodded.

He took off like a bullet, remembering to slow after a few paces. He'd been running like this for months and had grown used to the everlasting darkness, to seeing only so far ahead. He now trusted his balance in a way he didn't know possible before Black Quarry. But to Thea, it was all new. The weak glow of his helmet light was likely all she could see in the world. He couldn't draw it out of her range.

It pained him to go so slowly, but he did.

When the walkway ended, he stepped onto the long nose of the ship. Thea followed, clumsy and sluggish.

The infected were probably through the isolation chamber now. He swore he could hear the frenzy of their half-alive hearts beating in his ears, although maybe that was just the silence of Achlys. The planet was so quiet that the quiet became loud. Earsplitting, thunderous. A roar that echoed across the endless expanse of the planet and the stardust beyond.

The hull sloped aggressively. Thea slid up against his back, and he held his arms out, making sure she stayed behind him. His boot tips flirted with the edge of the ship.

The frozen earth waited about two stories below, pocked with craters and crannies. He could just barely see it. But here . . . he moved a few steps to the right. If they jumped here, they'd find a level patch of ground.

He readied to leap.

Thea's hand closed on his wrist.

"It's safe here," he assured her. "Bend when you land; don't lock your knees."

Her expression was doubtful.

The darkness was coming, and it would devour them—devour her. They could outrun it if they made it to the rover. But only then. He could have said all this. He considered it briefly, motivation by fear. He considered also reassuring her that the ground below wasn't going to swallow her whole or sink its jagged jaws into her limbs. But why would she believe what she couldn't see?

"Just trust me, okay?" he said, knowing she shouldn't. About this jump, yes, but not wholly. Not about so many other things that mattered.

Still, she surprised him. She nodded.

VII

THE ORIGIN

Rover2 / *Odyssey*

Achlys, Fringe-1 System

THEA'S KNEES FLARED WITH PAIN, and she buckled forward, barely getting her hands out in time to prevent her helmet from smacking the ground. The land beneath her palms was hard, but mostly level. A narrow trench yawned just meters to her right. To her left was a crater.

Beside her, Coen landed like a cat—graceful, nimble, like he'd jumped from nothing more than a sidewalk curb. He grabbed hold of her wrist, helped her to her feet. Then they were running again, sprinting around the massive nose of the ship, dodging shallow craters and rocky teeth. Thea followed the soft glow of his helmet, not bothering to worry about anything else. Not the terrain underfoot or where her boots landed. Not what waited in her peripheral vision. Coen was somewhat able to see, his two months of isolation on this night-soaked planet turning his vision sharper and keener than hers. In that moment, she trusted him fully.

They flew for the gangplank, where *Odyssey*'s Rover2 still waited. They scrambled inside, and then Coen had them flying again.

Thea swiveled in the passenger seat, looking out the hatchback window.

The woman who'd climbed from the medbay vent was mid-jump, leaping from the ship. Her shoulder clipped a rock spire before she was swallowed by the trench. Then the ship slipped from the glow of the rover's taillights, and Thea could see nothing at all.

"I can't fix it," Nova said, staring at the mess of wires beneath *Odyssey*'s flight dash.

She'd feared as much the moment she stepped onto the bridge and saw that the comm gear's compartment door was open. A closer look confirmed it. Half the wires had been cut clean through, their ends now dangling like colorful roots.

"What do you mean you can't fix it?" Dylan asked.

"Look at them." Nova grabbed a fistful of the severed wires and shook them at the captain. "Someone forced their way into the box and murdered the things."

"Can we splice them back together?"

"There are more than a dozen colors here, some repeating. I'd have to pull up a manual, and even then, I don't know if it's possible with this much damage." Nova bent lower and peered into the back of the compartment, searching for the compact black box that stored all the comm records and intercom exchanges. "Recorder's missing, too," she said. "Someone took it."

"What?" Dylan roared. "We've all been together this whole time."

"Tarlow maybe?" Nova offered. "She could have come here when we were at the drilling site."

Dylan was pacing now.

"We could do what Thea suggested," Nova said.

The captain glanced up. "Bail?"

"I could try to fix the comm gear while we fly. If I can patch things up, we contact Hevetz then, from off-planet. Otherwise, we just keep flying."

"All right, I'll go tell Cleaver." They'd left him standing watch down on the gangplank with the radio. "You get us ready to fly while I speak with Tarlow. The sooner she and the intern get their asses down here, the sooner we can leave."

Nova shifted off her knees and onto her heels. "What about Sullivan?" she asked as she used the dash to pull herself upright.

"I guess I'll see what Tarlow says. Just get us ready, 'kay?"

Nova nodded, trying to stay optimistic. But the reality of the situation dug in with its claws. There was no way Tarlow had had enough time to assess Sullivan's situation and reverse it. There was no breaking this down into small possibilities. The facts were against her. She'd run out of time.

Nova wondered for a moment if her father's motto was a giant scam. Some outcomes were unavoidable, inescapable, *impossible*.

She booted up the engine and initiated the preflight diagnostics.

A section of the dash lit up red. Nova zoomed in on the blueprint of the ship, her heart sinking as she pinpointed the issue.

Something was wrong with the landing gear.

"She's dead," Thea said, the image burned into her eyes.

"Maybe." Coen flexed his fingers around the steering wheel, eyes flitting to the rearview mirror before locking in on the treads of Rover1. The tracks from the team's first trip to *Celestial Envoy* had been cleared away in the storm, and this lone, fresh set were all they had to go by. "I've seen them keep coming after worse than a rock spire to the shoulder," he went on. "They don't feel pain the way we do."

"Not the woman from the vents," Thea clarified. "Dr. Tarlow."

"Ah." Coen's mouth twisted into a grimace before adding, "She's just infected."

"So she—they—can't die?"

"Oh, they can die. Broken neck, suffocation, blood loss—all the normal stuff. You've seen it on the ship."

She had, but she didn't remember any of those people having hemorrhaged eyes. Perhaps they'd been killed pre-emptively, at the first sign of a nosebleed. For the first time, she wondered how many of those kills had been Coen's. She glanced at his hands, gripping the steering wheel.

"But who'd want to get close enough to deliver one of those outcomes?" he continued. "Makes you wish for a real gun, huh?"

Thea touched the stun gun in her holster, silently cursing Julian Hevetz and his vendetta against traditional firearms. Then again, Pitch Evans had found a pistol that shot bullets and even that hadn't done him much good. No wonder nearly the entire Black Quarry team had fallen.

Thea's thoughts drifted again to Dr. Tarlow. All that knowledge, all those years of research and fieldwork, lost. The fragility of life struck Thea deeply in that moment. Humans spent so much time struggling to understand their world, learning to better exist in it, and for what? None of that knowledge could go with them. Dr. Tarlow had done great things for the Trios. But anything she'd yet to accomplish, any hypotheses she was still mulling over or contributions she'd yet to make had died with her.

An alert flashed on Thea's visor, informing her that her

oxygen reserves had dipped to forty percent. She checked her watch. They'd been on Achlys barely five hours, and she was already more than halfway through her oxygen.

"I think you'll find this interesting," Coen said, pulling a Tab from his door pocket.

"What is it?"

"Just watch."

Grateful for a distraction, Thea turned her attention to the Tab. A *play* prompt waited. She tapped the icon.

The footage showed a dark room. No, the walls were too rugged for a room. A chasm of some sort, lit by . . .

Thea squinted, trying to make sense of what she was seeing.

Metadata in the corner of the footage read *WH-Rover4 Cam*. Headlights, she realized. The light source was headlights. It must have been a tight squeeze to get the vehicle into such a narrow passage. The footage was focused on an oblong pool of water. If it wasn't for the man collapsed at the edge of it—his boots causing the liquid to ripple and dance—Thea might have overlooked the water altogether. There were two other people with him, a woman and a young girl.

"Lisbeth, get the medkit!" the woman yelled. She was wearing an environmental suit, but from what Thea could see of her face, she looked strikingly like Dr. Tarlow. "The medkit! Hurry!"

A young girl raced out of the frame. She, too, was wearing a suit, but her helmet had been removed. She reappeared with a carrying case. "Is he gonna be okay?"

"Yes, of course," the woman said.

"I should have been more careful. I shouldn't have tried to grab it. If I hadn't fallen—"

"If you hadn't fallen in, we wouldn't have made the most monumental discovery of the century. Seaweed! Growing here on Achlys! Now, he's only got a bloody nose. Pass me more gauze."

The young Lisbeth Tarlow did as instructed. Her mother saw to her father, having him tilt his head back. He was convulsing slightly, eyes pinched tight.

"I'm cold," Lisbeth said.

"Yes, well, we're lucky for the chasm. It's protecting us from the worst of the storm, and the thermal pool is heating the space some. Put your helmet back on. It'll help."

The father slumped into the earth, shaking more aggressively.

"We need to go back," the girl said, helmet dangling from her hand.

"We can't, Beth. Not in this storm. It won't be safe to travel in the open."

"But he needs help. There's something wrong with the water. He's sick because of it."

"If there was something wrong with the water, you'd be sick, too," the mother insisted. "Because of your helmet leak and— *Ouch*."

The woman fell onto her seat, shoved by her husband. Hands now free, the man grabbed at his face, his eyes. Blood seeped through his fingers.

"This is my fault," Lisbeth said, backing away. "If I didn't fall in and crack my helmet, he wouldn't have come after me."

"I would have done exactly what he did," the mother snapped. "There's no fault." She struggled against her husband, trying to hold his hands down. "Lisbeth, get in the rover."

"But—"

"Lisbeth," the man grunted out. "Listen to your mother."

Instead, she stood there frozen.

"Get in the rover!" he roared, blood streaming down his cheeks.

"I'm sorry," she cried.

"Lisbeth, now!" her mother yelled. "And lock the doors."

Finally, the girl ran. She had barely disappeared from the frame when her father lunged forward, his hands closing around the mother's neck. The woman was thrown backward, landing near the edge of the pool, her helmet practically in the water. Her feet flailed beneath her attacker. She shoved at his chest, kicked out. His fingers found the release on the edge of her helmet.

"It's me," she choked out as he batted the helmet into the pool. "Sweetie, it's me." He kept clawing at her neck. "Please. It's—"

An explosive bang sliced through the air, and the man staggered away from the woman before collapsing into the water. He floated there a moment, then began to sink, and it was only then that Thea realized he'd been hit not with a shock from a stun gun, but a bullet. Lisbeth reappeared in the frame, her back to the camera. A pistol tumbled from her hand. It looked remarkably like the pistol Thea had seen lying beside Pitch Evans on the bridge.

It was theirs—the Tarlows.

Lisbeth ran toward the water. "Mom?"

"Get away from me," the woman said, pushing her. Over Lisbeth's shoulder, the woman's face gleamed in the headlights. Her neck bore scratches, tiny rivers of blood.

"I'm sorry." The girl was sobbing, shoulders shaking. "But he was going to—you were—"

"Where are the others? The rest of the crew?"

"They were driving back. For the bunker. Remember?"

"Right, right."

"I'm so sorry."

"It's okay. It's going to be okay." The woman sat back on her heels. Lisbeth stood there, still as a statue.

Thea scrubbed ahead through their conversation, stopping after a few minutes had passed, when the woman abruptly jumped to her feet.

"The rover," she said, blood pouring from her nose. "Lisbeth, get in the rover!"

The girl backed away.

"You can't let it get back to the bunker," the woman said.

"Can't let what?"

"Me. *This*."

"Mom?"

Bright red spread through one of the woman's eyes, like ink dispersing in water. Her fingers twitched at her side. "I love you, Lisbeth," she managed, but the words were not loving. They were a snarl. Her body trembled.

And then she lunged.

The girl jumped back, tripping and tumbling to the ground. Her hand grazed the pistol. She grabbed the weapon and brought it up, getting a shot off without a second to spare. It hit the woman in the arm, sending her staggering.

"Mom, please."

The woman blinked, both eyes now completely hemorrhaged.

"Mom . . ."

When the woman lunged again, Lisbeth Tarlow squeezed the trigger and buried both her parents.

Thea stared at the end frame, dumbfounded. "Tarlow said they died in a storm," she said finally. "That's what she told Hevetz, told the world."

"She lied." Coen nodded at the Tab. "I found it under one of the Witch Hazel mattresses. I think she transferred the footage from the rover to a personal Tab, and then claimed the rover took damage during the storm. That her parents died in the storm, too."

"Why would she do that?"

"Because she was young? Scared? Maybe she figured Hevetz wouldn't let her come home if they thought she was sick."

"But then why not get rid of the footage completely?"

"Survivor's guilt? Denial that her parents were gone?" Coen shrugged. "I've walked through it a million times, and that's all I've got."

"Where did this happen—the same ravine Black Quarry drilled in?"

"I think so. Or at least one nearby, fed by the same water supply. From what I can figure, the whole Witch Hazel crew was out collecting data that day, and the other four adults really did die in the storm. Staying in that chasm was all that spared Tarlow. There are pictures of the seaweed on that Tab, too. I think she took them before heading back to the bunker, before she decided to bury what really happened."

Thea thumbed through the interface and pulled up the most recent photos. Shots of the water were illuminated by flashlight, showing a glimpse of the murky liquid. Ribbons of ink-black seaweed waved just below the surface.

"Photosynthesis . . . ," Thea murmured.

"Requires light," Coen concluded. "It's a never-ending dusk here."

"Which is exactly why the seaweed's black, to pick up all it can in the infrared." She looked back at the photo, the craggy walls of the chasm. The plant would have needed an incredibly strong and flexible root system to grow in such conditions. But if it could pick up light in the infared, if the water was heated by a geothermal spring . . . It was suboptimal conditions, but it had clearly been enough.

Thea's mouth hung open in awe. Until now, the fate of Black Quarry had been speculation. *Perhaps* there'd been a contagion in the water. *Perhaps* it entered via the blood and was passed in the same manner.

But here, preserved on a private Tab and presumably scrubbed from the Hevetz system by Dr. Tarlow as a child, was proof. It had originated in the water. If seaweed could grow in those freezing, desolate conditions, it was inevitable that bacteria flowed in those currents as well.

And Dr. Tarlow had known this. Her father had been Patient Zero, and she'd known all along.

"She should have warned us!" Thea spat out. "She knew just how dangerous Achlys is, and she covered it all up."

"That doesn't matter now."

"Doesn't matter?" Thea erupted. "Sullivan and Toby are dead because of her, Coen. They're *dead*!"

"They're infected," he corrected.

"She put us all at risk. She gambled our lives, and for what?"

"It's done. It happened. Nothing we say now will change things."

"You wanted to talk to her! You jumped at the mention of her name in the bunker."

"Because she's seen this infection before, and I thought she might have answers, not want to linger around trying to cure it. What matters now is that we stick together—you and me. When we get to *Odyssey*, I'll tell the others you weren't even in that isolation chamber when Tarlow was attacked. I'll say she was gathering blood and you were working at the computers or something. You argue my case, and I'll argue yours. We can both get off this rock if we work together, and if we make sure no one has a reason to doubt us."

"Why even show me this," Thea said, pointing to the Tab, "if you don't want to show it to the others?"

"Because it will only create panic. And Pitch's words are already in your captain's head. But I need someone to trust me so I can get off this planet, and you seem smart enough to make up your own mind. So what do you say? We keep this to ourselves, we stick up for each other, and then we show Hevetz and Galactic Disease Control and whoever else necessary once we're off this rock."

Thea could see the logic in his argument. Dylan had proved herself to be the true coward among the group. She'd let Sullivan take the fall, let others do the dirty work she as captain should have assumed. It wasn't a stretch to assume she'd leave Thea or Coen behind if their stories didn't match up. The safest move was to sit on this video footage for now and pass it on to a party that would make an educated, careful decision later.

"Why *did* Pitch write not to trust you?" Thea asked. "I mean, you don't seem particularly untrustworthy. You've helped me, confided in me, tried to warn our whole crew. I don't get why he wrote what he did."

Odyssey appeared as they crested a small rise. Coen squeezed the steering wheel, gaze focused on the ship. They'd get to it within minutes.

"Maybe he's talking about someone else. You're still

assuming that 'the kid' and I are the same."

She gave him a pointed look.

"I lied, okay?" he said. "Pitch found out, and then his trust in me shattered. That's why he wrote that note."

Thea started in her seat. She hadn't truly expected a confession. "Lied how?" she asked.

"To get this job. My name's not Lashley. It's Rivli. Coen Rivli."

"Then who the hell is Amos Lashley?"

"Some druggie who ODed in an alley near my place. I took his IDs—all of them. He worked for Hevetz and was due to report for a job the following day, so I just showed up in his place."

Hevetz had a larger labor force than any energy company in the Trios. Drillers reported to work like medics did to the hospitals—shifts constantly changing, new faces at each job. With a swipe of Lashley's company ID, Coen could have boarded *Celestial Envoy*, no problem. The real question was *why*. No one aspired to be a driller. It was awful work conditions, on awful sites, for months on end. The good pay was in the management jobs, in science and tech.

"I don't understand."

"My sister's sick, and we can't afford the treatment anymore," Coen said. "I've tried everything to help my parents. Side jobs didn't bring in enough money. Black market prices for scripts and meds are insane. I resorted to stealing, and all that got me was a record. No corp would touch me. So when I stumbled on that dead guy, already a driller, already with all the proper IDs, I just . . . ran with it. Got rid of his body. Never reported a death. Black Quarry was a long gig, with pay coming once a month. I set everything up ahead of time so the money would go straight into my parents' account."

"And they're okay with identity theft?"

"They think I got this gig on my own merit. And even if they didn't, I don't think they'd have said anything. We're all desperate for Gina. You do what you have to do."

Thea grabbed his backpack from the rear seat and unzipped it as far as she could without removing the pickax from its sheath. There, resting atop the other gear he'd packed in a hurry, was the framed picture from his nightstand. A wiry girl grinned up at Thea—thin hair, bony limbs, flagrant smile. It was Coen, sitting beside her, who looked grave, one arm slung behind his sister's shoulder as he forced an insincere grin.

"How old is she?"

"Fourteen."

"And you?"

"Twenty."

"I said *you*, not Lashley."

"Seventeen."

270

"What about school?"

"I dropped out last year so I could work, help bring in some unnes."

Thea zipped up the bag. She'd never considered that she had it quite good. The foster home felt like a prison. The conditions were far from ideal. But she had all she needed to survive—food, shelter, her health. She wasn't sick, had never been at the mercy of the pharm corps and the prices they attached to treatments or meds.

What was that thing Mel was always saying? *There's no money in the cure, only the continued treatment.* The cost of medication sometimes killed the less fortunate.

"And that's why Pitch didn't trust you—because you weren't who he thought?"

"Yeah."

It didn't seem big enough. Not when Pitch was finger painting that message with his own blood. Was this "truth" actually a lie, a way to win her sympathy?

"Everyone was going crazy," Coen continued, reading her hesitation. "It was impossible to trust anyone, and he didn't take it well when I told him."

"Why did you?"

"We were the only two left—at least the only two we knew of. He started talking about a suicide pact, escaping before things got ugly. I said I couldn't; that I had to make it back for

Gina, and that's when it all came out. It's easy to come clean when you think you're about to die. And I wanted to hear my own name again. Coen, not Amos. The same was true when you showed up at the bunker. Two months of no interaction and I just wanted to hear someone call me Coen."

And yet he'd originally given Thea the name Amos Lashley. Probably in case Dylan had checked the Black Quarry manifest. The captain *definitely* wouldn't have trusted him when the name Coen Rivli didn't appear among the Company's employees.

Coen stopped the rover.

They'd reached *Odyssey*.

"The odds were never good for me or Pitch," he added with a sigh. "I'm not that surprised he wrote what he did before shooting himself."

"Was he sick?"

Coen shook his head. "Nah. But he knew it was inevitable, and I think he wanted to go out on his own terms. A person's got a right to choose how they die, I guess."

Dylan appeared outside the passenger window, startling Thea so badly her visor flashed red.

"Took you long enough," Dylan said. Her eyes darted to the back seat. "Where's Tarlow?"

Coen glanced at Thea. *Well*, his look seemed to say, *are we together on this?*

For now, she thought, and handed him his backpack with a nod.

Nova felt like she was having an out-of-body experience as Thea updated them on the outcome of Dr. Tarlow's research. Sullivan was still locked in that isolation chamber. Tarlow hadn't found a cure. Hell, she hadn't even managed to do anything but draw blood before the men managed to attack. And now they were all lost causes—the doctor and Sullivan and Toby.

Nova slumped against *Odyssey*'s hull, hands in fists at her side.

What the hell was she going to say to Mikko? How could she ever tell the twins that their daddy wasn't coming home?

"There are more of them," Thea was saying. "They chased us from the medbay, and they'll be following."

"On foot," Coen added, "so it will take them a little while. We'll be out of here before we have to worry."

"That's kinda where we have a problem." Dylan glanced to Nova.

It's on me to break bad news to the team now? Nova thought. Exhaling hard, she began to explain. "We're not going anywhere anytime soon. Our landing gear failed in the storm. Cleaver's under there trying to fix it right now."

She waited as Thea and Coen dropped to their knees,

peering beneath *Odyssey*. Nova had done the same after the diagnostics warning. One of *Odyssey*'s legs had sunk a good meter into the ground, the hydraulic piping running alongside it bowed at an unnatural angle. There was no fixing it, at least not quickly, and still Cleaver was trying.

"Hydraulics can't retract properly under this much damage," she explained. "And even if they could, the damn boot's buried."

"Can you fly with the landing gear down?" Coen asked.

"It's not ideal," said Dylan. "But yeah."

"None of this is *ideal*," Nova snarled. "Flying with the landing gear down will force *Odyssey* into emergency protocol, which means our shields will be weakened and we won't be able to undergo cryo, and last I checked, we don't have enough food to keep us alive for two fucking months. Also, did you not hear the part about the boot being buried? We can't take off with it buried like that."

"Which is why Cleaver's trying to dig us out a little. Once we're off this rock, someone can put on an EVA suit and try to repair the leg. But one thing at a time. Okay?" Dylan gave Nova a pointed look. "Cleaver, you yell if you need a hand. Everyone else, spread out and form a perimeter. Those things are probably working their way toward us now. You spot anyone closing in on *Odyssey*," she said to the rest of them, "you drop them with a full shock. Am I understood?"

● ● ●

Thea did not know what help she would be in such darkness.

Barely more than an arm's length in front of her, the world seemed to blur into obscurity. Somewhere to her right, Coen, Nova, and Dylan stood at watch, but she felt disastrously alone. It was like being on Soter's ice caps, but at night, with a predator you couldn't see running in for an attack.

"How many of them did you say there were?" Dylan asked.

"Three in the vents and about a dozen in the hall," Thea answered. "At least that's what we could see."

"How long will it take them to get here?"

"Hard to say," Coen chimed in. "They're on foot, but they can follow our tracks. And the longer a person's infected, the slower they become, the more rash and chaotic their actions get. Your crew was contained, but if they somehow get out of isolation, they could be here any minute. Black Quarry will be slower."

"How did they even find you?" Nova asked.

"Probably just returning to the last place they remembered finding new hosts," Thea reasoned.

Dylan said, "So it *is* a virus?"

"Honestly, at this point, I'm guessing a bacterial parasite. Something that's essentially hijacking the host and driving them to pass on the infection." Despite her deal with Coen,

Thea considered sharing what she'd just learned about Tarlow—the doctor's discovery of the black seaweed as a child and the nature of her parents' death. But Cleaver suddenly swore behind her, his voice laced with panic.

For the briefest instant, Thea feared they'd failed to hold their perimeter, that somehow one of the infected had snuck past them and attacked. But as she turned toward Cleaver, she heard a deep groan of straining metal. The boot Cleaver was working on was about to give out completely. *Odyssey*'s exterior lights trembled, and as the ship jolted, sinking farther into the ground, Cleaver screamed in pain.

Thea ran for him, nearly colliding with Coen in the process. Dylan and Nova joined them, too. *Odyssey* was now at an incredibly awkward angle, one leg sunk deep into the earth. Cleaver had tried to crawl from beneath the ship, but hadn't made it completely to safety. He was facedown, visible from the waist up and pinned in place by the ship, which had come down on his upper legs. If he'd only crawled in the opposite direction, he might have been spared. That side of the ship was now raised well off the ground, landing gear suspended in the air.

"My legs," Cleaver panted. Dylan and Nova each grabbed one of his arms and tugged back, resulting in a string of curses from the man.

"You guys lift while we pull," Dylan said to Thea and Coen.

Lift? This was a UT-800 transport ship. Even as one of the smaller models in its class, it could only be moved in pieces, by industrial forklifts and cargo loaders.

"Shouldn't we dig instead?" Thea asked.

"And risk the ground caving in on all of us? Or pinning Cleaver further? Just lift."

They couldn't very well leave the man, so despite the absurdity of the order, Thea followed it. She positioned herself on one side of Cleaver while Coen stepped up to the ship on the other.

"One," he counted, "two, *three.*"

Together they heaved, and to Thea's surprise, the ship gave. Not much. Barely more than a centimeter. But with Dylan and Nova pulling on Cleaver at the same time, his body moved just slightly.

Dylan yelled with surprise. Clearly she hadn't expected much success either.

Coen and Thea looked at each other, confused. "Maybe the ground shifted again," he offered.

"One last time, then!" Dylan said. "Before it caves in."

At the count of three, Thea threw all the effort she could muster into the act. She felt the ground shift underfoot, the ship lurch slightly. It was enough to relieve the worst of the pressure on Cleaver, and Dylan and Nova were able to pull him back a few millimeters. That was all it took. With the widest part of his legs no longer pinned, the women dragged him to safety.

"Broken," Dylan said as they set Cleaver down at a distance. "Both legs."

"*Odyssey*, too," Nova said, still staring at it.

While not overturned, the ship reminded Thea of a bug stuck on its back, legs flailing, unable to get purchase with the ground. The damaged boot was now fully swallowed by the earth. There'd be no righting it, no chance at a liftoff.

"Maybe we can barricade the ship," Dylan muttered, mostly to herself. "Hole up there, wait for the backup Hevetz crew to land."

"They'll overrun it," Coen argued. "They forced their way past every barricade Black Quarry set up."

"What about the bunker you were hiding at?" Nova asked. "Will that hold?"

"If they don't realize we're staying there, maybe. But—"

"The short-range shuttles!" Thea shouted over them. They all looked at her like she was crazy. "Nova, you said *Celestial Envoy* probably had short-range shuttles."

The pilot nodded. "Yes, but they don't have enough fuel to get us anywhere. We'd take off and be dead in the water."

"Hevetz sent that specialized crew to meet us. We don't have to get home, just to them. If we get on a shuttle, we'll have wings and a working comm system. We can broadcast an SOS while flying for the Trios. With any luck—"

"Hevetz will pick us up," Dylan finished. "Lacking fuel cells won't matter."

"Not bad, intern," Nova said, but it was the way she said it that mattered. It was a compliment, truly and sincerely, and if anyone could relate to not being taken seriously because of their title, it was Nova.

Thea felt a smile crest her lips. Imagine that, smiling in a situation like this.

"We've got company!" Coen shouted, lurching to his feet.

Thea's smile vanished. She spun toward the rovers, searching in the direction of *Celestial Envoy*. The Achlys landscape was deathly silent. Coen was mistaken.

But there—something moved into the light of the rovers at an unnatural speed.

Thea blinked, and it was upon them, diving at the nearest crew member—Nova—and tackling her to the ground.

The air went out of Nova's lungs as her back hit the hard Achlys earth. She barely managed to get her rifle up in time, using the length of the barrel to catch her attacker beneath the chin.

It had happened so quickly—Coen's warning, the body slamming into Nova, the fall. It was only now, as the air returned to her lungs in desperate gasps, that she was able to make sense of things and see who had tackled her.

Sullivan.

Her cousin was a shadow of his former self. He'd left *Celestial Envoy* without his helmet, and his skin was now red with cold. A trail of frozen blood still marked the space beneath his nose and most of his neck. His eyes were two dark orbs.

He snarled like an animal, clawing at her. As his fingers grazed the glass of her helmet, she could see blood beneath the nails.

Would it matter that it had frozen in the elements? If he managed to get at her skin and scratch her, would she fall as he did?

Her forearms ached with exhaustion. She screamed for help.

No one was coming.

Behind her, she could hear a struggle. Dylan shouting orders. Cleaver yelling in pain. What they were up against hit Nova like a blow to the gut: Sullivan had been in Isolation One according to Thea's story. If he'd managed to get out, Toby must be free as well. The others likely had their hands full with the technician.

Nova tried to scramble from beneath Sullivan, but his weight was too much. Her arms trembled. *Keep your elbows locked, keep them locked!* If they gave out, it was over. As soon as they buckled, Sullivan would be upon her, his hands able to reach her helmet's release.

"Help!" she gasped out, her grip on the rifle slipping. "I need help!"

There was a flare of white, and Sullivan twitched with surprise. In that one small moment of limpness, Nova scrambled from beneath him. As she stood, she caught Thea in the corner of her vision, lowering a stun gun. The intern had just saved her ass. Again.

No time to dwell on it. Nova trained her rifle on Sullivan. He was pushing back to sit on his knees. He raised his head to meet her gaze, and when his mouth twisted into a smile, it was one of pure cunning. Evil, dark, murderous.

Nova pulled the trigger on her rifle.

And nothing happened.

She glanced down, slapping at the body of the weapon. From the panel that typically displayed battery life, two words shone up at her: *Charge Depleted.*

Sullivan's smile seemed to get more devious.

"Sull, please," she begged, backing away. Thea unleashed several more shots, but the small stun gun barely had any effect on Sullivan. He stood to his full height, plodding through the shocks Thea threw his way.

"Sullivan, this isn't you," Nova said, reaching desperately for the knife stowed in her utility belt. "Please don't make me do this."

But as the words left Nova's lips, she knew they were wasted. She wasn't talking to her cousin anymore. He lunged, and she sighted the muscular slope of his neck, accessible without a helmet. As he tackled her again, she brought the blade up and swiped.

Blood sprayed her visor. Nova slammed into the ground for a second time. She coughed in pain, yanked her arm from beneath Sullivan's limp body. Grunting, Nova pushed him aside and scrambled to her feet.

Sullivan lay gasping on his back, hemorrhaged eyes locked on the sky. A dark, ragged line was drawn across his neck. Nova watched the blood bubble and bloom, then begin to freeze before her eyes.

The bloody knife tumbled from her hand.

"Nova!" Thea said, grabbing the pilot's shoulder. "Nova, we have to go."

Sullivan was dead, but another threat loomed. Dylan was attempting to drag Cleaver into the rover while Coen used a stun gun—borrowed from Dylan, possibly—to hold Toby at bay.

The men had gotten free of the isolation chamber, which meant Dr. Tarlow was also free. Thea squinted toward *Celestial Envoy*, pulse pounding in her ears, but no one else was coming. Not that she could see. Maybe the doctor's head injury had been too severe. Maybe she died before the parasite could take over.

"Sull," Nova was muttering, still staring at his body.

"Nova, come on!"

Whatever miracle had kept Sullivan alive in the freezing elements—a slowed metabolism, quickly clotting blood—could no longer save him. There was no mending a ruptured artery, no easy way to stop the bleeding Nova had inflicted.

"The hatch! Get the hatch open!" Dylan was screaming.

Thea glanced over her shoulder. While Toby recovered from a shock, Coen had opened the hatchback of Rover2. Dylan was struggling to lift Cleaver into the vehicle as Coen continued to hold off Toby. With each blast, the technician stumbled backward, but just like Sullivan, he regained his footing easily and came in for another attack. Relentless. Tireless.

The longer a person's infected, the slower they become, the more rash and chaotic their actions get.

Toby had been infected for about three hours, and roughly half that time he'd spent either passed out or sedated. The technician was not going to tire, and Thea and Coen had left a small mob of infected Black Quarry members at the medbay. If they got through the air lock, or retreated back through the hangar bay . . . they'd be slower and clumsier, but there was no way the small *Odyssey* crew would be able to fend them all off.

"Nova! Thea!" Dylan's voice cut through the night.

"Coming!" Thea shouted back, but the pilot's grief had become a shackle, a chain of weights. Thea was forced to slow several times, yanking Nova to her feet. Thea's ankles protested the uneven, pocked ground. But she managed to get to Rover2, where she ordered the pilot into the rear seat. As soon as she slammed that door shut, Thea fumbled for the driver's door handle. Found the latch. Heaved it open.

Sliding into the seat, she looked over her shoulder.

Cleaver was halfway inside the vehicle, Dylan's hands hooked beneath his armpits as she pulled with all her strength. At his feet, Coen alternated between pushing him into the rover and firing on Toby, who was finally slowing after weathering so many shocks.

"One more!" Dylan yelled, pulling on Cleaver with all her might. The man slid into the vehicle, only his feet left hanging in the elements.

Coen leapt onto the bumper, fired one final shot at Toby, and shouted, "Go, go, go!"

Thea slammed her foot on the accelerator, and the vehicle sputtered and yawned. She tried again. Sometimes the cold played tricks on the rovers at Northwood Point, and all you had to do was give them a little extra juice before they turned over. Thea padded the accelerator. Battery lights flashed on

the dashboard, and as Thea looked up in desperation, something staggered into the glow of the rover's headlights.

Commander Lowe. Behind him, the men from the vents.
And others—perhaps a dozen infected crew members, bodies half frozen, faces distorted with blisters from the cold.

"Drive!" Dylan roared.

"I'm trying!" Thea smacked at the ignition button, revved
the engine.

The bodies collided with Rover2, hands slapping at the
hood and windows, fingers prying at the locked doors. Coen
shouted from the rear, firing again on Toby. The rover rocked
as the mob battered it, moving toward the rear. There were
too many for Coen's lone stun gun. Thea looked in the rearview mirror to see hands groping at Cleaver's ankles. Coen
kicked at them while Dylan struggled to keep the man from
being pulled from the rover.

"Goddammit, *drive!*" the captain screamed.

Thea held the ignition button, trying the accelerator
repeatedly. The engine whined with newfound energy and
finally turned over. A wave of relief knocked through Thea
as the rover surged forward.

Looking in the rearview mirror, her elation vanished.

The sudden speed of the rover had worked in the mob's
favor. Cleaver was now sliding toward them. He reached in
desperation, grabbing blindly for Coen, who was positioned

in a squat, firing on the very bastards Cleaver was so desperate to escape.

It happened in a heartbeat.

Cleaver's hand closed over Coen's ankle, and as he was pulled from the moving rover by the infected, he took Coen with him.

Pain shot through his back as he hit the ground.

If he hadn't been watching out for the others—watching what he said and did in their presence—he'd have seen the fall coming. But he'd been playing a game since the moment the Odyssey crew landed, and his deceptions had finally caught up with him.

He rolled, ignoring the pain and getting his feet beneath him.

As he straightened, he reached for what he'd been hesitant to use before. His hand closed over the pickax. He withdrew it by the arched metal, then let go swiftly, allowing the weight of the head to plummet for the ground. The handle propelled into his palm. Fingers closed over the carbon fiber shaft, he used his free hand to draw a second weapon from his thigh: a butcher's blade that he'd welded onto a piece of scrap metal.

Those things . . .

They were converging on the man the crew called Cleaver.

He ran, silent, and swung the pickax into the back of the nearest body. Pulled it free, slashed with the knife-sword. Yanked that free as he spun, burying the pickax into another skull.

He did not look into their eyes. He couldn't risk seeing a face he recognized, a crew member he'd worked beside. These people were not the friends he'd known two months ago. They were no longer human, but something . . . else.

Like him.

He'd become a thing he didn't understand since the incident, an eager, angry, vicious machine. There'd been a monster lurking within him, and he'd welcomed it in order to survive.

He kept swinging the ax, slashing the blade.

His helmet fogged with his breath, and sweat dripped in his eyes. His visor flashed with inconsequential vitals, as though an elevated heart rate mattered right now. As if slowing was an option.

He was a storm, a fury, a stranger to himself, and when it was over the Achlys ground was wet with blood. Over a dozen bodies lay scattered, dismembered.

He fought the urge to vomit.

The man called Cleaver raised a hand, searching for help as he had in the rover. His helmet had been removed, and his neck and cheeks were awash with scratches.

"Please," he said.

Please help me?

Please end it?

It didn't matter. There was only one thing to be done.

Coen kneeled, and the monster inside him snapped the man's neck.

288

VIII

THE IMMUNE

Celestial Envoy

Achlys, Fringe-1 System

THE THING LAY THERE, SILENT, facedown in the frozen dirt.

It felt cold, but only faintly.

It hurt, but not terribly.

The thing could hear the monster's attack, a flurry of slashes and stabs and tears. It tried to get up, move to safety, but its right leg felt heavy, wrong. Something had sliced through its calf.

It actually hurt quite a bit, the thing decided. It had been lying when it said it wasn't that bad.

Peering through the dark, the thing watched the others fall. One after the next until the monster finally slowed, then moved with careful precision, stepping over the dead to reach the lone survivor. Everything about the monster made the thing's insides writhe.

It watched the monster watch the survivor. Then snap his neck.

The thing no longer tried to move.

Not yet.

They'd fallen—Coen and Cleaver pulled from the rear of the rover—and here Thea sat, foot still on the accelerator, steering Rover2 back to *Celestial Envoy* as fast as the terrain would allow.

Some rescue crew they made. Half of their own dead. The only Black Quarry survivor now doomed, left behind in the clutches of a mindless mob. *Dylan ordered you to keep driving,* Thea told herself as she squinted at the ashy gray masses of rocks and ruts that flew by outside the vehicle. *You had no choice.*

But there was always a choice, wasn't there? It wasn't that they'd left Cleaver and Coen that bothered Thea so much, but that she agreed.

What could they have done for the men, truly? Her crew had just the few weapons between them, Dylan's lost when Coen was yanked from the rover, the charge on Nova's rifle depleted. And as they'd seen all too clearly, a stun didn't drop the infected the way it did a healthy person. It slowed them, but not sufficiently. They did not tire. They kept coming. And even if the Black Quarry crew was slower as Coen had explained, they were still a dozen strong. Perhaps there were even more coming. Commander Lowe was one of the first crew members to be infected. Was it possible, then, to believe he may have been one of the first to retreat to the ravines? That he'd been among the best preserved and one of the first to reanimate? Dozens of infected could have since emerged from the drilling base. Thea hadn't passed any other signs of life while driving, and while there was no way of knowing what awaited them back at the ship, turning around for Cleaver and Coen would only doom them all.

Besides, she reasoned, *they're probably already dead.*

Not dead, she imagined Coen saying. *Infected.*

Infected then. Beyond saving and nothing but a death sentence to the rest of the *Odyssey* crew.

Was this the person she'd become—heartless in the face of reason? She was putting herself above others, weighing her life as more worthy. Hers and Dylan's and Nova's. Dylan might have given the order to drive on, but neither Thea nor Nova had argued.

No one will get off this planet if you are not ruthless about the protection of your own life, Thea told herself.

Her oxygen reserves had just dropped below thirty percent. Time was of the essence.

She adjusted her grip on the steering wheel and sped on.

He was dead. Sullivan Hooper was dead, and it had happened at her hands.

Nova stared at her palms.

She'd dropped the knife back near the ship, but she could

feel the ghost of it against her skin as if she wasn't even wearing a suit. The rubber grip of the handle, the weight of the pommel against the heel of her hand.

Nova felt a tear slide down her cheek. She blinked aggressively to keep others from falling. She couldn't lose it now. If they didn't get to the short-range shuttles, they'd all be done for. And she needed to fly what remained of their crew to safety.

"I'm sorry about Sullivan," Dylan said softly.

"Don't talk to me," snapped Nova. The woman was kind enough to comply. Maybe it was cruel of Nova. Dylan had just seen her own father outside the rover, the ruined state of his eye, the rabid thing he'd become. Nova should have offered her own sympathies, perhaps, but she was too numb. And even in her numbness, a part of her couldn't stop comparing the two deaths. Sullivan's had only happened *because* of Dylan Lowe, who had pushed the team on blindly, stubbornly, without listening to those around her. Whereas Commander Lowe's death was in no way Nova's fault.

These losses weren't the same, and it drove a wedge into Nova's heart, letting her anger with Dylan widen.

When they reached *Celestial Envoy*, Thea brought the rover inside, and Dylan sealed the main hangar door.

"To keep them out," she explained.

"Or in," Thea replied. "More could have returned here

while we were gone."

A shiver ran down Nova's limbs at the possibility. She turned for the rear of the rover and began to search for additional battery mags as a distraction.

"I'm still closing it," Dylan said. "If infected crew members are running around *Celestial Envoy*, it's best we keep those numbers from growing. And we can continue to seal off sections as we make our way to the shuttle."

"What if we need to get back out?" Thea asked.

"If we need to get back out, we're fucked. Nova, where would the short-term shuttles be?"

Nova barely heard her. She'd retreated inside herself, busied her hands with the ray-rifle. She moved automatically, ejecting the drained battery mag and slapping a new one into place.

"Nova?" Dylan urged again.

She checked the panel on the side of the barrel. *Full Charge.*

"Nova!"

"The commander's chambers," Nova said, stowing two additional battery mags in her utility belt. She wouldn't find herself in the same situation again. "Maybe high-ranking officials, too. Their rooms probably adjoin emergency docking bays, and if there's a short-range shuttle, that's where it will be."

"*If?*" Dylan said.

"Also, an operation this advanced will have security protocol in place for those rooms. We'll probably need access codes to get through doorways and air locks."

"So we start in the lab," Thea offered. "The Tabs might have info on them."

"Or we start on the bridge," Dylan argued. "See if we can override the doorways altogether."

"We'd need Toby for that," Nova said. "And Toby's . . . Well, he's not going to be much help, is he?" She slid from the rover and rested the barrel of the ray-rifle against her shoulder. "It's a long shot any of the info we need is even stored in a public file, but maybe we'll get lucky."

"So the lab," Dylan concluded.

Nova watched Thea scan the hangar in desperation, as though she might find a rogue shuttle waiting in the shadows. She wouldn't. Nova had looked hours ago, when they first set foot in the hangar. It was filled with nothing but ground transportation, trailers, and cargo loaders.

"I'll lead," Dylan went on. "Nova, you take the rear. Thea, give me your stun gun and stay close."

Thea hated being unarmed. But Dylan's weapon had been lost with Coen's fall from the rover, and besides Nova's ray-rifle, Thea's stun gun was the only other weapon the women had between them. If she hadn't handed it over to Dylan willingly, the captain would have taken it by force.

Perhaps worse than being unarmed, though, Thea hated the ominous quiet of the ship. With each turned corner, each ascended stairwell, she braced for disaster, expecting an infected crew member to jump out at her from the darkness; but they were greeted with only the familiar and ominous flickering of lights.

When the women finally reached the research floor, it was still sealed off from the rest of the ship. The doors must have slid shut behind Commander Lowe and the small army of infected he'd brought with him when they took to following the rovers. That, or they'd managed to eventually breach the medbay and had followed Coen and Thea out the isolation chamber's air lock.

Dylan led the way through the doors, and they crept on.

As they edged past a vent, Thea heard a creak from deep within and froze, terror racing through her. But when she held a hand before the cover panel, she felt the softest kiss of air pushing back. It was just the ventilation system.

She checked the data in the corner of her visor, which told her that the air outside her helmet was unbreathable. She paused, confused. Maybe when Sullivan and Toby escaped Isolation One, the sedative continued pumping, slowly spreading beyond the medbay and throughout the entire floor. That didn't explain why these hall vents were running. Perhaps they were operating on an emergency protocol, circulating breathable air in an attempt to counteract the sedative.

There wasn't time to troubleshoot it. Her own oxygen reserves were now at twenty-five percent, and she doubted the other women had much more.

"What the . . . ?" Dylan stood frozen in the research lab's doorway.

Someone had been here—someone with a purpose.

Every last Tab had been removed from the charging caddy. Now, they lay strewn about the table, along with a variety of the freezer samples, and Evans's pistol that Dylan had taken from the bridge and left here ever since. The samples of drilled dirt had been separated from three canisters holding a viscous, black liquid. One had been labeled *corrarium-X*, and the subsequent two, *corrX*.

Thea followed Dylan into the room, walking in a trance.

Sitting at the edge of the table, behind all these canisters, was a small aquarium filled with water. Inside, blades dancing lazily along the surface, was a piece of the black seaweed Thea had seen in the WH-Rover4 footage. Up close, she could see that the stipe was slender but rubbery in texture, and that the blades were wide, flat ribbons supported by bulbous gas bladders that provided float. The entire plant was an inky black, save for the bladders, which gleamed with a greenish iridescent sheen. The roots were thick and gnarly, but they ended bluntly, as though someone had hacked the plant free while harvesting it. Still, many of the long blades intertwined in the small constraints of the tank. Unraveled, Thea guessed the plant was at least three meters long; easily taller than her.

"What the hell is—?"

"Don't touch it!" Thea shouted, putting an arm out to stop Dylan. The captain shook her off, peering intently at the seaweed.

"Where did it come from?"

Thea pointed to a hip-tall refrigerator in the far corner of the room. She'd overlooked it during her early times in the lab, but its lid was cracked open now, reflecting the overhead lights in a way that was impossible to ignore.

Thea glanced back at the aquarium. A label on the side identified the seaweed as *Laminaria achlys*, and also included a date that matched the day of Li's injury. The seaweed must have been found by Li himself or by others in his crew, perhaps when they'd reviewed the site where he'd fallen.

Interesting as all this was, none of it explained who had removed the sample from the fridge. Or what corrX was. If the substance was the same as that found in the Trios, it would surely be labeled *corrarium*. This sample—found deep in the ravine, below water and the rocky bottom where the seaweed had been anchored—must be some variant of the fuel source.

"Achlys has complex plant life?" Dylan murmured, still staring at the seaweed.

Plant life that grew in water that served as a conduit for a deadly parasite. It dawned on Thea that the bacteria might gather near—or even live *on*—the *Laminaria achlys* species.

She took a step away from the aquarium and said, "We should be looking for the passcode."

"These Tabs have been scrubbed," Nova said, glancing up from the devices.

"You're kidding," Dylan said.

"No. They're blank. Empty. Not a drop of data left."

"What?" Dylan rushed to join the pilot. "Who the hell would have done that?"

"Me," someone said behind them.

Thea knew that voice. She also knew it wasn't possible. But when she turned away from the aquarium, there she was— Dr. Lisbeth Tarlow, standing in the doorway, uninjured and very much alive.

"You should be i-infected," Thea stuttered.

"I'm fine," she said calmly. "What do you need the Tabs for?"

"I saw them attack you! They pulled off your helmet, and you were just lying there."

"I must have lost consciousness before they did any real damage. Maybe they thought I was dead."

The doctor was wearing her suit again, helmet and all. There'd been a cut along her brow, but it was missing now. In its place, Thea could see only a smear of dried blood. Had Thea imagined the injuries, mistaken Sullivan's or Toby's blood for the doctor's? Everything had happened so fast.

"Did you let Sullivan and Toby out of Isolation One?" Dylan asked. The stun gun she'd borrowed from Thea remained aimed at the floor, but her hand tightened on the grip.

"What? No! When I came to, the chamber's door was open and medical was empty."

"Then how did Sullivan and Toby end up attacking us at *Odyssey*?"

"I don't know," the doctor insisted. "I was alone, I promise."

"It's possible the group that attacked us saw people in isolation and forced the door open," Thea reasoned. "Maybe they assumed Tarlow and the guys were dead and just moved on."

"Yes," Dr. Tarlow said quickly. "That makes sense. Sullivan and Toby must have come to before me and also left."

"But I could have sworn you were bleeding," Thea went on. "Your brow, along your neck . . ."

"I'm fine," the doctor insisted.

It didn't make sense, but Thea could admit that Dr. Tarlow did, indeed, appear fine. She showed no signs of a nosebleed and her eyes were perfectly healthy. She wasn't twitching or snarling or clawing at her own face.

"I ran some brain scans and blood tests, and I know what we're dealing with," the doctor said. "Come to the medbay."

"Brain scans?" Nova chimed in. "On who? You said you were alone."

"I brought in two samples; infected that were roaming the halls."

Dylan swore in disbelief, and trained her weapon up.

Dr. Tarlow simply held up her hands and continued. "I can show you the results if you just come with me to the medbay. There's proof. It will all make sense."

"It doesn't make *any* sense!" Thea chirped out. "They're strong, wild, irrational. You never could have overpowered two of them without being injured yourself."

"I vented a sedative through the whole floor, brought in the subjects once they were unconscious."

That explained the air Thea had felt moving through the system. But it didn't explain why the doctor hadn't radioed Dylan when she came to, why she hadn't tried to contact anyone in the crew.

"It's not right," Thea said, shaking her head. "She's hiding something."

There was an air of sadness to the doctor's expression, but what had she expected? This was Thea's mentor, a woman who had told her everything would be fine. A woman who had been to Achlys before, as a child, and knew quite clearly that things would *not* be fine. That the planet was incredibly dangerous. That it should be under galactic quarantine, ensuring that no one ever set foot here again.

"How did you know *Odyssey* was damaged?" Dylan said, her weapon now aimed at Dr. Tarlow's chest.

"I didn't know anything. I assumed the storm would wreak havoc."

"Our comms were sabotaged. You did that, didn't you? When we went to the drilling base, you snuck out and cut the lines?"

"No! I was here in the labs the whole time. I'd tell you to ask Sullivan, but . . ."

"He's dead now," Dylan continued. "Cleaver's as good as infected, too. Same with Coen."

"The boy?" Dr. Tarlow gasped. "He can't be."

"I saw them get pulled from the rover by a mob of infected Black Quarry workers. I think I'd know! Now you better get your story straight, Tarlow."

"Listen," the doctor said, her palms still held up in surrender. "Just come into the lab with me, and I can show you the tests. I can explain everything."

"She's seen this before," Thea said quietly. "Coen showed me footage he found hidden at the Witch Hazel bunker. It started with her parents. They died in a storm, but not how we thought, not how all the reports claim. It's something in the water—a parasite. It got in her parents and drove them to attack each other. She killed them and covered it up."

"It's complicated," Dr. Tarlow said quickly.

Something seemed to crack in Thea's chest.

The doctor hadn't denied it. She'd known all along what they might find on Achlys, the risks the planet posed. She knew and she'd done nothing, even had the nerve to tell Thea everything would be fine. She'd warned the team about harsh land and rough storms, but not what mattered most.

She'd damned them all.

"I wanted to be you, once," Thea said.

"Thea, you don't understand. I had to keep it contained."

"Contained, sure! But you hid the footage. You didn't tell Hevetz all those years ago, and you didn't tell us now!"

"I was young during Witch Hazel, scared. I was terrified of lifelong quarantine, isolation that would never end. Tests and examinations. So I kept quiet. I isolated myself—in the bunker and then always. I isolate myself still."

"But you let us come here!" Thea screamed. "It's one thing to be scared as a kid, but now it's just cowardice. You could have stopped this. You could have prevented all of this!"

"I've dedicated my entire life to prevention," the doctor snarled, her expression hardening for the first time since she appeared in the doorway. "I've worked the same job for ages, always researching, always working toward an answer that might protect us—protect *everyone*. If a contagion of this magnitude exists on Achlys, it's only a matter of time until it, or something similar, appears elsewhere. In the Trios. Another system. Look at the devastation it's wrought! We need to find a cure. We need to understand this parasite so that we know how to eradicate it. I'll admit that at first I was terrified to set foot here again, but then I realized it was a gift, a chance to finish what I started." Dr. Tarlow swallowed heavily behind her helmet. "The responsible path is often hard. It has consequences. It is never easy. But this was the only way," she insisted. "Don't you understand? Can you imagine what they would have done to me if I'd told them the truth? It wouldn't have been a life. And it would never have resulted in answers. Science is about answers. About understanding. About making a better future."

"What the hell are you talking about?" Dylan said.

But Thea saw.

She saw and now she couldn't unsee. She saw so clearly she didn't know how she'd missed it when Coen had first shown her the footage.

The pool Tarlow had fallen into . . . almost drowning . . . mention of a helmet leak. She'd swallowed the water—the same bacteria her father had encountered when stripping off his suit and wading in to save her.

Lisbeth Tarlow's motives had been self-preservation, always.

As a child, it was somewhat selfish, a desire to merely survive. As an adult, that self-preservation drive extended beyond herself. To understand. To cure.

"You . . . you're . . ."

"Thea, let me explain. It's different."

"She's infected," Thea muttered.

Dylan's aim sharpened. "Is that true?"

Silence. The hallway was so still, Thea swore she could hear the whirring of the ventilation fans.

"Is that true?" Dylan roared. "Are you infected?"

"Yes, but—"

Dylan fired.

Dr. Tarlow didn't fall. She didn't even stagger. Her expression went blank as her hands moved to her stomach. When she removed them, her gloves were wet with blood.

Dylan Lowe was no longer holding Thea's stun gun. She was holding a pistol. Pitch's pistol. The very piece Thea had seen resting with the Tabs and drill samples. The captain must have grabbed it when Thea had her back turned.

"What are you doing?" she screamed as the doctor slumped to the floor.

"She's sick like the others," Dylan said.

"Yes, but it's different! This didn't just happen. She's been sick all along, since Witch Hazel. She's resistant to it."

"We can't prove that, and we can't take risks. Not when she damned our whole crew. This is *her* fault, all of it, and she can't be trusted."

"Thea," Dr. Tarlow breathed. "Thea, listen to me. This is imperative."

"Let's go," Dylan said, stepping over the doctor's legs and entering the hallway.

"She doesn't have symptoms!" Thea continued, rushing to check on her mentor. Blood oozed between the woman's fingers. "She could have helped us. She could have found a cure. She might be the *key* to the cure."

Dylan turned back toward them and dropped into a crouch. Ignoring Thea, she leaned forward, until her face was level with Dr. Tarlow's, and said slowly, "Is there a cure?"

The woman took a ragged breath, then gasped out, "No."

"Well, there you have it. No cure, and I most certainly can't bring someone carrying this contagion back to the Trios. Let's move."

"Wait." The doctor grabbed Thea by the arm. Thea couldn't help it. Even with the suit layers between them, she flinched.

"If you stay," Dylan said, staring down at Thea, "the next time I see you, I will assume you're sick and shoot you, too."

"Thea . . ." The grip on Thea's forearm tightened. She pivoted toward the doctor. The woman was now taking shallow breaths, her head leaning against the wall. "There's no cure . . . yet," she managed. "But there might be."

"How?"

"I'm sorry for lying to you. If I'm right . . . you were never at risk, not truly. And Coen . . . he's . . . You must . . ."

"The cure," Thea prompted. "How?"

The doctor's eyes rolled, and she fought to right them, to focus on Thea. "My research, in the medbay . . . Review it." A cough. Blood on her lips. "It's looking for . . . a match. . . . It's looking for . . . " The doctor's head slumped to her chest. Vacant eyes stared at the floor.

Thea pulled her arm from the doctor's grip, scrambled to her feet.

When she turned around, the hall was empty.

Dylan and Nova had left her. Again.

For the second time, Lisbeth Tarlow felt reality flex around her.

Before, she'd merely been losing consciousness, the strike of her head against that chamber wall too much to fight, the sedative then dragging her under. But this was different.

There was pain, for one. Unbelievable pain. She'd put a hand to the bullet wound on her stomach earlier, as if she could slow the bleeding with only a touch, as if something so horrifically deadly could be undone. Now her hand fell away. Her head slumped forward.

She couldn't move, could barely breathe, and yet she could feel the pain—and also the regret.

She'd done the right thing, hadn't she?

If she'd spoken up as a child, she'd have become a subject on an operating table. If she'd spoken up aboard *Odyssey*, the same would have occurred. They'd have turned her over to the authorities, or maybe not even believed her. And if she'd spoken up once the crew landed—when she found the *Laminaria achlys* or seen Toby's symptoms—she'd have been questioned, distrusted, suspected. At best, she would have ended up in an isolation chamber like Coen. At worst, she'd have been shot dead. Which was exactly what it had come to.

This was bigger than her. She'd had to sacrifice to ensure the safety of the Union. In the wrong hands, this could ruin a galaxy.

How she longed to explain that more thoroughly. It was likely she would now be viewed as the villain, and maybe she *had* damned the *Odyssey* crew. But it would have been worth it, had she developed a cure. Maybe Thea would do it in her absence. The research to understand the parasite was all there, and the girl was wise beyond her years. She just had to put it together. She just had to *see*.

The pain became white-hot and all-encompassing, and then it was gone.

The world went startlingly quiet, as though sound had been swallowed by the vacuum of space.

Lisbeth Tarlow's final thought was not of home or safety or a painless death. It was the same as before. She wished for more time. There was never enough time.

"We can't leave Thea," Nova yelled as she followed Dylan onto the bridge. "She's an intern, Dylan. She's not even out of high school."

"She's a Hevetz-trained science intern. If she's as smart as Tarlow has said, she'll follow us."

Nova looked over her shoulder, but Thea wasn't following. They'd already descended several floors to get to the bridge, and at the rate Dylan was pushing, they'd be off-planet within twenty minutes.

"Just look for a passcode, anything that might get us access to the admin quarters," Dylan said. Her expression was as stern and focused as ever. She'd just shot Lisbeth Tarlow in the stomach and didn't seem even remotely shaken.

The revelation that the doctor was infected had been shocking. Nova had been appalled, then furious. Tarlow had kept imperative information from them all, essentially damning some of their crew, and yet firing that bullet still seemed a step too far. They should have abandoned her on this rock to die. Or turned her over to Hevetz to become the experiment she so adamantly feared. But Dylan hadn't hesitated. As soon as she'd learned that Tarlow had betrayed them, she'd killed her. It was brutal. Merciless.

"Are you gonna help me or . . ." Dylan trailed off as one of the control stations blipped an alert.

A blueprint of *Celestial Envoy* filled the screen. A line flashed in the medbay, indicating that Isolation Three's air lock was open. But that didn't concern Nova. Thea had explained how she'd used that exit with Coen to escape a small group of infected. It was a second flashing line, down on the first level of *Celestial Envoy* that read *Main Hangar 01*, that concerned her.

"I closed Hangar One when we got back," Dylan said slowly. "You saw me close it, right?"

Nova nodded. "Do you think Coen and Cleaver made it back somehow?"

Dylan didn't answer. She simply tore from the bridge, and Nova followed.

Thea entered the medbay, her feet carrying her in a trance.

Dr. Lisbeth Tarlow was dead.

She couldn't wrap her head around it. She'd already been through this shock once, and it wasn't quite registering a second time.

Two frostbitten bodies were strapped down to the operating tables, their wrists slit. Most of the blood had found its way to the floor drains, but what hadn't now covered the floor in a winding, snaking pattern, drying beneath the overhead lights.

Well, at least part of the doctor's story was indeed true. Transporting these bodies from the hall and onto the tables alone must have been an exhausting feat. There were no needles near the bodies, but Dr. Tarlow's tremor would have prevented her from using them anyway. She must have gathered blood as they bled out. Effective, Thea could admit, if terribly messy.

She moved closer, examining the subjects. One was male, the other female. In the Trios tradition, both had a wedding band tattoo on their ring finger. The style had grown popular on the first generational ship that traveled for the Cradle, where classic bands weren't readily available. Instead, couples put their wedding date on their skin, the numbers encircling their fingers. Thea had seen a similar marking on Sullivan.

She turned for the computer, bringing up the most recently accessed report.

Results from subjects infected with Psychrobacter achli, Dr. Tarlow had entered into the summary overview. If Thea was remembering correctly, the genus *Psychrobacter* meant "cold-loving," and the species name the doctor had attached to it was clearly a nod to its origin on Achlys.

Thea scrolled through the report, scanning quickly until she found John Doe's file. She selected it, pulling the data onto the overhead monitor.

First, a brain scan complete with a looping animation of brain activity, with yellow patches marking firing neurons. It was unlike anything Thea had ever seen, nearly every section of the nervous system engaged and at work. The doctor must have recorded it before the man bled out. Thea swiped ahead, reviewing the blood work. Despite the impressive brain activity, John Doe's white blood cell count was freakishly low, his body trying to fight off an infection it wasn't going to win. Put simply: John Doe was dying.

Thea pulled up the woman's files. They looked incredibly similar. Jane Doe's white blood cell count was a touch higher, but still dangerously outside the average range. Thea didn't understand how this data was supposed to help her. It certainly didn't seem worth dying for. There was something Dr. Tarlow had seen that Thea was missing.

She closed the report, then paused.

There were results for a third subject in the report. *Lisbeth*

Tarlow, the file read. Thea opened it hurriedly, ignoring a visor alert that put her oxygen at twenty percent.

When the brain scan appeared on the screen, Thea couldn't keep her jaw from dropping. It was the same as the others, if not *more* impressive. Whole sections of the brain illuminated, neurons firing as though working overtime. It was unbelievable. Impossible. The doctor had entered a single note into her file: *Activity level in thalamus unexpected—tremor source?*

Thea frowned, moving on to the doctor's blood work. It confirmed what she already knew: that the woman had been the picture of good health. Her white blood cell count was perfect. She wasn't fighting any type of infection.

It's looking for a match. . . . It's looking for . . .

The truth slammed into Thea.

Symbiosis.

They weren't dealing with a parasite as she'd first hypothesized. It appeared that way, but in truth, the bacteria was looking for a host it could coexist with. Most often, it failed, driving the host mad and compelling that person to attack another potential host, passing on by blood. But for some reason, Dr. Tarlow had been a perfect match. She'd been able to offer *Psychrobacter achli* something everyone in Black Quarry—and her own parents—couldn't: a suitable home.

After that, she'd dedicated her life to trying to cure herself, to remove the bacteria lurking in her body. She'd lived an isolated life, cut off from family. She'd never married. Never dated. Never risked contact with another soul for fear of starting an outbreak. The doctor had spent decade after decade at research facilities in cold locations that mimicked Achlys's environment, searching for a clue that might help her solve the puzzle that was herself, and perhaps protect others, too.

If a contagion of this magnitude exists on Achlys, it's only a matter of time until it, or something similar, appears elsewhere.

Why, then, had she never enlisted the help of others?

She clearly wasn't a mindless host meant to pass the bacteria on. If her blood work was clean, she was safe. If her blood . . .

Thea bolted upright.

Her blood!

She grabbed a set of medical gloves and shot for the hall. Pulling them on over her suit, Thea carefully removed the doctor's helmet, then unzipped her suit and wrestled it down until Dr. Tarlow's arms were exposed.

On the top of the woman's left forearm was a faint white line, running from elbow to wrist. Her tremor would have prevented her from finding a vein with a needle, but she'd needed to extract blood, and so she'd simply cut herself. Thea stared at the faint line in disbelief. The cut had already healed, and not even as a scab, but as a faded scar. As though it were a wound that had happened months ago.

Thea pulled the suit down farther, revealing the gunshot wound in Dr. Tarlow's abdomen. Her undershirt was a bloody mess. Thea lifted the sticky material. Where there should have been a bullet hole, there was only blood. She wiped it away with her gloved hand to expose the skin underneath. Pale. Fresh.

Thea scrambled to her feet.

It was impossible.

The doctor had healed. As though the bullet hole was nothing but a paper cut, her skin had rejoined and mended. Even the faint shadow of the wound would probably have faded over the next hour if the doctor were still alive. Which she wasn't. Thea crouched down and put her fingers to the woman's neck, confirming there was no pulse.

But then . . . If Dr. Tarlow could regenerate skin and patch a bullet wound, it must have been the internal bleeding that killed her. Healing the entry point of the bullet wouldn't stop her from continuing to bleed out internally. A vital organ must have been hit, the damage too severe to reverse.

When had the woman discovered this ability? Thea wondered. A paper cut that closed instantly? A more serious wound that should have landed her in a hospital, but instead righted itself in the course of an hour? Come to think of it,

Thea couldn't remember ever seeing a single scar on Dr. Tarlow's person. The woman barely even had wrinkles. She had never looked her age.

This was why she'd been afraid to tell the truth, Thea realized. These miraculous side effects.

Hevetz would have reported news of the bacteria to Galactic Disease Control. Dr. Tarlow would have been studied, prodded. When the Union discovered she could regenerate skin faster than a Seckin bandage, she'd have become an experiment. In trying to replicate her, they'd have started an epidemic. If the odds of symbiosis here had taught Thea anything, it was that only one in several thousand were a match for *Psychrobacter achli*.

And the tremor . . . It had only started a few years ago, according to what Thea had been told. Perhaps it was a sign that the doctor's body had served its time as host, that the bacteria was beginning to itch for a new home and she would soon be compelled to pass it on.

Nobody lived forever, but the bacteria—with a new host—potentially could.

Thea stripped off her gloves and dropped them on the floor. The Company could never know about this. Same for the Union. They wouldn't be able to leave the knowledge alone. They'd comb Achlys for Dr. Tarlow's body. They'd gather water from ravines and beneath ice sheets. They'd unleash a plague on the Union, on the galaxy.

There was no cure that Thea could see. Perhaps Dr. Tarlow had come up with a few ideas, but they'd died with her. There was nothing in the medbay but a few brain scans and blood samples. The cure was to bury all of it—the doctor's findings, *Celestial Envoy*, Black Quarry. The cure was to leave while they could and never look back.

She had to get to the shuttle. She'd wasted too much time already.

Thea raced back into the medbay to scrub the data. As she pulled it up, a finger hovering over the *delete* prompt, something moved behind her.

She turned, ever so slowly.

Someone was climbing through the open air lock and into Isolation Three.

Nova and Dylan closed in on Main Hangar One, pulling up at the interior air lock door and peering through the small window. The far door was open, exposed to the elements, and someone was slumped over the control panel, back to them as he attempted to open the interior door. How he'd even managed the first door was a mystery. Dylan had locked them for security measures. They were only accessible from the inside.

"Coen?" Dylan said to Nova.

It sure couldn't be Cleaver standing there, not when both his legs had been broken.

"How the hell did the kid make it out of that mess alive?" Dylan muttered.

Nova had wondered the same on the bridge, but hadn't bothered to truly dissect the question. Now she felt the wrongness down in her bones.

"Something's wrong," Nova said, backing away from the door. "We should go."

Dylan gave her a sharp look, and Nova could understand the hypocrisy of it all. The captain was the one who constantly abandoned, who ran, who put herself above others. It wasn't Nova who typically argued for this path. But there was only one person Nova could think of who was capable of overriding security protocols, only one member of their team who could have hacked his way through locked doors.

The interior air lock whined and the doors began to part.

The crew member inside turned away from the panel, revealing his face.

Toby.

Thea grabbed for her stun gun, only to remember Dylan had borrowed it. Her hands flew over the counters, scattering vials and operating tools as she searched for the shock rod.

The interior door was closed and could only be opened

from her side of the medbay, but Thea didn't wait to see if it would hold under the onslaught of whatever was climbing into the chamber. As soon as the shock rod was in her grasp, Thea sprinted for the hall.

"It's me! Wait, Thea, it's me!"

She froze, glanced over her shoulder.

Coen Rivli stood in the isolation chamber.

Impossible.

She blinked, and he was still standing there, suit stained with blood, visor smeared where he'd wiped some clear. The orange backpack was slung over his shoulders, and what Thea could see of the pickax's curved metal looked wet.

"The hangar was closed," he explained. "This was my only way in."

"But you fell," she managed. "All those things . . ."

He motioned to the pickax.

They can die. Broken neck, suffocation, blood loss—all the normal stuff. But who'd want to get close enough to deliver one of those outcomes?

"Cleaver?" she asked.

He shook his head.

"And you're . . . None of them touched you?"

"I'm fine. Let me in."

She didn't move.

"Thea, come on. I'm not messing around. Open the door."

"There were a dozen of them," she muttered. "Maybe more."

"Look at me." He slapped the glass that separated them so hard, Thea flinched. But it was effective. Her gaze came up to meet his. Coen's brows were drawn, his eyes urgent. "There's no breach in my suit. See?" He turned around, arms held out. "You can search it yourself if you open the door."

It was impossible. One boy against all those things. Even if they were unarmed and slow, he should have injuries. *Something.* The nosebleed should have started by now.

She took a step away from the chamber, dread flooding through her.

Thea saw the truth. God, she had been so stupid. Dr. Tarlow had seen it, but Thea hadn't. A naive intern, she'd missed the obvious.

"It's in you, too," Thea whispered.

"Bloody nose, hemorrhaged eyes, uncontrollable attacks on your own crew. Does that sound like me?"

"It presents differently in some people."

"Thea, I'm fine," Coen insisted. He shed his backpack and let it fall at his feet. With his hands held in surrender he said, "Please just open the chamber. You can search me. I won't move a muscle."

But that wasn't the issue. She knew she wouldn't find any

injuries. If he was like Dr. Tarlow, every cut would be healed, any bruise invisible. She remembered the pristine state of his bare hands when she'd first met him in the bunker, how he didn't have the scrapes or cuts typical of most drillers.

But if he was like Dr. Tarlow, it also meant he was still in control of his mind. He didn't pose an immediate threat. She opened the door.

It slid to a silent stop, and true to his word, Coen remained motionless, hands clasped behind his head.

"Go on," he said. "You're not going to find anything."

True. She was going to *prove* something.

She moved cautiously into the chamber. Coen's forehead was slick with sweat behind his visor. Dark hair had fallen from his bun and now lay matted against his temples. Even in full gear, Thea didn't dare touch the blood on his suit. She searched with her eyes, working her way from where the helmet sealed at the suit collar and down over his shoulder, chest, waist, legs. There was no breach that she could see. And if there was, she was starting to suspect that it wouldn't matter.

"Satisfied?" he said.

It was then, with his guard lowered, that she brought the live shock rod to his back.

He buckled to a knee, grimacing. He should have been splayed out—writhing, jerking, screaming—but he only braced his palm against the floor, teeth gritted. The shock continued until the fail-safe kicked over, momentarily cutting the charge to ensure the person on the other end was merely stunned, not sent into cardiac arrest.

Coen sprung to his feet, wheeling on Thea with frightening speed. He deflected the shock rod, snatching it away and catching her at the wrist with his other hand. "What the hell are you playing at?" he snarled, pulling her close.

The strength to withstand that shock, to battle a dozen or more infected, to walk away without a scrape. The way Coen always seemed to be able to see things in the dark that she couldn't, hear things before the rest of the group. How he'd almost left the bunker without a suit, maybe because the environment barely affected him anymore.

Abnormal strength.

Miraculous healing capabilities.

Incredible eyesight and hearing.

On the surface, impossible, and yet, each ability was one that a species would need to survive on Achlys. Almost as if Coen had become a product of this planet, as if the bacteria had made him in its own image. Thea hadn't seen these abilities present in Dr. Tarlow beyond quickened healing and slowed aging, but she was willing to bet the doctor had just been better at hiding them. Or perhaps, she had not needed to utilize them. And if the tremor was a sign of the bacteria running its course, her inability to overpower

Sullivan and Toby in Isolation One might have been the same.

But there was one thing Coen and Dr. Tarlow had in common: they'd both been young when they were infected.

Could it be that simple? The bacteria simply needed a young host, a body already going through an array of hormonal changes and ready to adapt.

I'm sorry for lying to you, the doctor had said. *If I'm right . . . you were never at risk, not truly.*

Coen's grip tightened on Thea's arm, still waiting for an answer. She didn't doubt that he could break her wrist if he wanted.

"It's in you," she said finally, "just like Tarlow."

Coen swallowed.

"Instead of driving you mad like the others, it made you . . . more."

He looked away, let go of her arm.

"How long have you known?" she asked.

Silence.

"How long have you been lying to me?"

When he faced her again, his expression was pained. He was just like Dr. Tarlow, hiding the truth, endangering everyone to protect himself.

"Pitch Evans knew," she said. "That's why he wrote what he did."

"Thea," Coen said, his voice rough like gravel beneath a heel.

"Don't you dare say you're sorry. Answer my question. How long have you known?"

To explain, he had to go back.

Back to when he and the engineer were the only two sane ones left. Or at least, to when it felt that way. There was no telling how many had fallen to the parasite then, but they'd known it was bad. Comms on Celestial Envoy were down and malfunctioning, and the place was swarming with infected.

Coen had suggested contacting Hevetz from the old Witch Hazel bunker. The engineer agreed it was worth a shot. They took a rover, and the infected chased them on foot.

At the bunker, they found an honest-to-god pistol with a few bullets remaining but no working comm lines. After much deliberation, they decided to return to the bridge, record an SOS message, and set it to continually loop. If there was a break in the signal disruption, it might get out. It was a long shot, but gambles were all they had left.

When they returned to the rover, things went to hell. A group of bloody-eyed workers attacked. One managed to tackle Coen to the earth and wrestle off his helmet. He remembered the burning scorch of cold that hit his cheeks. It hurt worse than the fingernails that had gouged his neck.

The engineer wasted a precious bullet to save Coen, and then, in the rover, he watched Coen with a pointed gaze. They waited. The symptoms never came.

Later, Coen had wondered if the joint-suicide offer had less to do with mercy for them both and more to do with eliminating him. There was only one pistol, after all. The engineer had said he'd shoot Coen, then take care of himself. But perhaps he'd been lying.

In the weeks following Pitch Evans's death, Coen had thought it all a lucky twist of fate. Maybe he'd never been infected at all. Maybe he was somehow—miraculously—immune.

He explained away the oddities he began to experience. He'd gone so long without proper sunlight that his eyes had simply adjusted to the darkness. The freezing temperatures were so constant, they'd become nothing more than an annoying chill. After working months at the drill and fighting off relentless infected, his newfound strength was just a product of his labors. He truly believed this logic.

Still, he'd known the Odyssey crew wouldn't trust him if he'd told them the full story. It was too flimsy, too suspicious. And so he'd lied. He'd done horrible things to survive, yes. Probably, he would do more. But he honestly believed he was not infected.

That changed when he met Dr. Lisbeth Tarlow.

You're an official Hevetz employee, she'd asked when Thea wanted to release him from Isolation Three, are you not?

He had nodded, hoping that the motion looked convincing.

Why does it need to be convincing? *she'd asked, only her mouth hadn't moved.*

He froze, thinking he'd imagined it.

The doctor cocked her head at him, lips pinched, and then he heard her again. Are you lying about something?

She was in his head, speaking directly to him.

Impossible.

I'm seventeen, *he thought.* I changed my age so I could get the job.

She regarded him blankly. Of course she couldn't hear his thoughts. So foolish, to assume he'd heard words her lips never formed, to assume their thoughts were somehow linked.

And then, her response, cold and calculating: Well, isn't that interesting.

The doctor turned away, as though the private exchange hadn't happened, as if it was the most natural thing in the entire world, and answered Thea's original request. Aloud.

That's when he knew.

The doctor was infected, and so was he, only not in the same way as all the others.

IX

THE GAUNTLET

Celestial Envoy

Achlys, Fringe-1 System

TOBY'S ARM CAME FORWARD WITH frightening speed, closing over Dylan's wrist and yanking the woman into the air lock before toggling the door again.

Nova had one last look at the captain—the fear behind her visor as she shouted something unintelligible—before Dylan was dragged to the ground, disappearing from view as the doors slammed shut.

Nova stared, frozen in shock. Cleaver and Coen were as good as dead. They had to be, because Toby was wearing one of *their* suits. He'd stripped it off a dead body—cunning, sly— and used it to get close to them. And now Dylan was doomed.

It was over.

Nova needed to run.

For the briefest moment, she almost did. Then she thought of Dylan's grit and determination, and how she did not want to deal with a twisted version of the captain hunting her. But here, where she had them in an enclosed space . . . Nova could take out both threats waiting behind that air lock door. If she could use her ray-rifle to hold them off long enough to get her hands on the pistol Dylan had used to shoot Tarlow, Nova could end things right here.

She lunged for the controls and toggled the door.

It flew open.

Dylan was on her back, trying to fend off Toby, who had straddled her as he attacked. Both of their helmets had been removed, and Dylan's neck was red with blood.

Nova threw a blast at Toby, propelling him off Dylan. As he twitched momentarily, she trained her weapon on the captain. Their eyes locked. Dylan's were shockingly blue and frighteningly wide.

"Nova," the captain breathed, and Nova knew she couldn't do it.

It was still Dylan. The pain in her expression was too real. The way she continued to mutter Nova's name while crawling for the safety of the hangar, too desperate.

Nova couldn't pull the trigger. Her ray-rifle twitched to the right, finding Toby's form.

She fired another shot. He lurched away. Behind him, staggering toward the ship, was a cluster of infected. Twenty—maybe thirty of them, even—back from the ravine.

Dylan dragged herself over the threshold of the air lock, and Nova toggled the door as fast as possible. But Toby was quicker—lunging and grabbing. His hand closed over Dylan's boot. With a yank, she slid backward, finding herself in the way of the closing doors. She screamed as they slammed shut on her ankle.

A fail-safe kicked in, opening the door.

Nova should have grabbed the pistol from Dylan's waist and put a bullet in both of them. Right then. No questions asked. Sacrifices were necessary sometimes. It was a lesson drilled into her at the Academy. You might have to abandon a fellow pilot to save a dozen more. And those things were making their way up the gangplank. Soon it wouldn't be just a single threat Nova would have to deal with, but dozens.

But as the doors lurched open, Nova threw a final blast at Toby, grabbed Dylan, and pulled her to safety before the door slid shut for good.

"I didn't trust Tarlow," Coen explained. "Once it was obvious she was like me—that we'd been changed by whatever *it* is . . . Well, I assumed she was working for the Company. That maybe they knew what happened here during Witch Hazel and didn't care. Black Quarry could have been an experiment. Everyone was expendable in the hopes of finding people who could withstand the contagion like Tarlow. Can you imagine what the Union would pay for a discovery like this? The military would want to exploit it for the increased strength and pseudo—night vision alone, but for telepathic abilities? Think about it, Thea."

She *was* thinking. About all of it. Especially Pitch's warning.

"Tarlow was working only for herself," she said finally, and explained how she'd encountered her in the labs and uncovered the truth right before Dylan shot her. Coen said nothing. In fact, he didn't look that surprised, which made Thea wonder if maybe he'd known all along that the doctor was fine in that isolation chamber with Sullivan and Toby. Coen could have heard her thoughts, been assured she was healing. Sullivan and Toby might have even sensed that she wasn't worth the fight, turning their backs on her to instead home in on Thea in the medbay.

"What else have you lied about?" she asked Coen.

"Nothing."

"Did you cut *Odyssey*'s comm lines?"

Silence.

"Did you cut them, Coen?"

"Yes, okay. That was me. At the time, I thought that if you guys were able to contact Hevetz, they'd quarantine the whole planet, and we'd all be stranded. So I trashed the tech while you cased *Celestial Envoy*. I planned to meet you guys there, but then I saw you heading for the drilling base, and the storm was coming. I went to the bunker to wait it out."

"Why should I trust a single thing you've said?" Thea erupted. "You're just like Dr. Tarlow! You put yourself above the safety of our crew—above the safety of entire systems! You kept the truth from us, and we would have taken you back to the Trios while you're a carrier."

"So you're going to just leave me here, then?"

"Yeah, I think I am."

"Then you better be prepared to stay, too."

"Are you threatening me?"

"No, I'm reminding you of how I saved your ass. Mouth-to-mouth resuscitation, remember? I'm no fancy science intern, but correct me if I'm wrong: a contagion spread by a bodily fluid such as blood might just as easily be spread by saliva."

She reached for her lips, vision narrowing. Her hand merely came up against the glass of her helmet. The helmet he'd removed to save her.

"How long?" Thea gasped out.

Coen's brows pitched.

"How long before you started to notice changes?"

"I don't know, a couple hours, half a day? It got easier to move through the vents and avoid the others. It was like I could sense their presence. I think that's how it started."

Thea checked her watch. It had been roughly seven hours since she'd set foot on Achlys. Maybe four since he'd revived her.

"Can you communicate with them the way you

communicated with Dr. Tarlow?"

"No. They're just . . . loud. Like static. It gave me the worst headache. That's another reason why I went to the bunker."

"Can you communicate with me?"

"We wouldn't be having this conversation out loud if I could." A pause. "Then again, it hasn't been long enough since I . . ." His gaze trailed to her mouth.

There was no way to prove his theory wrong, to insist the contagion was passed only by blood. Dr. Tarlow must have feared that it could spread by saliva. She'd never dated, after all. Never married, shared a home, settled down. She'd lived an isolated life.

The shock rod slipped from Thea's hand, clattering to the floor. She staggered, feeling for the lip of the counter, desperate for something to support her. Her hand missed the edge, and Coen was suddenly in front of her, his palms pressed into her shoulders, holding her upright. Their helmets bumped.

"I swear I didn't know. I didn't know it was in me until I met Tarlow."

She pulled back, turned away.

"And even if I *did* know, I'm not sure I'd have done anything different," he added. "It was let you die or risk you becoming . . . *this*." He flicked a hand at his torso.

What was he, exactly? Just earlier, Thea would have

answered "a boy," but now he seemed frighteningly foreign. Was he still human if he could do inhuman things? Was he a monster wearing familiar skin?

The answer didn't matter, couldn't change the predicament they now faced.

"We can't leave, Coen," Thea said, quietly.

"Sure we can."

"It's irresponsible. Unforgivable."

"No, no, listen to me," he urged, grabbing her shoulders again. "We get out of here, and we don't tell a soul what happened. We'll set *Celestial Envoy* to self-destruct. We'll bury the evidence. And then you figure out a cure, a treatment, something. We purge it from me—you, too, if that becomes necessary—and then it's over. Tarlow managed to not infect anyone for decades. We can be careful for a few months."

His voice was almost joyful, the words said with such promise. He believed this fairy tale, this hopeful vision. Coen held her gaze for an uncomfortably long moment, and Thea tensed, praying his voice didn't whisper something in her mind. And just as she wished for silence, she could tell he was wishing for a connection, that he wanted so badly to not be alone.

"Thea, please. You have to be with me on this. Neither of us will get home if we don't twist the truth a little. The Company already sold out Black Quarry. If we don't look out for ourselves, no one will."

She considered, suddenly, if *this* was why Hevetz had sent an additional backup team to meet *Odyssey*'s crew. Maybe Toby's theories were completely wrong. Maybe it never had anything to do with the Radical movement and locking in an independent rock. Perhaps Hevetz had merely been searching for more corrarium, its intentions loyal to the Union, and it was only when they discovered the potential weapon housed on Achlys that their motives changed.

If the Company learned of the immunity that Coen and Dr. Tarlow possessed, they'd likely look to exploit it for their own means. And if the Trios military became involved . . . It would mean enhanced soldiers, just as Coen had said. Teen soldiers. Kids who likely wouldn't even get a say in the thing they'd be forced to become.

But what scared Thea above all else was how quickly things could go wrong. Just the smallest error could unleash an irreversible horror.

Maybe a lie was truly worth the risk.

If Dr. Tarlow had managed to live among people for five decades without incident, Coen could do it, too. Thea could also, if it came to that, and maybe even find a cure in the process. But stranding themselves on Achlys would solve nothing. There was a backup rescue crew already headed their way. They'd dig, unearth, meddle.

Keep it contained, Dr. Tarlow's mother had said in the video.

Best if there was no remnant of Black Quarry for others to investigate.

"If we do this," Thea said to Coen, "we need to get our stories straight. Because Hevetz is going to have questions. They're going to grill us, so I need to know everything that happened here. You keep nothing else from me. Understood?"

He paused, head tilting slightly.

"I said, understood?"

He moved a finger to his lips, then mouthed two words: *They're coming.*

Nova didn't think, she reacted.

She slung the rifle over her shoulder, then yanked Dylan's arm behind her neck and heaved the woman to her feet. Nova ran, rifle banging against her hip, Dylan muttering swears. She didn't slow until she realized her fear had sent her in the wrong direction, panic driving her far from the air lock, instead of toward the stairs.

Nova glanced around. She was deep in the hold, a door marked *Engineering Service 04* waiting just ahead. Behind them, the hangar door creaked open.

There was no time to go back.

She had to hide.

Nova pushed into engineering and secured the door. Peering through a small window, she watched Toby make his way into the hangar, limping slightly. He'd been injured at some point, potentially in the scuffle back near *Odyssey*. The mob of infected workers followed him.

Nova stood deathly still, holding her breath as Toby scanned the overrun hangar. Then his attention snapped to the far stairwell, and he staggered out of sight, moving deeper into the ship with the others on his heels.

Nova exhaled, letting Dylan slump to the floor. But there was no time to feel relieved, no time to feel safe. She grabbed the pistol from the captain's utility belt and trained it on her.

"You gonna shoot me?" Dylan grunted out.

Nova stared down the barrel.

The woman was taking shallow breaths, trying to breathe through the pain. The thrum of emergency generators and power reactors reverberated overhead. Nova tilted her head back, trying to see where the engine room ended. It was a mess of catwalks and service ramps, tech that dwarfed her like an ant. Her gaze snapped back to Dylan, waiting for the tremor, the nosebleed.

"If you're gonna do it, just *do it*," Dylan growled.

The weapon quivered in Nova's grasp. Her finger wasn't even near the trigger anymore. She couldn't. If the captain was showing symptoms it would be different. But right now she was still Dylan Lowe, and for all Nova's dreams about flying for the military and blasting ships into dust, it turned out killing a person was damn near impossible when you had to look them in the eye. Nova lowered the weapon.

The captain leaned against the wall, panting. "Fuck, it's hot in here."

The external temperature reading on Nova's visor confirmed it. Horrifically hot. Middle-of-the-summer hot. Nova just couldn't feel it in her controlled suit.

Dylan unzipped hers, pulling her arms out and letting the rest hang around her waist. Her undershirt was drenched in sweat, clinging to her frame. Her neck was covered in enough blood that Nova couldn't make out the wound itself.

"You should put pressure on that," Nova said, nodding at the injury, but Dylan just went on stripping, kicking off her boots, forcing the suit down over her hips. When she got to her bad ankle, she collapsed back against the wall, cursing.

Nova should have told her to put the suit on, to stay protected, but with the captain's helmet lost back in the air lock, there was no point.

"I'll get it," she said instead, peeling the suit over Dylan's ankle as gently as possible.

The captain yelled in response. Her ankle was surely broken. The joint was already swollen, Dylan's foot jutting out at an awkward angle.

Nova looked away. "We need to get you to the medbay,"

she said, staring at the door. "That cut on your neck needs a Seckin."

"It's not deep. And if we're going to the medbay, it's so you can put me in isolation."

"I could leave you right here if I wanted you isolated, Dylan. I don't think you can even walk."

Teeth gritted, sweat beading down her forehead, Dylan sat, then grabbed hold of a nearby service ladder and used it to heave herself up until she was more or less standing, bad leg hovering a few centimeters from the floor.

Stubborn brat.

"Why are you still here, Nova?" Dylan asked.

She glanced at her watch. Four minutes, and still no nose-bleed.

"Because I can't leave someone behind. Not when there aren't symptoms."

Can't leave someone behind, Sullivan whispered in her ear, *or can't leave* her?

"Can you do it if you have to?" Dylan asked. Her gaze flitted to the pistol.

"Yes. Absolutely," Nova said, not sure if it was a lie. Dylan didn't look like the person Nova was used to working with anymore. Fully clothed or suited up, the captain always appeared assertive, strong. But now, standing barefoot in the engine room, wearing only a tank top, spandex shorts,

344

and that thin silver bracelet on her wrist, Dylan appeared desperate. Scared. Small. Sweat dripped from her limbs. Her eyes were hollow.

Nova checked her watch.

Five minutes.

Maybe Dylan wasn't infected at all. Toby had attacked Dylan while wearing a suit, and maybe none of his blood had come in contact with Dylan's. Maybe the blood Nova had seen all over the suit was only Cleaver's or Coen's.

Nova moved to the door she'd used to enter the room and nudged it open. In the distance, she could make out the interior air lock door. It was open, but there was no one in sight, no movement in the hangar.

"Come on," she said. Hopping on her good foot, Dylan made her way to the door. Nova grabbed the captain's arm and hooked it behind her own neck.

"You're a better person than me," Dylan said. There was a softness to her tone that hinted at sincerity. Nova turned, the glass of her helmet grazing Dylan's nose. If it wasn't for that helmet, she might have considered kissing her. Instead, Nova only said, "I know."

Dylan would have left anyone else in the engine room by now, or maybe even shot them. She'd shot Tarlow after all. Nova expected an argument from Dylan, but the captain simply smiled. Wide and sincere, as though she wasn't experiencing an ounce of pain. The smile lasted only an instant, but it was there. That was three and a half in a single day. A new record, on possibly the *worst* day either of them had ever lived to see. Something was wrong with this woman.

Nova checked her watch. Six minutes and still no nose-bleed.

She shouldered her way out of the engine room, cursing her inability to leave a crew member behind. Perhaps she would have made a fine fighter pilot after all. She wouldn't have sacrificed one to save a dozen. She'd have been just like her father—sacrificing herself to save all thirteen.

Who? Who's coming? Thea wanted to ask.

But deep down, she knew. More infected had returned from the drilling base and had somehow made their way into the ship.

Thea transferred what she could of Dr. Tarlow's research to a nearly dead Tab and tossed it in a duffel Coen had found in one of the cabinets. After securing the unused blood samples in a sturdy traveling case, she packed those as well. Then she located the radio Dylan had left with Tarlow. It was still sitting beside the computer, right where the doctor had left it while she and Thea took blood samples in Isolation One.

"Dylan, Nova," she said into the device. "Do you copy?"

It was quiet a moment, then Nova's voice crackled back through the radio. "We're here."

"Meet me at the shuttle ASAP."

"On our way."

Coen gave Thea a nod, and she hooked the radio on her utility belt. Then she threaded her arms through the straps of the duffel so she could wear it like a backpack and followed him from the medbay.

They ran.

Coen's route was sporadic, filled with abrupt turns that took them away from the bridge before moving closer, sometimes going up a flight to then descend several more, only to go up again. Thea felt like a mouse in a maze, but then they were spilling onto the bridge and a new challenge awaited.

"Here," Coen said, leading her to a central command station. Three dials and one large lever were secured behind a panel of tinted glass. An eight-digit passcode was needed to open the compartment and initiate the self-destruct sequence.

Before Thea could so much as groan in defeat, Coen was punching in the necessary numbers.

"About a month back, I used the vents to access the commander's room," Coen explained. "I was hoping to find his passcode, but no such luck. Only an idiot would write it down. I did learn a bit from his files, though, and I started trying certain numeric combos, like addresses and birth-dates. I hit gold with this one." He nodded at the keyboard. "Turns out Commander Lowe's passcode is his daughter's birthday."

"You've done this before?" Thea said, staring at the now-open compartment.

Coen's mouth hardened. "Some days were horrible. I had no hope, no reason to go on. I just wanted it to end. I was too scared to try Pitch's gun. What if I fucked up and ended up dying some slow, awful death? But this seemed foolproof." He turned the three dials to *Engaged*. A prompt reading *Throw lever to initiate countdown* appeared, and the panel that had originally accepted his passcode refreshed with a clock bearing twenty minutes. "By the time I got this far, I always thought of Gina. How I couldn't help her if I was dead."

Coen raised a brow and nodded at the lever. "Well?" A red label reading *DANGER* was positioned across the palm-width handle, as if someone could get this far and not realize they were toying with something dangerous.

"What if Dylan and Nova don't get to the shuttle? Or what if they beat us there?"

"If Dylan doesn't guess her father's passcode, they'll need us to access the shuttle."

"And if she *does* guess it?" Thea asked. The captain had already abandoned her twice.

"We have to be okay with maybe going down with the ship. Literally."

Thea's heart beat wildly.

"We don't have much time," Coen added, his gaze jerking toward the hall.

Thea stared at the handle they needed to throw. Was this really the only way? Even if they got off-planet, it was possible Thea would be destroying something she'd later need. She only had a portion of Dr. Tarlow's research, and Thea was just a student, an intern. She couldn't possibly solve this alone. And if she didn't or couldn't . . . If it got out . . .

The responsible path is often hard. It has consequences. It is never easy.

She reached out, grabbing the smooth metal of the handle.

"Together?" she offered, before she could lose her nerve.

Coen covered the back of her hand with his palm, his fingers curling over hers.

They looked at each other. Coen nodded.

Together, they pushed the lever up.

As Nova and Dylan hit the medical floor, the ship was thrown into a state of darkness. Every light that had previously illuminated halls and stairwells was replaced with vibrant red strobes, flashing in synchronization as a shrill alarm sounded. A recorded voice boomed through the ship.

"Evacuate immediately. The ship will self-destruct in twenty minutes."

Dylan swore. "What the hell?"

"Thea?" Nova said into the radio. "Is that you? Did you initiate that? Abort it. We need more time!"

They were nearly to the medbay, and Nova needed to treat Dylan's neck wound. She'd been relieved to hear the intern's voice on the radio just minutes ago, but had she known this was part of Thea's plan, she'd have argued against it.

Visibility was terrible, the red alarm lights flashing off every reflective surface. To make matters worse, the halls were now venting in preparation for the inevitable blast. Nova could barely see where she was going.

When they burst into the medbay, Nova let Dylan crumple to the floor and ran directly for the storage cabinets to locate a Seckin bandage. She found a whole box and flew back to Dylan.

There was no time to waste cleaning the wound. The bandage would do its job. Nova simply tilted Dylan's head to the side and applied a strip, Dylan wincing in response.

Nova stowed a few more of the bandages in her utility belt and hauled Dylan to her feet. It was all she could do for the captain at the moment. A critical neck wound would have left Dylan dead already, and the good news was the woman still didn't have a nosebleed. Lucky as all hell.

"Thea?" Nova said, trying again.

"I've got the access codes for the admin quarters," came her response. "Just get there fast."

"Abort that sequence, Thea!"

"I can't."

"Thea!"

Silence.

"We have to get to the shuttles," Dylan said wearily.

Nova frowned, watching the strobes flash through the ship. "Why even initiate it?"

"I think you know the answer to that question," Dylan gritted out.

Nova spun, scanning the hall beyond the medbay. She couldn't see anything in the flashing strobes and venting air. Toby was out there somewhere, roaming the halls with that team of infected.

Getting anywhere could prove a nightmare, and require backtracking and stealth. It could easily take twenty minutes to reach the shuttles. Nova pulled Dylan's arm behind her neck, stood, and staggered into the hall.

The countdown clock was active, milliseconds ticking off in a flurry.

"Let's go," Coen urged. "Central elevator isn't far."

"You said elevators were dangerous," Thea reminded him.

"We've got a window if we're quick."

As they ran, Nova's voice came through the radio, begging Thea to abort the self-destruct sequence. Thea refused, telling Nova to get to the shuttles and praying she would comply. Without the pilot, they were all dead.

Visibility was awful. The strobes had thrown everything into a distorted sort of reality, shadows growing and shrinking. As the ship vented, wires hanging overhead swayed. Thea's visor became a constant flicker of heightened pulse and body temperature, and a new alert appeared, informing her that her oxygen reserves had dropped to ten percent.

They spilled into another hallway, so long Thea couldn't make out the end. The sound of the doors sealing behind her never came and she turned, startled.

That's when something grabbed her leg.

She fell backward, pain shooting up her spine as she hit the floor and came face-to-face with the thing that had grabbed her. An infected medic. Frostbitten flesh, eyes like black holes, dried blood covering its neck. The thing was crawling—or had been. Now it was splayed out on its belly, both hands on Thea's ankle, clawing and scratching. Thea kicked frantically, catching the thing beneath the chin and then bringing the sparking shock rod to its torso. The infected hissed and rolled aside.

Thea scrambled away like a crab. Something grabbed

her arm, and she lashed out again, but it was only Coen. He caught her arm before she could strike a blow, then helped her to her feet. She looked back at the thing that had attacked her. It wasn't alone anymore. As the strobe came around again, shining light down the hall, Thea could make out a sea of infected coming toward them. Their skin was blistered and cracked, their limbs stiff with cold. Some were crawling, others staggering, their shoulders bumping as they filed into the hallway. They were slower and clumsier than any she'd encountered so far, but much greater in number.

How had they gotten onto the ship? Coen had said the main hangar doors were closed. Were they always on the ship, or had someone—Dylan, perhaps—been back through the hangar?

She didn't have time to dwell on it. Coen tugged on her arm, and she fled with him.

Barely a half dozen steps and she spotted more shadows moving at the opposite end of the hall. They were just as slow and clumsy as the ones behind her, but it wouldn't matter. Thea had only the shock rod, and Coen the pickax in his backpack. He'd been able to protect himself against those infected back at *Odyssey*, but could he do the same in a cramped hall, with more than double that number steadily approaching?

Evacuate immediately. The ship will self-destruct in nineteen minutes.

Air hissed around them, filtering into the hall.

"The vents!" Thea gasped out.

Coen's head swung back, searching overhead. He found the nearest grate and reached up, his height just barely allowing his fingers to graze the screws. He stripped them as easily as if he was unfastening a button. The cover fell to the ground.

He laced his fingers together and held them out to Thea. She put a boot into his hands and he heaved her up as though she weighed nothing. Her palms and forearms slapped against the metal of the ventilation shaft, causing her to lose hold of the shock rod. It clattered to the floor below.

"Keep moving to the right!" Coen ordered.

She pulled her feet into the vent, only to hear a sickening crack of bones below.

No.

But when she looked, expecting the worst, Coen was standing over a collapsed infected, the pickax buried in the thing's chest. With a yank, he tore it free. Before he could raise the weapon again, another infected was closing in. Coen swung with his opposite hand, brandishing a sword-like blade Thea wasn't aware he carried. It sliced through a neck. The pickax came swinging down on another infected, catching him in the skull.

He wielded the weapons like a dance, like they weighed nothing and as though he was indifferent to the blood he sent speckling the walls and spattering the floor. As if the deaths didn't bother him. As if a part of him almost craved it. Thea could barely watch.

There was another slash of the blade, and then Coen had his opening.

He jumped for the vent, hands reaching for the lip, and then he was beside her. "What are you waiting for!" he yelled, kicking at the hands that clawed after him. "Go!"

She tried, and was immediately snagged in place, the duffel on her back practically clinging to the walls of the narrow passage. Thea wrestled it off, her elbow knocking the radio from her hip in the process. She fumbled blindly, trying to locate it. "Forget it," Coen said, kicking again at the infected hands pawing at the opening. "Just move. Fast!"

Thea rolled onto her stomach, shoved the duffel bag ahead of her in the narrow vent system, and started to crawl. Almost immediately, the muscles in her back began to protest the awkward position. Her forearms and shoulders burned. It was a relief, in a way, to know she wasn't growing strong like Coen, that she'd been spared. And yet, at the same time, this blessing was a curse—slowing her, slowing *them*.

Thea could hear the grunting of the infected far behind

them, still trying to fight their way into the vents. If they figured out how to work together and lifted someone up, she might find herself infected after all.

The metal vibrated beneath her, from her own efforts and Coen's, but all Thea could picture was the things crawling after them.

As they passed over another grate in the vent system, Thea made the mistake of looking down. A sea of shiny, dark eyes stared back. The infected mob was following their process through the vents, heads tipped back and fingers reaching.

"Just keep going," Coen said. "We're faster. Unless they try to cut us off and climb in elsewhere, we're fine."

Thea nodded, not sure if he could even see the response. "The vent splits ahead," she told him.

"Stay straight. We're almost to the elevator."

There was another grate ahead. They'd have to cross it. *Don't look through the cover. Just keep moving.*

The cover rattled, shaking from the assault of the things below.

"Faster," Coen urged.

Evacuate immediately. The ship will self-destruct in eighteen minutes.

Thea nudged the duffel onto the grate, inched herself forward.

Something collided with the vents with a newfound force,

and the cover blew into the shaft. Thea yelped and grabbed the bag by an arm strap, pulling it back toward her. A head appeared in the vent opening and swiveled to face her.

Toby.

He smiled at Thea, blinked those blood-filled eyes.

"Left!" Coen screamed. "Go left!"

Thea lunged to the side, taking the other path in the ventilation system. Toby's hand grazed her boot. She kicked out, and when she felt his grip slip, she dared a look over her shoulder. Coen was following her, also kicking. He caught Toby in the face, and the technician dropped out of view, slipping through the grate.

"You said they were all dead—that you took care of everyone back near *Odyssey*!" Thea shouted.

"Clearly I was wrong!" Coen yelled back. "Keep moving. We need to get out of the vents!"

Thea saw another grate several meters ahead. She threw all her energy into reaching it, trying to ignore the crying fatigue of her muscles, the sting of her own sweat as it dripped into her eyes.

When she reached the next grate, Thea kicked it with all her strength. It buckled. Another stomp with her boot and it fell.

Thea poked her head through.

Tables overrun with rotten food. Aluminum counters

reflecting the red strobes.

The mess hall.

Evacuate immediately. The ship will self-destruct in seventeen minutes.

She threw the duffel down, then swung through and dropped to the floor. There was a soft thump as Coen landed beside her. He drew the pickax from his pack and passed the makeshift sword to her. Back-to-back, they turned in a circle, surveying.

They'd dropped into the front of the room. Just a few paces off was a sliding bay door to access the hallway, currently closed. In the opposite direction were row after row of abandoned tables. The same deceased crew members Thea had found when first casing the ship still lay slumped where they'd been killed.

A bloody hand slapped against the large trapezoidal window of the mess hall door. Then another. Thea took a step away, watching as more bodies steadily filled the hall. Overhead something creaked.

"Toby," she breathed.

It was only a matter of time before he entered the mess hall. She was willing to bet he was sharp enough to unlock doors, too. He'd let the rest of the mob in.

"The kitchen," Coen said, grabbing at her shoulder.

They raced between the rows of tables, cutting deeper into

the mess hall, toward a buffet counter in the rear where the crew would have received dinner. Coen didn't even bother sidetracking for the adjacent set of swinging metal doors. He braced his hands against the counter and vaulted up, sliding over the buffet and into the kitchen beyond.

Thea did the same, only not nearly as gracefully.

"There's a dumbwaiter," Coen said. He pulled down a metal curtain that connected with the counter and slid a latch, locking it in place. "They used it to send meals directly to the commander's quarters." He moved on to the next curtain, slowly sealing off the kitchen from the mess hall.

"We can use it to get to the shuttle," Thea said, understanding.

He nodded. "I'll barricade things here to slow them. You make sure it's clear."

Nova made her way down three flights, toward a hallway that she knew had access to the central elevator. The medical floor surely had access to it, too, but the steam was making everything look the same, and she'd decided to take a route she was confident in. Now wasn't the time to get lost. Especially not when she had Dylan still slumped against her, making every step more difficult than it should have been.

Exiting a stairwell, Nova surveyed her position. To her left was the half flight of stairs to access the bridge. She moved away from it, grunting as she supported Dylan's weight, and headed toward *Celestial Envoy*'s central elevator.

Everything appeared to be moving in the flashing lights.

Nova passed through a strong hiss of steam, and her heart dropped.

Something *was* moving. Just ahead. A whole horde of infected, shuffling along in the hall, their heads tilted back to survey the overhead vents. Fingers clawed lazily at the ceiling.

Evacuate immediately. The ship will self-destruct in sixteen minutes.

The way to the elevator was blocked. She'd have to back-track. Maybe she could even return to the bridge and abort the countdown. It wasn't that far, and she needed more time.

Eyes locked on the infected, Nova retreated silently. She stepped on something slick, nearly losing her footing. The thing—a shock rod, she realized—shot from beneath her boot and went skittering into the wall. Even with the alarm, the noise it created felt earsplitting.

Nova froze. Dylan tensed at her side.

And the things froze, too.

Slowly, the one closest to them turned, peering through the steam-filled hall. It couldn't see them. Nova breathed a sigh of relief.

Carefully, ever so silently, Nova took a step away.

The thing's gaze snapped onto her, alerted by her movement. It turned completely, and began shuffling in her direction. The others joined the pursuit.

They were slow, but it wouldn't matter. Nova was slow, too, and with Dylan slumped into her shoulder, she'd never be able to get off a clean shot.

Nova snatched up the shock rod and, tugging Dylan along with her, bolted back the way they'd come.

The bridge was a dead end, but the stairs . . . She burst onto the landing. Down would be faster than up, especially with the added weight of the captain.

They'd descended half the flight when Nova heard the things entering the stairwell.

The dumbwaiter looked like a miniature elevator. Little more than a meter and a half wide by two meters tall, Thea estimated. It should fit them both, but with their bags it would be exceptionally tight.

With the swordlike weapon Coen had given her held at the ready, Thea threw a switch and the door slid up. She leapt back, waiting for something to come spilling from inside. It was empty save for a serving cart. Thea grabbed the handle and towed the cart into the kitchen.

Evacuate immediately. The ship will self-destruct in fifteen minutes.

Summoning her nerves, Thea edged toward the now-vacant dumbwaiter. She ducked inside, scanning. There were no lights, no adornments to the panels. But no threats either. It was a plain, hollow cube.

Thea leaned from the dumbwaiter and shouted, "All clear!"

Coen was already running to join her. Behind him, the metal curtains groaned as fingers threaded through the grating and pushed. Coen had moved a tall industrial freezer in front of the swinging doors, which now rattled against the obstruction.

There were so many of them.

"How did they . . . ?"

"Toby came through the vents and opened the main doors. Let's go," he said, ushering her back into the dumbwaiter. "Those curtains won't hold forever."

They crammed inside, Thea's helmet pressing into Coen's chest. She stared at the blood there, the product of the things he'd slashed through like paper. He'd been so fast, so merciless, a boy-monster able to push his humanity aside in that moment. It scared her a little.

Evacuate immediately. The ship will self-destruct in fourteen minutes.

Coen triggered the button that would send the dumbwaiter up and quickly withdrew his arm into the car. The door slid down, locking them in darkness. As they began their ascent, Thea heard the sound of the curtains breaking, followed by the freezer Coen had moved crashing to its side.

There was no way of knowing how many infected were now pouring into the kitchen. She was alone in the darkness, isolated, her thoughts drowning her in that small space. The darkness leeched into Thea, and for the briefest moment she considered that she should drive the knife-sword into Coen's chest and leave him behind. *He* was the risk to the galaxy, not her. He was just like the research they were attempting to destroy—a thing that needed to disappear, something the Union could never find. But Thea's arms were pinned at her sides. There was no room to lift the weapon, and even if she could, he'd be too fast, deflecting any attack with ease. Still, the thought lingered there: *Leave him. He's too dangerous. He could spell the extinction of the human race.*

"Are you okay?" Coen asked, the car rattling around them.

No. Yes. Did you just hear my thoughts?

"Thea, are you okay?"

Relief flooded through her, and her helmet squeaked against his as she raised her head to look at him. The detached expression she'd seen when he fought in the hallway was gone, replaced now with something heavy. Concern. Sincerity.

"I'm fine," she said. "As fine as I can be."

He touched her elbow—such a simple gesture—and she cursed herself for even considering abandoning him. Monster or not, he was the only thing that had kept her alive, and here he was, trying to reassure her as she considered trying to murder him. The least she could do was repay the debt she owed. A life for a life.

Thea would get him off this rock.

No sooner had she had the thought than the car lurched to a halt.

"Are we there?" she asked.

"No," he said, brows dipping. "Something's wrong."

The things were following. Nova could hear them half walking, half falling after her.

She burst onto the next floor with Dylan in tow. The elevator waited down the hall, but it might as well have been a kilometer away. They'd never reach it in time.

She yanked open the door to a small utility closet, shoved Dylan inside.

Evacuate immediately. The ship will self-destruct in thirteen minutes.

Nova squeezed in after the captain and closed the closet door just as the first infected exited the stairwell.

● ● ●

"What do you mean, something's wrong?" Thea asked. "What happened?"

"They cut power to the lift."

Her stomach clenched with dread. "I thought they had no logic this far gone. That they'd use only force and—"

"Shh!" Coen cocked his head to the side, listening.

Even Thea could hear something, a clang and ping beneath them, like someone was moving into the shaft.

"Toby," Coen whispered. "The heartbeat is faster, and his thoughts are . . . louder. We have to climb."

"Climb? Climb where?"

Evacuate immediately. The ship will self-destruct in twelve minutes.

Coen looked at the overhead panel. He wriggled against her, until his arms were free of his sides. Reaching behind his head, he grabbed the pickax just below the pick and thrust it up and into the ceiling, which buckled slightly. Coen breathed out, thrust the pickax up again, and this time it punched clear through the material.

By the dim light of her helmet, Thea could make out the shape of the hydraulic rails that powered the lift: two slender cylinders that extended up, up, up; one on each side of the shaft. They disappeared into darkness. What she could see of the shaft appeared to be just as smooth and slick; no hand- or footholds.

Climb *this*?

With the pickax finally free of the bag, Coen went to work at the hole, making it wider. When it was large enough to allow them passage, he stowed the weapon, grabbed at the edges of the opening he'd made, and lifted himself through.

Then he turned and offered her a hand.

"I'll slow you down," she said, staring beyond him, at the dark passage that tunneled up. The climb looked nearly impossible. She wasn't sure she could do it at any speed, let alone the pace they'd need to set to outrace Toby.

"I don't care," he said. "We're doing this together. That's what we decided in the medbay."

She grabbed his hand, and with a yank, Coen pulled her up.

Thea glanced at her oxygen readings—eight percent left—then tilted her head back to observe the shaft.

Evacuate immediately. The ship will self-destruct in eleven minutes.

Nova blinked in the dark, holding her breath.

From the sound of it, the infected were moving away, heading toward the elevator, which was precisely where Nova and Dylan needed to go. But still, it was better than them attempting to open the closet.

Dylan whispered, "Where are they go—"

Nova clamped a hand over the captain's mouth, smothering the words. They couldn't risk talking, not yet. Nova waited and waited, her pulse readings flashing in her visor. When she could no longer hear the things moving in the hall, she let go of Dylan. "I think they're heading toward the elevator," Nova whispered. "Or maybe the mess hall?"

"Why?"

"Who cares. As soon as they've cleared out enough, we're making a run for it."

Dylan gritted out, "So we just wait?"

As if *Celestial Envoy* could hear their conversation, as if the ship knew exactly how dire every second was, the alarm repeated its warning: *Evacuate immediately. The ship will self-destruct in ten minutes.*

Climbing was simpler than Thea had anticipated. That was not to say that it was easy—not by a long shot—but the material of Thea's suit kept her sweat away from the metal and her grip on the hydraulic rail firm. And there happened to be footholds after all. Every meter or so guide brackets secured the hydraulic rail to the shaft wall. They weren't large, and they didn't stick out far, but they were enough. Without them, Thea would still be standing on the lift.

Roughly four guide brackets up, just as Thea was feeling confident that she could manage this despite her aching muscles, something sparked beneath her. She glanced down—beyond her feet, past Coen a bracket below, and to the dumbwaiter car. Something was cutting through the floor. A laser saw.

Toby.

"Faster!" Coen yelled.

But she couldn't go any faster. Her limbs were already shaking with exhaustion. The duffel on her back had seemed to triple in weight.

Below, the sparks completed their circle, and an oblong section of floor was shoved up and into the car. Toby's face appeared next, eyes glinting in the light of the still-flared laser cutter, skin taking on a sickly reddish hue. He passed the laser cutter to his mouth, a smile appearing around the handle before he dissolved into darkness, disappearing as the laser turned off.

The car rattled beneath them, echoing through the shaft as Toby climbed through the hole Coen had made in the ceiling.

"Move!" Coen roared.

Thea's exhaustion was suddenly inconsequential. It was there still—her limbs were still shaking—but the instinct to survive was stronger. Earlier, she'd taken her time. Now she lunged for each new bracket, relying on muscle memory to navigate the ascent. She trusted her balance to not fail her and refused to overthink each movement. Her eyes stung with sweat, the shaft blurring as she blinked it away.

Evacuate immediately. The ship will self-destruct in nine minutes.

Coen swung his pickax, and Thea heard a feral hiss. The rails suddenly vibrated beneath her palms as the dumb-waiter sputtered back to life. The infected in the kitchen must have figured out how to recall the car. Soon there'd be dozens of those things scuttling into the shaft, climbing. Even if Toby fell, there would be others to replace him.

Thea lunged again, her fingers skimming the next bracket. Grimacing, she pulled herself up, found a new foot-hold, repeated the process.

Ahead, a bracket slightly larger than the others protruded into the shaft: a limit switch, so the car knew where to stop. She could make out a square of dull light in the wall. That had to be the edges of the door that opened into the com-mander's quarters.

They were almost there.

Red light from Toby's laser cutter sputtered and pulsed as Thea reached for the door. She could hear the struggle beneath her but only guess at what was happening. Coen swinging his pickax. Toby lashing out in return with the laser saw.

Clinging to the limit switch and toes braced against

another set of brackets, Thea felt blindly along the edges of the doors. There had to be a control panel, some way to override things and open the doors manually. But this was only a dumbwaiter shaft. The passage was never meant to transport people, and it would have different emergency features from a standard elevator. If there were manual override controls, they'd be outside the shaft.

Thea dug her fingers into the seam of the door and pulled with all her strength. The doors parted to reveal a sliver of the commander's quarters. Dark, save for the red flashes of the self-destruct alarm. A food cart holding an uneaten meal sat just before the doors. Behind it, a sitting area and the edge of a bed.

Thea pulled harder, the doorway widening slightly. She'd never be able to hold it this way. If she tried to crawl through, the doors would snap shut on her.

Evacuate immediately. The ship will self-destruct in eight minutes.

"Give me the pickax!" she yelled to Coen.

"No way!" There was a *whoosh* and the sound of the weapon striking the side of the shaft. The hiss of an angry animal followed.

Thea glanced down, only to wish she hadn't. Just a bracket below her was Coen, and another bracket beneath him, Toby, the laser thrumming in his hand, reflecting a pinpoint of red at the center of each dark eye.

"Give it to me, or we don't get out of here!" she screamed.

Coen swung again at Toby. The technician slid down the shaft, catching himself at the next guide bracket.

"I know what I'm doing," she insisted.

He looked up at her, their eyes locking.

"You have to trust me." Just as he'd said before she leapt from the nose of the ship with him into darkness.

Something flashed across Coen's face. She couldn't read it in the poor lighting, but she knew he could read so much about her. A spiked heart rate, for instance. The way she blinked constantly because she couldn't keep eye contact. How she'd just swallowed, trying to force away the obvious truth: that he *shouldn't* trust her. Not fully. Not when she'd considered abandoning him just minutes ago. And she couldn't guarantee that this would work, couldn't promise that he'd be able to get into the room before Toby managed to get to him.

Coen had to see it.

From what she'd come to learn, Coen Rivli saw everything.

But he passed the weapon to her anyway, handle first, the spiked ends grazing his helmet as she drew it up. Thea wedged the pickax into the seam of the door and pulled back. The doors yawned open. With one hand, she shoved them open farther. With the other, she shoved the handle of the pickax in place, so it spanned the width of the door's threshold. It barely fit, the length just centimeters shorter than the doorframe was wide.

The doors clamped down on both ends of the weapon, but the pickax held.

"Hurry!" Coen shouted below her.

She heard a kick and a wild growl and then a scream from Coen. There was no mistaking the panic in that scream. It was similar to the noise Toby had made when injured at the drilling base.

Thea flung herself through the dumbwaiter door, colliding with the food cart. It wheeled away from her, drifting deeper into the commander's quarters. She rolled over and sat up, coming face-to-face with Coen. His hands were braced on the edges of the doorframe, his shoulders bulging with effort.

Evacuate immediately. The ship will self-destruct in seven minutes.

Thea flung an arm out, and Coen grabbed it. He weighed a ton, more than seemed humanly possible. Her arm flared hot with effort as she helped pull him into the room.

When his torso was safe, she lowered him to the ground, attention snapping to movement in the dumbwaiter shaft.

Toby. The technician had grabbed Coen's legs and was still hanging from them. He'd dropped the laser cutter at some point, but not before using it to slice through Coen's suit and into his calf, the muscle slit open like filleted meat. The blood was everywhere, on Coen's legs, his boots, covering Toby's arms.

Toby continued to use Coen like a ladder, pulling himself up, desperate to reach Thea. As his face came into view, jaws snapping, Thea kicked him as hard as she could. There was a nasty crack beneath her heel, and Toby reeled backward, letting go of Coen. His scream echoed as he fell down the shaft.

Thea tugged Coen fully into the room—he seemed to weigh nothing now—and then kicked again. This time, at the pickax. The weapon sprung free of its hold within the doorframe and flew into the shaft. It pinged and banged as it fell, the noise cut off as the doors slammed shut.

After waiting through three more cycles of the alarm, Nova finally nudged the door open. The hall was blessedly empty. Afraid to waste their opportunity, she slipped from the closet and raced for the elevator, Dylan hobbling at her side.

When they passed the only fork in the hallway, Nova spotted a few infected staggering from the mess hall. Sensing her movement, their heads snapped up.

Nova muttered a swear and ran on, knowing they were following.

She hit the call button on the elevator, each second

painfully slow. Dylan slumped into Nova's shoulder.

As the infected rounded the corner, the elevator doors parted. Nova dragged Dylan in, and as the car jolted to life, she enjoyed ten seconds of utter bliss, complete safety. It was over too soon.

The car slid to a halt at its destination, and the doors opened. Nova scanned the hallway with her rifle. The only thing moving through the steam was the flashing lights of the alarm.

"Come on," Nova said, dragging Dylan beside her. It was the right hallway at least. The nearest door was labeled with an administrator's last name. She tried the handle. Locked. She tried the quarters opposite it. Also locked.

Evacuate immediately. The ship will self-destruct in six minutes.

The elevator doors clicked shut, and the car immediately descended. If the infected had recalled it . . .

"Take this," Nova said, passing Evans's pistol to Dylan. The captain now had Thea's stun gun in one hand and the pistol in the other, but she didn't particularly look like she had the strength to lift or fire either. Her shirt was drenched with sweat, her eyes droopy. It was amazing she hadn't passed out yet. "Anything comes out of that elevator," Nova continued, "you shoot it."

Dylan nodded weakly.

Nova lowered the captain to the floor, then moved up the hall, checking each door as she went.

They were all locked.

If it wasn't for the pulsing evacuation lights, the commander's quarters almost looked untouched by the madness that had spread throughout the rest of *Celestial Envoy*. The bed was made. The glass walls of the shower glinted as if they'd just been cleaned. A food cart waited near the table, reflective lid still resting on a serving tray that surely held rotten food. The glass was full of frozen water.

Thea could almost imagine it. This meal had just arrived when word of Jon Li's injury reached Commander Lowe. He'd been called away to visit the medbay. He'd left the food, untouched, and never returned.

If only he'd boarded his shuttle instead.

Thea ran to the docking bay and peered through the air lock's small hexagonal window. A short-range shuttle waited on the other side. She could make out its modest interior, including the pilot seat and a portion of the dash.

A visor alert flashed, warning Thea that her oxygen reserves were at a dangerous five percent. She reached for the radio, only to remember she'd lost it in the vents.

If Nova didn't show up soon . . .

Evacuate immediately. The ship will self-destruct in five minutes.

She turned back to Coen. He was still slumped against the wall beside the dumbwaiter, legs stretched before him like a rag doll. Despite the horrific injury, he was no longer gritting his teeth through the pain.

Thea watched as he shook out his leg, flexed his foot. Then Coen wiped the blood from his injured leg and peeled the suit back. The cut from the laser was gone, his calf marred by nothing but a pale line. "Not gonna lie," he said with a smile. "That is the strangest sensation I've ever felt. Even stranger than hearing Tarlow's thoughts."

"Well, enjoy it," Thea said. "'Cause we're going to be incinerated in a matter of minutes."

A bang in the hallway drew their attention to the main door. Springing to action, they raced across the room, and Thea used the control panel there to view what waited on the other side: Nova, pounding frantically at the door, with Dylan slumped against her. One of the captain's legs dragged, limp and broken. She was no longer wearing a single piece of her suit, and she looked close to losing consciousness. Dried blood covered her neck and shoulder.

Worse still was what Thea spotted behind them: a team of infected, flashing in and out of visibility on account of the emergency strobes, crawling over each other, jaws snapping as they made their way up the hall.

Evacuate immediately. The ship will self-destruct in four minutes.

"Let them in!" Coen said, elbowing Thea away from the controls.

"Look at the blood on Dylan!" Thea spat back. "She's infected."

"Then why would Nova be carrying her? She knows how this works. Dylan must have gotten hurt some other way."

"But—"

"If we don't let them in, we don't have a pilot, and we all blow up in four fucking minutes!"

He was right. Thea *knew* he was, and yet still she froze up. In her idleness, Coen toggled the controls. The door sprang open, and Nova staggered through, dragging Dylan with her. She lowered the captain to the floor and then buckled over, her own palms braced against her thighs as she gasped down air.

The door resealed with a hydraulic click, but Thea didn't feel an ounce of relief. Her eyes were glued on Dylan's neck and the Seckin bandage positioned below her ear. Scratches marred her skin.

"How did that happen?" Thea asked, pointing at the blood.

"Engine room," Dylan grunted out, her eyes on the floor.

It was a lie, and a bad one at that. They'd have had no reason to be in the engine room. Something had gotten its hands on Dylan Lowe.

Evacuate immediately. The ship will self-destruct in three minutes.

377

Outside in the hall, infected bodies slammed into the door, the sound of their nails shrill and piercing as they clawed at the surface.

They didn't have time for this, and Thea hadn't made it this far to be screwed over by Dylan Lowe—again. In fact, she saw the solution now. It wasn't easy or kind, but Dr. Tarlow had said that the responsible path rarely was.

"Dylan can't come," Thea said firmly.

"Of course she can," Nova replied.

"She's been infected. Look at her neck, those scratches."

"It's not from one of those things."

"Really? Would you bet your life on it? Would you bet ours?"

Nova stared directly at Thea, their eyes locked. Her silence alone was answer enough, but then Nova broke eye contact first, her gaze flitting to the floor as she swallowed. That was all the confirmation Thea needed.

"Let's go," Thea said. "Dylan stays."

"We can't just leave her!" Nova yelled.

"I'm fine!" the captain insisted through gritted teeth. But she wasn't. They were hiding something. Thea could sense the lie edging up against her intuition, a wrinkle she could feel even when they insisted there was nothing there.

"Coen?" Thea said, turning to him for help.

"Leave *him*," Dylan went on. "He's the one Evans told us to question. But I am getting off this damn rock." She braced her hands on the floor and, with her weight on her uninjured leg, managed to stand.

That's when Coen burst into action. His arms shot out, connecting with the captain. Dylan toppled away, arms windmilling as she collided with Nova.

Next thing Thea knew, Coen's hand was tightening on her utility belt, yanking her nearer. Thea's back slammed into his chest, and one of his arms came over her shoulder, pinning her there. The other trained a gun on the women.

Not a stun gun.

The pistol.

Thea blinked, sure she was mistaken, but there it was, Pitch Evans's weapon. The gun that had killed Dr. Tarlow. Coen must have lifted it off Dylan when he'd shoved her.

"Trust me," he whispered as she began to arch against him, his helmet grazing hers.

Across the way, Nova had managed to get her ray-rifle up and aimed. Dylan had slumped back to the floor, and though she looked close to passing out, her stun gun was now aimed in their direction as well. And Thea was serving as Coen's shield. If either of the women got off a shot, it was Thea who would feel the blow.

"Trust me," he said again quietly. "They can't hit you. I'll see it coming."

And she believed him, because she'd seen his speed, the unnatural reflexes that let him dance around attackers. *I could take that away from you before you even started to pull the trigger.*

Thea stood very still, her pulse pounding in her ears.

"I'm going to make this decision very simple for everybody," Coen announced. "We all get on the shuttle, or I shoot our pilot and everyone dies when that countdown hits zero."

"You wouldn't," Nova said.

"Want to bet your life on that?"

The pilot's face paled at the echo of Thea's original question.

"So what do you say, Captain?" Coen continued, now addressing only Dylan. "Should we die here because you've been brainwashed by Pitch Evans's warning, or do you wanna tell your pilot to stand down so we can all get off this rock?"

This was Coen's plan? To bring Dylan—the contagion in its most dangerous form—with them?

Evacuate immediately. The ship will self-destruct in two minutes.

"Nova, lower your weapon," Dylan ordered.

The pilot complied.

Nova dragged Dylan across the threshold and into the short-range shuttle. Coen and Thea were arguing behind her, but she didn't have time to make sense of their words. As they secured the air lock, Nova raced to the pilot's seat. Her fingers flew over dials and switches. The shuttle hummed with power. The dash blinked alight.

"Buckled in?" she shouted over her shoulder, though there was no time to waste even if they weren't.

Diagnostics flickered across her desk. The shuttle was ready.

As they undocked, Nova could make out a final, muffled alert: *Evacuate immediately. The ship will self-destruct in one minute.*

She steered them away, straight and hard. Like a bullet on an unalterable course, Nova Singh raced for the stars.

The blast chased them, a wave catching up to the shuttle's tail and rocking them violently. The dash flashed with warnings that quickly faded. The exterior hull was holding strong. The shields had done their job.

They were off-planet.

The thing couldn't move.

Spine broken, thoughts fractured, it watched the others scrambling up the dumbwaiter shaft, chasing the heartbeats it could scarcely still hear. Some crawled over the thing, no regard for where they stepped.

But there was no pain. Not until the ship exhaled and suddenly the pain was everywhere—a heat that seemed to originate in the thing's core and then explode outward, scorching down its limbs.

In the blink of an eye, the thing became nothing and everything, a billion pieces of dust scattered across the night.

And in that tiny eternity, the thing remembered that it had a name. It was an ancient memory, a flickering star, a whisper that danced just out of reach before reality collapsed inward, exploding with a blinding burst of light.

X

THE ESCAPE

Exodus

Interstellar Airspace

ONCE THE SHUTTLE WAS FLYING smoothly, the rattle of the blast behind them, Nova let out a heavy exhale. She breathed in and out. In and out.

Her pulse was still beating wildly in her ears, her visor flooded in red warnings. Probably it had been like this the past twenty minutes, only she'd been too preoccupied to truly notice. As her heart slowed and her visor cleared, she felt an unbearable pressure lift from her shoulders. She'd done it—the impossible. She'd gotten what remained of their crew off Achlys.

She'd need to program a distress beacon soon if they had any hopes of hailing the incoming Hevetz rescue crew. But Nova wanted just a moment longer of this relief, the quiet liberation.

She leaned into the pilot's seat and exhaled at the stars. They winked, exhaling back.

Thea unhooked from her harness but remained seated, too exhausted to move. Her oxygen was down to three percent, plus whatever she had left in her suit. She'd have to ditch it soon, but not yet. Not until she was sure it was safe.

She watched Dylan Lowe, who was breathing heavily in her chair, on the verge of passing out. The only thing holding the captain upright was her fastened harness.

Thea reached for the pistol Coen still held, surprised when he let her fingers close over the barrel and even more shocked when he let her take it from him. Maybe he'd known all along that it might come to this. Getting them all onboard had simply been a move to placate Nova, who clearly cared for the captain in a way Thea had not noticed before.

She looked at the weapon, then at Dylan Lowe. A gun on a shuttle this small was disastrously dangerous, but to not use it could be even riskier.

She would wait, and if she had to, Thea would pull the trigger.

The weight of the entire galaxy seemed to rest on her shoulders. Had Coen felt this, too, a responsibility as immense as space itself? To contain. To protect. To keep the contagion on Achlys.

She understood finally why he'd never tried to contact Hevetz after the outbreak, why he cut *Odyssey*'s comm lines, why he'd lied to her by omission. But his will to survive had been strongest, and he'd seen hope in the form of Thea's crew, seen hope in her. He hadn't been able to give up, to roll over without a fight, and now she was no different, willing to kill so that she could live. So the entire Union could live.

"It's empty," Coen said beside her.

"What?" she said.

"The gun. Dylan used the final bullet to shoot your doctor. It's been unloaded since then."

And yet he'd made his threats with it, known that Dylan would miss his bluff. All that time carrying the pistol after Dr. Tarlow's death, and the captain hadn't been aware that she was out of ammunition.

"There's one cryo bed," he said. "We can put her under. Wait and see."

"You think that really happened in the engine room?" Thea said, nodding at the Seckin bandage on Dylan's neck. "That she got gouged by some machinery?"

"Even if not, she still doesn't have a nosebleed." He glanced at Nova, who was deep at work programming a distress beacon, then dropped his voice to a whisper. "She might be young enough."

Young enough to harbor Psychrobacter achli, *Thea thought. Young enough to coexist with the uninfected—like Coen.*

She considered explaining it all to Nova, wondering if it would encourage the pilot to come clean about how Dylan's injury had truly occurred. But Thea didn't fully trust Nova—not after being left behind twice on that rock—and the last thing she wanted was to give Nova a reason to abandon her again. Thea was young, after all. So was Coen. Even if she left out that Coen was infected, they would both look suspect.

"Never mind," Coen said. "There's our answer."

Nova heard Dylan's harness unlatch and turned in time to watch the first drop of blood fall from her nose. It seemed to fall in slow motion, spattering on the floor between the captain's bare feet.

"Dylan?" Nova said tentatively.

The captain wiped at her nose with the back of her hand. It came away red. Her head snapped up, eyes locking with Nova's as blood dripped freely from her nostrils.

"I'm okay," she said, spinning the silver bracelet on her arm like a nervous tic. But her head twitched as she said it. A shudder racked her body. "It's okay."

It wasn't. Nova could see it now—the truth that she'd feared but had been too stubborn to confront back on *Celestial Envoy*. How had she ever believed that Toby's attack wouldn't prove fatal?

The captain lurched out of her chair and collapsed to all fours. She crawled toward the air lock, then pulled herself upright against it, fingers leaving a faint trail of blood across the stenciled letters that read *Exodus*. Those same fingers curled into a fist, and the captain punched the switch to open the internal air lock door.

"Dylan?" Nova muttered, darting forward. She was vaguely aware of the others behind her. Thea searching the floor for the stun gun Dylan had been carrying. Coen with Nova's ray-rifle now aimed at the captain.

"I deserve this," Dylan said, "after what I did." She glanced at the control panel, and for one sickening moment, Nova thought the woman might open the exterior door, too, flushing them all into space. If she couldn't live, no one could. It sounded just like Dylan. Stubborn to a fault.

"Don't," Nova spit out. "Don't you dare take us down with you."

Hurt flashed across Dylan's face.

"I'm sorry I wasn't the person you wanted me to be," she said. "If there was more time, I think I could have become her, though." A shiver racked her body. "Maybe." She backed into the open bay, shaking against her will as she unlatched the silver bracelet from her wrist.

"Take a piece of me home?" she said, tossing it at Nova's feet.

"Dylan . . ." Nova breathed. But she didn't know what else to say. There weren't enough words.

The captain grimaced as a tremor shook her body. "If I can't do it, I need you to do it for me."

"Can't do what?"

"I'm sorry," Dylan said through gritted teeth, "about everything." She toggled the interior door and it slid shut, separating her from the rest of them in the shuttle. Nova darted to the hexagonal window, peering through. Dylan hunched over, arms wrapped around her middle and sweat dripping from her as she convulsed.

"You can't leave her in there!" Coen shouted. "She'll just reopen the door."

Nova knew. She knew and she understood, but that didn't make the weight of the task less consequential.

A hand slapped against the air lock window, and Nova jumped back. Dylan was standing upright again, her mouth slick with blood, the whites of her eyes now bloodshot, a dark red ring around her blue irises. Nova stared but did not recognize the woman staring back.

If I can't do it, I need you to do it for me.

"Good-bye, Dylan," Nova whispered.

She slammed her hand down on the toggle. The external door flew open and Dylan Lowe was ejected from the air lock, the vacuum of space siphoning her to oblivion.

Thea felt supercharged, every sense alert and sharp as Dylan's final moments replayed in her head. She'd seen it through the small air lock window. The captain's eyes filling with blood. The exterior door opening. Dylan's body being sucked into space as though a rope was tied around her torso, arms and legs reaching for the *Exodus* in a final, desperate plea.

Nova had picked up the bracelet and retreated to the pilot's chair in a trance, staring numbly at the controls as she set their heading for Soter.

"It was the only way," Thea assured her. "If you didn't do it, one of us would have."

The pilot nodded meekly.

"That's two," she muttered. "Two people at my hands."

She'd have tallied many more if she'd ended up flying for the Union military, but Thea didn't say anything. She imagined it was much different to take a life up close, to see their faces. Especially if it was a person you cared deeply for. And it was obvious Nova had cared for Dylan. Even when all evidence suggested the captain wasn't worthy of it, Nova had felt something for her.

"You lucky bastard," Nova said, side-eyeing Coen. Her voice was no longer faint, but edged with anger. "How the hell did you make it back to us? All those infected at *Odyssey*, and you escaped without a single scratch?" Her eyes trailed the length of his suit. Facing her, the breach from where Toby's laser cutter had sliced into his calf was hidden from view.

"Luck, just like you said," Coen responded smoothly. "Thanks for leaving me, though. I'm sure it wouldn't have been any easier to fight my way free if I'd had some backup."

"Coen," Thea said, throwing him a glance. They didn't need an argument now.

"What? I'm supposed to feel bad that I survived when that pretentious asshole didn't?" He threw a hand toward the air lock. "She's the reason half your crew is dead. If she'd just *listened* to me from the beginning—if she hadn't been so stubborn . . ."

He didn't finish the thought, and he didn't need to. Thea knew where it was going. He was right, but that didn't change anything now.

"I can't sit here anymore," Nova said, lurching to her feet. "I need sleep."

Thea didn't understand how anyone could sleep after what they'd just witnessed—even if they *had* been running flat-out since stepping from *Odyssey*'s cryo chamber nearly eight hours earlier.

"But what if—"

"We're on autopilot," Nova said to her, "and the distress beacon will broadcast every thirty seconds. With any luck the backup Hevetz crew will intercept it in a few hours. You can pull me out when that happens."

"I'd feel better if you just napped," Thea argued, staring at the lone cryo pod. "What if we need you? You're the only one who knows how to fly this thing."

"It'll be fine," Coen interjected. "When a pilot says she needs sedated sleep, you don't stand between her and her deep, knocked-out slumber."

Or maybe Coen just didn't want their pilot to keep questioning him or discover his secret. It didn't matter. Thea was outnumbered, and she let the argument die.

The kiss of gas was blissful.

Nova breathed deeply, overjoyed at the way her pulse slowed and her thoughts calmed. How the guilt lifted free like dirt in water. How she could no longer feel the silver bracelet she'd fastened on her wrist.

She would wake to help dock *Exodus* with the rescue crew's ship, or she would die in the pod when life support failed. If it was cowardly to leave Thea and Coen facing the vastness of space, the thought did not occur to Nova. Her heart was too broken, her guilt too heavy. She couldn't sit in the pilot's chair, couldn't bear the thought of staring at the stars that used to welcome her home. They were still home, but they were tainted now. They'd become Dylan Lowe's grave, and it had happened at her hands. Just like with Sullivan. If only she'd listened to her cousin. He'd warned her from the beginning about Dylan Lowe, and yet Nova had put some level of faith in the captain, let the woman lead them into the ashes of destruction when everyone could have been spared if they'd simply been more cautious.

That woman ruined everything—even the stars.

Never again would Nova march forward so blindly.

Never again.

Reality faded, and Nova was dragged into a deep, peaceful sleep.

An hour later, Thea finally ditched her suit.

It had run out of oxygen as Nova settled into the stasis pod, and Thea didn't need it anymore regardless. It wouldn't keep her from freezing or running out of air if life support failed. The Hevetz backup crew would answer *Exodus*'s distress beacon, or she'd die. Those were the potential outcomes. She might as well be comfortable until then. Plus, she really had to pee.

She relieved herself in the ship's closet-sized restroom, wishing desperately for a shower. Her T-shirt was drenched and clinging to her body, and while her leggings had stayed mostly dry, she stunk. Badly. Still, her lips curled into a smile. It was a blessing to smell things so vividly. The filtration system of the suit had left her world bland and foreign.

She kicked the suit aside and used a wipe from the wash station to pat her face clean. Then she yanked her fingers through her tangled hair, peeling dark and sweaty strands from her neck and securing it back with an elastic.

When she exited the bathroom, she found that Coen had also shed his suit. With his coveralls once again tied at the waist and a plain shirt stretched tight at the widest parts of his shoulders, he looked like any other kid from Hearth City. Cocky. Young. Hungry to get out of town and make a name for himself. Just as she'd done, he was attempting to tame his hair. Thea watched him twist half of it into a bun, her gaze lingering on what she could see of the tattoo on his neck. Tendrils crept from beneath the neckline of his shirt, their shapes soft and organic. Nothing like the geometric Union flag that had been on Pitch Evans's neck.

Don't trust the kid.

It was Lisbeth Tarlow they never should have trusted. And Dylan Lowe.

Had they listened to Coen Rivli, fled to *Odyssey* at his very first warning, they'd all have been better off.

Thea closed the door to the washroom, and Coen's attention snapped to her. His eyes moved over her clothing. "Who'd have guessed you were so scrawny under that suit."

"Bony elbows can hurt, you know."

A smile touched his lips. "Only if you can land one on me."

She knew she couldn't. "What now?" she asked, feeling weary and wired at once.

"Now we wait."

Thea slid into the pilot chair, knees bouncing as she

scanned the dashboard controls. A light indicating that their emergency beacon was transmitting lit up, staying on for precisely six seconds as the message broadcast, then falling dark until the next transmission. Thea caught herself anticipating the pattern, glancing back to the light just a heartbeat before it would illuminate. The rhythm became a reassurance. Time was passing, even if nothing beyond the windshield appeared to change.

Exodus was designed for travel within a single system, as all short-range shuttles were. Quick flights between planets and moons, getting passengers to their destination in a few hours—or perhaps a day—by leveraging a powerful accelerator drive. This was the only type of travel legally allowed within the confines of a star system, and Thea could wish for an FTL drive all she wanted. It wouldn't change the fact that *Exodus* didn't have one. At their current speed, it would be years—*decades*—before the *Exodus* approached Soter, its passengers dead inside. If they didn't encounter the backup Hevetz rescue crew soon, they were doomed.

The emergency beacon flashed again.

The expanse beyond the window appeared unchanged.

It was three more hours before the ship's fuel reserves dropped very near the amount needed to safely return to Achlys.

"Should we wake her?" Thea said, glancing toward the cryo pod.

"So she could take us back?" Coen asked. "Is that really what you want to do?"

"No."

"Me either."

But it didn't feel right to push past this point without giving Nova a choice. Coen sensed Thea's hesitation.

"Even if we wake her and she votes in favor of returning, we outnumber her," he said. "Majority rules."

Thea nodded, turning back to the cockpit. For twenty minutes, with the beacon flashing in her peripherals, she watched the fuel reserves. When they crossed that point of no return, she felt dread but also freedom. It was out of her hands now.

They would be rescued.

Or they would die.

"If I could do it again, I'd have told you sooner," Coen said, leaning a hip into the dashboard.

Thea kept her eyes on the flashing beacon.

"Exactly what had happened," he went on. "And how it was in me, too."

"Why *did* you wait?" she snapped, turning to face him. "You knew you were infected after speaking telepathically with Dr. Tarlow, but when we drove to *Odyssey*, you still kept it from me. You fed me certain truths, but you hid the most important ones."

He thumbed his lip a moment. It had been so long since she'd seen him without a suit and helmet that she felt like she was looking at him for the first time. She noticed how tall he was, standing beside her. How his throat bobbed when he swallowed.

"I didn't know if I could trust you," he said finally. "I thought maybe you were loyal to Hevetz, or that you'd side with Tarlow no matter what I said. That's why I showed you the Witch Hazel footage first, tried to feel out your reaction to that. By the time I came clean, it was because I *had* to. I can see how I screwed that up now. But this is why I'm saying I'd have been upfront from the beginning if I could do it again. I'd have told you everything I knew, as I came to know it."

His gaze came up to meet hers. Everything about his expression was soft and vulnerable—his brown eyes calm and patient, his brows stitched with sincerity. He meant these words. Whether they were an honest apology or just something he needed to get off his chest, Thea couldn't say. Perhaps they were both.

She nodded to acknowledge them.

"Do you really think you can cure it?" he asked.

It was quiet for a moment, the only noise between them

the thrum of the ship's reactor. Thea glanced at the duffel that held the research, then back at Coen, his eyes bright with hope.

"Every problem can be solved," she said. "It's just a matter of having enough time."

"*Exodus*, come in," the intercom crackled. "This is the *UBS Paramount*. *Exodus*, do you copy?"

Thea tensed in the pilot seat. Coen perked up beside her. "A Union battleship?" he said. "Where the hell's the Hevetz backup crew?"

"Who cares?" Thea exclaimed. "We're saved!"

She reached to engage the intercom, but Coen lurched forward, his hand covering hers. It was the first bit of human touch she'd experienced since suiting up on *Odyssey* over twelve hours ago. It sent a jolt of heat through her, and she pulled her hand back.

"Our story," Coen said, keeping his hand in front of the comm gear. "What are we gonna tell them?" His desperation was obvious to Thea and thick in a way she had not yet witnessed. Even fighting off hordes of the infected, he hadn't appeared this vulnerable. Achlys had become his home, in a way. There, he was a king. But this was a strange, new territory, and she knew he could see how many ways things could go wrong.

"We'll say there was a deadly outbreak," she told him. "You're the lone survivor. I found you at the Witch Hazel bunker, and we reunited with my crew. End of story."

"And Nova?"

"She'll say the same thing when questioned, because it's all she knows."

"And you won't mention my abilities?" Coen said, his brows arching. "Or how I'm carrying it?"

Thea turned sharply toward him. His face gleamed with the lights of the dash, worry etched there. "Coen, they'll have us in quarantine for weeks regardless of what I say. I don't have any reason to make them more suspicious. I just want to go home."

He nodded, his understanding deep.

"*Exodus,*" the intercom crackled. "This is Lieutenant Christoph Burke of the *UBS Paramount*. Do you copy?"

Coen nodded, and Thea leapt to action.

"*Exodus*, here," she said.

"With whom am I speaking?"

"This is Althea Sadik. I'm an intern with Hevetz Industries. Our environmental survey crew at Soter's Northwood Point got called to investigate—"

"—a distress call from the Black Quarry crew. We know all about it. The Union military is working with Hevetz on this rescue mission."

Beside Thea, Coen bristled.

"We've got a team of Hevetz scientists onboard," Burke continued, "and we picked up Black Quarry's Decklan Powell during his transit back to Soter. What's your status?"

"Myself, one Black Quarry survivor, and *Odyssey*'s original pilot. The other five of my crew are deceased."

The lieutenant swore. "What the hell happened? You were supposed to sit tight on *Odyssey*, wait for us to arrive. We sent instructions while you were in stasis."

"If our captain got them, she didn't tell us." Thea glanced at the air lock, fuming. Dylan might not have seen that SOS, but she'd been informed of a risk on Achlys soil, and she'd gambled with her entire crew's lives anyway. All to go after her father, who'd been beyond saving from the beginning. "I'd ask her what the hell she was thinking," Thea added, "but she's dead."

Another swear. "How?"

"There was a deadly outbreak. We think the contagion originated in the water. It spread through Black Quarry's entire crew, and ours fell prey to it also, including our captain."

"What about the lone survivor?"

"He was holed up in the old Witch Hazel bunker. I found him when I was separated from my crew during a storm. He's not exhibiting any symptoms of the infection, but I can't urge you enough to put that rock under galactic quarantine.

No one should set foot there again."

"We'll make the decisions, Ms. Sadik. Where's your pilot?"

"She's in stasis. Let me wake her."

"No need for that. I just wanted to ensure she was safe. Let her rest, and once you're in range, we'll pull you in remotely. We'll see you in less than an hour."

"Thank you, sir."

"One last thing. Does that Black Quarry survivor have a name?"

"Amos Lashley, sir," Coen said, leaning forward. "General driller in the labor division. Do you need my Hevetz ID?"

"That won't be necessary. Our condolences for all you've been through, Mr. Lashley. This will be behind you shortly. Over and out."

The *UBS Paramount* overrode *Exodus*'s steering approximately twenty minutes later and began to draw them in. The *Paramount*'s credentials filled a screen on the dashboard, and Thea read them hurriedly. It was a Union battleship serving the Trios System with a home port on Soter. It was too good to be true. Not only were they saved, but they'd be returning to the Trios, escorted by officers and soldiers. Her nightmares were over.

When Thea heard the sound of the shuttle docking with the battleship, a surge of relief blew through her. She felt instantly lighter. The external air lock door parted and bodies marched into the bay. Thea could see the military seal on their uniforms through the small interior air lock window. They were tense and rigid as they stood at attention, helmets obscuring all but a fearful slope to their brows.

That fear was reassuring, though. If the crew was worried by what awaited them on the *Exodus*, it meant they weren't foolish enough to investigate Achlys, to go digging for what should be left forgotten.

Thea glanced at Coen, smiling, but his forehead had wrinkled and his mouth had gone thin with suspicion.

Her cheerfulness vanished.

She sensed it, too, suddenly, how the air seemed laced with electricity. She heard the interior air lock door crack open and turned in time to see a canister come rolling into the shuttle.

Thea leapt back, dodging the first and even the second. But soon there were dozens of cans being lobbed into the small space, knocking against her feet. Gas billowed. She coughed, sputtered. Even Coen wasn't immune, and he joined her in hacking.

A figure strode into view, the name *Burke* stitched in the breastplate of his spacesuit. Thea's mind felt foggy, her limbs detached. She could barely stay on her feet as the lieutenant strode toward the cryostasis pod and kicked the power switch. The light illuminating Nova flickered and went dark.

No! Thea tried to shout. The pilot could die without being properly revived, but the gas was everywhere, and Thea's mouth had stopped working.

She turned, searching for Coen. He was already on the ground, eyes falling shut.

Her knees buckled.

Darkness overtook her.

Nova was dreaming, again chasing a beacon that led to a space station. It wasn't breached this time, but she still found Dylan inside. The woman was trapped in an air lock, pounding on the window, begging to be let in. When Nova opened the door, Dylan would vanish and the banging would originate in another part of the station, the dream repeating.

On and on it went, and still Nova kept up her search.

She was making her way to another air lock when the station's lights flickered. That hadn't happened yet, not in all the times the dream had recurred. She paused, hand on the wall, and the hallways plummeted into darkness. The space station shuddered, and Nova was suddenly weightless, floating in the corridor.

She heard voices, distant and leery.

Then the crank of a handle, like a hatch being opened.

The air suddenly left her lungs and she was sucked through the station at an unnatural speed, flying toward the air lock. Somehow the doors had opened—both internal and external—and she could make out the freezing, silent expanse beyond. Nova hurtled toward it, spinning end over end, gasping.

A hand closed over her wrist, yanking her to a halt. Heat flared through her shoulder. She glanced up to see Dylan.

"Hang on," the captain whispered. "Stay with me."

The woman pulled Nova to safety, propelling them both through halls and corridors, defying the vacuum of space. It was impossible, and yet here they were, crossing a threshold into a new section of the station. Dylan sealed the door behind them, and the insane pressure stopped. Nova floated, weightless. She could breathe again.

"This area's secure," Dylan said. "For now. But that breach at the air lock is bad, and there's another in engineering."

"How do we fix them?"

"I don't know. The whole station's failing. We have to keep it operational."

"For how long?" Nova asked.

"Until you wake up."

Nova heard the voices again, tinny and bright, coming from beyond the station. But that didn't make sense. No one could be outside, not unless it was her crew, performing repairs. A beam of light drifted through a window like a spotlight, but when Nova floated over for a better look, she couldn't see anything but stars.

"What is this place?" she asked. "Where the heck are we?"

"Between."

"Between where?"

Dylan looked at her sadly, blinked those icy blue eyes. "You're in a coma, Nova. But I'll stay with you as long as you want."

Thea came to in an isolation chamber.

She flinched, only to find her ankles and wrists restrained by cuffs. Leather straps extended across her shins, thighs, waist, and chest, all tightly cinched. She'd been restrained like a subject on an operating table, only this table had been angled so that she was nearly in an upright position, feet dangling just above the floor.

Something moved before her, and her eyes zeroed in on Lieutenant Burke. He still wore a spacesuit, but she remained in her T-shirt and leggings. Even with such little clothing, she felt . . . heavy, leaden. The room was sedated, she realized. Not as thoroughly as the *Exodus*, which had made her pass out, but enough to keep her sluggish.

Thea craned against the restraints, looking at the medbay

beyond her chamber. The equipment was similar to *Celestial Envoy*'s, but the far wall bore the Union's military crest: a geometric shield sporting equally geometric eagle wings. Three stars sat above the shield like a halo.

"Where am I?" she said, already knowing the answer.

"The *UBS Paramount*," Lieutenant Burke confirmed. "You're safe now."

She yanked her limbs against the restraints. "*This* is safe?"

"There was a slight complication with your story. We had to take precautions."

"Where's our pilot? And Co—Amos?"

"Ah," Burke said with a small smile. "That's where the problem begins, doesn't it? With Coen Rivli?"

He knew Coen's true identity. Dread billowed through her.

"A quick search of Union records shows that Amos Lashley is presumed dead," the lieutenant said. "We ran a facial recognition program after docking the *Exodus*, which revealed that your Amos Lashley is actually Coen Rivli, a seventeen-year-old high school dropout, guilty of three felonies, the least serious of which is identity theft." Burke leaned forward, peering down at her. "Althea Sadik on the other hand . . . A promising student with exceptional grades. Top of her class. Winner of a prestigious Hevetz internship, with a fair shot at Linneaus Institute in her future. In other words: *smart*. Smart enough to not go down with a teenage felon." He rubbed the pad of his thumb against his palm for a second, then glanced up at her. "Care to change your story?"

"He's infected."

There, she'd said it. Chances were they already knew. And if they didn't, they'd find out soon enough. Coen was likely in isolation just like her, and all it would take was one body scan, one blood test. She felt terrible saying those two words—an ungrateful, backstabbing traitor—but they'd find something foreign in his results. Thea needed to warn them before it was too late. Before they unleashed the contagion a second time.

"So you see why we can't let you go," Lieutenant Burke said.

"Standard quarantine." She nodded. "How long until I'm out of this chamber?"

"You misunderstand me. You're not coming out of the chamber. Not any time soon." An unsettling grin spread over his lips.

"But I'm clean. I'm not infected."

"Black Quarry was an important research operation, and *Celestial Envoy* was not a military ship. It was protecting company secrets, not data pertaining to Union security. Activating the emergency destruct sequence simultaneously initiated a program that backed up all important ship data for Hevetz, from surveillance footage and audio files to documented reports." He took a step toward her. "Black Quarry used much of the infrastructure of the project before them as a foundation for their technical needs. Because of this, footage from the Witch Hazel bunker was also salvaged. We reviewed what we could while closing in on the *Exodus*."

Thea's heart dropped. She truly felt it drop, as though she were experiencing a moment of weightless free fall.

"After the storm," Burke continued, "Coen Rivli revived you with mouth-to-mouth resuscitation inside the bunker's air lock."

"It's passed by blood," she said quickly.

"Many diseases passed by blood are passed by *any* bodily fluid."

"There's no proof that's true here."

"But I think there is," Burke continued. "Think, Thea." He waved at the air, tapped on the side of his helmet. *"Think."*

The chamber being pumped with a sedative. The lieutenant, fully suited, and her still breathing without a mask or buffer.

Her pulse kicked as the pieces slid together. She'd passed out from the gas on the *Exodus*, too, but at roughly the same time as Coen. Earlier, Nova had been exhausted, desperate for a reprieve, and yet Thea hadn't been able to sleep—just like Coen. When had the symptoms begun?

She went back, searching her memories. She'd climbed the dumbwaiter shaft despite her body being racked with exhaustion. She'd pried open the hydraulic door that serviced Commander Lowe's room. Her endurance and strength had been a surprise. She'd chalked it up to adrenaline, but maybe it was from something . . . more.

It couldn't be true.

Thea didn't feel any different. Was it the sedative being filtered into the chamber, obscuring her senses, then? Coen said it had taken a couple of hours for signs to appear after he'd been infected, but that they'd happened subtly, taking about half a day to fully manifest. When the *Paramount* had pulled the *Exodus* in, it had been roughly ten hours since Coen revived Thea.

Lieutenant Burke took another step toward her, and the material of his spacesuit brushed against Thea's bare feet. The sensation of touch shot through her. Every muscle in her body tensed, wanting to lash out, attack, flee. Burke leaned in, lowering his eyes to her level.

And that's when she heard it: the muted thump of his heart. His pulse, in her head. Once she'd recognized it, she couldn't unhear it. And then there was more. The flap of valves opening and closing, lungs pulsing, oxygen moving. The ticking human machine.

A drop of sweat fell from the lieutenant's brow, hitting the inside of his helmet with an audible *plifft*.

Without the sedative, would she have heard all of this when he sat a meter away? Would she have known immediately that she'd become this *thing*?

"I'm not infected," she insisted.

"You are."

"Then get rid of us," she begged. "Put us to sleep. Throw us into space."

"Is that what you'd have recommended we do to your friend?" Burke's expression contorted with amusement.

"Yes! You can't bring this to the Trios. You can't bring it to any colonized planet in the Union! I've seen what it can do if it gets out, how bad it can be when it meets an incompatible host."

"I'd as soon launch two newly discovered alien species into space as I would extinguish you and Mr. Rivli. I watched a surveillance video where he fought off nearly three dozen infected in a *Celestial Envoy* hall—single-handedly. There's a good chance you can now do the same. If we can harness that power—if we know how to control it—the Trios will be unstoppable. We'll have the strongest military in the universe."

Thea caught the distinction: the *Trios* would have the strongest military, not the Union. One of Toby's theories flew through her mind.

The Trios has its own fleet of military vessels, just like the Cradle. . . . If enough Trios ships defect, they could stage one hell of a revolution.

The *UBS Paramount* hailed from Soter. It was governed by Union law, but it served the Trios first and foremost, the rest of the galaxy, second. Its crew could be Radicals.

"What if you can't harness it?" Thea snapped. "If *one* thing goes wrong, you'll have damned everyone on this ship! Potentially an entire system!"

"You let me worry about the details, Miss Sadik. I can see you're not a soldier. Cooperate, and when we've got what we need from you, I'll let you go home."

His pulse slowed with smug satisfaction, and Thea knew it was a lie. She was never going home. She sensed Burke's smile before it morphed into view behind his visor.

"You can't do this!" She flailed again against her restraints. "Where's Nova? What about that Hevetz pilot, Decklan? Does the Company know what you're doing?"

"Of course they know. I have a team of their scientists onboard. When Aldric Vasteneur saw Black Quarry's SOS, he feared the worst and contacted a friend at Galactic Disease Control. That friend pulled me in. We assembled our teams and shipped out on the *Paramount* as quickly as possible. But this outcome . . . what your crew found . . . It's incredible."

Incredible? Hundreds of people were dead. An inconceivable number could follow.

"I have rights!" Thea went on, still rattling the restraints. "You can't keep me here. You can't withhold a minor without their parents' or guardian's permission."

"You're an orphan. Your parents are *dead*! There is no one in the entire Union who will believe your story, and no one who will come looking for you!"

The truth behind his words hit hard enough to make Thea gasp.

There was no lie they couldn't spread convincingly. Black Quarry had been top secret, and no one would be searching for a crew they didn't know was even stationed on Achlys to begin with. Family of the crew members would get a variety of vague letters, apologizing for an accident that had regrettably stolen a life. And Northwood Point had been evacuated due to a storm. It would be easy to say *Odyssey* never made it off the ice caps, that its crew perished in the blizzard.

Thea pictured the warden at the foster home shrugging at the news of her death and passing the letter on to child services.

No one would miss her.

Coen and Toby had shared a fear that the Company was corrupt, that Hevetz had endangered all its employees for a large stash of corrarium. But Thea could see now how the truth was even bigger, more complex. It wasn't the Company she needed to fear but men like Lieutenant Burke—Radicals who would stop at nothing for Trios independence, including putting the lives of an entire system at risk in the pursuit of their own goals.

They would be the Trios's undoing.

"At least let me study the research," Thea said, desperate. "It's safe to have me working on it, and you need a cure—an ability to fight the bacteria if it infects someone incapable of hosting it. You don't know what you're tampering with!"

"We already have people going through the files salvaged from *Celestial Envoy*, and your duffel bag of blood work and brain scans is proving incredibly illuminating."

The dread coursed through Thea, and the lieutenant merely smiled.

"Let me go!" Thea screamed, pulling at her restraints, blood boiling. "You have to let me go!" She arched against the table as quickly as she could manage and heard a satisfying snap of the restraint across her chest.

Lieutenant Burke staggered away, shocked. "More sedative!" he called to someone.

But Thea's blood was already electric, every millimeter of her charged. She yanked her hands away from the table, snapping open the cuffs. There was a prick of pain followed by a wetness that blossomed, and then it was gone. One glance at her wrists and she could see the bleeding had already stopped, any cuts already healed.

Burke ran for the exit, his pulse beating a frenzy of noise into Thea's skull.

She reached for the remaining buckles, unfastening them as quickly as she could. Her own pulse kicked wildly in response. Burke was going to get away. Her window for escape was shrinking.

She yanked both her legs against the ankle restraints with all the force she could muster. The cuffs burst free, but not before slicing into her. Again she felt the whisper of the injury, a feather on her skin before it subsided.

Thea stumbled from the table, staggered after Burke.

The air was getting thick, her limbs heavy. Several paces from him, she slumped to her knees.

Darkness danced at the corners of her vision as she watched Lieutenant Burke slip through the doorway. He turned back to face her, relief painted on his features as he stared down on her through the glass that divided them.

His pulse slowed in Thea's ears, growing cloudy and muffled.

Just before passing out, she had a sickening realization: she would have attacked with more time. And if she'd been injured in the scuffle, if any of her blood managed to find its way into a cut she inflicted on Burke . . .

Thea had almost unleashed the horror of Black Quarry on the *UBS Paramount*.

‹ • • ›

When she awoke next, it was in a dark room. Before, it might have looked black to her. There were no lights or windows, but she could see to the room's edges, its darkness now nothing but a dim annoyance.

A cot pushed into a corner. Unadorned walls. A water dish set on the ground before a small window near the base of the door. The opening was large enough for a cat or small dog, but certainly not Thea.

She threaded her hands through her hair. If someone stood guard outside the room, she could not hear their pulse. She paced the room for hours, straining, listening. Eventually, she sat on the bed. She felt bright, springy. Almost weightless. Her thoughts were clear. Her breathing came easily. The room was not sedated.

Which made the silence that much more threatening.

She was alone.

Nova was at worst, dead, and at best, in a coma. The pilot Decklan Powell who should have been Black Quarry's salvation had likely been paid for his silence or had been silenced by execution. And Coen . . . His situation could be no better than hers.

She lay back on the cot. At first she thought about Althea Sadik and if that person was dead. She wondered who she was now. She wondered *what* she was now.

Each question brought her close to tears, making her feel small and weak.

So she began to think about things she could control. She had her head and hands. She didn't need Nova or Decklan or even the boy-monster Coen Rivli. She'd be her own savior. She thought about the water dish and the service window in the door, and as the minutes ticked by, a tireless Thea Sadik began to plot her escape.

He'd been poked, prodded, injected, inspected. They'd taken blood samples, skin samples, urine samples, probably a dozen other varieties of samples.

Coen had lost track.

He'd been on this table since leaving the shuttle. They'd believed him to be unconscious, and though he could hear the distant hum of the gas filtering into the isolation chamber, he wasn't knocked out completely. Still, his arms were useless, lying at his side like giant anchors. Even his eyelids were too much of a burden to open. But he felt the workers studying him, and he heard them talking.

He was a weapon, they'd said.

He could make the Trios stronger, help them earn their independence.

He was something they needed to replicate.

Well, be careful then, *a medic had snapped.* He's our only subject.

No he's not, *another replied.* There's a girl, too. Burke confirmed it.

Coen's heart had plummeted. He'd feared this. Ever since

421

speaking telepathically with the doctor, ever since realizing he wasn't quite human anymore, he'd worried he'd cursed Thea while resuscitating her. But the symptoms never arrived. The lieutenant must be mistaken.

Now, sitting in an empty cell with walls too strong for him to even dent, Coen wished otherwise.

He couldn't be alone again. Couldn't be the only one of his kind. He needed Thea to be like him. It was selfish, callous, and yet he still wished it with every fiber of his being. He'd saved her in the bunker, and she'd saved him in the dumbwaiter shaft, and now they needed to save each other from this prison. They had their differences, and he had much to make up for, but he knew with an irrefutable certainty that they'd only survive this if they worked together.

He'd tried shutting himself off from the world, fighting alone. It didn't work.

Sitting on the edge of his cot, he reached out to her.

Thea? It's Coen. Can you hear me?

Nothing.

He tried again.

Thea? Please say something.

The silence closed in on him, crushing, drowning.

He put his head in his hands.

Helplessness gnawed at his chest.

And then, he heard it: the thump of life. He paused, strained *his hearing. There it was. Again. And again. A steady, familiar rhythm. It came not from the hallway, where he'd already listened for a guard, but from directly beside him. He turned toward the wall and put a palm to it. The surface was cold.*

A faint creak, someone settling onto a cot, and the material beneath his palm warmed.

It was possible it was merely his own heat transferring into the wall, but the heartbeat was stronger in his ears now, and if he craned his senses, he could make out an exhale, too.

Thea? *he thought.*

The pulse on the other side of the wall kicked in his ears, momentarily faster, gleeful. And then, her voice in his head, the most beautiful four words he'd ever heard:

I have a plan.

ACKNOWLEDGMENTS

This book was a long time coming. I wrote the opening pages of what would eventually become *Contagion* back in early 2012, but the book didn't even begin to resemble what you hold in your hands today until 2016. It has been a labor of love (and oftentimes frustration) as I rewrote and revised and polished, but in the end, it was well worth it.

I owe an enormous debt to Susan Dennard, who brainstormed aloud with me as we walked through a cemetery in her hometown in the fall of 2015. I can still remember the weather (so mild for November!) and the moment we stumbled upon the twist that the entire book would hinge upon: Lisbeth Tarlow's backstory and secrets. *Contagion* only began to take its true shape after that. So thanks, Sooz. I'd probably still be writing in circles if you hadn't helped me puzzle that out.

Additional thanks to Alex Bracken, Amie Kaufman, Mackenzi Lee, and Jodi Meadows, who all provided invaluable feedback on early pages (once I'd finally found the story) and cheered me on as I attempted to reach the end.

To my agent, Sara Crowe, and everyone at Pippin Properties who championed this book. *Thank you.*

To my editor, Erica Sussman, who saw the book I was trying to write and helped me get there, and to everyone at HarperTeen who touched this project. *Thank you.*

To my family, my everlasting support net—Rob, who let me bounce ideas off him at any hour of the day, and Casey, who continuously reminds me that there are more important things than work (such as dance parties and sidewalk chalk). *Thank you.*

To everyone who has supported my writing endeavors over the years (you know who you are—friends, family, booksellers, librarians). *Thank you.*

And of course, to you, dear reader. Thank you for picking up this novel. I only have my job because of readers like yourself, so please forgive me for that cliffhanger? I'll wrap things up in the sequel. I promise.

DON'T MISS THE CHILLING CONCLUSION TO
CONTAGION

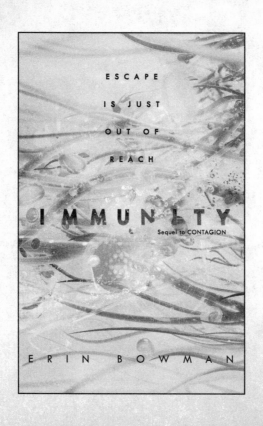

ESCAPE

IS JUST

OUT OF

REACH

IMMUNITY

Sequel to CONTAGION

ERIN BOWMAN

ALTHEA SADIK STOOD IN FRONT of the door to her holding cell. There was no mincing words; that's what it was. Not a room or personal quarters, but a cell. A prison.

She cocked her head, considering the small window in the base of the door. It was meant to serve as a passage for food, so that guards could pass meals to her. At least she assumed there were guards. No matter how hard she stretched the limits of her now extraordinary hearing, she couldn't make out their heartbeats. There was only Coen Rivli, the boy monster in the cell beside her. They were monsters together now, forever altered by the contagion they'd encountered on Achlys.

What plan? he whispered in her mind.

She'd told him she had one just moments earlier—her first words spoken to him telepathically. Now, she said only, *Follow my lead.*

When she'd first surveyed the room, Thea thought the window in the door was too small to fit her. But Thea was small, too. Little more than a meter and a half tall, roughly forty-seven kilograms in weight, with a figure like an inverted pyramid. The widest part of Thea was her shoulders, not hips, and she'd never been more happy for it. If she angled her body while sliding through the window, her hips would pass easily. But her shoulders . . .

Thea reached across her body, grabbing her left wrist with her right hand. Moving deliberately, she tugged. As her shoulder popped from its socket, a small gasp escaped her. The pain was a tiny blip in her consciousness, and then her brain pushed the feeling aside.

Thea? came Coen's voice. *You okay?*

Her pulse had quickened. He must have heard it.

I'm fine.

The glass was double-paned, secured with a latch on the outside. She kicked with her heel, shattering the first panel.

She froze, listening, stretching her hearing.

No one was coming. Motion sensors or cameras must not be watching the cells. Foolish.

She kicked again, breaking the second panel of glass. Thea was still barefoot, wearing only the tank top and leggings she'd been in when the crew of the *UBS Paramount* had taken her and Coen by force. She was still trying to process how the crew that she'd thought would be her savior had turned out to be an enemy. The *Paramount* had pulled in her shuttle not because it had been sent to rescue survivors from Achlys but because it was collecting a resource that would serve their agenda. Lieutenant Burke, *Paramount*'s acting captain, had made that much clear when interrogating Thea just earlier. Once he was done studying the *Psychrobacter achli* swimming in her—and Coen's—veins, he'd try to replicate. And control it.

Like all Radicals, Burke wanted the Trios to secede from the United Planetary Coalition. Even when so many citizens believed the systems were strongest united, he was hell-bent on Trios independence. And from what Thea had pieced together in her interrogation, it sounded like Hevetz Industries had allied with Burke as well, that the company's owner was another Radical lurking in plain sight. If Burke got his way, he'd create an army of soldiers—hosts like Thea—to force the Union's hand.

Thea bent, knocking the remaining shards of glass from the edges of the window frame. Then she lowered herself to the ground and poked her head through.

A dark hallway. No guards.

She wiggled forward. A stray piece of glass dug into her bicep, but she pressed on. Her shoulders slipped through the opening. The rest was easy. Just a quick tilt of her body when her hips reached the frame, and then she was in the hall.

She stood and moved to Coen's cell, her feet tracking blood

on the dark tiles. By the time she reached his door, she was no longer bleeding. The wounds had sealed, her body healing at inhuman speed.

A series of sliding metal bolts secured the door. She unlocked the first, second, third. Then tugged the door open.

Coen stood in the frame. Half of his shoulder-length hair was pulled back in a bun, a dark knot atop his head. The rest hung wildly around his face. His chest swelled with each breath, and beneath the collar of his T-shirt, Thea could make out the edges of his tattoo, black ink against his light brown skin.

Thea. His breathing was labored, as though it had been *him* forcing his way through that tiny window. His pulse beat with excitement.

Silently, he moved to her, crossing the threshold, gathering her in her arms.

Thea wasn't prepared for how the contact softened her resolve. His chest beneath her cheek, his arms warm and reassuring on her back. So unlike the hands that had dragged her to this cell while she was only half-conscious. It almost made her want to linger. Almost.

He backed away quickly, as though he'd heard her thoughts. Perhaps he had. Then he took her wrist in his and braced his other palm against her dislocated shoulder. *Don't yell*, he warned her.

4

She breathed out as he thrust her shoulder back in place. It was no worse than an annoying pinch.

Let's go, she said.

There was only one direction to travel—down a dimly lit, windowless corridor lined with doors. Thea led the way past the cells, all empty based on the lack of heartbeats. A part of her had hoped she'd sense Nova Singh here. Their captors had cut the power to the pilot's cryo pod when storming the *Exodus* shuttle—a gamble that could easily kill a person. Nova's absence from this row of cells could mean only one of two things: she was dead and had been disposed of, or she was in a coma and being held elsewhere on the ship.

None of that's good, Coen said.

Thea flinched; she hadn't realized she'd been sharing her thoughts.

Sorry. I wasn't trying to pry.

It's not your fault if I'm projecting it, Thea said, and hurried on.

At the end of the hall was a service ladder. Thea grabbed the rungs and climbed, coming up against a smooth hatch door. The hand wheel to open it was surely on the other side. She put a palm to the cover, using all her strength to try to turn it. *Help me with this.*

Coen scrambled up the ladder, Working together, they pushed until the cover groaned, then creaked, then began to spin.

A moment later, Thea was shoving it up and stepping through the opening. She blinked rapidly in the newfound brightness. The room was a white cube, locked off on all ends. She sensed heartbeats, though, and zeroed in on the guards. Dozens of them, on the opposite side of a sealed door. They spotted her and shouted orders. Gas began to fill the chamber.

Quick! She motioned for Coen.

He joined her at the main door, but the ground sparked to life beneath them. Shock rod plates lined the floor. Heat surged through Thea's bare soles, pain laced her limbs. When her legs betrayed her, she fell to her knees, waiting for the shock to subside. It didn't. The sedative continued to pump into the room, and Thea slumped to her side, writhing.

In his mind, Coen Rivli could picture the window in his cell's door, the tiny opening through which Thea had some-how managed to crawl. Without her, he'd still have no idea what waited on the other side—not the hall or the ladder or the dead-end room they'd never be able to breach. He won-dered, momentarily, if not knowing would be better. Not knowing meant he could hope. Now he knew escape was impossible.

He forced his eyes open. Blinked rapidly. Everything was bright and shiny.

For a moment, he thought he was still in the room above the hatch, but then he had the vaguest memory of a mask being put over his face. Not one to fend off the gas, but one to administer it, keeping him sedated as he was dragged . . . somewhere.

Coen pushed himself upright, finding a cot beneath him. Not the cot from his cell, though. One of the walls in this room was made of glass. Beyond was a space he recognized. A table he'd been on some hours earlier, nearly unconscious as medics inspected him and retrieved blood samples.

He was no longer in his cell, but an isolation chamber in the ship's medbay, which wasn't much better. Just a different kind of prison.

Coen swung his legs over the cot. There was a faint throb in his side. Probably a guard had struck him with a baton. He rolled his shoulder, stretched the muscles in his abdomen, and the pain faded with the movement.

A languid pulse beat in his ears. Thea's.

He shot to his feet. Standing, he could see over the operating tables and regenerative beds, to the other side of the medbay. Thea sat in a chamber of her own, massaging the back of her neck.

That went well.

Her head jerked up, and her eyes found his. *Didn't it?*

I wasn't joking, Thea.

Neither was I. Her pulse didn't twitch. Even the tone of her thoughts was even, her expression calm. *We're back on a main level of the ship. That's better than being locked below a hatch.*

It's still a ship, Thea. There's nowhere to escape to.

The medbay's main doors slid open and Lieutenant Burke marched in, a group of men on his heels. Two wore standard military uniforms; the third, a medical jacket.

"How'd they even get out of the cells?" Burke was asking.

"The feed door," one of the officers replied. "The girl dislocated her shoulder." He passed a Tab to the lieutenant, who watched the device, brow wrinkled.

I guess there were cameras after all, Thea mused.

Of course there were cameras. Maybe she hadn't fully processed the direness of their situation yet, but Coen had. They were on a Union battleship, a military vessel that hailed from the Trios. It would be equipped with the very best technology and staffed by officers and soldiers, presumably all of whom were Radicals. If even a single person on this boat was loyal to the Union, representatives from Galactic Disease Control would be present. Instead, Burke had Hevetz employees helping him. Coen had seen the Hevetz logo on the jackets of the medics who had inspected him.

Coen watched Lieutenant Burke take in the surveillance footage, the man's pulse blipping up a hair.

I nearly attacked him when he interrogated me after Achlys,

Thea said. *That why he's scared.*

The image made Coen smile, at least until he realized that a successful attack from Thea could have unleashed *Psychrobacter achli* on the *Paramount*. A small injury to her, a bit of that blood passed to Burke, and that was it. Madness, all over again.

Burke strode to Thea's chamber and stared down at her. "There isn't a scratch on her. She's bleeding in this footage."

"Sir, it is my hypothesis that *Psychrobacter achli* gave the hosts not only enhanced physical strength but incredible healing capabilities as well," the man in the medical jacket supplied. "And who knows what else. I'd love to run some tests on them."

"Negative," Burke said. "I'm putting them in cryo until we reach the research facility. We don't have adequate means of restraining them here."

"But sir—"

"This is not open to debate, Farraday. We only get one shot at this, and I'm not blowing it." Burke turned to the officers. "Get a fully suited unit in here, and tell them to bring shock rods and sedation masks for the hosts. We're moving them immediately."

Coen could guess what would happen next. A sedative would fill his chamber. Once he hit the floor, the suited unit would slip a mask over his face to continue administering the drug, and he'd be dragged to a new location, helpless. And once they reached the destination facility Burke had mentioned, Coen imagined security would only be tighter.

Thea seemed to be running through a similar line of logic because she said, *Maybe our best chance is to try again as soon as possible. Run for an escape pod?*

To what—land on Achlys again? Coen shook his head. *It's the only rock for hundreds of thousands of kilometers.*

What about a shuttle, then? she offered. *Maybe we can make it to a shuttle.*

And fly it . . . how?

"Nova," she blurted out. Thea threw a palm against the glass of her chamber and stared down Burke. "Where's Nova? Our pilot!"

The lieutenant folded his arms over the front of his uniform. "As good as dead. Try anything, and I'll see one of you ends up the same. I only need one host to accomplish what I'm after."

Dread rushed through Coen. Without Nova—without a pilot—they were truly stranded.

ERIN BOWMAN'S
PULSE-POUNDING, HAIR-RAISING, UTTERLY TERRIFYING SCI-FI DUOLOGY.

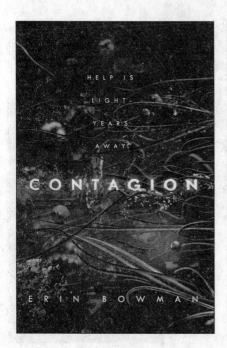

PRAISE FOR *Contagion*:

★ "Bowman's plot is intricate and action-packed, her worldbuilding is impressive yet economical, and the book climaxes in a gripping cliffhanger."

—*Publishers Weekly* (starred review)

JOIN THE

Epic Reads
COMMUNITY

THE ULTIMATE YA DESTINATION

◄ **DISCOVER** ►
your next favorite read

◄ **MEET** ►
new authors to love

◄ **WIN** ►
free books

◄ **SHARE** ►
infographics, playlists, quizzes, and more

◄ **WATCH** ►
the latest videos